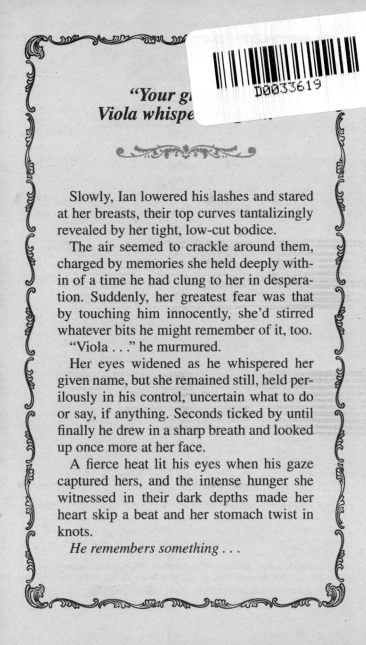

*"Your g...
Viola whispe...*

Slowly, Ian lowered his lashes and stared at her breasts, their top curves tantalizingly revealed by her tight, low-cut bodice.

The air seemed to crackle around them, charged by memories she held deeply within of a time he had clung to her in desperation. Suddenly, her greatest fear was that by touching him innocently, she'd stirred whatever bits he might remember of it, too.

"Viola . . ." he murmured.

Her eyes widened as he whispered her given name, but she remained still, held perilously in his control, uncertain what to do or say, if anything. Seconds ticked by until finally he drew in a sharp breath and looked up once more at her face.

A fierce heat lit his eyes when his gaze captured hers, and the intense hunger she witnessed in their dark depths made her heart skip a beat and her stomach twist in knots.

He remembers something . . .

ADELE ASHWORTH

The Duke's Captive

AVON
An Imprint of HarperCollinsPublishers

AVON BOOKS
An Imprint of HarperCollins*Publishers*
10 East 53rd Street
New York, New York 10022-5299

Acknowledgments

I'd like to extend my greatest appreciation to those who supported me through the ups and downs of this process and made this book possible: my editor, May Chen, and my agents, Denise Marcil and Maura Kye-Casella.

I also offer my deepest thanks to Kathryn Smith, an amazing author and wonderful friend who so willingly lent me her muse when mine strayed, hid in shame, or took an unannounced vacation. I humbly give it back to you. . . .

And my love to Ed, for always being there.

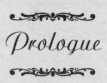

Prologue

Ian Wentworth stared out the window of his study into the dull, gray morning, the rolling hills of Stamford hidden by what remained of a nighttime fog. It wasn't yet eight and already he'd been awake for hours, poring over his financial books in an attempt to dull the daggers in his mind. As usual, he lacked the concentration to get much done, but it was enough just to be sober and living. Time healed all wounds, or so it had been said.

A knock at his study door made him jump, and his teacup rattled on the saucer in his hand. He doubted he'd ever get past being startled by a simple noise, even in his own home.

"Come," he grumbled over his shoulder.

Braetham, his butler, stepped inside the room. "Pardon, your grace, but a note has come for you by messenger."

Ian frowned and turned. "This early?"

"It's marked urgent," Braetham replied, the lines on

his aging face flat and noncommittal. "Courier rode all night."

Ian's first thought was that an emergency had struck his family, since his sister, Ivy, was expecting her second child within the month. Nerves on end, he placed his cup and saucer on his desktop.

"I'll take it," he said, his hand outstretched as he crossed the floor, meeting his butler midroom in three strides.

Braetham offered a letter-sized envelope, then bowed once. "Shall I stoke the fire, your grace? It's rather cold in here."

Ian hadn't even noticed. "Yes," he said absentmindedly.

He turned and strode back to the window for better light, tearing open the envelope and removing the small piece of paper inside in one swift action.

Unfolding it, he discovered it wasn't at all what he'd dreaded. It was worse. A single line of information, completely unexpected: *She's out of mourning.*

It took him all of five seconds to react. In a matter of moments, his future had changed.

Standing tall, he stared once more out the window. "Braetham, send in another pot of tea and a hearty breakfast. I think eggs and sausage. Then tell Cummings to alert the staff at Tarrington Square that we'll be arriving within a fortnight."

The iron poker clattered as it fell against the grate. "Sir?"

Ian's lips twitched at one end. It took quite a lot to surprise his longtime butler. "We're going to London for the season," he said, his voice but a whisper.

A staggering silence lingered. Then Braetham cleared his throat. "Of course, your grace. Tea and breakfast straightaway. Is there anything else for the moment?"

Ian shook his head vaguely. Seconds later his butler quit the room.

A mist curled up over the pasture to the east as the morning sun kissed the moisture away.

He crushed the note in his fist.

She's out of mourning. . . .

And now so was he.

Yes. It was time.

Chapter One

It's so dark inside, so cold, and in his sleep he weeps.
Although I wish I could, I cannot help him. . . .

London, 1856

𝓗er mother had always accused her of being too
whimsical, not pragmatic as a lady of quality should
be, but for the former Viola Bennington-Jones, those
days were long behind her. Widowed only eleven
months after her marriage to Lord Henry Cresswald,
Baron Cheshire, she had managed to escape the horrors of her past by the birth of their son, John Henry.
Widowhood had allowed her a time to fall in love with
her child, but now, at twenty-three, her official mourning was over and tonight she would begin to experience the world as a lady of quality should. Her closest
friend, Isabella Summerland, only daughter of the Earl
of Tenby, hosted excellent parties, and she could now
attend them in spectacular fashion. For Viola, this
season would become the debut she never had.

Of course there was more at stake than her own urge for company, or her desire for an occasional dance or tea with a dash of gossip. She needed the ease of moving in circles that would, over time, advance her son's placement in society as she mingled with those in elite circles. True, John Henry was only four years old, but as the son of a baron, he deserved the best. Though her life as his mother might be dwelling in secret scandals well kept, she'd promised herself at his birth that his good future would remain free of them. Always would she be careful, doing whatever necessary to protect his reputation above all else. Even Isabella, the closest of her friends, knew very little of the memories that continued to haunt her, and that's the way she would keep it, for the sake of her child, who would one day inherit everything due him through his good title and the connections she made for him.

Smiling with a genuine excitement she hadn't felt in years, Viola lifted a glass of champagne from a footman's silver tray as he passed, then walked with flawless grace across the sun-drenched promenade. Spring thus far had been rather warm, and she relished the chance to be outside in it, with the scent of flowers in the air and a string quartet playing softly at the side of the balcony. This, she vowed, would be the best time of her life.

Through a gathering crowd of London's elite, she caught sight of her hostess, who now stood in the midst of a cluster of colorfully dressed ladies, all eager to catch even the most minute bit of recent society news. Isabella spied her immediately and her eyes lit up with delight. "Darling, you look lovely," she said, scanning

Viola up and down as she left the group and walked forward to meet her halfway. "And dressed in ruby red! Good Lord, the stuffy crones will talk."

Viola leaned forward and kissed the air next to each of Isabella's cheeks. "Thank you, dearest, but I don't care." She stood upright and took a sip of champagne. "I was so tired of wearing nasty shades of gray, I thought I'd brighten my wardrobe. Be conspicuous and all that."

Isabella grinned and glanced around. "Well, you're certainly conspicuous. And if Miles Whitman sees you like this, he'll be down on one knee proposing."

"Heaven help me." Viola scrunched her face. "Is he here?"

Isabella almost snorted. "Of course he is. You know he never misses a party where he might woo a society wife. And everybody knows you're out of mourning now."

Viola had no intention of becoming the next Mrs. Anyone. Especially since her own late husband had left her with a perfectly satisfactory estate and a child to inherit it. She needed nothing else in life but her son, her friends, and her painting—the private side of her life that lifted her spirits when she needed it most.

"Where's Daphne?" she asked, glancing over her shoulder and scanning the crowd for their friend, daughter of the late Viscount Durham, granddaughter of the aging but extremely wealthy Duke of Westchester, and who, if she wasn't at her or Isabella's side, could usually be found in the company of an eligible gentleman. Or two. With her pedigree, she could have her choice of anyone, and she relished that knowledge. And the attention.

Isabella smirked. "Where do you think? She's intent on charming Lady Hollister into an introduction to her nephew."

"Ahhh . . ." Viola smiled in understanding. "This week she thinks to marry Lord Neville?"

"I suppose," Isabella replied with a lift of one bare shoulder. "He should be here tonight, as well."

"So . . . what happened to her fascination with Lord Percy?" Viola asked, almost afraid of the answer.

With a dramatic roll of her eyes, Isabella leaned in and enunciated, "Lord Percy, it seems, is intent on courting Anna Tildare this season since Daphne now seems rather bored with him."

Viola gaped, then lifted a gloved palm to stifle a giggle. "Poor Percy."

"Exactly what I thought." Isabella lifted her champagne flute in mock toast. "But here's to all the other available gentlemen who have yet to be swayed by the Lady of Horror's large fortune and tiny teats—"

"Isabella!"

They both laughed this time as Viola grasped her friend's arm and pulled it down, glancing around to be sure they weren't overheard discussing something so indelicate. They frequently called Lady Anna, daughter of the incredibly wealthy Earl of Brooksfield, Lady of Horror due to her obnoxious manner and overly imperious sense of entitlement. That she was pretty simply made it worse and particularly unfair, though it was quite true the lady had no bosom. Still, for all her conceited ways and lack of feminine curves, Anna Tildare usually managed to engage every gentleman in the room. For that reason alone, she would undoubtedly be here tonight.

"I heard the most intriguing bit of gossip, from Mother, if you can believe it," Isabella said, growing a bit cagey as she changed the subject.

"*Your* mother?" Viola gasped. Lady Tenby never gossiped and told her daughter frequently how much she abhorred the trait in others.

Isabella laced their arms together and pulled Viola closer as they began to walk slowly across the patio. "Well, perhaps it's not gossip, but more of . . . an interesting piece of news having to do with you."

Intrigued, Viola urged, "Go on."

Isabella leaned in, dropping her voice to a near whisper. "I heard Mother speaking to Greeley earlier today—"

"Your butler."

"—and she ordered a quick change of the menu to accommodate Fairbourne."

"Fairbourne's coming," she said blandly, pausing in her stride. "Does Daphne know?"

Isabella shook her head. "Not yet. And don't you tell her, either. I don't want her leaving before the dancing starts."

Lucas Wolffe, Duke of Fairbourne, was well known in London circles and had, through the years, attended several of Lady Tenby's events. Viola had met him once just after her marriage, and she remembered him as a handsome bachelor with a shadowed past and untold riches that made unmarried ladies swoon with the standard blend of shyness and calculation. Every mama in the land wanted him for a son-in-law, so it came as no surprise that he'd be invited this night, which Daphne would probably suspect anyway. But although Viola didn't know the man well, they were all perfectly aware that, despite the lack of details, a feud between Daphne's brother, Justin Marley, Viscount Durham, and the Duke of Fairbourne still remained strong and bitter. If they both had to be at the same party, Daphne would certainly want to avoid him.

"So, what has Lord Fairbourne's taste in food have to do with me?" she asked after a moment, returning to the original topic.

"It's not about the food, Vi." The corners of Isabella's mouth tipped up a fraction. "He's bringing a friend this evening. An art collector of considerable wealth. Or so Mother said."

A slice of apprehension coursed through her, though Viola had trained herself these last few years to hide such fear well inside an elegant demeanor. Instead of reacting, she sighed through a gentle smile. "That's it? That's the gossip?"

Isabella bit her lower lip, gazing at her askance. "He must be an important person, don't you think, to be escorted by Fairbourne? It's possible he's even heard of you and is, in fact, coming here to meet you, though of course I couldn't ask Mother his name. I'd be chided for eavesdropping."

Viola took another sip of champagne, her eyes once again grazing over the growing party before her. She noticed several people she knew, others she didn't, and almost nobody paid any particular attention to her arrival beyond the expected formality. But she'd learned to be cautious nonetheless.

Even now she carried a fear that she would be discovered as the legendary erotic artist Victor Bartlett-

James, a fear well founded, though usually without warrant, since that short element of her past had long since been retired. Nobody on earth knew she and Victor Bartlett-James were one and the same, save her highly paid solicitor, who'd been the man to place her work at auction. When her husband died, so did Victor, and that's when she began to develop a far more acceptable avenue for her talent, and an exemplary name for herself as Lady Viola, Baroness Cheshire, one of England's finest painters of still life and formal portraits for the nobility. Still, she couldn't brush aside the notion that she'd eventually be discovered, exposed as a fraud, and, worse, ruined socially for being the infamous artist of nude men and women posed in various positions of ecstacy. And she would never, ever forget that such ruination was a danger to her son. Always would she be careful, doing whatever necessary to protect his reputation above all else.

"Don't look at everybody so suspiciously," Isabella murmured, demanding her attention once more. "He's not here yet."

Viola glanced back at her friend. "How do you know, if you don't know who *he* is?"

"Be*cause*," Isabella stressed with wide eyes, "if he's with Fairbourne, you can be certain Mother will let us know the moment they arrive so we can begin the appropriate flirtations."

Viola grinned at that truth and, in a sweeping motion, interlocked her arm with Isabella's once more, turning them back toward the party. "Then let's bask in the evening before we're forced to flirt with arrogant dandies who make our teeth hurt."

For the next several hours, she tried very hard to ignore a certain lingering uneasiness and enjoy herself. The mood of the celebration delighted her, and because she was finally able to be free of the rigidity of mourning, she relished each bit of gossip, each person introduced to her, the food and champagne, and at last, by early evening, the dancing as the gathering moved inside Lord Tenby's luxuriously decorated ballroom.

Viola hadn't danced in years. Since the night of the masquerade ball in Winter Garden five years ago—the night her life had changed forever—she'd danced only once, at her small wedding. Soon thereafter she'd gone into confinement, and not long after her son had been born, her husband had caught pneumonia and died suddenly. It had been a most shocking year in so many ways, but keeping their estate running and raising her child had been exhausting, the restrictions of mourning depressing. Now she could dance, and even her two waltzes with Miles Whitman were enjoyable. She truly wished he'd keep his eyes on her face rather than her bosom when he spoke to her, but she supposed all men had such a natural propensity. Tonight she vowed not to care.

And then at five minutes to nine, her comfortable life shattered.

Viola stood near the buffet table, sipping her third glass of champagne and feeling marvelously lightheaded. Daphne and Isabella were beside her, and the three of them scrutinized the crowd for morsels more delectable than those on their plates.

"I see Lady Anna is flirting as usual," Daphne said with disgust, licking a dollop of sweet cream off a teaspoon.

"And with Seton, no less." Isabella blew out a quick puff of air, lifting a thick slice of chocolate cake from the sideboard. "I don't know where she gets the idea every gentleman wants her hand."

Viola snorted. "Knowing Lord Seton's reputation, I don't think it's her hand he's after."

Isabella and Daphne giggled—then stopped abruptly when Lady Tenby came into view, striding quickly toward them, her carriage erect, her flustered face nearly as pink as her wide, flounced gown.

"For heaven's sake, stand up straight, Isabella," she scolded in a low voice as she approached her daughter's side. "There are numerous titled gentlemen in attendance, and no gentleman of such high quality wants to dance with a lady who slouches."

Isabella leaned forward to kiss her cheek. "We were wondering where you were, Mother. Viola and Daphne were only just commenting on your salmon pastries. They enjoyed them, but I think there's a bit too much dill in the cream tonight."

Viola lifted her champagne glass to her lips to choke down a laugh, noticing Daphne do the same. Nobody had more ability to invent stories, to lie for her own amusement, than Isabella. Had she not been well born, she would have been an actress.

Lady Tenby sighed in affectionate annoyance. "We all know there are no salmon and dill pastries on the menu, Isabella."

Isabella's eyes lit up. "Oh. Well then, I'm thoroughly confused." She glanced at Daphne, then down to her plate. "What have we been eating?"

"Hopefully very little. Now put that down and stop

the gossiping," Lady Tenby carried on, exasperated as she patted her upswept gray hair. "You girls shouldn't be spending so much time at the buffet table anyway. You'll never find husbands if you don't keep your trim figures."

Her daughter complied by placing her yet untouched cake back on the sideboard. "Viola has already experienced the joys of marriage, Mother," she said with false sweetness. "I don't think she needs or wants another husband."

"Nonsense. Joy has nothing to do with it," the older woman huffed. "All ladies of good breeding need husbands, including young widows. Now stop the unbecoming chatter and go, all of you. *Mingle.*"

With that pronouncement, Lady Tenby straightened, turned, and disappeared into the ever-growing throng of inebriated but apparently worthy nobles in need of wives.

"She exhausts me," Isabella said, raising her fan and swishing it in front of her.

"Mothers always do," Daphne replied through a groan.

Viola smiled. "When you two become mothers, you'll understand. We want nothing but the best for our children."

Isabella scoffed. "You have a son."

"And he's four years old and titled," Daphne chimed in as if that explained everything.

Viola rubbed the back of her neck, feeling tension rise again, as it always did when she worried about her son and his future. The Duke of Fairbourne had probably already arrived, without ceremony as was his nature, which meant his friend roamed the ballroom as well. Most of her recent artwork wouldn't be considered the collectable kind, though if this particular gentleman wanted his garden painted, she would be the one to contact. What made her apprehensive, she supposed, was his calling himself a collector of art. Most of her original V. Bartlett-James artwork had been sold to gentlemen collectors.

"Oh, good heavens, who is that?" Daphne asked excitedly, cutting into Viola's thoughts as she pulled on her sleeve.

Viola turned toward the dance floor, seeing nothing but a scurry of colorful skirts and bobbing heads, hearing the usual blur of conversation and outbursts of laughter intermixed with a perfectly played Bach Minuet in G.

"Who is who?" Isabella asked, raising up on her tiptoes to try to get a better view.

"Fairbourne?" Viola offered.

Daphne shook her head. "No, someone else. Someone *much* more attractive. But—he's disappeared now."

"Nobody is more attractive than Fairbourne," Isabella said forcefully.

Suddenly Daphne stiffened, lifted her chin a fraction, and said flatly, "I was wrong. It is him."

"And he's coming this way," Viola added, catching her first glimpse of the man's magnificent stature striding easily around lingering couples, who parted automatically for him.

"He is so handsome," Isabella whispered through a sigh.

Daphne said nothing to that, even though, still yards

away, the undeniably handsome duke stared directly at her for a long, intimidating moment.

Abruptly, Daphne cleared her throat and turned. Brightly, she said, "Excuse me, dears, but since I refuse to cross paths with the deplorable duke, I think I'll look for Lord Neville. I believe it's time for our second set."

With that, she lifted her skirts and slipped around the buffet table, head held high, her dark curls bouncing with every forceful step as she disappeared into the crowd.

"When will their ridiculous feuding end?" Isabella asked seconds later, brows pinched as she stared after her.

Viola shook her head minutely. "She's protecting Fairbourne. Her brother would call him out if the man so much as requested a dance."

"Lady Isabella, and Lady . . . Cheshire, is it not?"

Viola flipped around, dazed for a second or two as Lucas Wolffe, tall and domineering, stood directly in front of her, acknowledging her in a deep, cool voice.

"Your grace," Isabella said at once, breaking the spell first with a proper curtsey.

Viola automatically followed with the same, lowering her body gracefully as she tipped her head down in respect, her heartbeat quickening as it always did when she found herself in the company of someone so important. And then past and present collided in swift, brutal force when, as she pulled herself upright and raised her lashes, Fairbourne moved to his left to offer full view of the man standing behind him.

Oh, my God . . .

She blinked, instantly spellbound by a new and vivid unreality.

"Ladies, may I present to you Ian Wentworth, Earl of Stamford, Duke of Chatwin."

The room began to spin. Her throat tightened. She couldn't breathe.

Ian Wentworth, Earl of Stamford . . .

He's found me.

Isabella curtseyed again, mumbled something. He nodded brusquely in response, then slowly turned his attention to Viola.

Those eyes . . . Ian's eyes. Pleading . . .

Run!

She couldn't move. Their gazes locked, and for an endless moment, time stopped, if only between them. History suddenly became now, their shared memories, both distasteful and passionate, fearful and vibrant, passing intimately between them in a heartbeat.

Viola stumbled back a step; her champagne glass fell from her fingertips to shatter on the marble floor at her feet. And still, she couldn't take her gaze from his face. That beautiful, expressive face, so changed. Perfected in time.

"Viola?"

Footmen scattered around her to quickly sweep up the glass and pale liquid that pooled at the hem of her gown; others in their vicinity backed up to make room. The bluster of sudden activity jarred her and she blinked quickly, glancing down, bewildered.

"I—I'm sorry." Her voice sounded clipped, hollow.

Isabella wrapped an arm around her shoulders. "Are you all right? You look ready to faint."

"No, I'm—I'm fine. Really." She tried to lick her lips though her tongue felt thick and dry. "I'm just—hot."

Concerned, Isabella opened her fan. "Take this. And sit. Catch your breath."

Fairbourne chuckled, interrupting her disorientation as he reached out and grasped her elbow, helping her into a chair a footman placed beside the sidebar. She looked at him, attempting to draw a full inhale as she fanned herself without thought. "Thank you. I—I apologize, your grace."

"Not at all, I'm very flattered," he returned in a good-natured drawl. "It's not often I have such an effect on a lady."

She tried to smile—then shot a glace at the very real cause of her turmoil.

He stared down at her, his sharp gaze focused intently on her face, his expression unreadable. Then his lips curved up at one corner. "Nor do I. You swooned even before we'd been properly introduced. I usually have to speak before that happens."

Isabella laughed lightly at his charm and cleverness. Viola, however, had no idea what to say to him. But his voice . . . oh, how she remembered his voice! It mesmerized her then as it did now—husky soft, low and rich, begging—

"Forgive me," Fairbourne said after an awkward pause, his tone slightly amused. "Lady Viola Cheshire, his grace, the Duke of Chatwin."

The man took a step forward to tower over her, blocking the brilliantly illuminated chandelier with his powerful form. Then, with a gentle nod, he reached out with his hand, palm up.

Viola stared at it for several long seconds, unsure what to do. But her head had begun to clear. The music played around them, the champagne flowed, and the party carried on as the first great event of the season. They were only two among many. She also realized something else: he'd inherited a new title, and a grand one at that. As a gentleman of such distinguished rank, he certainly wouldn't expose her, or their past, in front of his peers. Not tonight. Not here, like this. She had no idea why he acted as if he didn't remember her, and he no doubt enjoyed her discomfiture, but for now her reputation was safe, and that was all that mattered. She had time.

Feeling relief wash over her, more confident for the moment, she inhaled another deep breath. Then staring at his long, hard fingers, she lifted her gloved hand and placed it gingerly atop his.

He closed his thumb over her knuckles, then, second by second, gently helped her rise. Standing before him once more, she curtseyed with elegance, playing the part she'd learned.

"Your grace."

"Lady Cheshire."

Her name seemed to roll off his tongue as if the sound of it fascinated him. Or perhaps it was only her imagination. But the strength she felt from him as he touched her now, hand to gloved hand, permeated her skin to shock her thoroughly, inside and out.

Strong. Vibrant. *Alive*. Because of her.

He released her and took a step back, standing tall, arms behind him. "Feeling better, I hope."

She shook herself and rubbed her palm down the bodice of her gown. "Indeed. Thank you."

He nodded once.

Another strained moment skipped by. Then Isabella said, "So . . . Mother informed us you're an art collector?"

"I am," he replied without elaboration.

Viola swallowed. "And a friend of Lord Fairbourne. How delightful for him—for you. As it were." It was likely the most ridiculous thing she'd ever said, and she felt like cowering inside the moment it was out of her mouth.

Isabella glanced from one to the other, then thankfully saved her more embarrassment. "Uh, Lord Chatwin, Lady Cheshire is an exceptional artist. Perhaps you've seen her work?"

Viola felt Ian's stare on her again and she forced a flat smile even as she felt renewed heat creep up her neck.

"I've no idea," he replied evenly. "Are you perchance famous, madam?"

The tenor of his voice teased her to the core, just as it did all those years ago. But there also appeared a telling confidence about him. She raised her lashes to capture his gaze once again, immediately sensing an undefined boldness in their dark depths, something calculating that sent a ripple of warning through her body.

Fairbourne, who'd been silently watching for the last minute or two, crossed his arms over his tailored evening coat. "No need to be humble, Lady Cheshire, you may admit it. I've already told Chatwin you've painted most of the nobility's formal portraits in recent years and are celebrated as one of the finest artists in London. It's why he's here."

"Why he's here?" Isabella repeated.

Viola reached up to wipe a stray curl from her forehead, not because it bothered her but because she felt more uncomfortable at that moment than she had in the last five years and desperately needed something to do.

"I apologize if I've been vague," Ian murmured, his smile pleasant as he continued to scrutinize her. "But I've just returned to London and expect to remain only for the season. Since your good reputation precedes you, I wanted to meet you straightaway, Lady Cheshire, in the hope that we can discuss a commission of your work while I'm here?"

Again, she felt dumbstruck, numb. She had no intention of working for him, being alone with him. Not ever. And yet when he asked like this, standing before her in a crowded ballroom, dressed formally, and presenting himself as a man of great wealth and power, she simply could not deny him his request for one innocent meeting. Not if she was to maintain her status as a lady of quality and her reputation as a professional artist.

There was something about this entire encounter that just seemed bizarre. No mention of their past, no recognition from him at all, really. And yet she felt a tension between them that threatened her composure, forcing her to play his hand for the moment.

Overcoming her reluctance, she nodded once, clutching Isabella's fan to her waist in a measure of defense. "I'll have to review my schedule."

"Of course," he replied at once, as if expecting such a standard response.

The orchestra struck up a waltz. Isabella cleared her throat and Fairbourne took the cue.

"Would you honor me with a dance, my lady?"

She smiled beautifully as she placed her silk-covered palm on his arm. "I'd be delighted, your grace."

Suddenly, watching her friend wander into the noisy group of mostly inebriated nobility, Viola felt more isolated in the crowded ballroom than she would have in a dinghy in the middle of the sea. With growing trepidation, she lifted her gaze one more time, meeting his.

Don't ask me to dance. Please don't ask me to dance—

"Lady Viola Cheshire," he drawled in a whisper.

She felt an instant thundering in her breast as he used her given name. "Yes, your grace?"

His lids narrowed, and very, very slowly, he studied the length of her, from the hem of her full, ruby red gown, through her tightly corseted bodice, pausing briefly at her low, rounded neckline and the golden locket resting in the crease of her bosom before moving up her throat to her flushing face. When at last he looked back into her eyes, her breath caught in a whirlwind of panic. For the slightest second she felt hunger within him. Not lust as she knew it, but something else. Something she couldn't possibly define.

His lips twitched. "I don't feel much like dancing at the moment."

A palpable relief swept over her even as she felt the slightest twinge of disappointment.

His voice dropped to a husky whisper. "Would you care to walk with me on the promenade instead?"

She swallowed, simply unable to look away from him, or answer.

He smiled again as if sensing her hesitation, a beautiful smile that softened the hard planes of his face, then lifted his arm for her.

She took it because she didn't dare deny him, and in the course of ten seconds, they were heading out of the ballroom.

Chapter Two

He is drugged again, but still so restless and in great pain. Oh, please, God, tell me what to do. . . .

Darkness had fallen and Viola shivered as they stepped into the cool night air. He couldn't have felt it, though, as she only touched him with her gloved palm to his forearm. Instinct told her she needed to get away, and quickly, but running would bring suspicion upon her. For the moment, she had no idea what to do or say.

He remained quiet as he led her toward the balcony's edge, which overlooked a large garden and pond below, lit up beautifully by torchlight. There were others around them, couples strolling or mingling in the distance, muted laughter and music coming from the ballroom, and knowing they weren't completely alone gave her at least a small sense of security.

At last he stopped and turned to her, resting his elbow casually atop the railing as he studied the side of her face. She stood rigidly erect, gazing down to the pathway that wound through the flower garden below, clutching Isabella's fan in front of her. Any moment now she suspected he would tell her he knew who she was, that he had found her purposely to confront her, that he'd wanted to get her alone outside to accuse her of being privy to his kidnapping five years ago and doing nothing to help him escape. Part of her wanted to blurt out an apology before he could mention it, explain her actions, but she knew it would sound hollow at this point, and she just didn't want to be the one to break the silence anyway.

"It's a perfect night to be outside," he said, interrupting her thoughts.

The small talk disconcerted her. "Yes, lovely."

"Lady Viola Cheshire," he repeated very slowly.

The richness of his voice when he said her name again enthralled her. Bravely, she looked up to his face, now hidden partially in shadow, illuminated only by faint light from the ballroom behind her, revealing nothing in expression. Suddenly she knew he was about to reveal his intention, and she waited, unable to tear her gaze away from his. Silence lingered for several unbearable seconds, and then he cocked his head to the side to eye her speculatively. She couldn't move. Or breathe.

Then, with a crease of his dark brows, he murmured, "Forgive me for being blunt, but there is something so . . . oddly familiar about you. Have we met before?"

For the second time that night, Viola nearly fainted. She blinked quickly several times, unable to avoid gaping at him as the blood left her face and a deep confusion enveloped her. "I—I beg your pardon?"

He continued to gaze at her, seemingly unaware of her incredulity.

"I apologize for staring, but your . . . face, and voice, have arrested me." He shook his head, mystified, his eyes narrowed. "I know I've seen you before. I just can't pinpoint the time, or where it might have been."

A rush of air escaped from Viola's partially opened mouth and she sank momentarily into her stays, feeling a sudden, inexplicable exhilaration at the possibility that maybe he didn't actually remember her, hadn't come here to challenge her at all. Yet the mere notion seemed so totally unbelievable. True, he'd been drugged almost all of the time he'd been in captivity, kept in near total darkness, and she'd never given her name to him during those few respites alone where he'd appeared more lucid. But could he really not remember her as the woman who'd shared his horror?

"Lady Cheshire?" he prompted softly.

She straightened, heeding the warning within that if he truly didn't recognize her, she wouldn't be the one to enlighten him. "Sorry. I was just thinking, trying to place you, but alas, I cannot." She sighed and gave him a half smile. "If we've met before, I can't recall the time or circumstance."

His lips turned down and he nodded. Seconds ticked by as he continued to study her, making her ever more uncomfortable under his scrutiny. Then he grinned slyly. "Perhaps you're right, though I rarely fail at remembering beautiful women, and you are very beautiful."

His unexpected compliment warmed her inside as much as it surprised her. Aside from the shape of her face and her coloring, she looked nothing like she did five years ago, and nobody would have called her beautiful then. Pretty maybe, but not beautiful. Still, his flattery seemed genuine even if she didn't now understand where the conversation headed.

"That's a lovely thing to say," she murmured. "Thank you, your grace."

He continued to watch her, and she held his gaze steadily, her smile polite as she waited for his next move, her heart pounding so hard that she could feel it in her chest.

"You are a widow," he stated seconds later, "and Fairbourne tells me this is your first season out of mourning."

"That's true. My husband died nearly four years ago."

"I see." Turning, he faced the garden below and leaned over a bit, resting his forearms on the railing, interlocking his fingers in front of him. "What did your husband think of your artistic talent?"

She blinked. "My talent?"

Shrugging a shoulder, he replied, "Did he encourage you to pursue it as a profession?"

His line of questioning concerned her, and she shook herself mentally, prepared to be as vague as possible. "I wouldn't say he thought of it as a profession, your grace," she answered carefully. "But then he died not long after we were married, at which time it became a moot point."

"And since that time you've acquired quite a name for yourself and are considered one of the best portrait artists in London, are you not?"

He already knew that, but she decided against reminding him. "I am, though there are several others who are also very good."

Looking back into her eyes, he asked, "How much do you charge for each portrait?"

"That depends," she replied honestly. "There are various fees involved, and each situation is different, from the simple to the complex."

He studied her for a moment. "And how do these . . . situations differ exactly?"

"Well," she explained through a long exhale, "my time is generally what charges are based upon, although I also consider how many sittings might be needed, if the subject is a child or adult, how many individuals are in the portrait, how large the painting is to be, cost of supplies, traveling expenses, and the financial situation of the buyer."

His brows rose. "The financial situation of the buyer?"

She shouldn't have revealed that. Fidgeting a little, she said vaguely, "I try to be accommodating when I can be. Some people are less fortunate than others, even in the gentry, as I'm sure you're aware."

"Indeed I am," he readily agreed, dropping his deep voice to just above a whisper. "And in what manner do the less fortunate gentlemen repay you for your . . . accommodating talent, Lady Cheshire?"

Her eyes widened a fraction at the suggestiveness of the question. Heat suffused her, creeping up her neck and into her cheeks, though she held her ground, refusing to look away or cower from embarrassment, since he probably couldn't see how she flushed in dim lighting.

With a slight tilt of her chin, she returned, "Sometimes their *wives* bake me *pie,* your grace."

Very slowly his mouth curved up into a grin. "You work for pie, madam?"

His handsome features, caught up in genuine amusement, nearly made her heart stop.

"Cherry is my favorite."

"Is it."

"But I also enjoy blueberry and apple," she added rather mischievously. "Sometimes, if the portrait is very large and time consuming, I demand one pie each in all three flavors to satisfy the debt."

He almost laughed; she could see him fighting it as his gaze brushed over her face again, taking in each feature, from the curls in her hair, to the tiny pearl earrings that dangled at her lobes, to her lips when she licked them from sudden nervousness.

He turned to face her fully once more, his smile fading as he took a step toward her, close enough that his shins brushed her gown.

"I'm assuming your husband left you with a satisfactory estate, then, since you can work for pie," he maintained, his expression and manner unreadable.

Trepidation filled her anew. He was close enough to touch, to smell a trace of his fine cologne, to sense a hidden meaning in the dark depths of his eyes.

She swallowed, attempting to remain composed. "Forgive me, your grace, but I'm—I'm not certain what my taste in pie or my husband's estate has to do with—"

"Us?" he finished for her in a whisper.

She wasn't going to say that, and it stunned her thoroughly that he did. He entranced her utterly.

He smiled again, slyly. "If I am to commission work from you, Lady Cheshire, I need to know more about you, and just how accommodating you can actually be."

She didn't know how to take that statement at all. But she was quite certain she didn't want to paint his portrait. Every second in his presence increased the danger of being discovered. And right now he was acting far too . . . familiar.

She took a step away from him and opened her fan, swishing it in front of her face, immensely thankful she hadn't given it back to Isabella. "As I mentioned before, your grace, I'm not certain I'll have time to begin a new project."

Thoughtfully, he said, "I have learned that time is indeed precious. You are a widow, so I'm sure you understand that better than anyone."

Her fanning slowed. "Of course."

Shifting his gaze toward the garden, he expounded. "I don't attend many formal functions, Lady Cheshire. I prefer to keep residence at my country estate due to . . . an unfortunate ordeal that changed me when it nearly took my life in the winter of fifty-two."

Under her assumption that he had no idea of her involvement, the shock of hearing him mention his kidnapping made her sway on her feet. Instinctively, she reached out to wrap her palm around the railing at her side.

"The *ton* revel in gossip, as I know you're aware," he continued, his voice growing somber. "For just that reason I've stayed away from the city as much as possible these last few years, refusing to offer myself to my peers as a spectacle, or worse, a subject of pity."

He paused as a laughing couple strolled by them, then straightened and turned to face her again. He took a step closer, though he clasped his hands behind his back to stand formally erect, his dark countenance unreadable as he regarded her closely.

Viola shifted from one foot to the other, uncomfortable under his scrutiny. "Your grace, I'm not sure—"

"Lady Cheshire, several months ago I inherited a new title through my mother's Scottish ancestral line," he cut in with ease. "Unusual, to be sure, and although it was not unknown to me, I was not expecting it so soon. However, with this title came the acceptance that I must finally do my duty and marry. That's why I've come to London for the season."

Her mouth dropped open a shade. "You're here to choose a wife?"

"I need an heir, madam."

Viola nodded as if in complete understanding of his plight, though suddenly experiencing anew every vibrant, tumultuous emotion she'd ever felt for him bubble to the surface, heating her face and muddling her rational thinking.

"You—have you a lady in mind, sir?" she asked in a near whisper.

He frowned, shaking his head. "Not at the moment, but the season has only just begun."

An odd relief swept over her, and she quashed it at once. "I see."

Seconds later, he asked, "Do you have any acquaintances you'd recommend for an introduction?"

If she hadn't been so befuddled by this entire confrontation she would probably have taken offense at his question. He hadn't wanted to dance with her, but he had no trouble asking her for advice regarding other ladies to pursue? Viola shook herself. Such thought was irrelevant. Whom he chose to court was none of her business. Frankly, she had a far greater concern at the moment—like doing what she could to assuage him, then getting away fast, before he recalled their former encounters.

"I'm sure there are many ladies to choose from, your grace," she replied matter-of-factly, standing tall and fanning herself again. "I'm also certain any one of them would be proud to be your duchess."

He smiled again, crookedly. "Such a formal response, Lady Cheshire."

She had no idea how to take that remark, so she ignored it. "Perhaps you should tell me what you'd like from me, your grace."

He watched her silently for several long seconds, then replied, "I would like you to paint my ducal portrait for me to give to my bride as a wedding gift, then later hang in the halls of Chatwin. Of course I will pay you well for your time and the final product." He leaned over a little to add, "I don't bake, so it'll have to be payment in the bland and ordinary form of a banknote."

She almost laughed at the incredibly silly thought of a baking duke. Clearing her throat, she replied, "I'll see what I can do. I'll need to—"

"Check your calendar, yes, I know," he cut in again,

still amused. Then, reaching into his coat pocket, he removed his card and handed it to her. "Please let me know if you're available as soon as possible. If not you, I'll have to commission work elsewhere."

She glanced to his card but couldn't read it in the darkness. "I'll send word, your grace."

He bowed slightly. "Until then, Lady Cheshire."

She looked back into his eyes, and for the briefest moment a current passed between them. His dark gaze raked her figure for a final time, and then, with a nod, he stepped past her, heading back toward the ballroom.

Viola nearly collapsed on the spot. It took her several minutes before she dared return to the festivities herself, and when she managed it, her emotions got the best of her as she caught him dancing with Anna Tildare, a beautiful smile planted on his handsome, masculine face.

Head held high, she went searching for Lady Tenby and made her excuses, leaving the party before ten, the brightness and excitement she'd felt when she'd arrived all but dimmed to a dull ache of regrets.

Chapter Three

I sat beside him today, for a long while, hoping to comfort, but he never knew I was there. . . .

Ian stood in his bedroom, straightening his cravat, then smoothing his sleeves as he stared at his reflection in the mirror. She had accepted his offer, and in just minutes, he'd be on his way to her town house to discuss the fees and details of the portrait she would paint. He intended to be late, to keep her waiting on purpose, not only to increase her uneasiness but also because he wanted to clarify every detail in his mind before this final masquerade began in full.

She was nothing like he expected, or remembered. True, his memory of her remained hazy at best, intermittent and appearing more in his dreams and nightmares than in his thoughts. But it hadn't occurred to him that she'd be something other than the timid girl he vaguely recalled, that she might have matured into a woman other than his vision of the despondent young widow who grew fat from laziness, tended her child, and kept to herself.

Her sophistication had surprised him immediately. Even as she'd fully gratified his five-year wait to confront her by nearly fainting in shock at the sight of him, he'd still felt a twinge of dismay course through him when he'd caught his first glimpse of her. Although only twenty-three, she exuded an elegance, a cultured loveliness, of someone ten years older. To be honest with himself, he now conceded the fact that in a relatively short time she'd transformed herself magnificently, from the shy, plain village girl to the confident and stunning widow of high society. And everything about his initial reaction to her last night infuriated him.

Admittedly, he'd been taken aback by her beauty, caught up in striking hazel eyes, shiny dark hair curled into a mass upon her head, flawless fair skin, and swirls of brilliant red that covered her body appropriately yet hugged each curve to perfection, only hinting at the treasure beneath the silk. Fairbourne had warned him, calling her something of an enchantress, but he'd ignored a notion that hadn't fit his memory. Still, he'd managed to conceal his amazement well. At his weakest moment he'd almost kissed her, feeling a quick and troublesome urge to pull her close and enjoy a few minutes of mutual desire. But he'd stopped himself by remembering who she was and why he had come to her. There would be plenty of time for a deliberate seduction if he chose to bed her, and moving too fast could be dangerous. He wouldn't be so careless to forget that again.

Ian stared at himself in the mirror, neither happy nor unhappy with his appearance. His once handsome demeanor had been replaced long ago by cold cynicism.

At thirty-one, he was a fully grown man, experienced in most everything that mattered, yet yearning for a contentment of body and peace of mind that remained obscure. His purpose for the last five years had been about healing terrifying wounds and overcoming a bitterness more difficult than most men of his position should ever contemplate, but thus far he had failed. His heart had slowly hardened as his hopes for any sort of vindication had dwindled, and with it a dream for lifelong happiness, however fanciful, had died. Even his twin sister had distanced herself from him these last few years as he'd pursued his demons relentlessly, to no avail.

But everything had changed eleven months ago when he'd unexpectedly inherited a distinguished, formidable title, and all the wealth, land, and power that came with it. He suddenly had the ability and means to reshape his destiny. And it all centered around a calculated, slow, and meticulously designed ruin of the former Viola Bennington-Jones. She remained the only person to have escaped justice for the wrongs committed him five years ago when, after having him knocked unconscious, her two sisters had dragged him into a centuries-old dungeon, chained him to a wall, drugged him repeatedly, and eventually left him for dead. And although Viola, the youngest of the three, had been innocent of the initial kidnapping and the plot to hold him for ransom, she'd been there from time to time as he'd awakened from his drugged stupor, hearing her soothing voice, recalling . . . a certain warmth, even vague impressions of her face and form as she'd tried to console him. Yet all her meager efforts at providing some kind of comfort had meant nothing when she'd refused to free him or summon help. In essence, she had left him there to die. Both of her sisters had received judgment—one through suicide, the other through prison—but Viola had denied to the authorities that she'd known anything about it, had lied to escape paying for the crime of inaction. In the end, there had been no solid proof she'd been involved in, or even witness to, the event. It had become the word of a girl against those spoken by him, an earl with influence but who had been so incapacitated and frequently delirious that he'd had no idea how much time had passed until he'd been told. She'd disappeared soon after his rescue, leaving town to escape the scandal and reinvent herself, marrying well above her station, succeeding as an artist, and living a life of ease even as he'd suffered from nightmares and an inner pain she could never possibly imagine. Now all of that was about to change, to his satisfaction, and her well-deserved detriment.

The unexpected attraction he felt for her troubled him, though. It was the only part of his plan he hadn't anticipated, and he would fight it. Teasing her, seducing and bedding her as he must would be acceptable; caring for one small strand of hair on her head would be nothing short of embracing the indignities she'd witnessed and forced him to suffer for five horrifying weeks. He would never forget how she'd passively allowed and observed his keen humiliation then, and if it cost him his soul, she would pay for it now.

Ian reached for his jacket and donned it, smoothing the silk as he adjusted the collar. Then, devoid of guilt, his mind centered and controlled for the meeting ahead, he turned and walked from his bedchamber.

Viola paced her parlor, staring at the rose-colored carpeting, reminding herself every so often to relax, to *think*. If she used her head, she would get through the dreadful ordeal to come with her composure intact and her future safe. She refused to accept anything less, and had decided hours ago that she would do what she must to avoid a confrontation that could cost her son everything. His good reputation was all that mattered to her in the end.

A sense of alarm had been building throughout the day as she'd awaited their appointed meeting time of two o'clock. After a fitful night's sleep, she'd spent the morning in discussion with servants, writing letters, and making careful plans to send John Henry away to stay with her late husband's sister Minerva. At half past one, she headed downstairs to await her guest, nearly sick with anxiousness as she attempted to control her restless thoughts. She'd made arrangements for tea to be served at his arrival, but now, after waiting by herself for three quarters of an hour, most of her nervousness had been replaced by irritation at his delay. That was probably a good thing.

Aside from the formalities, she had no idea what they might discuss, though the fear raged that he'd reopen the wound of his captivity in the dungeon in intimate and gross elaboration. That he didn't seem to recall her involvement was surely a blessing, but it didn't mean he wouldn't remember over time, or that he wasn't lying outright and knew exactly who she was, pursuing this formal business association with her for nefarious reasons. She kept mulling over their conversation on the balcony, trying to interpret what might have been unique inflections in his tone or hidden meanings in his words. And although his mild sexual suggestions left her a little rattled, the only thing she could recall that disturbed her were his questions regarding her husband's estate and her profession.

True, she made a modest income from the selling of proper portraits, but it was Victor Bartlett-James, her secret persona, who'd taken London by storm five years ago with the auction of the first charcoal drawings of lovers embraced in carnal acts. Her husband had insisted on taking charge and developing a career of sorts for her, enlarging his purse by selling her lascivious art, only asking that she continue the pretense for their mutual financial benefit. He had been an impoverished noble when they'd met, but he had married her, taking her away from the nightmare in which she had been living, and for that reason alone she'd agreed to the risk. For their combined efforts, she now had not only a title and a son but also a sizable and debt-free estate for him to inherit.

Her work had been a sensation, partly, she supposed, because of her talent, but also because the artist's hidden identity had created a stir of intrigue and gossip. Even ladies had discussed Bartlett-James and his drawings, though in a vague manner that had amused her when she'd had opportunity to be part of such an interesting, albeit delicate, conversation. Her husband's solicitor had been the one to place her artwork—the less explicit at very respectable auctions, the more lustful and bold in exclusive gentlemen's clubs—and although she'd retired long ago, she continued to pay the man well enough to remain silent about the details for the remainder of his years. The likelihood that Ian Wentworth had learned of the precise nature of her husband's wealth seemed beyond remote, and yet why should the man wonder if Henry had encouraged her to pursue her talent as a profession when ladies did not have professions? Why would he even *mention* a connection between the Cheshire estate and her artwork?

Of course it was entirely possible she was reading far too much into two or three casual sentences. She'd been careful, and successful, in staying away from him these last few years, knowing he lived a rather secluded life on his estate in Stamford after returning from an extended trip on the Continent. After she'd married and left Winter Garden five years ago, her sole ambition had been to create a new version of herself in the hope of never having to reveal any part of her former life, and in so doing, never having to see him again. Thus far she had succeeded beautifully. Nobody in her circle of friends and acquaintances knew who she was, or where she came from originally. She never spoke of the time before her marriage, aside from very general references when asked, because just the mention of a sister shipped to a penal colony and the horrors her family had forced upon a titled man would ruin her and destroy her son's good name. Her innocence in his abduction had saved her from arrest, and until now her prevarications and avoidance of detail had been effective in hiding both her identity and her middle-class upbringing by a mother who'd valued manners and breeding above all things, allowing her to flourish in a class in which she hadn't been born and didn't actually belong.

Unfortunately, she now carried two grave secrets that would disgrace her should the Duke of Chatwin, with all his wealth and influence, choose to investigate her past in detail and announce his findings to society. And if by chance he'd come back into her life to hunt her down and destroy her, she would need a plan to save herself and her son. She would remain alert and strike back deviously if she must.

A sharp knock at the door jarred her from her thoughts, and she paused in her stride. "Come in."

Her butler, Needham, entered and offered a quick bow. "Madam, his grace, the Duke of Chatwin, has arrived," he said stoically.

She nodded once. "Send him in."

He turned, leaving her momentarily to fluff her skirts and run her nervous hands down her tightly corseted waist. She'd donned her most conservative, high-necked day gown in rich blue satin, and she'd instructed Phoebe, her maid, to dress her hair in braids and coil them neatly upon her head. Her look, she supposed, might be a bit severe, but then her appearance fit her mood as well as her determination to hold a proper and imposing carriage in his presence. Assuming such a thing was possible.

Moments later she heard his footsteps on the parquet floor. Trying her best to control a renewed trembling within, Viola couldn't help but stare in awe as he walked into her parlor.

The man made a striking presence, his tall, chiseled form filling out his tailored suit to perfection, the olive green silk, white linen shirt, and brown-and-green-striped cravat providing an excellent contrast to his dark brown hair and the eyes she remembered so well.

"Lady Cheshire," he addressed her, his voice deep and formal.

"Your grace," she replied with a quick curtsey. Then, with a glance to her butler, she said, "Needham, we'll have tea at once."

"Of course, madam," he returned with a nod before he quit the room.

Alone with Chatwin for the moment, she gestured, palm up, to the green leather chair beside the cold grate. "Would you care to sit, your grace?"

He strode with ease across the carpet, his gaze roving over the parlor, taking in each floral painting in gilded frames she'd hung on nearly every available space on the walls.

"Did you paint any of these?" he asked as he lowered his body into the chair.

"I did," she replied, moving to the pink velveteen sofa across from him. She sat gracefully on the edge of the cushion, spreading her gown out around her knees and ankles, stopping short of sinking into the softness by keeping her back erect, her posture stiff. Folding her hands in her lap, she added, "I painted all of them, actually."

His brows rose faintly as he stared at the picture of a flower garden in full bloom above the mantel. "Very impressive."

He didn't elaborate, which left her wondering if he

meant her talent or the sheer number of pieces she displayed in one average-sized room. Fortunately, Needham saved her from an awkward reply by knocking and entering once more, his stocky hands clutching the handles of a large silver tray.

"Is there anything else for the moment, Lady Cheshire?" he asked, walking to the tea table in between them and placing the tray gently on the polished walnut.

"No, we'll serve ourselves."

He bowed, then turned on his heels and made his way quickly from the parlor, leaving the door ajar as propriety demanded.

She immediately reached for the pot and began pouring a perfectly steeped Darjeeling into one of the delicate china cups, the sweet, floral aroma curling upward with the steam.

"Sugar, your grace?"

"Please."

She complied, adding a teaspoon full, then offering the cup, saucer, and serviette to him before filling her own. That done, she sat back a little to regard him, trying not to stare as she gently stirred the sugar in her own hot brew.

He looked fairly relaxed, his elbows resting upon the arms of the chair, his tapered fingers, dusted with fine, dark hair, pinching the handle of the china as he waited for his tea to cool. She'd never seen him in full daylight before, and although it was filtered through her pale pink curtains, a ray of sun played across his face and chest from the window to his left, brightening his features for her view. He truly looked spectacular, robust and healthy. On the outside, at least, he had healed with no damage at all and remained one of the most incredible-looking men she had ever seen in her life.

Suddenly the entire moment struck her as absurd. Not only had she just served exquisite tea in imported fine china to Ian Wentworth, the man her sisters had nearly starved to death five years ago, but he'd also accepted with graciousness her company as a high-ranking member of the nobility. Her mother, God rest her, a woman who'd struggled all her life to improve her modest social standing to no avail, would have fainted in joyful astonishment at first sight of her youngest daughter entertaining such a marvelously handsome, *available* duke in her fashionable home in the city.

"You look amused," he drawled, lifting his cup to his lips.

She smiled faintly and shook her head. "I apologize, your grace, but I haven't entertained a guest in my parlor in a very long time. I've only been out of mourning a short while."

"Ahh." He took a sip from his cup, then lowered it back to the saucer. "Well, I'm certainly delighted, and honored, to be your first . . . diversion, shall we say."

She dropped her gaze as she slid the edge of her teaspoon across the china rim, then placed it on her saucer, assuring herself that he couldn't possibly know how unsettled he continued to make her by using suggestive words as he focused on her person so directly. She just wished she could tell if he was trying to rattle her on purpose. Thankfully, he saved her from an embarrassing comment by getting to the point of their visit.

"So," he began, leaning over to place his cup and saucer on the tea table, "I suppose we should get to the details of what exactly is required of me during a sitting."

Lowering her own cup to her lap, she replied, "Perhaps we should discuss my price first, your grace."

He brushed that aside with a shake of his head. "That won't be necessary. I'll pay you whatever you ask."

Her brows pinched in skepticism. "Whatever I ask? I'm very flattered by your apparent trust in my ability, sir, but I assure you, I'm no Peter Paul Rubens."

The side of his mouth twitched up as he raked his gaze over her rigidly sitting form. "I am aware of that, Lady Cheshire, though after viewing what you have to offer, I'm certain your talent will be worth every penny I spend."

Again, the double meaning in his remark disconcerted her, and a familiar warmth crept up her neck and into her cheeks. He probably noticed it, too, which only made the matter worse. She lifted her cup and drew a sip of her tea.

Straightening a bit, he shifted his large body in the chair. "But I do realize my request is sudden, so of course I expect to pay more. Time is of the essence where I am concerned as well."

"I see." She waited, assessing him and his formality, especially considering all they'd shared in the past—a past he claimed to not recall. "So . . . if I asked for ten thousand pounds for a four-foot portrait, you'd comply?"

She'd been more or less teasing with that outrageous

offer, but he didn't look at all fazed by it. Instead, he offered her a beautiful smile that nearly took her breath.

Dropping his voice, he replied, "I would."

She laughed. "That's ridiculous."

His brows rose as he leaned back casually once more, lacing his fingers together over his stomach. "I think, madam, that if the worst thing I must do is pay ten thousand pounds for the enormous pleasure of sitting and staring at you for several hours a day, for perhaps weeks, it would be an investment well spent."

The satisfaction she felt from his compliment wrapped her in a seductive heat she simply could not brush aside. Why he flirted with her, she couldn't fathom, but she decided to attempt to get an explanation from him regarding his intent.

"Since you said time is of the essence, your grace, and I've made it known how my time is the greatest cost," she expounded matter-of-factly, "I suppose one can assume you've chosen a lady to court and marriage plans are in the making?"

His eyes widened fractionally, and he almost looked surprised. Almost. Then he tipped his head a bit to gaze at her askance.

"Would that have an effect on the price?"

She grinned. "Perhaps."

He smiled. "Why?"

She lifted her cup to her lips, taking another swallow of tea without moving her gaze from the directness of his. Seconds later, she replied, "If you propose to a friend of mine, I might be more willing to give you a generous offer."

"You're a matchmaker now?"

She lifted a shoulder delicately. "I wouldn't call myself a matchmaker exactly, but I think I should be rather pleased if someone I care about married so well."

"Indeed. So you find me an excellent catch, do you?" he asked, his voice low and taunting with amusement.

Without pause, she countered, "Wouldn't you if you had a daughter?"

His eyes lit up. "Touché, Lady Cheshire."

She nodded once, feeling enormously satisfied that he seemed to admire her polished comeback.

He regarded her closely, tapping his thumbs together in his lap, his eyes narrowing even as he continued to smile.

Moments later, he remarked, "Lady Isabella is beautiful, and she is a friend, is she not?"

The fact that he would mention Isabella as a possible wife for him irked her for a reason she couldn't define, though she really should have expected it. He had appeared at her party, after all, and she would make an excellent match for him, at least socially.

"Yes, she's actually my closest friend, and she is beautiful," Viola agreed pleasantly, masking her feelings well. "But you do know if you show even the slightest interest in courting her, you'll be forever at the mercy of Lady Tenby."

He chuckled, his dark eyes sparkling. "Thank you for the warning. But truthfully, I think I'd prefer a wife who's more . . . vibrant."

She had no clue what that could mean. "Vibrant, your grace?"

Shrugging, he replied, "I tend to prefer ladies with dark hair, someone more like . . . an enchantress than an angel."

Her stomach fluttered, and for a slice of a second, Viola wondered if he considered her more attractive than Isabella, though in a million years, she'd never ask him. Instead, lifting her cup to her lips, she finished off her tea in a swallow, then placed both cup and saucer on the walnut table in front of her.

"I see your point," she maintained with a forced sigh. "Isabella does look like an angel, and she's rather too innocent to be called an enchantress."

"Agreed." He paused, watching her closely, then said, "And what do you think of Lady Anna Tildare?"

He couldn't have shocked her more. "Lady Anna?" she fairly blurted. Then, catching herself, she smoothed her skirts and cleared her throat. "I'm sorry, your grace, but a man of your . . . um . . . stature can surely find someone more suitable than Lady Anna."

"You don't care for her?" he asked, his tone warm with continued good humor.

She shouldn't have said anything. If he told a soul, gossip would surely spread, and in the end, she could be excluded from certain social events that would no doubt dampen her impeccable reputation. Then again, perhaps she worried too much, though it never hurt to be careful.

Smiling, she replied, "That's not what I meant, your grace. Lady Anna would make a lovely wife, I'm sure."

His brows rose. "And yet she's not suitable for someone of my stature?"

Viola couldn't now tell if he was teasing her or simply didn't believe her meager explanation. Suddenly she felt uncomfortable in her stays and she fidgeted a little on the sofa.

"Please forgive me," she said with feigned meekness, "I only meant that she is very social. She adores the city and attends every ball and festivity. You told me yourself that you prefer the country. And while it's true that I don't know you very well, I do know Anna. It just doesn't seem quite a . . . suitable match, but that's only my opinion."

"Ahh . . . I understand."

Frankly, she couldn't tell if he understood or not.

"And yet she does come with a remarkable dowry," he added seconds later.

So he already knew the marriageable value of Lord Brooksfield's only daughter. That irritated her more than the thought of him courting Isabella.

She smiled flatly. "But you don't appear to be in need of it, your grace."

He blinked, as if he couldn't believe she'd said that. Then, grinning widely, he murmured, "Thank you for the compliment, Lady Cheshire."

His good-natured response, when he could have re-proved her for her gauche interjection into his personal affairs, consoled her a little, and she decided to make light of it. In a low, conspiratorial voice, she acknowledged, "And think of it this way, if you court Lady Anna, I'll have to charge you more for your portrait, since she's worth a fortune."

He grinned again, slyly. "Really? You'd charge *more* than ten thousand pounds?"

She ran a palm down one long sleeve. "You must admit it would be difficult to pass up such an opportunity to enlarge my own coffer."

He nodded very slowly. "For both of us, I should think."

"Except that Lady Anna is also blonde," she reminded him. "And you said you prefer ladies with dark hair. I wouldn't call her vibrant, either."

He didn't reply for a moment, just continued to eye her candidly, as if he studied her for some unknown purpose, trying to delve into her very female thoughts. Not only did his overt attention make her nervous; it made her hot all over as well, and she immediately regretted wearing such a conservative gown, which scratched her neck and didn't allow her to breathe. She should never have permitted the conversation to become so intimate.

With a wave of her hand, she tried to dismiss it all. "Of course who you choose to court is your affair, sir. And naturally I won't charge you a penny more than I would anyone else, which is far, far less than ten thousand pounds. I suggest we get started with our first sitting tomorrow morning, and if we work quickly, it shouldn't take too long to finish." With a rush of air, she finalized their meeting by saying, "And please forgive me for infringing on your privacy. It isn't for me to discuss."

"Not at all, madam," he fairly drawled, lifting a hand to rub his chin with his fingers and thumb. "I rather enjoyed your insight."

Enjoyed her insight?

"And watching you squirm," he continued as his

amusement faded. Leaning forward, he confessed, "You are far more clever and beautiful than Lady Anna Tildare, and I'm certain she knows it, which is why she disregards you and flaunts her wealth and class whenever you're near. You, in turn, are flustered by the notion of her marrying a man *you* find attractive." With a deadly smile, he finished in a whisper, "You needn't worry, madam. I won't tell a soul that you tried to dissuade me from her charms, whatever they may be."

She flushed deeply then, her eyes growing wide with astonishment as she sank into her corset. He had rendered her speechless, which he apparently noticed, or expected, because he stood at that moment, adjusted his coat, then walked around the tea table to gaze down at her face. She just stared at him, unsure what to do, thoroughly confused by his motives. He reached out with his hand, palm up, and after several seconds of gaping at it, she realized he wanted her to take it and stand before him. Reluctantly, she grasped his fingers as gently as possible, and he helped her rise on shaky legs to meet the level of his gaze, his thumb closing over her knuckles to keep her from pulling away.

"Your price sounds reasonable and I accept it, madam," he murmured softly. "I will be here in the morning for our first sitting. Is ten o'clock a good time?"

She nodded in slight, jerky movements, captured by his mesmerizing eyes.

He raised her hand to his mouth, his gaze never moving from hers as his lips lingered and his warm breath caressed her delicate skin, making her shiver within.

"I'm very much looking forward to tomorrow," he said huskily. "Until then."

She didn't argue. With a brief curtsey, she simply muttered, "Your grace."

And then at last he released her and turned, walking out of her parlor, his shoes echoing on the parquet floor as they had at his arrival.

It took minutes, it seemed, for her heart to stop pounding, for her body to move again. But instead of leaving the parlor herself, she fairly fell into the sofa, her skirts crumpling around her in a heap she hardly noticed as she tried to put some rationale behind their most atypical conversation.

He had changed dramatically from the thin, dying man she'd tried to help all those years ago. That he had filled out muscularly to become a stately, virile gentleman was a complete understatement, though she couldn't quite decide why such an acknowledgment of his amazing recovery intimidated her. And it wasn't just his appearance that caused her so much worry. The fact that he had reentered her life so unexpectedly, and in such a peculiar manner, made her question every single thing he said and did. Frankly put, she didn't believe in coincidences this great, which meant she couldn't trust him at all.

But she had her own card to play should he threaten her in any way. After spending hours with him in the dungeon, where he'd spoken in a drug-induced haze, sometimes incoherently, sometimes clearly, she knew a secret or two about him that, should he endanger her or her son's future, she would use as a weapon in confrontation. True, her confusing feelings for him were as acute as they had been five years ago, but now she understood herself better, and she realized with fortitude that she wouldn't be so quick to fall victim to her attraction this time.

No, all things considered, she had a power to stay ahead of whatever game he might be playing, or even worse, whatever war he intended to wage. That thought in mind, she stood, straightened her skirts, then walked swiftly out of her parlor to make the needed arrangements for their first sitting tomorrow—while considering every possible angle to ensure her social and financial survival.

Chapter Four

He tried to stand today, but soon realized they'd chained him. Watching him struggle makes my heart ache so. . . .

Ian sat at the large oak desk in his study, listening to the steady rainfall outside, staring at a letter he was trying to write to his sister, Ivy. It was of little use, however, as he simply couldn't concentrate on mundane topics that might interest a marchioness and expectant mother. And he certainly wasn't going to let her know of his contact with Viola. The two ladies had met five years ago, during his captivity, as Ivy had tried to find and free him, but even as a famous seer, his sister had never felt any malicious intent from Viola, as she had from the woman's sisters. Ivy could be very stubborn, too, and he knew from either experience or some shared intuition that his twin would be mighty mad at him to learn that he intended to establish some justice of his own where the former Miss Bennington-Jones was concerned. But even as he tried to simply answer the trivial questions she'd posed in her last letter, his mind, usually centered and controlled, kept wandering to the fascinating Lady Cheshire.

He would be leaving shortly for his first portrait sitting, and he expected her to try to keep the conversation between them formal, the topics general and of a social nature. Keeping his own words and thoughts in check would likely prove to be difficult, however. He knew he made her uncomfortable each time they were together, and that she was drawn to him—something he would use to his advantage. When he'd first started this quest for justice, he hadn't been exactly certain how each detail in his plan would be accomplished. But after spending a bit of time with her and witnessing her inability to hide her confusion at his unexpected return into her life, her unsettling attraction to him, and, most of all, her fear of being discovered, he now had a better idea of how to bring a woman like Viola to her knees.

A light rapping on his study door cut into his musings.

"Come."

Braetham entered. "Your grace, Mr. Cafferty has arrived."

Ian looked at the large clock over the mantel. Three minutes to nine. As always, Cafferty arrived precisely on time.

"Send him in," he said, sitting forward and adjusting himself in his oak rocker.

Braetham nodded. "Very well, your grace."

Ian had hired Milo Cafferty, a distinguished and rather exclusive investigator who worked only for those with the means to afford him, to do his level best at uncovering each secret the Lady Cheshire kept to heart. He'd been well worth the hefty expense, too, as the man had been able to discover her whereabouts in London within four days of his hiring, learn some of the more intimate details of her marriage and the state of her finances in less than two weeks, and let him know the moment she'd officially come out of mourning. They generally met once a week for updates, but late last evening the man had sent word of new information regarding Lady Cheshire and had requested they meet as soon as possible. Ian had obliged him, asking Cafferty to be at his town house before he left for his sitting. As always, his well-paid agent of inquiry did his bidding without question or argument.

Ian stood as he heard footsteps in the hallway, taking note as he always did of the man's extremely lean and tall frame when Braetham admitted him into the study seconds later. Now in his midfifties, Milo Cafferty had been retired from the metropolitan police force for some seven or eight years due to a foot injury incurred during a building collapse at the docks, which had resulted in a very pronounced limp. And yet what struck Ian every time he met the man was his overtly cheerful nature, emphasized by his oiled, thin mustache that he curled into the shape of a long smile in front of his cheeks. Quite a contrast to the image one would have of a retired, injured police officer who no doubt lived in a measure of constant pain.

"Good morning, your grace," Cafferty said in fair English, staggering somewhat inelegantly across the Persian carpet, arm extended, the usual grin spanning his gaunt face.

"Morning, Mr. Cafferty," Ian replied, moving around his desk to greet the man. After shaking hands, he directed him to one of the wing chairs across from him.

Cafferty lowered his body with effort, then stretched his injured foot out in front of him. "Shall I begin, your grace?"

Ian returned his rocker. "Please. You said it was important news?"

"Fascinating news, more like it, sir," the man countered, his conspiratorial-laced excitement charging the air. "And I'm not sure what to make of it."

Ian remained silent, allowing the investigator to gather his thoughts.

Cafferty pulled at the collar of his shirt as if it strangled him. Then after clearing his throat, he asked, "Have you ever heard of the artist Victor Bartlett-James, your grace?"

Ian's brows rose very slowly. "I have. I believe his artistic endeavors border on the salacious, do they not?"

"Precisely," Cafferty acknowledged. "Most of his art was sold privately, to gentlemen of means, usually at auction for great sums. He's been retired now for quite some time, and because he apparently no longer works, his portraits and drawings are highly prized." He chuckled. "Where one might hang a salacious portrait is beyond my imagination, sir, but there you have it."

Intrigued yet totally puzzled, Ian rocked back in his chair. "And somehow this artist of provocative work is connected to Lady Cheshire?"

Cafferty rubbed his fingertips across his mustache. "I'm not certain if they know each other as professional artists, your grace. His identity is unknown, at least to the general public. But last evening, through one of my contacts, I learned that Lady Cheshire met with her solicitor yesterday afternoon, and during a twenty-minute conversation, requested that he put a rare Bartlett-James charcoal drawing that she apparently owns up for immediate auction."

Ian slowly sat forward. "Are you certain?"

Cafferty nodded heartily. "I am indeed, sir. My sources are quite reliable. It's to be auctioned Saturday, at Brimleys." His thick brows creased in thought. "Rather exclusive gentlemen's club seems like an odd place for an auction, though."

"Not necessarily," Ian maintained. "Not for exclusive, suggestive art that only gentlemen would be interested in purchasing. But—why now?"

The investigator shook his head. "Don't know what excuse she gave her solicitor, since my contact was in the building, not the private meeting itself."

Ian tapped his fingertips on his desktop, eyes narrowed. "The only reason I can think of for selling something like that now, and for her to risk being caught doing so, is to raise money," he said. "Lots of it."

"And quickly," Cafferty added in agreement.

He remained silent for several long seconds, his mind racing as he attempted to understand the meaning of such an action and the possibilities he could use to his benefit.

She'd obviously made this decision after their tea yesterday. He didn't know this as fact, but it made sense. He knew he'd shaken her with his sexual innuendos that hadn't quite been advances, flustering her and perhaps even distressing her with discovery so deeply that she'd felt threatened and had needed to act immediately. But for what purpose?

Ian stood and walked behind his rocker to stare out the long window to the gray and misty morning, folding his arms over his chest as he watched rain pellets strike the sidewalk of his small garden in mind-numbing rhythm. Cafferty remained quiet, waiting for comment or instruction, likely as confounded by this news as he was.

He'd paid to have Viola followed by Cafferty's men for several months now in order to learn her established routines, who she knew and the places she frequented. Thus far there had been nothing surprising or out of the ordinary about her as a widow of her station. She had a son, whom she kept close at heel, but that in itself was unremarkable. She painted in her own studio in the back of her town house, lived on her husband's assets, and rarely entertained, though that would no doubt change as her mourning period had ended. And all of this information had been relayed to him on a regular basis while he'd waited patiently at Stamford, hoping to be rewarded by any shred of news that he could use against her. But nothing about her movements or daily habits had been startling or even remotely interesting— until now.

This unusual development troubled him. Obviously she couldn't sell certain assets of her husband's estate, nor would she if she could, with her son as legal heir. But the selling of one of her husband's personal extravagances, one that perhaps had embarrassed her at the purchase, made sense if she needed money quickly. And the only reason she might take such a risk was if she planned to run from him. He might actually have done the same thing had he been in her shoes.

Still, he had the advantage of knowing her plans ahead of her actions. The problem for him was how to use this piece of information.

Suddenly he flipped around to stare at Cafferty. "How much is she asking for the piece?"

Cafferty blinked. "Your grace, she's asking two thousand pounds as the starting bid for the work."

Ian scratched his jaw, thinking. Then the fog of uncertainty cleared in his head, and a small smile of triumph spread across his face. "I need you to meet with her solicitor," he said. "Today, if it can be arranged."

Cafferty struggled to sit up straighter in his chair. "Pardon me, your grace, but don't you think it will raise his suspicions when I reveal my identity to him?"

"It doesn't matter. We're making an adjustment to the plan," he said, walking toward his desk once again. Instead of sitting, he stood behind his rocker, clutching the back of it with both hands as he looked at Cafferty directly. "I want you to have Lady Cheshire informed, through her solicitor, that you are an agent of inquiry, hired by a secret buyer's private banker. You don't know the buyer, just the banker, and his name is also confidential. This secret buyer of erotic artwork has heard of the upcoming auction, but he doesn't want to bid for it because the situation with his wife is . . . delicate, and he does not, in any way, want her to know. He will, instead, pay the owner three thousand pounds for the Bartlett-James piece before the end of the week."

"Make an offer to buy directly from the owner?"

"Precisely," Ian replied. "And you don't know who the owner is, of course, just that the artwork is for sale."

"She might not sell for that sum, your grace, especially if she's counting on competition for the piece to bring in more."

Eyes narrowed, Ian thought about that for a second or two, then said, "If it's not enough, increase the increments by a thousand pounds until a sale is established."

Cafferty's mouth dropped open so far that his thin mustache curled up tightly. "Sir, that could grow to an outrageous amount of money."

"Yes, I know," he agreed, his tone matter-of-fact. "But I want you to bid, offer to counteroffer, until she yields."

The investigator shook his head, his expression dubious. "And if she questions how this . . . buyer learned of the upcoming auction?"

Ian shrugged. "It's irrelevant, though probably through gossip at Brimleys. Certainly the club is looking forward to the publicity. Regardless of how, you don't know the buyer anyway, so you can't possibly say."

Cafferty nodded minutely. "There's always the possibility she won't sell at all—"

"She will," Ian cut in with assurance, feeling strangely satisfied that he could so easily manipulate the woman's situation without her knowledge. "If she's looking to raise money quickly, Cafferty, she'll be more than eager to accept a private sale than risk a public auction where someone might learn she's the owner, even if she suspects my involvement, which is unlikely." He dropped his voice a fraction to add with wry amusement, "And if she retracts and chooses not to sell the piece because someone has learned of her predicament, it will put her in a tight spot financially once again, and I will have the advantage of knowing she isn't prepared to make any significant moves yet."

Cafferty remained quiet for a long moment, appearing hesitant, even slightly uneasy as he eyed Ian closely, his characteristic smile gone from his mouth, his lank form rigid in his chair. Ian understood his concern. The man had no idea on earth why the Duke of Chatwin wanted information regarding an average, aristocratic widow so badly he would have her followed for weeks, then pay such an enormous sum for a piece of lascivious artwork she'd tried to secretly sell. Cafferty wasn't paid to ask questions, and he'd so far not been required to do anything dangerous or illegal. But this new request grew very close to compromising their working agreement because it aroused a suspicion that hadn't been there before. And Ian didn't need him suspicious.

Smiling pleasantly, he released the back of the rocker, straightened, and clasped his hands behind him. "You needn't be concerned, Mr. Cafferty," he assured the man, his tone and bearing regal. "My intentions toward the Lady Cheshire are entirely noble. But they are private, as I'm certain you also understand."

The investigator nodded as he drew in a long breath, his apprehension quelled for the moment. "Of course, your grace," he answered formally. "I'll see to this matter immediately. Is there anything else for now?"

Ian shook his head as he walked around the desk. "No, that'll be all. But do let me know as soon as you confirm the sale and I'll have a bank draft drawn at once. If she insists on placing it at auction even after you've continued to make offers, or withdraws the sale completely, I need to know that as well."

Cafferty leaned heavily on the armrest of his chair and raised himself awkwardly. "I'll do what I can, sir." He paused as he adjusted his posture and put weight on his injured foot. "I suppose you want the drawing?"

He hadn't thought of that, but having it in his possession might prove useful should he decide to use it against her in some fashion. "Yes, have it brought here. But under no circumstances let anyone know I'm the purchaser."

"Certainly, your grace." Cafferty's smile lit his face. "And I wish you all the best in finding a place to hang it."

Ian chuckled, reached out, and shook the investigator's hand. "Braetham will show you out."

"Good day, your grace," Cafferty said with a slight bow. Then turning, he hobbled from the study.

With ten minutes remaining before he had to leave for his sitting, Ian returned to the window. The rain had finally eased to a sprinkle and the color in his flower garden gleamed vibrantly as the morning began to brighten. It reminded him of Viola, so vibrant and lovely and full of color, whose dewy soft cheeks would one day gleam from her own tears of sorrow.

Chapter Five

*I spoke to him at last, whispered words of comfort as
I tried to soothe his brow. He first called me Ivy, then
opened his eyes when he realized a stranger sat beside
him. . . .*

*V*iola stood at the window of her bedroom, pushing
the lace curtain aside just enough to watch the Duke
of Chatwin descend from his carriage and stride with
confidence toward her front door. She couldn't see him
very clearly, as he wore a light overcoat and top hat
pulled low over his brow to ward off the lingering mist,
but even the sight of his powerful form made her insides
flutter with apprehension. Every instinct she possessed
warned her about being in his company again, and the
fact that she felt that certain strange pull of attraction
just by looking at him at a distance made her angry at
herself for being so gullible. And maybe being angry
was the best thing to keep her on her toes.

Suddenly, just before he passed out of view below,
he paused in his stride and glanced up. She quickly let

the curtain drop and stood back, feeling irrationally violated as her pulse began to race, uncertain if he'd noticed her or not. But it didn't matter. She would play her part and receive him as she would an ordinary client, pretend to be enamored of his good charm while she kept her mind alert for any reason to escape. Just this morning she'd sent her son to stay with her late husband's sister for at least two weeks, getting him far from the city and the mess she feared to come. If she needed to, she was prepared to take him to the Continent for a while. For as long as necessary.

Turning, she glanced at her figure in the full-length mirror next to her bed and fluffed her skirts. She'd chosen a vivid yellow day gown with white lace flounces and sleeves in the hope of presenting a sunny disposition on such a dreary day. The fact that it also had a very low neckline and she'd donned her finest corset to lift her bosom in compliment meant nothing more than a desire to appear feminine and sophisticated. Or so she told herself. With her hair plaited and pinned becomingly atop her head, and satisfied that she looked the part of the elegant young widow, she pinched her cheeks, bit her lips lightly, and left her bedroom.

It took her only a few moments to descend the stairs to the first landing and walk the hallway toward her studio on the east-facing side of her home, a room she'd chosen because of its wall of long windows that captured the morning sun and lightened her workstation, at least on most days. She'd also brightened the area by adding yellow wallpaper adorned with pink rosebuds, and a cream-colored sofa on which she did her sketching before painting. For her son, she'd placed a child-sized chair and table in one corner so he could draw with her when he got bored in the nursery. It was the sunniest room in the house, and on many days, she remained inside it for hours.

Today, however, she hoped the time spent would be short. She'd instructed Needham to take Chatwin to her studio immediately upon his arrival, and presumably the man already awaited her. As she approached the door, she paused just long enough to draw a deep breath for confidence, then silently entered.

She spotted him at once as he stood in front of her main easel, staring down at a still-life painting she'd begun a week ago. He wore fine silk dinner clothes in black, with a white silk shirt and an olive, white, and black striped cravat, tied perfectly, highlighting his coloring and accentuating his handsome, chiseled face. Of course he only wore such magnificent clothing at this hour because of his portrait, but the mere sight of him so spectacularly adorned made her falter. She had always been drawn to him as a man, though now the feeling concerned her more not only because he knew it but also because he looked so formidable and strong and powerfully . . . sexual. Like a man whose passionate nature could not be refused. She knew the consequences of such an irresistible desire, and until she left him for a final time, she would do everything in her power to fight it.

He glanced up to catch her staring at him, and a sly grin spread across his face. Planting a pleasant smile on her lips, she pretended not to notice by acting nonchalant.

"Good morning, your grace," she offered with a curtsey.

"Lady Cheshire," he replied, standing fully erect to face her as he clasped his hands behind him.

"Shall we get started?" she asked, walking toward him at a steady pace.

His gaze smoothly scanned her figure when she approached him, then he turned his attention back to the easel.

"How much time do you take on a painting like this?"

She moved closer, lightly holding her hands in front of her. "It depends on how much work I put into it daily. If I'm busy with other things, it could take weeks to finish."

"I see." He studied it for a moment. "What is the point of painting fruit?"

She laughed outright. "It's not the fruit that's so intriguing, your grace, at least not for me. I enjoy vibrant hues and rich color blends, which is why painting floras and fruit are appealing." She shrugged a shoulder lightly. "And of course fruit and flowers are inoffensive."

"Inoffensive?"

"Still life appeals to almost everybody and can be hung in any room in the house."

He looked at her askance. "And may I ask, what kind of artwork can't be hung in any room?"

She wavered. The double meaning behind his words nearly took her aback, and for the slightest second she had to wonder if he purposely baited her with knowledge of the more sensual side to her artwork. Then again, she was probably overreacting. He should know nothing about it.

Seconds later, she replied, "I suppose any artwork

can be placed in any room the owner chooses. But what I meant, your grace, is that when a painting is full of various colors, it's possible to blend them with any decor, in any room. Or most rooms." She smiled. "Perhaps it's different for other artists, but I enjoy the boldness of great color in my work."

He nodded very slowly. "As you obviously do in your wardrobe."

She blinked. "I beg your pardon?"

One side of his mouth twitched up seductively again, making him look so handsome of a sudden that it nearly took her breath.

"I only meant that you seem to enjoy bright colors on your person as well," he explained, voice lowered. "The night of the ball you wore scarlet, yesterday it was vivid blue, today sunny yellow. They're obviously colors that enhance your appearance and make you stand out in a crowd."

It struck her as quite odd that he'd not only remember what she'd worn yesterday but also remembered the color of every gown he'd seen on her. Men, in her experience, didn't notice such things, or even care. Then again, she had always considered him an extraordinary kind of gentleman, and at this point she could hardly let his comment go without response.

"How very . . . unusual of you to notice my taste in attire, sir," she said pleasantly.

"Not at all," he countered at once. "It simply occurred to me how difficult mourning must have been for you. I'm sure being confined to black and gray would be rather unappealing for a young widow who prefers bright colors."

That seemed like such a staid answer, and yet somewhere deep within she found it suspect.

"I'm sure you flatter me too much, your grace," she maintained cautiously, her tone and manner formal. "But I do thank you for your kind words." Instinctively, she moved away from him and busied herself by pulling the curtains on the east windows aside, one by one, to let in as much light as possible. "I'm assuming you want a formal background, sir?"

"You're the artist, madam. I'll do exactly as you say."

She tried not to smile as she returned to the easel, lifted her still-life painting and leaned it against the wall, then picked a large, blank canvas to use for his portrait.

"If you'll sit on the stool provided, your grace, I'll begin."

He glanced around to note the wooden stool beside the south-facing window. "Here?"

"Yes, please," she said, placing the canvas on the easel. "The light next to the window is the best we have for now. Hopefully, when we begin the actual painting, the sun will shine and make it brighter in here."

"You're not going to paint now?" he asked as he walked to the tall wooden stool and climbed upon it easily.

From the small desk beside her, she lifted her sketchbook and needlework basket, filled with sundry craft items and supplies, then carried them both to the sofa about five feet across from him and sat comfortably. "I'm going to sketch your likeness first, then I'll get to the painting, though it probably won't be today," she clarified. "One can only stand, or in your case sit on a stool, for so long."

"That's why you get the comfortable sofa and I'm left with the small wooden stool?" he asked, amused.

She smiled as she untied her needlework basket and began to rummage through various types of paint-brushes and different-sized charcoal pencils until she found one to her liking. "I usually stand or sit on a stool when I paint, as well, your grace."

"Ah," he replied casually, "so we'll both be uncomfortable."

He couldn't possibly have any idea just how uncomfortable she was at the moment. "Indeed," she offered, sitting back to regard him, her sketch book in her lap. "Though I'm used to it, and as I get involved in the process, I must admit I hardly notice."

"I'm sure that's true."

Another staid and very ordinary comment that, if she pondered it, could contain a world of subtle meanings. Considering their background, she was beginning to find their conversations amusing in their extreme primness, and bordering on the ridiculous. If she hadn't been so ready to bolt from him, she might have snorted a laugh and told the man to tell her what he *really* thought.

She worked quietly for a few minutes, sketching his form into the pose she would use should he approve it. He watched her from a distance, and the most unnerving part was his rapt attention to her. She could positively feel his gaze on her as if he studied each strand of hair, each curve of her body and line of her face. In her experience, most subjects, even the adults, grew bored or distracted after a short time. Some became quite chatty or impatient. The feeling she got from the Duke of Chatwin was that there was nowhere on earth he'd rather be at the moment.

"You know," he said, cutting into her thoughts, "the more I look at you, Lady Cheshire, the more I know we've met before."

Viola had to force herself to remain composed, fighting the urge to look him directly in the eye.

"I suppose it's possible," she replied rather vaguely, sketching furiously as she pretended to concentrate on her work.

Another few moments drifted by in silence. Then he murmured softly, "I'm sure you realize I enjoy looking at you."

Her breath caught in her chest, and she paused almost imperceptibly in her pencil strokes, but she didn't dare glance up to reveal how his frank comment startled her. And how in heaven's name did he expect her to respond?

"I'm sure you flatter me too much, your grace," she yielded, her voice taut, smile forced.

He chuckled. "Does mentioning my attraction to you make you uneasy?"

Oh, my God.

She sighed, closing her eyes for a second or two before replying, "Perhaps it's best not to discuss such things, your grace."

He didn't argue her statement, thankfully, though she wished he wouldn't stare at her quite so intensely. At this point, she decided she'd rather keep their necessary interactions formal and mundane. She didn't want to know at *all* what he really thought.

Moments later, he asked, "Do you hope to marry again, madam?"

Finally. A subject she could discuss. "I don't think so, no," she answered without reservation. "Or at least not soon. My life is very full at the moment, and I'm quite happy."

"That sounds like an answer one would give the queen."

She did look up then. "I beg your pardon?"

He shrugged a shoulder, eyes narrowed as he held her gaze. "It sounds as if you've rehearsed that response for any formal inquiry on the subject."

She licked her lips, hesitating only briefly before she turned her attention back to her sketch. "Actually, your grace, it's the truth."

He waited, then asked, "You didn't enjoy marriage?"

She thought about that for a moment, deciding to answer him honestly. "On the contrary, I did enjoy much of it. Although we had little time together before his passing, my husband was very kind and generous." She smiled again. "And I am proud to have my son, his heir, to dote on."

"Well, you either have an excellent nanny, or he's very well behaved. I've yet to hear or see any evidence of a child in your home, Lady Cheshire."

Peeking up through her lashes, she decided he offered the comment sincerely. "Actually, he's not in the city, but visiting my husband's family in the country."

"Ah." After a short pause, he added, "And you didn't go with him?"

She blew across her sketch to rid it of pencil dust. "I'll join him soon, I'm sure. But for now I have your portrait to paint."

"So I'm keeping you from time with your child, am I?"

She smiled and glanced up. "Don't feel guilty, your grace. I miss him terribly, of course, but this is my first season out of mourning, and frankly, I think a bit of separation will be good for him. He's nearly five, and as a baron's son, he needs to begin learning his place in the family."

"My, you are indeed a proud mother," he replied with amusement.

She gave him a nod. "As you will be a proud father, I'm certain, when you have your own children, sir."

"I suppose that's true." Seconds later, he asked, "And what is his name?"

Warmly, she returned, "John Henry Clifford Cresswald, Lord Cheshire."

"Is that what you call him?"

She stopped sketching and looked up. "Call him?"

He chuckled again and ran his fingers through his hair. "Dear Lady Cheshire, that was such a long and formal answer I have to wonder if it's indeed what you call him even when the two of you are alone in the nursery."

She pressed her lips together to keep from laughing. "Forgive me, your grace, but as you said, I am a proud mother. In point of fact, I call him John Henry—unless, of course, he's very naughty, in which case using his full name and title tends to produce a better result in getting him to behave."

"I see. You use the inbred tricks of motherhood, I suppose."

She did laugh at that. "My dear Lord Chatwin, there are *no* inbred tricks of motherhood, I assure you. We do only the best we can and hope the love and discipline we provide our precious children give them each a worthy heart to build a solid and respectable future."

He shook his head, grinning. "Even that sounds rehearsed."

"That's because it is," she replied, her tone lowered conspiratorially. "I heard my own mother say it day to day for years, though she never used the word 'love'; she used 'example' instead." She frowned gently, then added, "I never understood how we could give our children a worthy heart if we didn't show our love to them first. I should think that's the *best* example."

The amusement on his handsome face captured her, and for several seconds they gazed at each other silently, with some kind of mutual, intimate connection she couldn't quite define, or exactly comprehend.

"You love your son very much," he stated softly.

Her heart melted from the mere thought of such a gift. "Beyond measure, your grace. Everything I do in my life is for him and his well-being."

For a long, lingering moment he just stared at her candidly. And then very slowly, his eyes narrowed and his smile began to fade, as if she'd said or done something to irritate him.

Shifting his weight on the stool, he sat up a little straighter. "I suppose you want more children, then?"

His voice had grown edgier as a sudden coolness prevailed. His change in mood made her remember her place in his life precisely, reminding her to avoid revealing too much about herself. The less he knew of her personal affairs, especially the lengths she would go to protect John Henry, the better.

Lowering her gaze back to her sketch pad, she said matter-of-factly, "Not necessarily. I would have to marry again first, which for now isn't something I care to contemplate. And I already have a son and heir to my late husband's estate."

"You don't want a daughter?"

Her lips tipped up slightly. "A daughter cannot be guaranteed, your grace. And to be perfectly honest, I loathed carrying."

That surprised him. She could sense it in him without even glancing up.

"How odd to hear a lady say that," he replied.

She shrugged, tilting her head to the side a little. "Perhaps for the lady who has no physical ailments during her confinement and delivers with ease."

"You had physical problems?"

His eagerness to discuss something so personal and delicate made her wary, especially in light of the formality of their working acquaintance. Frankly, discussing childbirth with any gentleman assaulted her sensibilities, though after a quick peek at his face, she decided he truly looked curious and didn't seem at all embarrassed by the subject.

She sighed. "Yes, I was ill much of the time. He was also delivered with his feet first, after three days of labor, which caused me to nearly die at his birth. I thank God every day that I was in the city and had the expertise of a good doctor at my disposal. Had I been in the country, I suspect we would have both perished, as most children do when born the wrong way."

"That's . . . unfortunate," he muttered, subdued. "I suppose your husband was beside himself with worry."

She shivered within, as she always did at the memory of those dark days. "I'm sure he was," she agreed, probably too brightly. "In any case, the . . . experience was very difficult for me, and not something I long to repeat."

"My sister is expecting her second child any day now and she's ecstatic," he disclosed almost absentmindedly. "Or so I gather."

So Lady Ivy was carrying. Viola wasn't about to ask him to elaborate. "Well, I shan't be gloomy for her sake. How very lovely for her."

"Indeed," he agreed, nodding lightly. "I suspect her husband is beside himself as well."

Smiling fully at that, she remarked, "No doubt he is, but probably with joy if her first delivery held no problems."

He didn't reply to that statement, just continued to watch her, his features unreadable. She turned her attention back to the sketch, now nearly done to her satisfaction, hoping the man would grasp her desire to leave the topic of childbirth, his sister, and especially the past, alone.

"May I ask you another question, Lady Cheshire?" he murmured seconds later.

He certainly didn't expect her to deny him, with his

suddenly silky-smooth tone and the intimacy it implied. Her pulse began to quicken with renewed uncertainty, but she didn't dare look at him.

"Of course, your grace," she replied as primly as possible.

He drew in a long breath, then let it out slowly. "You've never asked me a single question about my past or interests, my family or home in the country. I wouldn't find it so unusual in most circumstances, but given that I explicitly told you I believe we've met before, I'm . . . curious to know why that is."

She stilled, staring down at her sketch pad as her mouth went dry. Trying to sound nonchalant, she admitted, "I—I hadn't really thought about it, actually."

"No?" he prodded. "You never thought to ask me even general questions about my daily affairs or acquaintances who might be mutual? Never thought about where our paths might have crossed? I even mentioned my sister and you didn't ask her name, much less where she lives or if she's titled."

His gentle affront almost made her angry, though in truth that anger should have been directed at herself rather than him, because his query was perfectly reasonable. If she'd been smart, she would have exchanged pleasantries before now, and not doing so only made such an oversight on her part seem evasive. Then again, she had no reason to think he knew her motives, only that he questioned them.

"I apologize, your grace," she said sweetly, placing her charcoal pencil back in her needlework basket, then standing, sketchbook in hand. Gaze direct, she continued, "Honestly, I never gave it a thought. Of course I'm curious, and I just assumed your sister was titled and lived in the country." She spread her free arm wide. "But, as I've already said, if we've met before, I can't recall anything about it. And of course it's not my place to question clients in such a manner, or become too intrusive into their lives, especially those with titles as grand as yours. I'm sure you understand."

For a second or two he looked as if he might laugh. Then he drawled, "I do, indeed. It's very . . . noble of you to respect my station, Lady Cheshire."

His use of such a phrase sounded a bit deriding, and she resisted the ridiculous urge to give him a deep curtsey. Instead, she brushed over his mock praise and walked bravely toward him, chin lifted a fraction for confidence, a satisfied smile planted on her mouth.

"I've finished the first drawing, your grace," she said as she moved to his side, the sketchbook held tight to her bosom. "Perhaps you'd like to see it?"

His brows rose slightly, but he remained sitting. "Absolutely, I would."

With him still on the stool, the top of his head met her shoulder. She scooted as close to him as she could without touching, then held the sketchbook out at arm's length so they could view it together.

"It's only a rough image, but you can better see how the portrait will appear."

He studied it for a moment, then said, "The likeness is excellent. I'm actually quite . . . delighted with your talent."

"Thank you, your grace," she replied politely, though she really felt annoyed, because if she didn't know better, she'd say he sounded more surprised than pleased. That suddenly made her determined to explain her effort. "May I show you a bit of the process?"

He shot her a fast glance. "The process?"

"How I put the drawing together."

Confusion crossed his features, and then he acquiesced. "Of course."

She tipped her head to the side minutely as she turned her attention to the drawing. "The background will be as you like it, probably your form in front of a sunny window in a library, or wherever you wish. Likewise, the colors of your attire can be to your liking, regardless of what you wear to each sitting." She began skimming specific lines with her fingertip. "You'll notice the angles of the cheekbones and the squareness of the jaw. Your side whiskers are somewhat short for the average gentleman today, but the look is quite appealing on you. I also tried to give depth to your eyes. You've got stunning, dark eyes that tend to show a great vitality, but if I paint the brow too high or thin, the likeness on the portrait may appear too cheerful, and I'd rather give a serious tone to one this formal."

He nodded very faintly, seemingly engrossed in the work.

She turned her attention to him. "You've got a good forehead—not too wide or long, and your skin is excellent. I think, for a stately appeal, I'm going to comb your hair from your face to reveal it." She reached forward and began to brush the silky strands away from his brow with her fingers. "I think—"

He grabbed her by the wrist, jerking his head back as if she'd scalded him.

She gasped, startled.

He didn't move, just held her tightly, his gaze intense, penetrating the depths of hers intimately, searching.

Viola swallowed hard and tried to pull away, but he refused to let her go. Her heart began to beat wildly in her chest, now merely inches from his face, their bodies so close she felt instantly enveloped—trapped—by his presence.

"I'm sorry, your grace," she said hoarsely, trying to wriggle her wrist from his grasp to no avail.

And then he blinked, shaking his head negligibly as if returning from a trance, his brows furrowing in confusion.

"Your grace?" she whispered again.

Slowly, he lowered his lashes and stared at her breasts, their top curves tantalizingly revealed by her tight, low-cut bodice. She grew breathless and warm from the scrutiny as his gaze lingered, and for a timeless moment she feared he might actually lean forward three inches and lay his cheek against them, kiss them with need.

The air seemed to crackle around them, charged by memories she held deeply within of a time he had clung to her in desperation. Suddenly her greatest fear was that by touching him innocently, she'd stirred whatever bits he might remember of it, too.

"Viola . . . ," he murmured.

Her eyes widened as he whispered her given name, but she remained still, held perilously in his control, uncertain what to do or say, if anything. Seconds ticked by until finally he drew in a sharp breath and looked up once more at her face.

A fierce heat lit his eyes when his gaze captured

hers, and the intense hunger she witnessed in their dark depths made her heart skip a beat and her stomach twist in knots.

He remembers something. . . .

And then, abruptly, the fire died. The mood in her studio shifted as she watched his lids narrow seductively and his handsome mouth curved into a wry smile. As if he willed himself to completely alter his demeanor, he no longer seemed disoriented or aroused, but rather returned to the disarming, intimidating gentleman he'd been when he'd arrived. He still held her wrist, but his grasp had become gentle as he began to rub the pad of his thumb along her sensitive skin. Seconds later, he raised her hand and gingerly placed his soft lips on her curled fingertips.

Stunned, her knees wobbled beneath her and she almost dropped the sketchbook she still clung to like a lifeboat. But she couldn't look away.

He watched her closely as he moved his head back and forth to caress her knuckles with a delicate, side to side brushing of his mouth. She shivered from the contact, her insides heating with an immediate sexual longing she remembered but hadn't felt in years. Then raising her hand even higher, he cocked his head slightly and kissed her wrist, peck after small peck, his warm breath teasing her deliciously until she nearly fainted.

"You're beautiful," he whispered against her. "I can't help myself when you're so near."

In a manner, she believed him, and yet his attention to her now wasn't anything like the desire she'd instinctively felt from him and beheld in his eyes only moments ago. Now it seemed forced—as if there were two sides to his thoughts and feelings. As if his actions were planned.

With a renewed strength, her emotions grounded, she attempted to pull her hand away from him again, and this time he released her.

He stood as she took a step back from him, and in some form of self-defense, she clutched her sketchbook to her bosom with both hands.

"You know I want to kiss you, Viola," he murmured huskily.

She raised her chin a fraction, growing furious with his apparent notion that he could dominate her as he pleased, that she would abide by his every desire or whim. She had given up such allowances when she'd left her overbearing family in Winter Garden, and for a final time when her husband had died, and she didn't need another man making choices for her now. Especially one who used her female nature against her. But worst of all, the worst *feeling* of all, after the last few moments, was that she couldn't be sure he wasn't acting. Or lying for a nefarious reason.

Holding his gaze, pulse racing, her face no doubt bright pink to his satisfaction, she smiled flatly and replied with prim sarcasm, "You do strike me as a man who would enjoy that kind of small diversion, your grace, but I don't think it would be in my best interest to let you. And of course it would get in the way of our professional association."

His brows rose; his lips twitched. She couldn't tell if he was surprised or amused, but if she had to guess, she would say he was both. She didn't bother to wait for his response, however. Quickly, she stepped past him and walked back to her small desk, placed her sketchbook atop it, rang the bell for a servant, then turned and faced him squarely, hands folded in front of her.

"I believe we're done for today anyway. My butler will show you out—"

He was upon her in three strides.

As swiftly as he grabbed her upper arms with both hands, he yanked her against him, his mouth coming down on hers not harshly, but firm with purpose.

A squeal escaped her at the initial contact, and for a slice of an instant, she thought to shove him away and scream. Then all negative thoughts vanished as he began to coax her lips apart with his, tease her into submission with a gentle urging that melted her within and forced a whimper from her throat.

Her sound of submission encouraged him. Releasing her arms, he wrapped his own around her and pulled her closer, hugging her fully with a palm to her back, another on her neck, his fingers brushing the hair at her nape. His mouth assaulted hers exquisitely, making every nerve in her body come alive, reminding her of the pleasure that only a man could give. His tongue skimmed her upper lip, then drove inside, and she welcomed it with a teasing of her own, mesmerized by his feel, his taste, his scent. Locked in his embrace, she could do nothing but accept him, and just as she wrapped her arms around his lower body and surrendered to desire, he paused, and then very slowly raised his head.

Viola felt him reach for her hands and pull them from him as he took a step back. Her lashes fluttered open, and in a daze, she looked up at his face.

He stared down at her, his eyes dark and unreadable, his breathing coming fast and hard as he tried to gain his own control.

Suddenly, she heard a low cough behind him, and remembering that she'd rung the bell before he'd charged at her, she realized, with total mortification, that they were not alone.

"Don't underestimate me, Lady Cheshire," he whispered for her ears only, a smirk upon his mouth. "I'm not easily brushed aside."

Furious, wanting to slap his handsome face for taking advantage and embarrassing her, she tried to react but realized at once that he still held her hands. And then as he smiled and released her fully, stepping away to allow her to view a newly hired footman sheepishly fidgeting in the doorway, she cringed inside as she began to understand exactly what he'd done. Servants talked, and by the end of the day the entire neighborhood would know that the young Widow Cheshire, so recently out of mourning, had been caught kissing the Duke of Chatwin in her studio, not innocently, but with passion. Within the week, most of good society would be heeding the delectable news, and although it likely wouldn't ruin her, she had now become the gossip of the season.

As if sensing her fury, her humiliation, he said loud enough for all, "Forgive me, madam, but I was . . . overcome by your good charms. Of course I didn't mean to take advantage."

He cleared his throat, then shot a quick glance to her footman before looking back into her eyes.

"I'll see you Friday for our next appointment."

He'd posed that as a statement, not a question, which didn't allow her to criticize his actions and turn him away to save herself a bit of disgrace. Frankly, he *dared* her to deny him, a man of power and prestige, which he knew she would not do.

Coldly, she replied, "Perhaps we'll work in the garden next time, your grace. Being out in the open air will do us both some good, don't you think?"

For seconds he did nothing as a sly grin spread across his mouth. And then, to her utter astonishment, he winked—*winked*—at her, then nodded once, turned, and walked toward her footman, who led him from her studio.

Viola clenched her fists at her sides, willing herself not to smash the windows in her rage. The man had nerve, she was forced to admit, but she was smart, too, and wouldn't again be so cleverly cornered.

He had upped the stakes, indeed. But by Friday, she vowed, she would be ready for him.

Chapter Six

I put the candle behind me today, so he couldn't see my face inside my cloak. He asked me my name, but I didn't dare speak. He is frightened, and his heartache is so intense. . . .

*V*iola stepped inside the Chelsea office of Leopold Duncan, Esquire, her solicitor of many years. The morning had been quite warm and sunny, and the small room in which she now stood felt as stuffy as the coach she'd just exited. But that was irrelevant. She didn't intend to stay long, and hadn't actually planned to see him today until she'd received an urgent note from him insisting upon an immediate meeting.

After closing her parasol and hanging it on the rack beside the door, she removed her peach lace gloves and greeted the man's assistant, Calvin Bartlett, with a nod and a brief good morning. Moments later he ushered her into Duncan's private office, where she found the man seated behind his massive desk, pen in hand as he scribbled on a sheet of paper.

He looked up when he heard her enter, then stood abruptly, his deep-set eyes bright, his round, pock-marked face cheery as always.

"Ahh, good morning, Lady Cheshire," he said with an abundance of gaiety, pulling down on his waist-coat in an attempt to cover his wide belly as he moved toward her.

She smiled and held out her hand. "Good morning, Mr. Duncan. I see you're looking well."

"As are you, madam," he replied, taking her fingers with his and bowing quickly to brush them with his lips. "Please be seated."

She did as directed, walking to an oversized, velve-teen chair and lowering her body with grace to sit upon the edge. He only had two chairs in the room besides his own, and they were both so full of fluff that one naturally sank into them inelegantly if not careful. In fact, everything in Duncan's office was either fluffy, enormous, or both, including his curtains, desk, chairs, artwork and frames, even the fireplace, and she knew for a fact that it had been decorated by his wife. Every-thing, aside from his dark brown desk and the large painting of red roses above the mantel, was the color of the summer sky and accented with yards of frilly, white lace.

"So, what information do you have for me that's so very important?" she asked breezily, folding her hands over her gloves and reticule in her lap. "I assume it's about the auction Saturday?"

Duncan fairly grunted as he plopped his round figure down onto the seat of his chair again. "Indeed, it is," he replied, leaning forward to fold his hands together on top of all the scattered paperwork. "I received an unusual visit yesterday from an agent of inquiry, requesting that I speak to you immediately about selling the Bartlett-James drawing."

Forehead creased, she repeated, "An agent of . . . inquiry?"

"An investigator," he clarified. "Privately hired."

She shook her head, thoroughly confused. "I'm sorry, Mr. Duncan, I don't mean to sound ignorant, but . . . privately hired to do what, exactly?"

"Apparently to broker a purchase," he replied at once.

She blinked. "I beg your pardon?"

"I admit I was a bit puzzled myself at first. I'm a solicitor, not a museum curator." He chuckled at that, reaching up to scratch his side-whiskers. "But what I gathered from our brief conversation is that apparently this agent works for a banker who represents an anonymous individual who would like to make an offer to buy your drawing before the auction, sight unseen. He's also willing to negotiate the price."

It took her several long moments to fully grasp the implications of all that he was saying. She'd never been personally approached by a buyer for a specific sale before, and at any other time, in any other instance, she might have brushed such information off as somewhat surprising but rather trivial. Yet for more than one reason, this new and unusual development made her uneasy.

"What is the man's name?"

"The agent?"

She nodded, waiting, feeling a nagging tension begin to coil up within.

Duncan rummaged through sheets of paper on his desk until he found a card. "Ah, here it is. A Mr. . . . Milo Cafferty."

Milo Cafferty. She'd never heard the name before. "And you say he's representing an anonymous buyer?"

He reached across the desk and handed it to her. "Actually, he's representing the banker of the buyer."

She stared at the printing, seeing nothing but a name and title on an ordinary, inexpensive white card.

"Why would an investigator be hired as a third party to speak to you about buying art, even art of this nature?" she asked, looking back at Duncan. "What is there to investigate?"

"I had to wonder that myself," he remarked with a half-grin. "Even for a work by the elusive Victor Bartlett-James, this seems a bit extreme, doesn't it?"

"Indeed." Viola tapped the card against her fingertips, thinking. "Did you find this Mr. Cafferty suspicious?"

He shrugged. "Not particularly. Seemed like a regular chap. But I do find the entire circumstance a bit suspicious."

"How so?"

"Well, why wouldn't the potential buyer just send his banker? Or for that matter, why not trust me as a solicitor to manage the anonymity in the best interest of both parties—buyer and seller?" He shook his head as his features grew serious. "I suppose it could be said that this gentleman—I'm assuming it's a gentleman—might simply be a private collector with a great deal of money and influence, trying to protect his reputation by being secretive. But what strikes me as most odd is his going through such ridiculous, roundabout channels to acquire something an intermediary could bid for in just a few days. Even if he's hiding such a purchase from a suspecting wife, she would surely not attend an auction at Brimleys." Frowning deeply, he eyed her candidly. "It's one thing to remain anonymous; it's another to hide one's identity to this extreme. Cafferty refused to tell me even the name of the banker."

Silence ensued as he gave her a moment to contemplate his words. Viola turned and stared out the small window, seeing only the ivy-covered brick wall of the building next door. It wasn't much of a view, but it did allow daylight to enter the office. And if nothing else, staring at a brick wall allowed for no distractions when one tried to think, as she did now.

Although this turn of events disturbed her, she refused to panic. It was entirely possible that this anonymous buyer truly had reasons to keep his identity hidden from everyone, especially if he was a very important individual, perhaps working in government or high office, or for the royals. On the other hand, with all the unusual events that had transpired in her life these last three weeks, she couldn't help but be as dubious as Duncan seemed to be. And she trusted Duncan. He was the only person alive who knew she was the actual artist of the infamous erotic work, and in all these years, he'd never once belittled her for creating it, treated her with disdain for selling it, or betrayed her secret for any reason. And for his good judgment, she paid him handsomely.

But this new situation seemed to bother him, and that in itself alarmed her. Duncan knew nothing of her past and had no reason to wonder if what she'd been through five years ago had suddenly caught up with her in the name of Ian Wentworth.

A sudden thought occurred to her, chilling her enough to make her visibly shiver. With a quick glance back to her solicitor, she asked, "Could someone suspect I'm the artist, then hire an investigator to find out if it's true by coming to you and pretending to be interested in a purchase?"

Instead of answering her immediately, he cocked his head to the side to regard her thoughtfully.

"Did you mention the upcoming auction to anyone, Lady Cheshire?"

Her lips tipped down a fraction. "No, nobody, though I'm certain many people know about it by now since it's less than a week away."

He nodded, thinking. "But *you* didn't tell anyone?"

"Absolutely not," she repeated a bit more forcefully. "I think you know my reputation would not remain unblemished should others learn of my connection to Mr. Bartlett-James's work."

That firm answer satisfied him for a moment. Then he asked, "What about your staff?"

His ardent inquiry sent a whirlwind of new and frightening thoughts through her head. "I keep my staff completely ignorant of details, but even if they knew I was the artist of such work, I don't think any of them are reckless enough to risk unemployment without a reference, especially if they have no proof."

"Have you received any threats to your person or husband's estate?"

Just Ian Wentworth's threatening kiss. . .

She fidgeted. "Not that I'm aware of."

"And nothing's been stolen?"

"Stolen?"

He gazed at her shrewdly. "I'm just wondering if this might be the start of some sort of blackmail plot against you."

That thought had never occurred to her before, and hearing such a warning put into words made her mouth go dry and her body turn cold. "I don't actually keep any of my Bartlett-James work out in the open in my home," she answered, trying to control the shake in her voice. "All my paintings and sketches, when finished, are locked in my attic, the only key in my possession, and I never leave unfinished work unattended in my studio—for obvious reasons."

Duncan nodded in understanding. Then with a large inhale, he sat back in his chair, his thick brows furrowed, palms resting on his rounded stomach. After a few seconds of silence, he stated matter-of-factly, "I hope you'll not suspect anyone in my employ of being indiscreet, Lady Cheshire."

That notion hadn't occurred to her, either, though it led to greater doubts. "You're still the only person who knows I'm the actual artist, correct?"

"Absolutely," he replied, nodding firmly. "I've never said a word to anyone. But my secretary and book-keeper both know you're the individual placing a rare Bartlett-James drawing at auction. Such information couldn't be avoided, I'm afraid. I assure you, however, that they assume it belonged to your husband and you

are simply now wanting to rid yourself of this . . . uh
. . . risqué piece of art." He squirmed in his chair a little.
"If you'll pardon me for being blunt, Lady Cheshire."

"Of course," she said with refined grace. It was the
closest Duncan had ever come to a personal remark
about her work, and if she hadn't been so suddenly
worried about her future, she might have smiled at his
attempt to be tactful. Instead, she returned to her original question.

"Let's assume, Mr. Duncan, that at this point in time
nobody but you and I know I'm the artist," she maintained. "Would it even then be *possible* for Mr. Cafferty to somehow learn this secret as an investigator in
some indirect way?"

"Indirect way?"

"Through . . . record keeping or old books, maybe
from miscellaneous notes regarding past sales or inquiries?"

Frowning, he replied, "I truly don't think so. I keep
my closed files and old records locked in a safe at all
times, and even if he tried to access my accounts or
files to discover something incriminating, directly or
indirectly, I would be made aware of it immediately."

She didn't know whether to feel disheartened or relieved. "I see."

He scrutinized her for a second or two, then suggested, "Perhaps it would be better if we look at it from
the reverse perspective. Can you think of anyone who
would go to such trouble and pay an investigator to
learn certain secrets about you that could then be used
against you personally?"

Don't underestimate me, Lady Cheshire. . . .

She swallowed hard and evaded the question. "I'm not sure. Is this what an agent of inquiry is hired to do?"

His thick eyelids thinned as he considered it. "Not usually, but I suppose anything is possible for the right price. In my experience, these investigators are former runners or policemen, hired to track down stolen items, follow husbands to learn of certain indiscretions, or find missing people, though not necessarily to investigate them."

Find missing people. . .

A violent wave of incredulity washed over her at that moment.

Don't underestimate me, Lady Cheshire. . . .

"Impossible . . . ," she breathed.

Duncan's brows shot up. "Pardon?"

Viola stood, tossing her gloves and reticule on the cushion of her chair before walking slowly to the center of the small room, staring at the tiny yellow tulips on the light blue carpeting, her palm closed over her mouth as she began to put the pieces of the puzzle together to form the most outlandish picture imaginable. And one that in an instant made so much sense.

He'd hired someone to find her, and when that deed had been accomplished, he'd made a grand entrance back into her life, startling her at her first party out of mourning, pretending to not recognize her, doing his best to control their discussions, to confuse her into believing their encounter again had been pure coincidence and that his attraction to her was genuine. And he'd called himself an art collector, just like this so-called buyer who now wanted to purchase her artwork, sight unseen.

The fog in her mind lifted as it all suddenly became so clear—every conversation, every question, and the motives behind every action. He blamed her for her family's deeds all those years ago, and as she'd been the one to escape unscathed, he had reentered her life to enact some kind of despicable or costly revenge. She supposed she had always suspected that he would come for her one day, a reason she'd stayed in the city, but after so much time had passed, she had slowly lowered her guard. She just really wished she knew how much he remembered from his drug-induced haze, how much he'd learned about her and her life from his investigator, why he'd waited so long to return. At this point she had no proof that he *knew* she had once painted as the famous Victor Bartlett-James, only that she was trying to sell one, which, as Duncan had confirmed, his investigator could more easily have discovered simply by following her and asking a few questions. If that was the case, Chatwin would certainly want to know why she would suddenly be attempting to part with one. And until his motives for trying to purchase the work from her directly became clearer, she didn't dare give him the benefit of learning she had created it. She could easily believe that a man held hostage, freezing and dying for five long weeks, would seek his own revenge if he thought justice had not been served, and the greatest revenge she could think of would be blackmailing her about her Bartlett-James persona. That he hadn't done so yet hopefully meant that he didn't have the necessary information to put the clues together. She could only thank God that she'd had the good sense to send John Henry to the country before Chatwin had pounced. For now her son was safe, though should the man decide to go after him, he wouldn't be so difficult to find.

Still, for the moment she had the advantage; wealthy, distinguished, *charming* Ian Wentworth didn't yet know she'd caught on to his scheme. At least there seemed no reason to think so, though he had to realize she wasn't stupid or naive and would certainly be skeptical of his every move. And there could be no middle ground in her assumptions. Either she and Duncan had uncovered the truth of his masquerade by their suspicions and careful deduction, or she was completely wrong about everything and her imagination had finally gotten the best of her. What she needed now were facts and her own plan of action—before he ruined her future and her child's destiny, which she vowed to protect with her life.

Cursing both her fears for controlling her and the handsome man who continued to take advantage and fill her with misgivings, Viola groaned and put her entire face in her palms.

"Lady Cheshire?"

Several miserable seconds passed before she said, "I may know who this person is, Mr. Duncan." Raising her head and crossing her arms over her breasts, she looked back at her solicitor and admitted, "But I can't be certain, so you'll forgive me if I don't give you his name at this time."

Duncan nodded. "If that is your wish."

He didn't sound at all offended or wary, and she supposed that he knew his place, like any good solicitor.

She began to pace the carpet in a large circle. Duncan

remained in his chair, watching, waiting for comment or instruction. Finally, she asked, "Is there any way to discover, beyond question, who hired this investigator?"

After a fast exhale, he replied, "Frankly, I doubt it, especially if he's paid well. The main reason these men are retained is because they tend to be extremely discreet."

Of course. And this one would certainly be well paid if he worked for the Duke of Chatwin, she conceded. That meant she might not learn of Ian Wentworth's definite involvement unless she confronted him herself.

Abruptly, she paused in her stride and glanced up, a small grin of triumph spreading across her mouth.

"Mr. Duncan," she said with utter satisfaction, walking back to her chair, "please inform Mr. Cafferty that I would very much like to accept his client's offer, but I won't settle for anything less than five thousand pounds for the work, since it's what I would expect to get at the auction."

Duncan sat forward very slowly again, nodding. "As you wish."

"Also," she continued, lifting her gloves to don them again, "please advise the owner of Brimleys that your client has sold the drawing privately and the auction for this Saturday has been canceled. However, your client may be interested in auctioning a larger Bartlett-James painting in the near future, which would bring in substantially more money for everyone. That should placate them for the trouble."

Duncan's brows rose as he placed his palms on the arm of his chair and pushed himself to his feet. "Is there any need to explain the change?"

She shrugged a shoulder delicately. "I don't think so, but do please let them know that this particular painting, if I choose to sell, should startle the gentlemen who frequent Brimleys into spending plenty of money on whiskey and driving up the final price. As the club receives ten percent from the sale, they should be more than pleased."

"You'll have the work for Cafferty delivered here as usual?" Duncan asked, pulling down on his waistcoat.

She offered him her gloved hand. "If Mr. Cafferty's client is agreeable to my terms, I'll send it at once."

He took her fingers in his and gave her a slight bow. "Very good, madam."

"And I know you'll remain as discreet as always."

"Of course, Lady Cheshire," he replied without any hint of offense. "I'll send word as soon as I hear from Mr. Cafferty that his client has accepted or rejected your offer."

With an unusual sense of elation, Viola bid her solicitor good day, then turned and walked swiftly from the office.

Chapter Seven

*I stole the key to the dungeon today and went to him
just after she drugged him. I could finally nurse him
and care for his needs without him knowing. . . .*

Ian sat at his desk in his study, staring out his
window to the darkness of nightfall, holding a full
glass of whiskey in one hand. He'd poured it himself
nearly three-quarters of an hour ago, but his mind had
been so overwhelmed by confusing thoughts of Viola
that he really hadn't been interested in taking a sip.

He couldn't stop thinking about that kiss—a kiss
he'd never planned but one he'd wanted urgently the
moment she'd defied him in her studio. She hadn't just
teased him coyly into forcing her hand; she had chal-
lenged him directly, and no man alive would allow a
woman to remain in charge after denying his demand
with such a sarcastic, albeit clever, rebuke. And kissing
her into submission in front of a servant only helped his
cause. By now, the entire neighborhood would know
that not only had the Widow Cheshire come out of

mourning literally but she had also already begun to offer her charms to another man, and one with a greater title than her late husband. In the end, such speculation might work perfectly into his plans. What bothered him, though, was realizing just how much he'd actually enjoyed kissing a woman he despised and vowed to ruin.

He really didn't want to feel anything for her aside from contempt, even as he now realized how difficult staying focused on that goal was going to be. She no doubt had some decent qualities, most notably that she loved her child and would risk much for his well-being. But he didn't need the complication of admiring her for something any mother would feel and exhibit. He would need to be very careful not to allow compassion for her to develop as he pursued her.

He supposed he should have expected his desire to be intense. He hadn't been with a woman in a long time, and since his captivity he'd never felt a thing for any of those he'd bedded beyond the need of the moment. They had been a means to an end, as Viola would be now. But to his dismay, he suddenly couldn't wait to bury himself within her soft, warm walls and give in to the momentary pleasure. And what truly angered him was accepting the fact that for now, the only person he wanted to satisfy him was Lady Cheshire. Naturally, his desire for her would diminish once he bedded her, as it had with all the others, but since that first sitting a week ago he hadn't been able to focus on anything but the memory of her tantalizing breasts so close to his face, and kissing luscious lips that had surrendered to him without any real persuasion.

His disorientation had started the moment she'd innocently touched his brow. By brushing his hair back from his face, she had disarmed him, sparking a memory that he still couldn't quite piece together to form a complete picture. He'd always known she'd been in the dungeon with him, but he didn't know how often, or the length of time of each visit, and quite frankly, due to the constant darkness and the drugs given him day to day, he hadn't often been able to tell the difference between her and her sisters. But as if awakening after a violent storm, he now recalled a specific instance when she'd brushed that same hair off his forehead while he'd lain on his cot, the warmth of her body as she'd spoken to him in a muffled voice that had soothed regardless of the words that, at the time, he hadn't understood.

Tomorrow, at their second sitting, he intended to draw her further into his web. He still wasn't certain how to go about getting her to succumb to his charms without forcing the issue, and he didn't want to frighten her into running before his final act of vengeance. He needed her trust. That's when she would be the most vulnerable. That's when she would help him remember every horrifying moment as he had been forced to live it—alone and scared and chained in darkness.

A fast knock at the door jarred him from his musings and he turned back to his desk, his posture erect.

"Come."

Braetham entered a second later. "Forgive the intrusion, your grace, but the package you've been expecting has arrived."

Ian stood immediately as his butler walked across the carpeting toward him, the frame, approximately three feet long by two feet wide, wrapped in newspaper, held firmly in his hands.

"Place it here on my desk," Ian said, making room by moving pen, paper, and his whiskey glass to the side.

Braetham did as ordered, laying it gently flat in front of him.

"Anything else, your grace?"

Ian shook his head. "No, not now. I'll call if I need you."

His butler bowed, turned, and left his study, closing the door behind him.

Ian stared at the newspaper for a long moment, hands on hips, hesitant about tearing it open to view the erotic piece of famous art he'd purchased from his nemesis for five thousand outrageous goddamned pounds. He hoped it would be money well spent and that in some manner he would be able to use the piece against her.

That thought in mind, he lifted his glass and finally took a sip of whiskey, then began pulling at the corners of the paper until he ripped it from the frame, exposing the entire picture to his view.

Pure and unequivocal astonishment washed over him as he stared down at the most incredible, sexually suggestive drawing he'd ever seen.

The sketch, though simple and elegant of design, exposed a nude woman in full form, standing with feet spread about a foot apart, her head turned sideways as she leaned it against the shoulder of a man hidden behind her, her long dark hair flowing so that it obscured the features of her face, her arms reaching up to clutch his shoulders behind her. The man, head down, pressed his lips against her bare neck, his arms wrapped loosely around her, one hand clasping a breast, fingers teasing her nipple, the other hand pressed fully into the dark triangle of curls between her legs, his fingertips hidden inside her delicate, feminine warmth.

Ian took a step back, staring in utter fascination at a spectacularly good drawing. Although he'd never call himself a critic of good art, it was quite obvious to him why Victor Bartlett-James had become a sensation. The sketch had clearly been drawn by a talented hand, and the subject matter, though certainly erotic, managed to tastefully depict a pose without making the act between the two seem debauched.

Indeed, as he gazed at each intricate detail now, the hourglass form of the female, the strength of the man's arms and hands on her body, his delicate kiss and the hidden planes of her face beneath flowing hair, it struck him as it should, as it was intended to do. Ian felt himself grow hard with a rush of desire, not only from looking at such a titillating picture but also because it just occurred to him that Lady Cheshire had seen and likely stared at this work with longing herself. And it was the thought of Viola getting physically aroused by such work, just as he did now, that enticed his imagination, making him wonder what she had been like in bed with a husband twice her age, if the man she'd married had satisfied her, what she did now to relieve her own sexual tension without him or any man to fulfill her fantasies.

Reaching for his whiskey glass, Ian downed the contents in one gulp, then turned, stepped around his chair, and walked to the window to lean his shoulder on the frame, arms crossed over his chest as he gazed out to the blackness of a moonless night.

He felt a little annoyed at himself for never considering that in his quest for justice he might discover a different Viola Bennington-Jones with her own sensual secrets, that the girl he remembered from five years ago might have turned into a fiery, experienced woman. She hadn't just gotten older; she had become an independent widow who would not now be so easily manipulated by her naivete. But she wouldn't be able to deny her sexuality. Nobody who'd at one time tasted the fruits of the flesh could give up that particular sweetness forever.

Still, something more than merely knowing that Viola had seen, owned, and then sold such an explicit drawing nagged at his curiosity and, warranted or not, gave him pause. As an artist herself, she had to have noted the nature of the talent, critically considered each line and blend of the charcoal, just as she'd done for his benefit when she'd drawn the sketch of him. She certainly would have studied Bartlett-James's specific gift to improve upon her own, regardless of the fact that she only drew and painted still lifes and formal portraits.

And perhaps that's what intrigued him. An artist could study erotic art for its precision and elegance, its beauty and form. But could that same artist do so and not find the picture as a whole arousing?

Ian glanced over his shoulder to the drawing again. He could imagine the prelude to passion the artist had chosen to convey with each stroke. But had it come from memory or from models standing before him?

Could Viola draw such a lascivious portrait if paid the right price? A slow grin of satisfaction spread across his mouth at the thought of witnessing her expression if he actually asked her to draw him nude. And of course if he was watching her draw him like that, he wouldn't be able to avoid having an erection in full view.

Suddenly a thought struck him soundly.

Why do you paint fruit?

It's inoffensive . . . one can hang it anywhere. . . .

Not just inoffensive. It was safe.

Ian quickly moved around his chair and back to his desk, peering down at the picture once more, a bizarre theory beginning to take shape in his mind.

And how do they pay you?

Their wives bake me pie. . . .

A coquettish answer, and yet probably truthful to some degree. Yes, still life was safe, and didn't pay all that well. Erotic artwork would no doubt bring in far more money as a sensation within the *ton*.

But Victor Bartlett-James had been retired for several years, or so Cafferty had said. Perhaps this drawing wasn't actually one of his but a copy forged to bring in fast money. Could a female artist be so forgetful of her station as to purposely duplicate an erotic piece of art for auction? Yes, he decided at once, if that female artist was a lady of the nobility and desperate to protect her child. And he had made Viola desperate.

He tried to eye the work skeptically this time, to envision the artist's hand in creating it. Viola had shown him the lines of his face in the drawing she'd made of him, and although he'd paid some attention, he couldn't say this drawing was anything like the one she'd so quickly created for his benefit. They were entirely different, at least in subject matter. And one more problem occurred to him. If Victor Bartlett-James got any notion of a forgery being auctioned, Lady Cheshire would surely find herself in a terrible quandary with authorities and likely charged with fraud. The only reason she would take such a risk, he concluded, was if she planned to leave the country. If forgery was her intent, he had no doubt done her an enormous favor by purchasing the drawing privately.

Ian reached out and touched the picture with his index finger, skimming the figure of the woman, aroused again, not because of the drawing itself but by the intriguing notion that Viola might have drawn this very image herself, perhaps even from the memory of a specific time with a man.

Indeed, it was an incredible thought, but not necessarily impossible to believe. And even if she hadn't, if this *was* a Bartlett-James original that had belonged to her husband, he could still use the forgery aspect against her in some way. He just needed to think it through.

"Viola, Viola, Viola . . . ," he whispered aloud, his bitterness returned with an absolute satisfaction. "You are far more vulnerable to me than you will ever know. . . ."

The darkness engulfed him, the damp cold made him shiver. And then she curled up beside him, offering her warmth, her softness. He felt her touch him on his cheek, drape her leg over his, press her head into his shoulder. Her hand caressed his chest, and he tried to pull her close, but the chain kept him defenseless, unable to respond even to her affection. She began to move her hand downward, rubbing his stomach over his ragged shirt, then his legs, all in an effort to keep him warm. And then she realized he wanted her, and with a soft sound from her throat, she timidly closed her hand over his erection. He moaned, uncertain of time, of events, but so desperately needing! He couldn't think clearly, couldn't speak, but he felt her fingers explore him, her lips on his neck, heard a raw sound come from his throat as he jerked his hips into her—

Ian woke with a start, sitting up quickly, breathing in gulps of air as he looked around in the blackness, confused. His heart thundered from the intense fear that enveloped him, and he shivered from the cold sweat that coated his body. For seconds he sat there, breathing deeply to calm his racing pulse, and then the haze began to clear and he realized he was safe in his bed, in his home, and all was silent.

It had been weeks since he'd had one of his nightmares, the scenes of the dungeon so vivid they always caused him to awaken in a panic. But this one had been different, erotic in nature, and as he now became more alert, the terror of the moment all but gone, he realized he had climaxed in his sleep.

That kind of physical reaction to a dream hadn't happened to him in ages, no doubt caused this time by his need for a woman and the erotic nature of the drawing that only hours ago had brought such base feelings to the surface. But what troubled him was that this nightmare stemmed from a memory he'd apparently repressed during his experience in the dungeon. Or perhaps repressed wasn't the right word. He'd always known he had been touched intimately during that time, though whether it had been an intentional, criminal act in itself or a matter of nursing, he couldn't be sure. But *this* memory didn't fall into either of those categories. Regardless of the fact that it had been sexually pleasurable for him, regardless of whatever comfort he'd found in it at the time, someone had taken advantage of him in the most despicable way possible, leaving him vulnerable and humiliated. And because of the nature of the drugs he'd been given, and the utter darkness of the dungeon, he couldn't remember the specific details, or who exactly had been with him.

Pushing his bedcovers aside, Ian stood and walked to the basin beside his wardrobe. He poured half a pitcher of water into the bowl and splashed it on his face and neck, relishing the icy tremor that shot through him.

It was time for the nightmares to end. Time to take back control of his life from those who had stolen his innocence by making him face his own mortality in their hands five years ago. Time to demand retribution from those who had assaulted his masculinity by stimulating him sexually without his consent.

It was time for Viola to pay.

Chapter Eight

He begged me not to leave him, and so I sat at the foot of his cot for a while and held his hand until he slept. . . .

$\mathcal{U}$nfortunately, due to a steady rain, they couldn't have their sitting in the garden, out in the open, as she'd hoped and fairly threatened the last time they'd been together. So, with fortitude, Viola braved another uncomfortable morning as she sat on her own stool in her studio, several feet away from him, trying to concentrate on the painting she'd begun at last. He made it difficult for her, though, just by his bearing. He hadn't said anything more than the usual superficial nonsense one spoke in greeting, and she hadn't offered anything else. But she was overly nervous this morning, and he probably noticed it.

She knew he had to be watching her with the eyes of someone fully aware that not only had she sold a Bartlett-James original for the money it garnered but she had also certainly examined the erotic image for herself. He knew it had belonged to her, but she remained convinced that, at least for now, he didn't suspect she and Bartlett-James were one and the same person.

But she only had to bide her time. With Duncan's help, she'd quietly and discreetly finalized arrangements to retrieve her son and leave for the Continent in less than thirty days, and if it killed her, she would keep Ian Wentworth unaware of her plans. He knew that she corresponded with her solicitor, but only she and Duncan knew of her arrangement.

"May I ask you a question, Lady Cheshire?"

His continued civility under the circumstance quite annoyed her, and it took everything in her to hide her irritation from him. Still, the way he scrutinized her this particular morning left her brush strokes lacking their usual elegance.

Smiling flatly, focusing on mixing a shade of blue on her palette, she replied, "Of course, your grace."

He waited for a moment, then lowered his voice a little to continue. "Do you miss your husband?"

Her lashes flickered as she looked up at him. "I beg your pardon?"

He offered her a half smile. "Your husband. Do you miss him?"

She couldn't for the life of her decide why he would drop the formality and ask her such a personal thing now, and so, in quick response, she relied on the usual answer. "I'm sure all widows miss their husbands, your grace, especially those husbands recently lost."

"Were you in love with him?"

That question, coming from Ian Wentworth, so startled her that she nearly dropped the palette of paint in her hand.

"Of course," she replied, repressing the desire to tell him it was none of his blasted business. Lifting the paintbrush, she motioned with it in an attempt to change the conversation. "Now, if you'll tip your head just slightly to the left."

He did as she ordered. "How did you meet?"

"Meet?"

"Your husband."

She didn't want to look at him now, and so focused intently on her work. "He asked me to dance at a masked ball several years ago."

He waited, then said, "I see. And how long after the ball did he propose?"

She laughed in an effort to lighten the mood, trying her best to make it sound sincere. "Goodness, why all the questions, your grace? I assure you my past is quite dull and unremarkable."

He inhaled deeply, then lowered his voice to reply, "Not to me."

Her pulse began to race; perspiration broke out on her upper lip. Without a glance at him, she reached for a fatter brush and began mixing two different shades of yellow together on her palette. "And how are you managing in your search for a wife?"

For ages, it seemed, he said nothing. Viola refused to look into his eyes for fear of giving herself away by showing anxiety and a desire to discuss anything but the past she shared with him.

Finally, he murmured, "Answer my question first."

She held her tongue from a sharp refusal. "I'm sorry, your grace—"

"When did he propose?"

She swallowed at his perseverance. "Shortly thereafter, if I recall."

"After the ball?"

"Yes."

"Were you his first wife?" he asked, brows furrowing in thought.

Suspicion began to bubble up inside her, but since she had neither any idea why he was quizzing her about her husband nor knowledge of his intent, she decided to just answer forthrightly for now. "Actually, he had been married once before, and was a widower before we met."

"Ah. I see. How long was he married to his first wife?"

She chanced a glance at him before looking back at the paint in her hand. "Perhaps you'll first tell me why you find my late husband so fascinating."

"I wouldn't say I find *him* fascinating at all, but I am rather . . . curious." He lifted one side of his mouth in a smile. "Humor me, Lady Cheshire."

Humor you, indeed. . . .

Cordially, she maintained, "I think they were married for twelve or thirteen years, though I really don't know. It was a long time ago, and long before he and I became acquainted."

He reached up and ran his fingers through his hair. "He must have been older than you by several years, then."

She felt like throwing the paintbrush at him to get him to stop the meaningless inquiries. Good breeding prevailed, however, and after adjusting her bottom on her stool, she acknowledged, "He was seventeen years older than I at the time we married."

"And he had no other children from his first marriage?"

She hesitated in answer, then gave him the standard response, "Unfortunately, they were not blessed."

Nodding, and somewhat bemused, he remarked, "Then he met you at a ball, made you a baroness, and you gave him a son. Quite a whirlwind, and fortunate for all of you."

She didn't know how to take his comment at all. Somewhere deep within she felt a certain resentment from him, and a blatant curiosity coupled with a palpable anger that went far beyond the superficial, as if he was trying to sort out the timing of events and how they related to him and his captivity five years ago. If he was indeed concocting a brilliant revenge against her as the only remaining Bennington-Jones daughter left to disgrace, understanding the sequence of each occurrence between the time of his capture and her escape from Winter Garden could be vital to any plan he might have in store for her. And for that reason alone, for John Henry's protection, she needed to remain as vague as possible.

She relaxed a little on the stool and sighed. "Perhaps my marriage seems rather romantic in that particular light," she said with calculation, eyeing him directly, "but I wouldn't say the death of my husband has been fortunate at all, sir. I don't think losing someone close ever is."

"I understand," he agreed soberly. After a pause, he grinned and attempted to lighten the mood. "I certainly hope my questions aren't making you uncomfortable, Lady Cheshire."

"Not in the least," she lied, forcing a smile as she turned her attention back to her painting. "But you have yet to answer *my* question."

He straightened a bit, pulling down on his waistcoat. "Ah, yes. The bride hunt."

"Is it going well?" she prompted, more inquisitive than she ought to be. From the corner of her eye she saw him lift a shoulder in a shrug.

"At this point I believe Lady Anna is the best choice and will no doubt make a perfectly adequate wife."

Perfectly adequate? She cringed inside, then scolded herself for caring. "I'm certain she will, your grace. I commend you on your choice."

He chuckled. "Commend me on my choice?"

She ignored that. "So, I suppose you've been courting her?"

"Not especially," he replied, amused. "Frankly, she doesn't interest me all that much."

Viola paused in her brushstroke and looked at him askance. "If she doesn't interest you, sir, why on earth would you want to marry her?"

He continued to watch her, intensely it seemed, the humor fading from his handsome face.

"Why does anyone marry?" he countered at last. "She comes from a long line of nobility, an excellent family with a father who will not think twice about giving her hand to me, and she brings with her a large dowry."

Her forehead creased a little. "You don't even know if you enjoy her company, your grace. Wouldn't it be advisable to at least court her for a season to see—"

"I'm sure you know that in our class, marriage has very little to do with such trivial feelings as enjoying each other's company," he cut in, his tone thoughtful. "It does, however, have everything to do with lineage, heirs, and necessity."

And sometimes desperation . . .

"Of course, you're right," she acknowledged with a nod. "And you are in need of an heir."

"I am, indeed. It is the most important reason for a man to marry, is it not?"

Viola nodded once in acquiescence, then returned to her painting, trying, but hopelessly failing, to remove the image of a nude Ian Wentworth making love to the stubborn and obnoxious Anna she knew. The thought made her queasy.

"Or did your husband marry you for love?" he asked rather nonchalantly.

Heat suffused her, and she decided not to look at him. "I'm certain there was a great deal of duty in his decision to marry me as well, your grace."

"Was there?" He paused, then added, "I can't imagine a gentleman ever growing tired of looking at you, Lady Cheshire. He must have been thoroughly content in his married life with you warming his bed night after night."

She fumbled the brush, inelegantly dropping it onto the palette into the yellow paint, splattering droplets onto her smock.

Ian chuckled again at her discomfiture, then stood

and began to saunter toward her. "So, how is my portrait coming along?"

If not for the fact that he'd decided to observe her work up close, she might have been quite relieved by his easy return to the safe subject of painting. But seconds later she felt his warmth at her back, his chest nearly touching as he peered over her shoulder to view the artwork she'd so diligently created.

"You are certainly very talented with your brushstrokes, aren't you, Lady Cheshire," he said rather than asked, his voice low and intimate.

Viola pulled back a little from his overbearing closeness. "Thank you," she mumbled, throat tight. "But perhaps it's best if you reserve judgment until I'm finished, your grace." She gestured to his stool with her forehead. "Please."

He stepped around her slightly so that he could look down at her face. She felt his eyes on her, and it took her a long moment before she managed to lift her lashes and meet his gaze.

"I wonder if your husband admired you for your gifts as he should have," he speculated, denying her veiled suggestion to return to his stool. "Did you satisfy him, Viola?"

His question rendered her speechless, which he obviously expected, as his handsome mouth curved up slyly and his dark eyes narrowed.

"I had a fascinating dream last night, a memory brought to light," he whispered in a husky timbre, reaching up to brush a stray curl away from her cheek. "About a woman with very nimble fingers and soft, delicate, *talented* hands. I awoke thinking of you."

His intimate insinuations silenced her, and by standing so close, he all but blocked her escape. A sudden fear coursed through her. Her eyes widened and she felt a hot flush creep up her neck and into her face.

Without hesitation, he lifted the palette from her hands, then leaned across her and placed it on the small desk at her side. When his own hands were free, he reached up and pressed his fingers gently through her loosely coiled hair until he cupped her cheeks in his palms.

She blinked quickly several times as her pulse begin to race. "What are you doing?" she whispered.

His gaze locked with hers. "I know who you are."

It took ages for that statement to register. And then clarity struck her as a blow to the gut.

She jerked back in horror, but he held her tightly in his grasp, expecting her reaction to his whispered pronouncement, refusing to release her or allow her to move.

In an instant, his expression turned to stone. "Yes. I know who you are, Viola. And this time I'm in charge of *your* future. It's time for me to take back what you stole from me, and give you what you deserve in return."

She started trembling. "No—Your grace—"

His mouth closed over hers in a tantalizing, determined kiss of hardness and power. She squirmed to no avail; a quick sob of defiance tore from her throat, but he pursued her relentlessly, provocatively, forcing desire upon her until she yielded and accepted his will.

She stilled, permitting him to take what he wanted, giving in to the madness, allowing his tongue to seek hers as he desired. She felt his need, his anger, and a cheerless passion borne of loneliness. Tears stung her eyes, not from the harshness of his demand but from her own knowledge of what he had endured at her hands, of what he so desperately wanted her to experience now. Of how much he despised her and resented all that she had become because of him.

He softened his advance as he felt her give in to his urging. As suddenly as it had started, he pulled away.

Viola gasped for air, shaking, squeezing her eyes shut as she felt his fast, warm breath on her skin, his gaze on her face, his hands clutching her, fingers intertwined tightly in her hair. She couldn't speak, couldn't look at him, but his rigid stance conveyed his rage.

"You have taken everything from me, and yet I want you," he murmured, his voice hard, his breathing erratic. "That is something I can't accept."

"Please . . . ," she whispered, her voice barely audible.

He relaxed his grip slightly, pulling back even more as he inhaled deeply to calm the storm within him.

"Look at me, Viola," he insisted, his tone low, hoarse.

Her lashes fluttered open, her gaze locked with his, and the coldness he conveyed through those dark depths sent an icy fear through her body.

"You cannot ruin me as I can ruin you," he whispered. "Tomorrow night it begins. You will be at my town house for dinner at eight or I will expose you as a fraud. Is this clear?"

Her chest constricted; she felt suffocated, couldn't breathe.

His lips twitched. "The masquerade is over, my beautiful, clever lady. The masks come off now."

He released her at once, and her body fairly crumbled on the stool.

Turning, he left her then, numbed to the core, and utterly terrified.

Chapter Nine

I watched him in the dark for a long time, afraid to let him know I was there. But when he started shivering from extreme cold I risked everything and went to him, lying down on the cot beside him to lend him my warmth. . . .

She had no idea what the night would bring, though Viola felt certain she wouldn't be eating a pleasant, relaxing dinner in his dining room. At least she doubted it, as she hadn't been able to stomach anything since he'd left yesterday. But she would arrive just as he'd ordered, dressed fabulously in a low-cut gown of lavender satin and royal purple lace flounces, her hair adorned with pearls and piled high on her head in loose curls. He could certainly scare her with his threats, but she had always known this day might come, and she had long been prepared to counter his every move. Or so she prayed she would be able to do tonight.

He'd lit up his home in Tarrington Square like a torch, she mused as she stared out the window of her private coach toward his beautiful dark brick home. The circular driveway curved through perfectly clipped hedges and lush flower beds before it sloped and ended at the large front doors, beside which stood two footmen in pristine livery at the ready. Seconds later, one of them opened her door and offered her his hand, and she alighted, pausing at the bottom of the stone steps to gather her wits, draw in a deep breath, and fluff her skirts for the show to come.

And it would be a show, she concluded after a day of careful thought. She didn't know what he wanted with her, but she suspected it would have something to do with his demanding kisses and their thoroughly undesired yet overwhelming attraction to each other. She, of course, had a prepared response to his demands, which was the sole reason she hadn't fled the city during the night. That, and the fact that she knew without a doubt that he really could damage her reputation to the point of ruin, and believed wholeheartedly that he would if she ran. Her only consolation was knowing one or two things about him that she could use against him should she need to. Her weapons weren't as mighty as his, she realized, but they would do nicely in battle should it come to that.

The tall front door opened as soon as she reached the top step, and an aging butler, graying and stalwart, nodded once to her, then moved to the side to allow her to enter.

"Good evening, Lady Cheshire. Braetham at your service," he said prosaically. "May I take your wrap?"

She pulled the light silk cover from her shoulders and passed it to him as her eyes scanned the foyer, its enormous chandelier lit up brilliantly, casting crystalline diamond shapes of illumination on every gold-papered wall, the rich, colorful tapestries, and the brown and gold marbled floor. By first look, Ian Wentworth had inherited well. He truly had a stunning home.

"Follow me, please. His grace is expecting you and will meet you momentarily in the green salon."

"Very good," she replied, attempting to sound regal but probably failing horribly. At least a good butler would never claim or appear to notice her discomfiture, and she suspected the Duke of Chatwin would only employ the best.

Braetham turned to begin a silent walk down the hallway to their left, and she followed, making a conscious effort not to squeeze her hands together in her lace gloves. She tried not to gape at the view before her, his wealth so clearly obvious by the thick Persian carpeting, the wrought-iron stands which, every few feet, raised ornate golden vases filled with fresh, vibrantly colored flowers that scented the air like a lush summer garden. And this was only one hallway.

Trepidation continued to grow as she neared the salon, knowing he was about to receive her in his grand and elegant home, not formally as the Duke of Chatwin but as the wronged man of five years ago who had cleverly ensnared her in an intricate web of deceit, shocking her with the demand to come tonight for a specific purpose yet unknown to her. But she had grown strong through the years, had conquered every storm blown her way with grace and fortitude, and she refused to allow him to destroy the life she'd built for her child because of a personal past he couldn't overcome. Hell hath no fury like a mother scorned, and if he brought war between them, she would fight him with her claws.

Braetham paused as he neared the end of the corridor, then reached for the handle of a door and opened it for her.

"If you'll wait here, madam. His grace will be with you momentarily."

She nodded, took three steps inside, and stopped short, dumbstruck at the sight before her.

The green salon was a magnificent room, decorated exquisitely in rich browns and vivid greens, with tall windows spanning the north wall that looked out over a luscious, full garden, now resembling a forest at twilight. In the center of the room two matching velveteen sofas the color of emeralds faced each other, a dark tea table between them, accented by two brown leather wing chairs at each end. Floral paintings in gilded frames hung in abundance from the remaining three walls, all papered in woodland green velvet. But what made the salon so vibrant were the vases of all shapes and sizes filled with live green plants, placed on end tables, the tea table, the mantel, and even the wooden floor in enormous golden pots, all of them lending an atmosphere of botanical radiance. Truly, her mother would have fainted at the sight of such beauty.

"This is my favorite room in the house."

Viola twirled around at the sound of his voice, as rich and luxurious as the salon itself, her heart suddenly racing, eyes growing wide at the sight of him.

He stood in the doorway with stately bearing, hands clasped behind him, wearing a magnificent dinner suit of black silk on cream, his cravat of royal purple tied perfectly at his neck. His hair had been combed back to expose every plane of his hard and handsome face, now freshly shaven, his expression unreadable as he scanned her up and down.

I know who you are. . . .

Her mouth went dry from his thorough scrutiny, though she managed a curtsey. "Your grace."

"Do you like it?"

"Sir?" she replied awkwardly, her cheeks warming.

His mouth tipped up a fraction. "The green salon."

"Oh." She glanced around. "It's . . . spectacular. I've never been in a room like it."

"Indeed. I often come to this room to think, to make the difficult decisions one must make." Moments later, he said, "You look especially beautiful tonight, Viola."

She couldn't tell if he meant that as a compliment or if his soothing words only served the purpose of intimidating her. But it didn't matter. She was ready for him.

"You look especially wonderful tonight as well, your grace," she returned matter-of-factly. "I've never known a more handsome man in my life."

For a slice of a second she saw surprise flicker in his beautiful brown eyes, and then they filled with wary amusement as he began to slowly walk toward her.

"Viola Bennington-Jones, now the lovely Lady Cheshire, how you've changed," he said, his tone a deep drawl. "From plain, country miss to an elegant, sophisticated widow; from a mere sister of criminals to a defiant protector of their secrets. Here you are after all these years, beautifully dressed and standing so . . . regally in my home."

She swallowed, clutching her gloved hands in front of her, lifting her chin minutely in an effort to bravely hide the fact that his statement left her trembling inside. "My, you're certainly full of compliments this evening. And a plethora of information."

He smirked as he neared her, fully aware of her fear and uncertainty. "Merely observations, darling."

She blinked at the intimacy he conveyed sarcastically in his words and manner, taking a step away from him as he approached.

"What do you want from me?" she whispered.

He came to a halt in front of her, his smile fading as he skimmed her face with a dark, cold gaze. "I want what any man in my position would want from you."

A tremor of sheer terror sliced through her, though she managed to hold herself steady before him, her eyes flashing obstinacy. "Which position would that be tonight, your grace? Duke of Chatwin seeking conversation with his portrait artist over dinner? Or are you just a wounded soul who lives only for revenge?"

He cocked his head to the side a little, studying her features intently. "If all I wanted was revenge, I would have come after you years ago. And you wouldn't be standing here now."

She had her suspicions about that, since she didn't think he'd known of her location until he'd hired Mr. Cafferty. But at this point such speculation on her part was irrelevant.

"Why didn't you admit you knew who I was at Lady Isabella's party? You had to know I wouldn't believe you'd not remember me."

"And yet my evasiveness worked, didn't it?" he replied. "All I needed was to introduce a bit of doubt."

She shook her head minutely, brows furrowed. "Why did you do that? Why not let everybody know who I am and create a scandal that evening?" Before he could respond, a sudden thought occurred to her. "Unless mentioning your imprisonment causes you . . . discomfort."

His cheek twitched, though he never moved his gaze. "I will never be ashamed for being a victim, madam," he countered icily. "No, my intent was to evoke your curiosity and confusion, which would keep you from leaving the city until your fears were confirmed."

And she had done exactly as he'd planned. She probably would have left that night had he simply confronted her. By setting up such an elaborate ruse, he'd drawn her further into his web, making it harder, or more complicated, for her to leave. And the only reason he could possibly want that would be to draw out a lengthy ruin.

Oh, yes. He'd organized meticulously, though the nature of his scheme still remained a mystery.

"So why tonight? Why am I here now?" she asked, feeling bold despite his commanding form. "I can't imagine that you simply want to chat about the wrongs my family did you over a lingering dinner and a bottle of fine wine."

For a long moment he did nothing but stare into her eyes, his jaw fixed, tension radiating from his body like a tiger posed to strike. Then, without any hint of propriety, he glanced down to her breasts, enhanced by her low-cut gown and a tightly strung corset, and the heat she suddenly felt from him made her nearly swoon. Instinctively, she raised a gloved palm and covered her cleavage from his view.

He chuckled at her vain attempt at decency, then stepped away from her and walked to the window, shoving his hands into the pockets of his dinner jacket as he peered out to a looming, deep green twilight. She just watched him, unable to move, barely able to breathe.

"I find it remarkable," he finally revealed, "and a perplexing stroke of irony, that the only woman I've been attracted to in ages is the one person in all the world I should despise on principle."

She didn't know how to take that at first. Her heart fluttered from his honest disclosure, but reservation grounded her in her own determination, and so she remained unwilling to divulge anything about her feelings or thoughts without careful consideration. And she certainly wasn't going to admit how much the inexplicable, alluring force between them bothered her, too, and always had.

Trying to be rational, she said, "I suppose it would be a good idea to discuss what happened five years ago."

He exhaled fully and looked at his polished shoes. "Even if that were true, and we discussed every aspect of the cruelties done to me, it would never be enough to right the wrongs."

"Is that why I'm here? To help you right the wrongs?"

He said nothing to that. After a long moment, she clasped her hands in front of her, shoulders stiff, legs trembling beneath her skirts, and asked bravely, "How much do you remember?"

He glanced at her askance, eyes narrowed. "I believe, madam, that I remember the important things."

She swallowed. "Then you must remember how much I did for you—"

"How much you did for me?" he cut in, incredulous, standing fully erect and turning to face her squarely. "You left me there to die, Viola."

Her heart tightened with anguish. "I helped them rescue you."

"You did?" His brows rose. "And how exactly did you do that?"

Raising her chin a fraction, she replied, "I left the key—"

"You did nothing."

His dark, whispered words expressed a cold detachment rather than hot rage, and she took a step back, baffled by his demeanor, and more than a little alarmed.

"You knew I was there and did *nothing*," he continued, his tone low, expression grim. "You protected your despicable family by allowing me to suffer in chains and darkness for five long weeks while they blackmailed my sister into trading me for diamonds. That is what you *did*, Viola. And you are as culpable as they are."

"If that is what you think," she remarked bravely, voice shaking, "then you don't remember much at all."

His nostrils flared; his jaw tightened. "I remember being abused, starved, and drugged. I remember being teased and humiliated while I lay helpless on a cold cot. I remember nearly dying."

"Do you remember that I nursed you? Comforted you? Talked to you?"

The tiniest flicker of hesitation crossed his features. Or perhaps disbelief. And then it disappeared, masked by ruthless calculation.

"What I *know,* Viola, is that you escaped justice for allowing the torment to continue when you could— *should*—have had me rescued. And that's all that matters now."

At last he said it, admitting the reason he'd hunted her down after all these years.

Tense, she asserted, "Everyone involved has been punished—"

"Except for you."

She shook her head bitterly. "Oh, sir, I have been punished more than you know."

"Don't mock me, Viola," he murmured with disgust. "Your life since leaving Winter Garden has been a fairy tale for which any country miss with a tarnished past would disown her family to savor. You are a lady now, a wealthy lady at that, and have fashioned a new and marvelous life for yourself. I, madam, am the one who suffered, and suffers still."

Suffers still . . .

The hurt he exuded coiled around her like a snake, suffocating and painful, tightening its grip on her emotions even as she fought to come up with an explanation of her motives all those years ago. But clearly she couldn't argue with him now, and he obviously didn't want to hear details as she remembered them, even the ones she thought were valid. If she told him anything more, tried to describe from her perspective all that had occurred, he certainly wouldn't believe her, at least not now, and might instead try to use her words against her.

"So now you want me to suffer, is that it?" she asked softly.

For several long moments he watched her intently, his head tipped to the side, hands still in his pockets, his beautiful face partially hidden by the plants at the window as dusk deepened to nightfall. She waited, expecting nothing, uncertain and afraid, desperate to tell him everything but knowing he'd reject her words strictly because he'd drawn his own conclusions that fit the facts as he remembered them.

"Suffer is a harsh word," he acknowledged at last, "and whether you believe this or not, I would never want you or anyone to experience what happened to me at your family's hands."

Relief shot through her even as her suspicions heightened.

"But there is a price to be paid, Viola," he continued, his voice contemplative. "I've spent these last five years thinking of you every day, trying to decide what to do with you."

His arrogance gave her anger fresh energy and she fisted her hands at her sides, facing him squarely. "What to *do* with me? What right do you have to do anything? Why not just leave me alone? You must know I would never talk of that shameful time in my past to anyone."

Slowly, he began to walk back to her, his gaze sharp as he focused on her face. "I believe you. And while it's true you weren't involved in my abduction as your sisters were, there is no denying that you were negligent, and for that negligence, that *in*action, you were never held responsible." His features hardened as he added, "There has been no justice."

"This isn't about justice, it's about simple revenge," she retorted, her voice low and firm. "Perhaps it would be better for both of us if you would get to the point of this pretense, sir."

He smirked. "Revenge is never simple. *That* is the point."

"I don't understand you," she whispered. "Why am I here dressed like this when you so obviously despise me and every bad memory of yours you believe I caused?"

He eyed her speculatively for a moment before offering her a daring smile. "Because, Viola darling, there are two things I know about both myself and this . . . situation in which we now find ourselves."

She just stared at him, exasperated and confused.

"The first," he carried on, closing in to stand before her again, "is that having you simply disgraced by ruin or arrest, if such a thing were possible after all this time, wouldn't bring me lasting peace. It would be too fast, too unappealing, and would offer me no satisfaction. The second thing I know is that I'm dumfounded by the fact that I want you sexually, and I've finally realized I won't be able to rid myself of that desire until I have you in my bed."

A small mewl of shock and helplessness escaped her.

He chuckled. "My admission can't be all that surprising to you."

"Does it matter?" she whispered, glaring at him. "I think you know I will never risk social disgrace and my son's good name by giving myself to you willingly."

Lifting a hand, he rubbed his chin with his palm,

eyes narrowed in speculation. "Just as *you* know you really have no choice."

Swallowing tears of anxiousness, she mumbled shakily, "I suppose your desire to make me your mistress is the reason for this elaborate ruse."

"Not initially. But after seeing you again after all these years, I can't help the way my body responds, and so I've chosen not to fight it."

"That's disgusting," she said.

He shrugged. "It's the nature of being a man, Viola."

Caustically, she said, "And you've used this base excuse for forcing yourself upon me—"

His chuckle cut her off. "Forcing myself upon you? You enjoyed our kissing as much as I did, sweetheart. I think it would only take me minutes to get you naked on my sofa."

She flushed under his scrutiny, the truth behind his words filling her with embarrassment. "To be perfectly honest, you grace, for the sake of my son, I would rather marry you and live the rest of my life with your hatred and insults than submit to you as your mistress."

His amusement faded at once. "And I would see you dying in prison before I willingly gave you the value of my name."

He'd said that so quietly that she almost hadn't heard the words. But there could be no mistake in his meaning and his ruthless determination to see her slowly destroyed for his gratification.

"You're a monster," she breathed.

"Maybe," he admitted, "but you and your beloved family made me that way."

Slowly, she shook her head and replied, "I will never accept blame for a situation that was out of my control."

He ignored that to whisper, "You can't fight me, Viola."

She gathered strength from his audacity. "Oh, I most certainly can fight you, sir—"

"And you will lose."

A final statement, offered firmly, and with absolute conviction. Appalled, she realized he had already won this battle, whether by tactic or his own stubbornness, and he knew she understood the depth of his purpose. Arguing with him further now would do no good. She needed time to think before giving in, time to plan and organize her weapons against him.

Inhaling a deep breath, chin raised, she lifted her skirts and stepped past him. "I'm leaving."

"I think it would be in your best interest to stay," he said in quick response. "Our guests are no doubt starting to arrive."

That stopped her in her tracks. She spun around at the door. "What guests?"

"I'm hosting a small party for artists and collectors. The highlight of the evening will be the unveiling of my newest piece, the Victor Bartlett-James original I purchased from you."

Her heart seemed to stop as she held his gaze, positively mortified by his revelation.

"You cannot be serious," she whispered.

"Oh, I am most definitely serious, madam," he replied as he began to stroll toward her. "But what shocks you more? The fact that I would show a piece of erotic art with ladies present, or that I'm aware you knew I was the buyer of your work?"

God help me. He knows everything. . . .

She started trembling. "How—How did—"

"I'm clever," he finished for her very softly. "And I can afford to buy any information I desire."

She fought her own desire to slap him hard across the mouth, to cringe in defeat, to lash out at him in utter disgust. But she refused to lower her lashes and give him the satisfaction of knowing he'd made her truly defenseless to his will.

"And should I refuse to attend?" she charged, mouth dry, pulse suddenly racing.

He casually shook his head. "You won't risk it, I'm sure. If you don't attend, your curiosity about what I might reveal will drive you mad."

He was right, of course. He had no reason on earth to protect her virtue or her good name. She had become his puppet, and they both knew it.

"The depth of your humiliation of me is astonishing," she breathed, fighting back tears.

He bit down hard. "I felt the same five years ago."

"I will never forgive you for this, Ian," she whispered in abject sorrow.

Whether it was her feminine display of helplessness, or her use of his given name, for a second or two she watched him hesitate, saw a flicker of doubt cross his features. Then as quickly as it appeared, it vanished.

With rigid demeanor, his eyes dark and passionless,

he replied, "That, madam, is not something that concerns me."

Recoiling inside, she turned her back on him and opened the door, refusing his escort as the two of them silently walked from the encroaching darkness of his beautiful green salon.

Chapter Ten

I tried to bathe him today, while he slept from the drug. He is so masculine, so handsome, but he is beginning to lose strength. I want to help him, but they will keep me from him if I do anything else. He needs me, but I am so afraid. . . .

*V*iola ignored him completely as he walked by her side down the hallway, past his fabulous foyer, and farther into his impressive home. As they neared the drawing room, she heard voices in what appeared to be a festive gathering, then a deep male laugh. Instinctively, she slowed her stride and paused several steps before the door.

"How many people are here tonight?"

He turned to face her. "Counting us, there are now ten, though several others may arrive later in the evening."

Livid, she glared at him. "And how are you going to explain my participation in this farce, your grace?"

He rubbed his cheek with his palm, eyeing her speculatively. "That depends on you, Viola. For now, you're simply my guest, as are the others."

Through a fast, exhaled breath, she demanded, "What is your plan?"

He smiled. "I wouldn't want to ruin the surprise, darling."

"Don't call me that," she ordered in a huff.

Unfazed, he reached out and pushed the door handle down, then stepped back and motioned for her to enter.

The sight of the drawing room itself struck her first, amazing her almost as much as the green salon had. No amount had been spared in its decoration, both elegant and sophisticated, colored in deep reds and gold, with dark brown oak furniture, scarlet settees, chairs and drapes, rich Persian rugs of lavish design, two large crystal chandeliers hanging from the gilded ceiling, and intricate artwork displayed on every papered wall. But her appreciation of such beauty quickly turned to uneasiness when she at last gazed upon the party guests. She took in the scene with an odd mixture of anticipation and amazement. For a party this small, the Duke of Chatwin had set up a rather elaborate display of hors d'oeuvres on one side of the drawing room, the aroma of fine meats and pastries filling the air, while on the other stood footmen at the ready, pouring champagne at the sideboard. And directly next to the large mantel and cold grate stood her large Bartlett-James sketch on an easel, covered with black velvet, ready for the unveiling to all.

Suddenly she felt as if he'd put *her* on display. Of those he'd invited who were here now, most she knew either personally or by reputation as prominent members of London's art society, and at their entrance, everyone ceased their conversations and turned to look at them with varying degrees of curiosity.

"Ladies and gentlemen," Chatwin said as he moved into the room, "I'm certain you all know Lady Cheshire, an extraordinary artist in her own right, who has graciously accepted my invitation to join us this evening." He looked back at her, offering her a smile that never reached his eyes. "Of course you know Lord Fairbourne, Mr. Whitman, from the London art museum, Lord and Lady Brisbane, Lord and Lady Freemont, and Mr. and Mrs. Stanford Quicken. The Quickens only just returned from the Continent with some lovely French pieces to add to their collection."

She'd never met the Quickens, but she offered pleasantries to all of them as they did the same in return.

"Mr. Quicken is also one of England's finest art authenticators," he added casually. "His expertise should be especially helpful this night."

Confusion enveloped her, followed by a feeling of cold trepidation that settled in the pit of her stomach.

He noticed her hesitation and explained. "I hope to verify with certainty that the painting I only just purchased is in fact an original and not, I fear, a forgery."

Her eyes widened with shock; her cheeks grew hot again with renewed fury. He must have expected her reaction, for his brows rose as he looked at her, daring her to make excuses, to challenge him in front of everyone or flee in shame.

But instead of giving him the satisfaction, she swallowed a scream of rage and, with remarkable poise, pulled her gaze free of the penetration of his to offer his guests a delicate smile.

"I'm certainly honored to be included among such distinguished art patrons," she said, her voice sounding raspy and dry to her ears. It was a ridiculous statement, and yet she had been so completely caught off guard by Chatwin's audacity in assuming her a fraud that she truly had no bearings for the moment.

Fortunately, the party resumed as a footman announced that hors d'oeuvres were now being served at the buffet and several people moved toward the food.

Lucas Wolffe, Duke of Fairbourne, stepped toward her instead.

"It's a pleasure to see you again, Lady Cheshire," he said with a slight bow.

She curtseyed. "And you, your grace."

"And you're looking as lovely as ever," Miles Whitman added as he moved to her side and handed her a glass of champagne. "I daresay you're the most talented among us as well. I had no idea you'd be with us for this event."

She smiled and took a much-needed swallow from her glass.

Whitman, curator of London's modern art museum, would marry her next week, for the prestige alone, if she showed just the slightest measure of interest. She hadn't seen either man since Isabella's party, and although Fairbourne appeared only slightly amused by her presence, Whitman once again stared at her with a growing grin of excitement on his round, middle-aged face, patting down his oiled, thinning hair and licking his lips as if he couldn't wait to take a bite out of her neck.

Ian took a step closer to her so that she could now feel his warmth at her back, his shoulder behind hers, his legs pressing fully into the folds of her wide skirts.

"Lady Cheshire is in the process of painting my formal portrait," he maintained pleasantly, "and in that capacity, she is my special guest this evening."

Miles looked from her to Ian, and then back again, his countenance falling as he slowly came to the conclusion they were indeed a couple, probably as the insufferable man had planned. Suddenly she felt smothered, felt her cheeks growing hot, and had it not been for the piercing laughter of Lady Diana Freemont from the buffet line, reminding Viola that she was in the safety of other ladies of the peerage, she might have shriveled up into a ball in the corner, hoping not to be noticed until she could make an escape.

"So, what have you got planned for us tonight, then?" Whitman asked after clearing his throat, abruptly bemused.

"Heard it's a Bartlett-James original," a voice from behind them cut in. "So, Chatwin, when are we going to see what's behind the velvet?"

Viola turned to see Bartholomew St. Giles, Baron Brisbane, walking toward them, his small china plate piled high with edibles, his portly stature stuffed snugly into his waistcoat and dinner jacket. She knew Brisbane because she had painted his wife's portrait last summer. He'd also, years earlier, been one of the first to purchase several of her Victor Bartlett-James original sketches as a collector highly interested in erotic art. Of course he didn't know she was the artist of such risqué work, just as all these men and women now in the Duke of Chatwin's drawing room had heard of Bartlett-James or collected various erotic pieces but remained ignorant—at least until tonight.

"You've heard correctly, Brisbane," Ian replied.

The baron chuckled with delight as Whitman looked at Ian, aghast. "There are ladies present, Chatwin. It—it must be especially . . . artistic?"

Viola bit down to keep from laughing. Miles looked as if it had just been announced that nude dancers would be the evening's entertainment.

"They're all married ladies, Whitman," Ian countered, "and they've all seen questionable artwork before."

Miles nodded sheepishly. "Yes, I . . . suppose. It is art, after all."

"Have you heard of the erotic artist Victor Bartlett-James, Lady Cheshire?"

That from Fairbourne, who continued to look amused by the entire event.

She took another sip of champagne. "I'm sure everybody has heard of him, sir. At least everybody in the London art world."

Seconds later, he asked, "Where do you suppose one would hang his kind of art? Certainly not the parlor."

Brisbane chuckled, then coughed and waved himself away from the small group as he seemed to choke on a pastry. Whitman's eyes widened and he shifted uncomfortably from one foot to the other, his round face reddening. And although she'd never felt more ill at ease at any other time in her life, Viola managed to keep herself from cowering by maintaining a false air of dignity.

After clearing her throat, she suggested, "I would think if a person could actually afford to purchase a Bartlett-James original, he could hang it anywhere he wanted, your grace."

Fairbourne almost smiled. Then he nodded to her once and replied, "I hadn't thought of that, but I do suppose you're right, madam."

She tried to ignore the flush in her face as she took another sip from her glass. Thankfully, Whitman turned away to speak to Mrs. Quicken, and Fairbourne excused himself to attend the buffet. For a second, she almost relaxed—until Ian reminded her he still stood at her back.

Leaning over, he whispered in her ear, "I think the best place to hang erotic art might be the bedchamber. What do you think, Lady Cheshire?"

She wanted to scream. Instead, she turned to look at him, her features flat. "If you're trying to startle me, your grace, it won't work," she said mildly.

"Startle you?"

She inhaled a deep breath, then let it out heavily. "You know I'm a widow and artist and therefore not at all shocked by erotic work, or viewing it in public."

His eyes bore into hers. "What about viewing it in private?"

Nervously, she glanced around, noting with some assuagement that nobody appeared close enough to hear them.

"Viola?"

She glared at him again. "I believe viewing it in private is what gentlemen do, your grace."

"Ah." He glanced down her bodice again. "So the

piece I purchased never hung in your bedchamber for you and your husband's viewing pleasure?"

She gaped at him, then whispered, "That's none of your business."

He gave her a genuine smile, the first she'd seen from him, and the look of cunning delight on his handsome face made her suddenly falter.

"I'm hungry," she lied, turning away from him.

Quickly, he reached out and took her hand in his, pulling her gently back. Leaning over, he whispered, "I'm hungry, too, Viola, and your sketch, which I'm going to hang in my bedroom after tonight's showing, has whet my appetite."

She couldn't look at him, though she did notice one or two people watching them curiously. Fighting the urge to toss her remaining champagne in his face, she instead gently pulled her hand free and murmured, "Hang it any damn place you like. Now leave me alone. People are staring."

That said, she lifted her skirts and walked around him toward the foodstuff, listening to his chuckle with prickly nerves and heated flesh she tried very hard to ignore.

For three-quarters of an hour, she mingled restlessly, unable to do anything but pick at the roast beef, cucumber sandwich, and ginger cake she'd placed on her plate, listening to Lady Freemont and Lady Brisbane discuss charity work and social news while staying removed from the men. Finally the ladies turned to the subject of art, and the conversation became far more intimate.

Lady Freemont, a woman of nearly sixty, with broad

hips and shoulders, thick silver hair piled high on her head, and now more than a little tipsy from drink, leaned closer to say conspiratorially, "Have you ever created one of those, Lady Cheshire?"

Viola blinked. "I beg your pardon?"

Lady Freemont laughed, then clarified in whispered excitement, "A naughty painting!"

Lady Brisbane giggled like a woman half her age, and Mrs. Quicken walked toward them, leaving her husband's side to discover what might be so entertaining in their discussion.

"Yes, do tell," Lady Brisbane insisted, huddling closer. "I wish I had the skill, myself. Just think of the fun Bartholomew and I could have watching it come to life at my fingertips!"

They all laughed again. Viola forced a chuckle, feeling more annoyed than amused. Mrs. Quicken, younger than the others by a decade or so, took a rather large gulp from her champagne glass, then said, "There are quite a lot of good artists who can emulate his style, but I daresay there's not one who captures the mood of love like Victor Bartlett-James does."

"The *mood* of *love*?" Lady Freemont leaned back with another laugh, sloshing a bit of her drink on her skirts without notice. "Oh, goodness, what a thought!" With bright eyes, she glanced back at Viola. "Come, Lady Cheshire, you can tell us. Have you ever thought of creating your own brand of risqué art?"

Grinning, she shrugged lightly. "I'm sure if I did I wouldn't tell a soul."

"Which means," Ian said from behind her, "that perhaps she already has?"

Someone gasped, then everyone giggled as if they'd been caught in a bawdy tête-à-tête. Except her. Forcing a smile, she glanced over her rigid shoulders to find him standing perhaps a foot away, champagne in hand, looking at her with mild speculation on his handsome face.

"Your grace," she replied, "I think if I attempted to re-create the Victor Bartlett-James *mood* of *love,* you would be the last to know."

He nodded once at her coyness, taking a step toward the small group. "Duly noted, madam, though after seeing your work on portraits, I suspect your . . . talent would shine in any form."

She had trouble deciding if she should take that as an actual compliment, though the ladies no doubt did. Smiling, she carefully replied, "Such praise, coming from you, sir, is beyond gracious."

He raised a brow at her quick, ambiguous retort and she grinned in triumph before turning away from him and looking back at the ladies. Suddenly she felt his palm against her lower back and she instinctively stiffened, startled that he would display such a manner of intimate possession in front of the others. She didn't move an inch, praying nobody in the vicinity would notice.

"I think it's time to for the unveiling, don't you?" he maintained softly across her shoulder.

"Oh, goodness, yes," Lady Freemont said, fanning herself with her hand. "I don't think I need any more champagne."

Lady Brisbane laughed jovially, as if finding some outrageous joke in Lady Freemont's consumption of drink. Mrs. Quicken's eyes lit up as she glanced across the drawing room. "My husband always seems to disappear the moment he is needed."

Viola opened her mouth to offer a comment, and at precisely that moment, she felt Ian's palm move smoothly down her gown and rest momentarily on her bottom.

Her breath caught and her face flushed hotly as he caressed the lower half of one cheek with his fingertips. She didn't move, couldn't register anything except the racing of her pulse.

"Actually, your husband and Lord Fairbourne went to the balcony to enjoy their pipes in open air," Ian offered, his voice low and formal. "I just sent a footman after them."

"Oh, good," she replied, pulling at a stray brown curl at her cheek and bending it behind her ear. "Perhaps I'll take a moment then to freshen my beverage. Excuse me, your grace?"

"Of course, please," he replied at once, gesturing with a nod toward the table of unopened bottles.

"I think I'll do the same," Lady Freemont said, clearly changing her mind about having more champagne after taking the final swallow from her glass. "Margaret? Lady Cheshire?"

She couldn't speak. He continued to subtly caress her bottom, and although his palm and fingers remained atop layers of satin and petticoats, she felt the touch as a scorch to nude skin.

"I think I'd like to have a private word with Lady Cheshire," Ian said seconds later. "If you don't mind?"

Both ladies looked at her with wide eyes, then back at him.

"No, no, of course not," Lady Brisbane sputtered. "If you'll excuse us, then?"

They curtseyed in unison and stepped away, their heads huddled together in whispered words until Margaret giggled again as they neared the sidebar.

"If you move away from me, Viola," he warned softly, "I'll grab you and kiss you in front of everyone."

She swallowed, seething, then managed to whisper furiously, "What do you want?"

He leaned over and put his lips next to her ear. "I have nothing more to say. I just wanted to feel your softness and imagine you naked and moaning for a few seconds longer."

She clenched her fists at her sides to keep from striking him. "I rather think you enjoy embarrassing me, sir," she murmured tightly. "You've made everyone here tonight think we're intimate."

His warm breath teased the back of her neck. "Not necessarily. Nobody can see my hand on you, Viola. Everyone is in front of us."

Drawing a shaky breath, she pivoted slightly to look at him, and the stark lust she beheld in his eyes took her aback. Suddenly he dropped his hand from her and she took a step away, turning to face him fully.

He held her gaze for a moment, his features hard, his lips thinned grimly, his skin as flushed as hers.

She couldn't believe that his touching her over her gown for a few seconds could arouse him. But in silence, she glanced down to note the rigid erection beneath his trousers, and her mouth opened slightly in shock.

"I haven't been with a woman in a long time," he

murmured, his tone thick and low. "It doesn't take much to make me respond."

She blinked, gazing back into his eyes, uncertain what to say, the urge to run overwhelming her more than at any other time since he'd come back into her life. Yet she also felt the sharp pull between them, luring the memory of his beautiful nude body to the surface of her thoughts, reminding her of just how much she had desired him then—and how difficult it would be to resist him now.

"How can you want me physically and yet hate me enough to humiliate me at the same time?" she whispered as cold confusion swept over her.

He shoved his hands in the pockets of his dinner jacket. "I don't know."

She shook her head in disbelief, noting with a sinking heart how he didn't at all deny his need to shame her.

Drawing a long breath, he admitted solemnly, "But I *do* know that only you will do, and I intend to have you, in spite of your class, your own desires, and your future. In spite of *everything*."

That appalling certainty, coupled with the obvious contempt he showed for her in everything he did and said, acted like an abrupt icing of her veins.

"I detest you, Lord Chatwin," she breathed, her words coated with loathing. "And I've never, in my life, felt sorrier for such a lost soul."

Before he could respond, she turned and walked away, shaking inside, moving as quickly as she could to the sideboard for a long, full glass of his excellent champagne, vowing that by this time tomorrow she would be gone from his life forever, regardless of the price to be paid. Nothing mattered more now than escaping his clutches with her son in her protection and her pride intact.

Nothing.

They gathered around the covered easel in front of the mantel, Ian on one side, Mr. Quicken on the other. Several others had joined the party in the last half hour, drinking and eating and awaiting the showing of great, erotic art. Viola stood back a little, between Fairbourne and Lady Freemont, refusing to look at Chatwin even once since she'd left him in rage nearly an hour ago. But she could feel his gaze on her face as intensely as she noticed the expectancy in the air.

Chin held high, she waited as Chatwin began a short monologue of his ambition to buy fine, excellent art in various forms, from sculpture to paintings, and how he'd never purchased erotic art before but had heard of Victor Bartlett-James and had taken this opportunity to expand his collection. Finally, he raised his hand and pulled the black velvet from the frame.

An audible gasp could be heard among the group— then whispered comments of praise and a nuance of graphic language to describe the sketch in detail as they all started talking at once.

Viola sipped her champagne, nodding when Lady Freemont offered her thoughts, trying to stay as inconspicuous as possible. At last Mr. Quicken moved in to study the artwork with the precision of an authenticator, scanning each inch of the piece and speaking in hushed tones to Chatwin. She paid little attention to her surroundings, waiting for the perfect moment to slip away and head quickly home, when she heard him say her name.

Mr. Quicken turned abruptly and looked at her. "Lady Cheshire?" he repeated, his thick brows furrowed deeply.

Suddenly all eyes were on her as silence fell across the drawing room.

Her mouth went dry. "I beg your pardon?"

Ian cleared his throat. "I had to tell him where I purchased the sketch, madam," he said very smoothly. "I'm sorry."

She had no idea what was happening. Momentarily stunned, she finally looked at her nemesis.

He watched her with cool, calculated eyes and a coldly satisfied demeanor. And the look he gave her caused a shiver of fear to run through her. "I—Forgive me for being confused, but—"

"Did this sketch belong to your husband, Lady Cheshire?" Quicken asked, his tone one of concern.

Her mouth dropped open; she felt the blood drain from her face as the shock of that question sank in. He had exposed her secret, at least partially, and she couldn't deny it now. Not in front of everyone in attendance here tonight.

With firm resolve, she replied, "Yes, it's true. My late husband purchased it years ago, and I only just discovered it during a cleaning of my attic. My solicitor sold it on my behalf to Lord Chatwin."

It was the best she could do under the circumstances, but at least the explanation sounded reasonable. She would deal with the little gossip her revelation might create tomorrow.

Stanford Quicken rubbed his jowls with his plump fingers, his frown deepening. "I'm so very sorry, madam."

"Sorry?"

The man's cheeks grew pink as he shifted from one foot to the other, casting a fast glance at Ian before looking at her once more. "I know this is quite . . . I realize how shocking this must be."

An uncomfortable stillness filled the room. Viola glanced around her as the sliver of fear Ian's calculated gaze had evoked moments earlier turned to alarm. "I don't understand," she whispered.

"My dear," Mr. Quicken said, "I'm afraid you've been cheated. I'm well aware of Victor Bartlett-James and his work, and this sketch was not created by him. It is a forgery."

For the longest moment she had trouble stifling a laugh of absurdity. "That's impossible," she blurted, scanning the group for some sort of assurance. She got nothing in return but glances ranging from awkwardness to pity.

Quicken rubbed the back of his neck, ignoring her insistence altogether. "I'm certain that under the circumstances you will want to compensate Lord Chatwin for the . . . uh . . . blunder."

And that's when it hit her—his lie, his deception, and the ultimate social humiliation he had planned from the beginning.

The painting was an original, and they both knew it. So did Quicken, if he was truly an authenticator. But Ian Wentworth had planted the seed of doubt tonight, setting up an elaborate ruse to begin her social ruin.

He'd trapped her into admitting that she had sold this sketch to him, and now they all knew she would also be expected to return payment. He'd even made certain the ladies might consider the possibility that she had created this piece herself as the forger. There was no real proof that she hadn't cheated the Duke of Chatwin by attempting to sell her own art in place of an original, and every reason to doubt her word. Even Miles Whitman couldn't seem to look at her as he stared instead at his shoes. And she couldn't tell all, explain anything, without revealing to everyone that she was the artist Victor Bartlett-James, which, at this point, not one of them would believe.

For the first time in her adult life, Viola felt betrayed to the center of her soul. And by a man she had once cared for, ached for, and even for a time had thought she'd loved.

She looked at him again, noting his bland expression, his narrowed eyes daring her to deny his integrity, to call a gentleman of his wealth and station a liar at his own elegant party.

Bastard.

Quashing tears of anguish, helplessness, and growing fury, she backed away from the group, her gaze never moving from his. And then she turned her back on them all and walked out of the drawing room, her head high, back rigid with newfound determination.

Everything had changed. She would most certainly not be leaving tomorrow.

They were now, officially, at war.

Chapter Eleven

I couldn't stop looking at him today, and when I finally touched him to care for him, his body responded and he reached for my hand, pleading deliriously for me to caress him. I have never experienced anything so shocking, so intimate, in my life. . . .

*I*an stood at the back of the room, watching with only half interest as the club gradually filled with well-respected, finely dressed gentlemen. Many were drunk already and it wasn't yet six in the evening, though the crowd remained rather well behaved considering the subject of tonight's auction. He'd only had one whiskey so far in an attempt to stay alert through the process so soon to take place, his lingering doubts overcome by a growing curiosity at what he was about to witness.

He'd dressed with care, choosing evening attire in black and white silk, his cravat knotted precisely yet making him feel uncomfortably choked at the neck, probably due to both the stuffiness of the crowded room and his sour mood. Fairbourne stood at his side, sipping from his glass, engrossed in a political discussion with an older gent next to him. Ian didn't much feel like joining in, or talking at all, for that matter. Although the evening had yet to truly begin, his thoughts kept straying to the wily Lady Cheshire.

Since she'd left his home in shame three nights ago, he'd done nothing but think of her face. Her beautiful face so stunned by his actions and intent, her bright, hazel eyes so overcome with despair and confusion and a centered hatred of him. Strangely, the searing look of fury and frightened vulnerability she had given him seconds before her departure haunted him, making him feel more annoyed at himself for caring than anything else. He should be rejoicing in her slow destruction, as he'd envisioned for five long years, but for the moment he just felt hollow. Empty.

The party itself had continued well into the evening, but his heart had gone out of it the minute she'd left. He'd played his role as he should have, though with her exit the triumph and excitement, at least for him, had quickly vanished. He'd slept little that night as he'd contemplated his next move and obsessed more than imaginable about how she might respond to him physically, finding no help at all from the stirring sketch he'd hung over the mantel facing his bed.

The problem, he mused, was how to get her to come to him, to crawl between his sheets and give in to him willingly. He had no doubts that he could seduce her, and as much as he despised her and all she stood for, forcing her wasn't an option. She craved his touch as much as he did hers, something he'd witnessed in her gaze when he'd first caught her standing so beautifully in his green salon. Viola admired him, felt their mutual attraction, and clearly desired him. He'd seen that as well when she'd exposed flushed cheeks and a lust-filled gaze after he'd done no more than caress her behind over her gown in a crowded drawing room, a memory that amused him even now. She hadn't been shocked by his obvious need for her, just bewildered. And that bewilderment she felt for him would be her undoing—if he could figure out how to play to it for his benefit, a problem without an answer, which was why he'd let her simmer these last three days rather than going to her with his demand.

She hadn't been in contact with him since the night of the party, but Cafferty kept him informed of her whereabouts and intentions as much as he could. She had stayed in her town house these last three days, except for yesterday morning, when she'd made a short visit to her solicitor. Hours later the news had spread that Brimleys would be holding an exclusive auction for a prized Victor Bartlett-James painting—and the reason he found himself here tonight, dressed uncomfortably, and acknowledging the drunken crowd with building anticipation as to what Lady Cheshire had working in her very clever female mind.

The painting to be presented had created quite a stir already, although nobody had yet even seen it. It stood on a large wooden easel beneath a brightly lit chandelier, covered by a black velvet drape, and guarded by a burly man with fists the size of melons. Just the secrecy alone had started a drone of speculation, as most auctions allowed bidders to view items before the start. Apparently a Victor Bartlett-James piece created a flutter of excitement regardless of what it looked like, which managed to make it all the more valuable, he supposed. Nothing like a bit of titillation to increase its worth and, thus, the bidding.

"You think it's an original?"

Ian straightened and looked at Fairbourne, who had turned his attention from the elder gentleman and back to him again.

"The painting?" he clarified.

Fairbourne nodded once and took a long sip of whiskey. "Surely she can't create a forged painting in three days."

Ian shook his head, glancing out over the crowd. "No, I think that would be impossible, even for her," he agreed. He hadn't mentioned even to his closest friend that he'd paid Quicken to deny the authenticity of the sketch, which, as he'd subsequently learned, was indeed an original. That fact didn't matter in the least to his pursuit, though he did find it curious that she owned more than one piece of Victor Bartlett-James art, and he had to believe the painting to be auctioned this night wasn't a forgery either.

"What, may I ask, is your . . . relationship to the lovely widow anyway?"

That question made his nerves fire irritably. "No need to ask. No relationship at all."

Fairbourne laughed outright. "Good God, Chatwin, you don't even lie well about her."

Ian turned to face his friend squarely, his body tensing, features grimly set. "The truth is irrelevant," he said with a measure of hostility. "But the fact is, I don't like her."

Growing serious again, Fairbourne eyed him candidly for a moment, then motioned for the barkeep to refill their glasses. "I think she finds you rather appealing, actually."

He almost snorted. "You don't lie well, either."

Fairbourne shook his head. "That's . . . not a lie. I saw the two of you together, and although you hide your feelings well, whatever they may be, she does not."

Ian glanced at him askance. "Frankly, my friend, what she thinks of me isn't something you would know."

"Maybe I don't know a thing or two about ladies in a general sense, but I do know a smitten woman when I see one. I couldn't decide if she wanted to kiss you or strike you at your ridiculous art party."

Ian chuckled and reached for his glass. "She wanted to strike me. The lady may find me physically to her liking, but the woman in her despises me."

"Why?"

That simple question caught him off guard, making him realize at once that he should have said nothing, acknowledged nothing. But Fairbourne, his newly poured whiskey untouched, now seemed truly curious, even concerned, as he leaned his hip against the small table at his side and crossed his arms over his chest, waiting for a reasonable explanation.

Ian exhaled a long breath, then in two swallows, finished the contents of his glass, feeling the sudden burn down his throat as a needed reminder of the pain often caused by sweet things desired.

"It's a complicated tale, Fairbourne," he admitted at last, licking the rim and then placing his empty tumbler on the table. "And not one I feel like repeating."

"She had something to do with your kidnapping, didn't she?" he prodded, tone lowered.

Ian stretched his neck, ready to jump out of his skin, hot and annoyed at the smoke-filled air and voices of loud, inebriated gentlemen rising with each passing minute as they all awaited the grand display of nothing more than a titillating painting. After a brush of his palm down his face, he replied, "She wasn't involved with the kidnapping, but she was there."

Fairbourne scratched his jaw. "There in what capacity?"

He looked at his friend again. "What capacity? As a goddamned helper."

"I see." Seconds later, Fairbourne raised his glass and added, "As a helper I suppose she took care of you in some manner?"

Ian's brows furrowed with incredulity. "She left me there to die, Lucas," he said through a bitter whisper. "She took part in a vicious crime, and in the end she was never found guilty of anything."

"But what exactly did she *do* that she should have been found guilty *of*?" he persisted.

"Inaction," he shot back.

"And what else?"

That confused him. "What else? What the devil does that mean?"

Fairbourne sighed. "Was she actually with you in the dungeon, or just aware that you were a captive?"

"She was there."

"So what did she do to you when she was with you?"

Ian resisted the sudden urge to slam his fist into the brick wall at his side. Instead he drew in a long, deep breath and attempted to steady his fired nerves like a gentleman.

"The truth is, I don't remember clearly," he muttered. "They had me drugged much of the time."

"I see."

"No, you don't," he countered without clarification, unwilling to tell a soul that he believed he had been taken advantage of as a man. He couldn't even mention such a shame to Lucas, the only person in the world he trusted right now.

Fairbourne took a sip of whiskey, watching Ian closely over the rim of his glass. Then slowly he lowered it to the table, his expression turning thoughtful. Voice subdued, he asserted, "And now here you are, alive after having survived a horrible ordeal, wealthier than God, able to live the rest of your life in comfort, with any lady of your choice, and yet you're relentlessly pursuing a young, beautiful widow with a child to ruin. Is that it?"

The casual manner in which his confidant of several years said his thoughts aloud, and uttered them so distastefully, made Ian cringe inside. Perhaps it sounded like revenge to Fairbourne, and when stated bluntly, the ignorant would no doubt find him guilty of offense, but the truth of it was simply inexplicable.

Taking a step closer, Ian eyed the man candidly. "I don't expect you to understand, Lucas," he said with caution. "But I do ask that you refrain from judging me or my actions. You weren't there, and you haven't lived in my hell for the last five years."

For several long moments Fairbourne studied him in silence. Then with a sigh of acceptance, he lowered his gaze to the table, tapping the wood with his fingertips.

"I would never presume to know the horror you experienced, Ian," he said quietly, "and perhaps she isn't at all innocent in your suffering." His eyes shot up once more, narrowed as they bore into his. "But I do think you need to take care. The woman is young, inexperienced, and feels something for you other than hatred. That I can tell." He paused, then lowered his voice to add, "I can understand your anger at her inaction or . . . inability to set you free, but it doesn't appear to me that you've thought of this from her perspective, or tried to discover if she actually did anything for you to lessen your struggle."

Ian bit down hard to keep his frustration in check. "She should have gone for help. She didn't, and now she should be in prison."

Fairbourne lifted a shoulder in a shrug. "Maybe. Then again, perhaps like you, and because of what her family did to you, she's been living in it herself for five long years."

That notion jolted Ian, sparked his anger anew, and yet he couldn't exactly find fault with his friend, who spoke so honestly.

Subdued, he ran his fingers through his hair. "I don't intend to destroy her, Lucas, I merely want justice, for me and for her crime."

Fairbourne scanned the crowd for a second or two, then looked back at him. "There is a difference between justice and revenge, Ian," he argued, "and revenge goes much deeper, ends with far graver consequences. Justice requires diligence, but revenge goes to the trouble of spending whatever funds and time are necessary, hiring anyone to do or say anything for the right price, and calculated planning regardless of all else. And you've done all of that, haven't you?"

Ian said nothing.

Fairbourne leaned his forearm on the table and moved closer. "If you intend to bed her in this scheme of yours, take warning. I think you'll find it's not so easy to walk away with your dignity intact after you've done everything in your power to ruin her, especially if you seduce her and then discover your own desire for her remains unsated because you've grown to care for her as a woman." He waited, then very softly added, "She will never forgive you, and she will never let you return to her. The revenge will be complete, but in the end, you could very well experience the loss of your honor, probably the greatest loss of all."

Ian felt as if he'd been splashed with icy water as cold perspiration broke out on his body. Fairbourne wasn't one to talk of his own fractured past, though Ian knew he referenced it here in a warning of the truest sense. But he wasn't Lucas, and he had no intention of having his heart broken or his integrity damaged by a revenge gone wrong. Bedding Viola had less to do with wanting her than it did a need to take everything she had, including an intimate passion she offered nobody else. That he actually found her desirable was simply sweet cream for the berries. And leaving her in the end would be the easiest part, the sweetest thing of all. With his time in the dungeon brought to a gratifying conclusion, he could then move on, think about a future worthy of his title. No regrets. Sexually sated. Justice done.

"I know what I'm doing," he grumbled.

Fairbourne studied him for a long moment, then once again stood upright. Sighing in acquiescence, he raised his empty tumbler. "That calls for another, I should think."

Ian didn't want more to drink, he wanted to get home, to relish the quiet, to lie on his bed and consider his plans for the seduction to come, to look at his sketch that he knew—just *knew*—Viola had stared at while she'd satisfied her own lust. But then he wasn't sure ladies ever did such a thing, and just imagining it now, in public, aroused him enough to hand his glass to Fairbourne for a refill to quell the need.

He glanced around the room, nearly filled now to capacity, thick with smoke, the chatter almost unbearable. And just as Fairbourne returned with his third shot of whiskey, Brimleys's owner walked to the dais next to the draped painting and attempted to hush the crowd.

"Gentlemen!" he bellowed, his puffy hands patting down the air in front of him. "Gentlemen, please!"

A surge of excitement pulsed through the room as the noise dimmed. Ian and Fairbourne stood at the back, quietly watching, sipping their drinks.

"Are you bidding?" Lucas asked.

Ian smirked, calculating the size of the artwork to be larger than his sketch. "I don't suppose I need two of them. And the cost for one of these is outrageous."

"And yet . . . won't she be returning payment for the forgery? Certainly you can afford an original now."

It was a biting comment, meant to sting, and Ian ignored it. "I didn't come to buy it. I came to see what she could possibly offer this time." And to discover how much she might acquire for the sale, though he didn't say that aloud. He also had to wonder why—why she had two, and why she chose to sell this one now if not to be used against him in some nefarious manner he couldn't yet fathom.

"Gentlemen," the burly owner began, "tonight's auction is an original painting by the celebrated artist Victor Bartlett-James."

Ian tensed, realizing he felt the anticipation almost as much as those who intended to buy. Viola had obviously seen this erotic painting as well, and the notion stirred his interest even more.

"Tonight's bidding," the man carried on, "shall begin at five thousand pounds."

Whistles and a rumbling of voices ensued.

"This obviously isn't a dignified auction," Fairbourne mused.

"It isn't dignified art," Ian replied.

The guard with the melon fists came forward and clutched the bottom of the black velvet drape. The owner and auctioneer stood to the side, one hand raised. "I now present to you tonight's painting, titled . . . *Gentleman Chained*!"

The drape flew up to gasps of astonishment.

"Holy Christ," Fairbourne whispered as a low murmur began to spread through the crowd.

Ian felt his heart stop and a freezing blanket of fear and dread envelop him. He backed up to the wall, his glass dropping from his hand to shatter on the wooden floor at his feet.

On the easel stood a wide portrait in mostly bronze, tan, and peach, the background dark brown, of a nude couple in carnal embrace, painted in side view. The man lay flat on his back, his right arm lifted slightly and shackled to the stone wall behind him at the wrist, his face in profile, eyes closed, jaw clenched, and head lifted at the height of ecstasy. The woman on top sat upright, her bare hips melding with his as she rested her visible leg to the side of him, foot pointed back toward his, her waist long and slender as she arched up and forward, her own head tipped back, the silky strands of dark brown hair barely skimming his thighs. Most of her face remained obscured in shadow, though her lips could be seen as the brightest part of the art-work, slightly parted as if gasping, and painted a sear-ing scarlet. Most shocking of all was the placement of hands, hers cupping her breasts, fingers pinching her erect nipples, his free hand lost between her thighs. And they were both clearly at climax.

The form was exquisite, the colors—aside from the centered, red mouth—subdued and perfectly blended, the painting masterful, shocking, dark and erotic. And Ian knew at once that the man in chains was him.

Suddenly he began shaking with rage, with confu-sion and absolute panic. The features weren't exactly defined, but all of society knew he had been held in a dungeon, shackled to a wall, and anyone who looked at this famous Bartlett-James work would surely think of him.

She had exploited his terror and now thought to sell it publicly for profit. The whispers would begin, and soon the entire country would know that Victor Bartlett-James had created an erotic painting in the image of Ian Wentworth, prisoner.

Fairbourne put a palm on his shoulder. "Ian—"

Instinctively he jerked back, shoving it aside. "She did this," he whispered harshly, teeth clenched, hands fisted at his sides. "She did this to me."

Voices grew louder as the bidding began.

"Is it—Is that *her*?"

Ian shook his head, blinded by disbelief, by suddenly sparking memories and thoughts he couldn't control or understand. "I don't know . . ."

"Who *painted* it?" Fairbourne asked, clearly as appalled and bewildered as Ian was.

Ian drew a staggered breath, swallowed harshly. And then he knew.

She did.

"God . . . she's Bartlett-James."

Fairbourne blinked. "What?"

The bidding continued, the loud chatter grew to a deafening pitch. Ian turned to Lucas. "Buy it. Bid for it and buy it, no matter how high the final price." He scrubbed a palm down his face. "I have to leave."

"Wait a minute," Lucas insisted, glancing around them. "What the devil is going on?"

"I think you know I can't let anyone else own that piece," Ian replied quickly, his anger consuming. He slammed a fist on the table. "Jesus, just bid until it's yours. I'll repay you, whatever the cost."

"You're going to her," Fairbourne stated rather than asked.

Ian didn't reply, though the fury in his eyes said everything.

Fairbourne grabbed his arm. "Don't hurt her," he admonished carefully. "I'm warning you, Ian, confront her if you must, don't hurt her. *You* started this war. Remember that."

Ian couldn't reply, couldn't think clearly. Pulling free once more, he turned and disappeared into the crowd.

Chapter Twelve

It's been almost five days since I've seen him. Mama kept me in to take care of her needs, whining about how she suffers in the cold. I'm afraid for him when he's alone. Much of the time I'm only there to listen to him speak. Sometimes I laugh at his tales, sometimes I tell him a story or two, even when I know he doesn't understand. I'm starting to think he needs me more than anyone does, or ever has. . . .

It took him forty-five agonizing minutes to reach her town house. The congested traffic in the city kept his driver to a crawl, and at one point he almost left his coach to walk instead. In the end he decided he would use the time before their confrontation to think, to center his thoughts and calm himself lest he unleash his fury on her smug and deceitful charms in ungentlemanly fashion the moment he laid eyes on her.

Fairbourne had been right. He had started this war, and she had merely fought back, and fought back hard, though it wasn't in his nature to hurt her or any other woman physically. But she would know his wrath, and after nearly an hour of thinking about the humiliation that had just taken place, he finally came to the conclusion that she had probably expected it, had to have known that he'd attend the auction and would be waiting for him to arrive at her home, her claws sharpened, exposed and ready to lash out.

Viola Bennington-Jones. Victor Bartlett-James. God, he should have suspected it sooner. But would any soul alive imagine a lady painting bawdy art? Then again, objectively he had to admit her work wasn't exactly common in expertise or subject. There truly existed a beauty to her form, a talent that went beyond the vulgar, which, he supposed, was the reason for the high price the artwork demanded. It also explained why Bartlett-James remained such a mystery. She could hardly expose herself as the artist and expect to live and raise her child in high society. But had her late husband known? Ian couldn't recall when Bartlett-James's work had first appeared on the stage, whether it would have been during her marriage or after Lord Cheshire's death. Such thoughts nagged at him, and the longer he sat waiting in a stifling coach to confront her, the more troubled he became, and the more questions he intended to have answered before the night was through.

At last they turned onto her drive and pulled up in front of her brightly lit town house. Ian jumped from his coach the second it stopped and climbed the stone steps to the large front door two at a time before using a heavy hand on the brass knocker. Several long moments later, the door opened a crack to show the surprised expression on the face of a parlor maid.

"The Duke of Chatwin to see Lady Cheshire," he said, amazed that his voice sounded far more steady than he felt.

The girl, who couldn't be more than sixteen, curtseyed with bright eyes. "Sir, Lady Cheshire isn't home."

Of course she was home, likely hiding from him, and this girl probably knew it. It took all of his effort not to barge in and search every room for himself.

He smiled, trying to appear charming as he replied, "I rather thought she was expecting me. Perhaps you could check with the staff?"

The parlor maid's thick brown eyebrows furrowed deeply. "I—I'm sorry, your grace. I'm certain she's out, but maybe you'd like to speak with Mr. Needham?"

Viola's butler. At least he'd have specific answers. "That would be most excellent, thank you."

She looked him up and down, then, apparently deciding he didn't appear very frightening, opened the door enough to let him step inside.

He noticed the artwork first, frame after frame of paintings stacked along one wall of the brightly lit foyer.

"Is Lady Cheshire moving all of these?" he asked, forcing a congenial demeanor and what he hoped was a dashing grin.

The girl paused, shifting her gaze uncomfortably over her shoulder and back. "We're leaving for the country in two days' time. These are the paintings Lady Cheshire is taking with her."

"Leaving for the country?" he repeated, unable to mask his concern and urgency. "To Cheshire?"

She bit her lip, afraid she'd blundered. "Yes, but I

think—I think perhaps you'd best speak to Needham, sir. Wait here, if you please."

With another quick curtsey, she turned and scurried down the hallway.

Ian stared at her departing back, paralyzed with uncertainty and feeling as if Viola had kicked the wind out of him just as he prepared to go on the attack.

She's running. And one step ahead of me. . . .

Immediately, he moved into action. If she'd chosen these particular paintings to take, they were important, at least to her, which meant the possibility existed of one or more portraits or sketches of him. He couldn't imagine her exposing erotic art to servants by just leaving it here in the foyer, but then perhaps they all knew of her persona and the details of her work already. Or she had sketches and paintings of his time in the dungeon that weren't erotic but remained nonetheless revealing. Regardless of her motives, he needed to know if she had anything here that could incriminate or expose him to even greater indignity.

Quickly, hearing nothing as yet from the staff, he walked to the first stack and began pulling the frames away from each other, just enough to catch a glimpse of the art before moving to the next. The first row was nothing more than still lifes, gardens and ponds, paintings ladies displayed at tea. The second stack—more of the same, with one sketch of puppies sleeping on a blanket, probably something she'd created for the nursery.

The third stack held his attention longer. Five gilded frames displayed portraits of individuals he assumed to be family. He recognized the first instantly, causing a deep rush of chilling anguish to slice through him as he gazed upon the faces of his captors—all three sisters, looking solemn and contemplative, Viola so young, expression lost. He shoved it from his view.

The next two paintings were of individuals he didn't know, followed by a remarkable family portrait of Viola, her baby, and her husband, Lord Henry Cresswald, Baron Cheshire, a man nearly twice her age and so unappealing physically that it astonished Ian. He stared at it for a moment or two, unable to imagine Viola married to the likes of this gentleman, so lean as to be gaunt, with deep-set eyes, a long, pointed chin, thin, curling mustache, and enormous ears he attempted to cover with fine, oiled hair he combed straight down from the center part on his head to his lobes.

Fascinated and slightly appalled, Ian turned his attention to Viola, probably no more than twenty, noting an expression that suggested a smile but never revealed one, her beautiful hair piled high on her head, eyes vibrant and focused, dressed in a modest blue gown and standing beside her sitting husband, one hand on his shoulder, the other holding her swaddled, infant child. They made a striking couple, in every way they shouldn't have, and for several seconds he felt a stirring of sympathy and sadness for the young woman in the portrait.

Ian shook himself. She had made her bed, marrying above her station and moving from Winter Garden and her despicable past before he had even gained enough strength to walk without help. She would receive no sympathy from him. Her choices were hers and she could suffer with them. That thought in mind, he shoved the portrait forward to expose the last one in the group.

The intensity of the color struck him first—bright reds and brilliant blues of all shades, creating a stunning portrait of a boy of about four, wearing short pants, stockings, and a velvet jacket buttoned to the ruffled neck of his white collar, as he stood formally in front of a massive staircase, each step accented by a vase filled with blooming red roses. At first glance the child looked very much like Viola, especially in his subtle expression and the shy tilt of his head. But as Ian finally focused on each distinct feature of his face, he felt a stir of a memory deep within.

With narrowed eyes, he studied the color and cut of his light brown hair, the shape of his hazel eyes, the line of his cheeks and chin. And although a boy of his age hadn't yet reached the maturity when facial characteristics became defined, if he had been wearing a girl's dress and had had ribbons in his hair, this child could have passed as his sister at that age.

He looked like Ivy. He looked *exactly* like Ivy.

"Your grace?"

Startled, Ian jumped back, shifting his gaze to Needham, who now walked toward him from the rear of the house.

"I'm sorry, sir, we've been preparing for a return to the country and I've been rather busy. Liza says you're looking for Lady Cheshire?"

The man's words didn't register. Momentarily disoriented, Ian blinked quickly several times, then glanced back to the painting. "Who is this?"

Needham looked at the stack of frames. "You mean the boy? That's Lord John, Baron Cheshire."

Ian's mouth went dry; his pulse began to race. "Lady Cheshire's son," he said as a confirmation to himself.

"Indeed. She painted this portrait last year. One of her favorites." Needham frowned. "Is there anything wrong, your grace? You look a bit . . . winded."

Not winded. Alarmed. There could only be one possible reason this child of Viola's looked nothing like her husband and very much like Ian's twin sister, Ivy. As a slap to the face, it all became clear.

"My God . . . ," he whispered.

"Sir?"

Ian staggered back, reeling inside, his eyes opened wide in astonishment as he stared at the painting. "How old is he?" he asked, his voice choked and barely audible.

Needham pulled at his waistcoat, shifted his weight to the other foot uncomfortably. "He will be five come October."

Five in October. She conceived in January five years ago.

"Jesus . . . ," Ian breathed, stumbling as he began to move away.

"Your grace?"

Ian had trouble taking his eyes off the portrait. She had given birth to his child—*his* child—and he couldn't even recall being with her. Did that mean she'd forced him? Was it possible for woman to rape a delirious man? And for what purpose, when the greatest risk would be pregnancy? He couldn't imagine such a thing happening, and yet he'd been chained, drugged, and altogether helpless under her control. All the nightmares and vague reflections that occasionally surfaced of that horrible time in his past suddenly had new and even darker meaning.

This child was living proof that they had been together in the dungeon, just as the erotic artwork auctioned tonight suggested. He had already suspected she'd touched him intimately until he'd responded, but this confirmed without doubt that she had, at least once, taken him inside of her.

Ian's throat tightened, his stomach lurched in sudden revulsion as it also occurred to him that he might have been abused by all three girls at different times, fondled as a plaything until he'd grown hard for their perverted, disgusting enjoyment, then stroked or raped to release. Yes, in the inky blackness of an ancient, abandoned dungeon, he had been used sexually, and, in the end, when they'd finished with him, they had left him to die.

"Your grace, you've gone ashen," Needham said, cutting into Ian's thoughts as he stepped toward him. "Perhaps you should sit—"

"Where is Lady Cheshire?" Ian demanded, voice shaking, taking a deep breath to control his nausea, the bitterness within as a new chill of enlightenment took hold.

The butler straightened, his features going slack at the sudden cold formality. "She's not at home, sir."

Sweat broke out on Ian's body and he wiped his upper lip with the back of his hand. "Yes. *Where* is she?"

Needham cleared his throat, raised his chin a fraction. "She said she had an errand or two to complete before leaving the city, one of which was a visit to her solicitor. I've no idea when she'll return."

Of course. She'd gone to Duncan, the man who sold her work and kept her secrets. She intended to hide there, evading Ian's immediate wrath, making plans to escape the city, or even the country, while his anger cooled, thinking he'd eventually return home from the auction humiliated and defeated, his tail between his legs. It made sense, and clearly she told her staff very little about her plans. Duncan would be the only person with details, the only man she could trust.

And there wasn't a bloody chance in hell he'd let her get away with it. She had painted him at his most vulnerable, a time when she'd held power over him, then exposed his likeness to the world tonight, selling it for profit. And that after knowing she had carried his son. The injustice was done, and there could be no turning back, for either of them.

With a nod to Needham, Ian offered a stiff thanks and walked to the front door, opened it himself, and climbed down the steps to his waiting coach.

Chapter Thirteen

He was very distressed today, thrashing, mumbling incoherently, pulling on his chained wrist so hard I feared he'd break the bones. And yet still, I wonder what would happen to my life if I helped him escape. My future seems as bleak as his. . . .

*V*iola stood at the window in the Duke of Chatwin's green salon, staring out at the thick garden foliage, now dark except for shadows cast by moonlight. She'd spent the day packing, making arrangements with servants, writing letters, and taking care of final necessities that had to be done before they left. But she'd come to his home to confront him as soon as the auction had ended and Mr. Duncan had informed her that Lucas Wolffe had purchased the painting on Ian's behalf.

She'd been sitting alone in this gorgeous room for nearly two hours now and had yet to hear his voice or learn that he'd finally arrived, and she was getting anxious. True, he might have gone to her town house to confront her, but she'd just assumed he'd come here after learning she wasn't home. Perhaps that hadn't been a clever calculation on her part, but her main concern had been avoiding a confrontation where her own servants could overhear or come to wrong conclusions. She also wanted her sketch back, since he expected her to repay him, and she refused to leave this night without it. So, while waiting for the clash of wills to begin, she'd twice accepted Braetham's offer of a sherry, sipping it slowly to give her something to do while the sweet elixir warmed her body and helped keep her nerves as calm as possible.

She'd never intended to auction or sell her most intimate portraits—those of her and Ian. They had always been her personal treasures, created to give her solace and remind her of the intimacy the two of them had shared during a time of fear. But he had left her no choice in fighting back after he'd more or less called her a schemer and exposed her as a possible fraud, though now, three days after his party, she felt more subdued than angry. She was tired of the fight and just wanted to leave, to get out of the city quickly, retrieve her son in Cheshire, and head for the Continent. With the sale at auction this evening she at last had adequate funds, and with her title, she could settle in any number of cities, begin life anew, afford good tutors, and raise her son to an age where he could return to his land as a young adult with promise. Of course the Duke of Chatwin might follow her to the ends of the earth, she supposed, but after she'd unveiled her greatest weapon tonight, in front of his peers, she truly hoped he would take the message to heart and his crazed pursuit of her would end.

It really didn't matter what she said to him. He ignored explanations and would never forgive her for the pain her family had caused him. Even if she revealed everything that had happened in the dungeon, she knew instinctively that he wouldn't believe her. Leaving the city was now her best option for living a normal life, and as much as she had looked forward to a grand season out of mourning, the notion now seemed as far removed from her world as it had been for the country girl from Winter Garden, her past of years ago.

Viola raised her glass and took a sip of sherry. He would be fuming mad when he finally laid eyes on her, though she felt relatively prepared for whatever he might do or say, trusting her keen intuition that he couldn't do her physical harm in his own home with servants present. In the end, regardless of his anger, she just wanted to get this confrontation behind her so she could leave him once more with good riddance, and for a final time.

The sound of slow-moving footsteps interrupted her musings and she glanced over her shoulder, her pulse beginning to race seconds later as he at last walked into view.

He looked disheveled, his evening jacket discarded, waistcoat unbuttoned, dark brown cravat loosened at the neck and his shirtsleeves rolled up to midforearm. He studied her from the doorway for a long moment, the dim lighting of one lone lamp on a sofa table shadowing his expression as he very slowly skimmed her figure, from the top of her elegantly upswept hair to the hem of her plum embroidered satin skirt.

Viola felt a stirring of uncertainty in her belly. She

turned her body so that she faced him squarely, holding her sherry glass with both hands to keep them steady. Finally, after a long, uncomfortable pause, she broke the static silence.

"Are you going to speak, your grace, or just stare at me for a time?"

For seconds he did nothing. And then, very slowly, he closed the door behind him, isolating them from the outside world.

"Why are you here?" he asked, his voice low, controlled.

Shoulders back, chin lifted defiantly, she replied, "I'm offering you a truce."

"A truce?"

"Yes. For my part, I'm leaving the city," she said without pause or pretense.

He nodded almost imperceptibly. "I know. I just spoke with your solicitor."

She blinked; her mouth dropped open. "How did you—Why?"

He shrugged negligibly. "I was looking for you and thought you might be at his office, awaiting information or payment from the auction."

She licked her lips, then swallowed, uncertain how to respond.

"Don't worry, darling Viola," he drawled, smirking. "Your secrets are safe with him, though he did inform me you were on your way here." He looked her up and down again. "To be truthful, I didn't think you'd actually have the nerve to come to me, to my home, after what you did tonight."

She couldn't read his mood, and the notion that he'd

sought Duncan's counsel about her made her squirm a little in her stays. Obviously he'd gone to her town house in search of her and Needham had offered too much information. For her butler of several years to do so meant that Chatwin had either threatened or coerced him in some unusual manner. Suddenly she just wanted to get away fast.

Clearing her throat, she said, "I came here to offer you a bank draft in exchange for my artwork. "

His eyes narrowed as he watched her. "I'm keeping the sketch."

That simple statement unnerved her even more. He wasn't acting at all as she had expected. Instead of heated anger and a quick demand for answers, he analyzed her with a cold calculation that filled her with escalating dread and an immediate regret for baiting him tonight. Still, it was too late to back down now. She just wasn't sure how to respond to such icy calmness.

He apparently sensed her confusion. Inhaling deeply, he clasped his hands behind him and began to stride toward her, his gaze never wavering.

Viola backed up a step as he approached, feeling her skirts spread out as satin and crinoline pressed up against the glass window behind her. "Forgive me, your grace," she replied curtly, "but I cannot imagine you wanting to keep a *forgery,* which you so craftily proved to my disgrace—"

"We both know it's not a forgery," he cut in, coming to a halt two feet in front of her. "And we both know you sketched it yourself, as Victor Bartlett-James, along with the very explicit painting you auctioned tonight."

Of course he would make that assumption, and she'd

expected it after he'd laid eyes on the portrait at Brimleys. It had also been her hope, at least in part, that it might in some way spark a bit of memory in him, and perhaps it had. Still, hearing him acknowledge her as the artist in such a cold, measured tone rang the first bell of warning deep within.

"There is no way you can prove I am Victor Bartlett-James," she replied boldly, "and I'm sure you know that if you tried to announce it to the world, nobody would believe you. I also know Duncan would never betray my trust and give you details about me and my artwork, my past, or my future plans."

"I don't need details about you, Viola, or to prove anything to anyone," he said. "What matters is that I own both pieces of art now, and I'm sure you realize, madam, that the painting I bought tonight will never again see the light of day."

Alarmed, she fairly blurted, "You wouldn't destroy it."

He dropped his gaze briefly to her breasts, then raised it again. "And yet I can't sell it, or display it, especially when it's so obviously painted in the likeness of me, the nobleman famously kidnapped and held captive by common women."

She recoiled inside from such a callous remark overflowing with enmity.

He moved a step closer. "How many others are there, Viola?"

"Others?"

"You know what I'm asking." His cheek twitched. "How many other paintings and sketches of me, of us, did you . . . create from memory?"

Her heart skipped a beat as he seemed to suddenly tower over her. "There are no others."

Shaking his head, he replied, "I don't believe you."

"You've no choice but to believe me, your grace," she maintained, trying to sound braver than she felt. "And if you agree to a truce between us, leave me alone forevermore, you can guarantee it."

He cocked his head to the side a fraction, studying her intently. "You are the brazen one, aren't you?"

"Not so brazen as determined," she admitted in fast reply. "And you know we *both* have secrets we'd rather not have revealed."

His eyes grew stormy and he tightened his jaw with that implied threat. Silence reigned for seconds until he whispered huskily, "What happened in the dungeon, Viola? Between you and me."

Stalling, she took another sip of sherry in a vain attempt to disguise her discomfiture. "Nothing happened."

Incredulous, his brows rose. "Nothing?" He brought his arms forward and crossed them over his chest. "I know *something* happened, and you must as well, since you had the gall to paint us together, show it to the public, and sell it for profit."

"I did no such thing," she shot back defensively. "I would never paint myself in such a . . . an *indecent* position, I assure you. I painted a portrait of lovers without defined features, and if you choose to see the man as you, or think that's what I think *you* look like when—when—"

"When I make love to a woman?" he finished for her.

She swallowed as heat suffused her cheeks, then she brushed the unseemly question aside with a flick of her wrist. "If you think it's you, that's your own conclusion entirely."

"And the conclusion of every other gentleman at Brimleys tonight."

She said nothing to that, knowing he was right, just as he knew his humiliation had been her only intention this evening.

The air crackled around them, the tension grew palpable as she fought to contain her growing anxiety. Still, she couldn't look away from him.

At last, he murmured, "You have stirred a scandal, Viola—"

"*You* stirred the scandal—"

"—at my expense, knowing very well that by tomorrow I will once again be the joke and pity of society. You exploited my suffering for profit, for one last laugh, and I intend to make certain you pay for it."

"*Pay* for it?" she retorted caustically. "And what would you do? Have me arrested for *painting*?" Chin lifted, she shook her head defiantly. "No, do not *think* to threaten me, sir. Everything had been settled, all was fine, until you came to London to pursue me, to purposely ruin me. Now here you are enraged that I got the best of you instead. You thought to embarrass me and damage my reputation at your party, and you succeeded. I simply fought back to warn you that I will stop at nothing to protect my honor and my son's good name."

"Your son's good name . . . ," he echoed in whisper. Suddenly he sneered. "You have no honor. You're nothing but a fraud and a liar, a beautiful whore who will do anything in your power to climb the social ladder on which you don't, and never have, belonged."

She gaped at him, stunned and deeply hurt by his assertion, more so because he said the words with such utter repulsion. Fighting tears of anger and frustration, she countered, "You don't know me, Ian. You don't know my life and what I've done. You're filled with a hatred for something you can't define, for a past you couldn't control and can't now escape, and you've placed all your bitterness on my shoulders, making *me* guilty for *your feelings*. I realize you've been wronged, but I refuse to have my future ruined by a bitter, *lonely* man and his foolish quest for revenge—"

He slapped the glass of sherry from her hands. She gasped, stunned as it shattered on the floor, the amber liquid splattering on her gown, his shoes. And then just as quickly he was upon her.

In one swift move, his warm palm spanned her neck as he shoved her shoulders against the glass window behind her, pinning her tightly with the length of his body, his grip firm and steady on her delicate throat.

"What happened in the dungeon, Viola?" he demanded in quiet rage. "Between us."

She began to tremble, her terror realized, her eyes opened wide with shock as she stared into his.

He tightened his grip. "What *happened*?"

She smelled the whiskey on his breath, witnessed the controlled fury in his expression, his hardened jaw and rigid body. Shaking her head, she whispered, "You don't . . . understand, Ian."

His nostrils flared, his lips thinned. "I *understand* the lewd painting I saw. I also *understand* I was violated—"

"No," she countered, her own anger at his terrible assumptions crushing the fear. "I stayed with you, cared for you—"

"You're lying. I remember being touched intimately, Viola, when I couldn't defend myself. Did you do that, or did one of your sisters? Maybe all three of you? Maybe you made a game of it, a mockery of me?"

Appalled, she raised a hand to slap him hard, but he caught it instead, wrapping his palm around her wrist as he shoved her arm against the glass, locking her in place without defense. He leaned into her, his entire body touching her, chest against chest, his legs enveloped in her skirts.

"Tell me, Viola Bennington-Jones," he whispered huskily, "was I there for your pleasure alone?" He swallowed so violently that he appeared ready to choke. "Was I drugged daily just enough to affect my memory but not my body in the hope of getting one of you with child?"

Made speechless, she could do nothing but stare into his eyes, her absolute horror exposed to his view, his crushing weight and strength keeping her in his total control. His warmth seared her through the layers of her gown; the scent of his musky skin struck a sudden memory of him so potent that it took her breath and made her legs weaken beneath her.

His dark eyes narrowed to slits; his forehead beaded with perspiration as the veins in his neck grew taut with tightly controlled rage.

"Did you rape me, Viola?" he whispered.

She trembled, said nothing.

"How did you do it?" he goaded, baiting her, his voice scratchy and thick with an innermost pain. "How does a woman rape a man?"

Her eyes filled with tears. "Ian—You don't—"

"Understand?" he said for her. He rubbed his thumb along the length of her neck, paused at the quick pulse beneath the skin. Seconds later, he murmured, "I saw the painting of my son, my *bastard* son, conceived through whoring and without my choice."

It took a long time for those words to sink in, for her to clearly comprehend what he was saying, the line of his thinking, to grasp the foundation of his fury.

My bastard son. . .

Her eyes grew wide with newfound fear. "No . . ."

He snarled. "It was a secret well kept, I'll give you credit for that, Viola. Were you waiting to blackmail me with this information when I announced my betrothal to the perfect, innocent lady of quality? Did you expect me to pay you for your silence?"

Bewildered, she shook her head, tried to free herself from his tight grasp. "You don't know what you're talking about."

"Oh, I know precisely," he charged. "I know the only reason you'd take advantage of an earl, risk getting yourself with child, would be to extort money in the end." His nostrils flared; his own lips trembled. "I just wish I could remember the details for my trouble."

Her entire body flushed as shame and renewed anger radiated from every pore. "You don't know anything, Ian." She struggled in his arms again, to no avail. "You're despicable. Let me go."

He shook his head. "I want the truth. I demand to know what happened. Exactly."

She clenched her teeth. "Nothing happened. John Henry is *my* son, my husband's son—"

"Who happens to look nothing like him and just like me," he said snidely.

Refusing to turn away from his burning gaze, she retorted, "Your arrogance is astonishing. My son, Lord Cheshire, is of noble birth, and everyone who knows my child will say without the slightest doubt that he looks *just like me*."

His hold of her loosened slightly as he furrowed his brows, and for the first time since he entered the green salon he looked less infuriated than perplexed.

"You're actually denying I'm his father?"

After a long, still moment of silence, of lingering regret and sorrow filling her heart, she whispered with harsh intent, "My son is not a bastard. There is nothing else to deny."

For ages, it seemed, he stared into her eyes, attempting to probe her thoughts with an intensity she felt to her bones. And then, with a sharp inhale, he apparently grasped the meaning behind her carefully chosen words, releasing her so swiftly and unexpectedly that she nearly toppled over.

He backed up a step, arms to his sides, his gaze never wavering. Now well after dusk, the only light in the room came from a dim lamp behind him, leaving nearly all of his face in shadow, his expression masked, though he radiated a tension that enveloped her, compelling her to flee.

Voila righted herself and smoothed her skirts with

trembling hands. "Keep the sketch," she said in a shaky breath as she slowly began to move away from him. "Keep everything. Just leave me alone—"

"I can't do that."

That powerful pronouncement stopped her cold. "What did you say?"

"It's time for full disclosure between us, Viola."

Panic seized her. "There is nothing left to disclose. Or discuss."

"I disagree," he revealed very slowly, "and so I informed Mr. Duncan that my sister, the Marchioness of Rye, has gone into confinement and needs your assistance in Winter Garden, where you're anxious to visit her and . . . extended family for a time. And because her baby is due any moment, you're needed at once. *That* was the reason I went to him this evening looking for you, and *that* is why he told me where to find you."

"I'm barely acquainted with your sister, and I don't have extended family," she argued, knowing that was a ridiculous thing to say even as her mind began to race in an effort to discern the depth of his resolve. "Mr. Duncan knows me well, and wouldn't believe any of it."

He shrugged a shoulder. "I don't think he'd disbelieve a gentleman of my station, especially after he receives your note."

"What note?"

He moved closer, his eyes conveying a certain lurid delight in his command over her. "You'll only need to write two, one to Duncan, the other to your staff, and my butler will see that they're delivered tonight by messenger."

She shook her head sharply. "I'm not going back to Winter Garden. I will *never* go back there."

He almost smiled. "Of course not. You're coming with me instead, to the country, and a place of my choosing where we can be alone."

At last, she understood. "So you can bed me at your whim? Do you really think I would give in to you so easily?"

He didn't reply for a moment, though his eyes narrowed with the tightening of his jaw. "There is more involved now than simple lust, Viola. Everything has changed between us."

Nothing had changed at all, and that broad statement left her dazed, embarrassingly intrigued, and more than a little scared that everything she held dear remained in jeopardy, threatened by a man who blamed her for certain failures over which neither of them had ever had control. It would take a mighty influence for her to disclose the truths behind John Henry's conception, but if she refused Ian now, the danger of him exposing every suspicious detail regarding the birth of her child grew more plausible by the second. Suddenly the fear of her lengthy deceptions and ignoble past being laid bare before society's eyes overshadowed any other. If nothing else, going with him to the country would buy her time.

"If you'll find me pen and paper, sir," she said haughtily.

For a slice of a second he looked surprised by her easy acceptance. And then with a nod, he gestured to the door.

"In my study, madam."

She glowered at him for a long, charged moment, feeling helpless but determined, and especially regretful for taking care of him all those years ago, for trying when no one else would. And she would never, ever forgive him if he attempted to destroy her son's future.

She lowered her lashes. "God help you."

Then, with as much dignity as she could muster, she lifted her skirts, and with regal bearing, stepped past him to walk to the door of the green salon.

Chapter Fourteen

I sat beside him for a long while today, listening to his quiet, steady breathing. When at last he woke, he pulled me against him, wrapped his arm and leg around me, and hugged me close. I think I could stay in his arms forever. . . .

*I*an fidgeted on the leather seat of his private carriage, unable to find a comfortable position, though thankfully the air had grown cooler by the hour as his driver now meandered through the countryside toward Stamford. It was closer to the city than his lands in Chatwin, and less populated this time of year, exactly as he wanted for his captive of the next few days.

He glanced at her, sitting across from him, rigid and silent, her eyes closed as she huddled beneath a coach blanket he'd tossed her when she'd taken her seat, though he knew she hadn't slept since they'd left his town house. She was livid and worried, and he hoped she stayed that way for a while. At least that's what he kept telling himself.

He truly hadn't been prepared for the range of emotions that had swept over him the moment he'd caught sight of her in the green salon—everything from fury, to regret, to outright lust and a stirring of something warm and comforting deep in his memory that he didn't at all understand. She had been fully prepared to do battle, he supposed, and in any other situation he might have found her bravery compelling in a sweet and refreshing sort of way. But it was his increasing physical attraction to her that bothered him more than anything else because he simply did not understand it. By all accounts he should find her manner unappealing and unrefined, her appearance disgusting and offensive as one who fostered harm on the innocent. But he didn't. Although others certainly thought her a lovely woman, and although he knew several ladies he would consider more classically beautiful, there was something about Viola that made his breath catch in his chest and his heart beat faster each time he laid eyes on her, and tonight had been no exception. At first glance she'd appeared lost, confused, and most of all stunning with the muted lighting of nightfall playing across her pale skin, her shiny, upswept hair, perfectly curved body, and those frightened, vivid hazel eyes. It had been difficult to stifle his desire to charm and seduce her on the spot, to forget himself, and his goals—until she'd once again evaded his questions and denied him answers.

He hadn't planned to force her to go anywhere with him. It had been a last-minute decision borne of anger, restlessness, and a mounting frustration in his inability to drive the stake in far enough for his satisfaction, just as he'd realized she had gotten the best of him once more that evening. And maybe he would never be satisfied and able to move on to grasp a much brighter future. Some deep part of him wanted to fault her for his actions toward her, and yet he knew she'd been absolutely correct when she'd said he blamed her for his feelings. That had been a striking moment for him, a slap to his face that had jarred him, reminding him all too clearly that he had been the one to target her first. He had pursued her, with nefarious intent, but the moment tonight when he'd laid eyes on the painting of her child, *his* child, he'd suddenly wanted explanations more than revenge.

She had given him a son. His first son, and a bastard just like him, conceived during a bond he couldn't exactly remember, and into which, in his weakness, he'd been very likely forced. Such a notion appalled him, and yet it was the fact that she wouldn't acknowledge to his face that the boy was his that angered him so much and made him rationalize his deplorable actions toward her. And he didn't know what to feel about it, either. Should he demand a meeting with the child? Should he take any responsibility for him, when Viola refused to acknowledge the relationship? Did he even *want* to know the boy? In one long, eventful evening, his entire life had changed to become far more complicated than he could have imagined. He now had a mind full of questions with no apparent answers.

He supposed she might never admit that he'd fathered her child, and as he'd now had hours to consider it rationally, he finally thought he understood her reason. If she denied it, her son would grow up a baron and inherit all to which his name and rank entitled him. It would be far smarter than claiming the child a bastard and attempting to blackmail the father; she could never have envisioned him marrying her for any reason. Perhaps blackmail had been her initial intent, but by getting a titled gentleman to propose instead, she'd settled on the better surety. But had the honorable Lord Cheshire known this fact when they'd married? When he'd died? It was just such speculation about how and why she'd taken a chance on getting herself with child, every implication and detail, that had been haunting him since they'd left his town house.

Ian turned his gaze to the small widow and stared out to the inky blackness. It wasn't safe to travel at night, and yet in some manner he delighted in the danger, especially if it made her more uncomfortable. The next few days were going to be miserable for her, and if he could keep his guilt suppressed, he might delight in that misery as well.

"Are we nearly there?"

Ian turned to her shadowed figure, feeling her stare upon him, her expression unreadable in the darkness. "Yes, nearly."

She huddled down further into the blanket. "Where are you taking me?"

He didn't reply immediately, uncertain how much to tell her of the next few days to come.

Her tone flattened as she asked, "You're not planning to murder me when you're finished ravishing me, are you?"

He almost laughed at a notion so outrageous. "Murder? Good God, Viola."

Pulling the blanket tighter around her neck, she replied, "I'm sure you can see why I have my doubts. You clearly despise me, have taken me captive, and nobody on earth knows where I am. You also have enough wealth and authority to deny any involvement in my disappearance, and everybody would believe you."

He adjusted his large frame in his seat. "You're exaggerating both my importance and my dislike of you."

"Am I? As a high-ranking gentleman of the peerage, you know as well as I that you're a rather important person." She softened her voice to add, "And quite honestly we both know I wouldn't be here now if you hadn't turned your hatred of what happened to you into a retaliation against me personally."

For seconds he debated a caustic retort, then decided against it as he turned to gaze out the window again. The sadness and frustration she exuded in words and form shrouded the nagging remorse he felt in taking her from the city by reminding him of just how innocent she thought she was in his captivity five years ago. But he refused to contemplate that now. She would understand his perspective soon enough.

They sat in silence again for the better part of an hour, until at last he could see the shores of the lake at Stamford through the tiniest flicker of dawn creeping into the eastern sky. Then his fishing cabin came into view and he sat up, glancing at her huddled form.

"We're here," he said, tapping her on the knee with his foot.

She blinked and sat up a little straighter, glancing around. "Are we at Stamford?"

"We're on my land," he replied vaguely. "We're not, however, going to the house."

She frowned as she caught his gaze. "I don't understand."

"You will shortly."

After a quick glance out the window, she shifted uncomfortably on the leather seat. "I . . . um . . . need to freshen up a bit. And I'm hungry."

He groaned inside. It hadn't occurred to him that she might require more than a bush to crouch behind. He knew there was a chamber pot at the cabin, though he hoped to God she wasn't on her monthlies, something else he hadn't considered in this inane plan to abduct her without thought.

"All in good time, Viola. We're almost there."

The coach slowed as it crept through a thicket of trees, the road growing rockier as they neared the small lake. Viola sat forward and peered out the window.

"What exactly are you planning, Ian?"

"You'll see—"

"This pretense has gone on quite long enough," she interjected as irritation took hold once again. "You've taken me into the country with no notice, not a stitch of clothing aside from what I'm wearing, without any idea of how long I am to be your prisoner—" She gasped, her eyes opening wide as her fear of his full intentions dawned. "You're not going to chain me."

"And have you suffer such an indignity?" he replied at once, purposely leaving her to wonder. Sardonically, he added, "At least you know I have no artistic talent and won't paint it for the world to see."

"I never expected the world to see that painting, Ian," she retorted. "You have to know that. You forced me to act when you threatened my reputation and everything

I hold dear." After a pause, she added, "You also made me angry."

Amusement swept over him as he relished that truth. Suddenly he cared more about her secrets than her motives. "Did your husband see it?"

Her brows creased in a frown. "No, not that one."

"Not that one? You mean he saw others? He was aware of your erotic work?"

"I couldn't very well sell it without his knowledge," she replied with exasperation.

He hadn't thought of that. "Did he . . . encourage it?"

She fidgeted on the leather seat. "Of course he encouraged it. He championed all of my artwork. As a good husband does."

Ian allowed that revelation, and her formal choice of words, to sink in a bit before deciding he wanted more. "Is that what a good husband does, Viola? Encourage his wife to create artwork designed to arouse other men?"

Her eyes flashed in renewed irritation. "I think you should be the last person to judge what a good man does, Ian, after abducting me for a vile purpose. I don't suppose you'll want to give these details to Anna when you ask for her hand."

She was trying to incite him, and truthfully, he didn't at all want to consider how unheroic he'd behaved these last few hours. Right now all he wanted was answers.

"Why didn't he see the one you auctioned last night?" he continued, voice lowered.

Without hesitation, she glanced away and replied, "I painted it after his death."

"Why?"

"I don't know."

He didn't believe that for a second. "You don't know? You already told me you had no intention of selling it. Or maybe that's not true at all and you were, instead, keeping it as blackmail in the event I came forward and charged you with a crime."

She looked back at him, scrunching her face, thoroughly appalled. "Why do you always think the worst of me?"

A certain guilt gripped his chest, which he tried very hard to dismiss. "I'm just hoping to understand your motives, that's all."

She scoffed. "I don't think you care a fig about my motives. All you want is to hurt me, and in any way possible."

He wouldn't deny it even if he wanted to. But since she'd been a bit more forthcoming, he decided to press her for more intimate detail. "Did your husband know you carried another man's child when you married?"

"I believe we've settled this notion," she articulated very slowly. "John Henry is my husband's son."

He eyed her speculatively, his head tipped to one side. "And yet you conceived in January."

Her features grew brittle as she glared at him in the early morning light. "I conceived on my honeymoon, your grace, in early February, though this is really none of your business."

"And your son was born nearly two months early? Your husband must have been very . . . concerned."

"My husband was overjoyed."

She'd stressed that with complete conviction, her voice dripping with caution, and yet Ian could not imagine the gentleman he saw in the portrait overjoyed at anything at all. Then again, if he'd thought the child had been his, and since one could hardly distinguish features on a newborn infant, perhaps he'd simply been overjoyed at having an heir, especially when his first wife had never carried at all. One would think he'd have been suspicious that his second wife would deliver him a child so soon after their marriage, but in the end he'd had a son. Perhaps that was all that had truly mattered to the man.

"Did you marry for love, Viola?" he asked softly.

He'd managed to ruffle her feathers so much that she looked momentarily confused by the sudden intimacy of the question.

"I loved Lord Cheshire, of course," she admitted with only the slightest hesitation.

"Is that why you married him?"

She sighed. "I married him for the same reasons anyone might marry—companionship, children, stability, and yes, love."

"And a title?" he drawled.

The side of her mouth lifted fractionally. "Although many a lady hunts for a husband with the grandest title, that wasn't the reason I married mine."

"What, then, did you find particularly . . . compelling in Lord Cheshire?"

"Compelling?"

He shrugged, watching her closely. "If not for his title, what attracted you to him?"

She squirmed a little on the seat, turning her attention outside again. "He was very charming."

Ian almost snorted. If there was one thing he could

not envision at all in the baron, it was charm. "Did you also find him handsome?"

"He was handsome enough for my tastes," she snapped. "Not every lady is graced with the opportunity to marry a man as perfectly proportioned and marvelously appealing as you, sir."

She'd meant that sarcastic retort to sting, and yet such a backhanded compliment coming from her stirred his blood, thoroughly warming him from head to toe. Masking an immense satisfaction, he replied, "Frankly, I think you were far too beautiful for him. I'm certain he knew it, too, and counted his blessings that he could bed you every night."

After casting him another fast glance, she scooted down further into her huddled blanket. "I think it's inappropriate to discuss my late husband in such a manner, your grace."

He would have debated that, but the coach abruptly halted. "We're here," he said flatly. "Let's go."

She didn't budge.

Ian grabbed her wrist from beneath the blanket and pulled as he opened the coach door, relishing the rush of cool air from the lake that struck his face as he lifted her with him and alighted.

"Take the horses to the stable, Larson," he ordered his driver. "I'll walk to the house later."

"As you wish, your grace," the man replied without even a glance at Viola. Seconds later he snapped the reins, made a quick turn, and headed back through the trees.

Ian began striding toward the cabin, holding her hand, more than a little impressed by how she managed to keep her head high and shoulders rigid when her skin felt cold and she had to be scared to death.

"What is this place?" she asked as they reached the small, wooden door six feet from the edge of the water.

"It's a private little cottage," he said, releasing her and reaching into his jacket pocket for the key.

"It doesn't look much like a cottage."

He didn't respond to that indisputable observation as the door creaked open. The cabin smelled of wood smoke and fish, and its small one room would likely fit inside his town house pantry. It was dark, sturdy, and perfect.

Clasping her elbow, he fairly pushed her inside.

"You can't expect me to stay here," she remarked, stepping over the threshold and into semidarkness. "Ian, I refuse—"

"This is the perfect place for an intimate discussion."

"Discussion?" she said incredulously. "You can't be serious."

He walked with purpose to the east wall and lifted a thick black linen curtain, allowing sunlight to filter in and warm the room.

"Why are there bars on the window?"

"To keep vagrants out," he answered, turning once again to face her.

Her eyes narrowed suspiciously. "Or to keep the ladies locked inside?"

He smiled. "You're the first lady ever allowed in my humble fishing cabin, Viola. You should feel quite proud of that distinction."

She shook her head in disgust, crossing her arms over her chest. "I'm not staying here."

"I want to know what happened in the dungeon," he said quietly, watching her closely. "Every sordid detail."

She fidgeted in her stays. "There is nothing I can tell you that you don't already know, Ian. I wish you would understand that."

"I don't know how you coerced me into getting you pregnant. That's something I'd like to discuss."

She swallowed, uncertainty washing over her. "I never coerced you into anything."

Her stubbornness would likely be the death of him, but he was too tired to argue or to put his own plan of coercion into action. It was time to leave her to think. And worry.

"Are you having your monthlies?" he asked abruptly.

She gasped.

He brushed over her surprise. "I suggest you answer truthfully."

"I . . . that's none of your business."

He sighed loudly. "The cot is clean, and there's a chamber pot beneath it. You might want to sleep for now—"

"You're not leaving me here," she said, suddenly alarmed.

"You cannot win this battle, Viola. Think about that until I return."

She blinked in total disbelief. Then she lunged for him.

He stepped onto the porch and quickly shut the door,

locking it and slipping the key back into his pocket as she banged on the wood with both fists.

Disregarding her shouts of anger, and feeling far more worried and far less smug than he thought he should, Ian walked away from his fishing cabin and began the mile-long trek to the main house—discouraged, irritated, and uncertain how in hell he was going to get her to tell him anything, least of all the truth.

Viola stopped banging on the door almost immediately, knowing perfectly well that he had every intention of letting her rot there for a time. Screaming would do nothing, and since he'd locked her up in a remote area on his land, nobody was likely to hear her anyway.

Glancing around the cabin, she took in her surroundings. The air smelled stale and musty, and her first thought was to open the window. It took her three shoves before it finally lifted an inch, just enough for the slight breeze to make its way inside. For now, she just felt drained, more tired than frightened or even angry. He obviously expected her to remain here, uncomfortable, alone, and suspicious of every little sound.

Her stomach growled and she kicked the wooden wall, which did nothing but remind her that she would remain trapped in this hovel without food or water until he felt the need to check on her. And he forced her to use a chamber pot for the first time in years. That was indignity enough for the moment. Thank God her monthlies had only just ended, though now that she considered it, she felt mightily relieved that she hadn't discussed her cycle with him. She couldn't believe he'd asked her about it, though it made sense if he wanted to bed her and not get her with child. If she played on her fear of another pregnancy, maybe he would leave her alone. Or maybe not.

Insufferable man.

Exhausted suddenly, Viola stared down at the cot for a moment before lifting the battered quilt and shaking it of bugs or other sundry undesirables that might be hiding in the folds. At least it and the sheet beneath it appeared clean.

She sat upon the surprisingly soft mattress, fluffed the feather pillow, and, after deciding no rats had gnawed through the cotton to make it a home, lay flat upon her makeshift bed, covered her body with the quilt, and closed her eyes.

Chapter Fifteen

His body responded to me again today. I was so fright-
ened, afraid of being discovered, but he needed me,
begged me, and I couldn't resist the desire to be with
him. I've never felt anything so intense and wonderful,
and doubt I ever will again. . . .

The hazy vision of warm lips and soft breasts
stirred him to semiconsciousness. He vaguely knew
he lingered in that state where sleep and wakefulness
mingle and blend, yet he wanted to remain for just a
while longer, to explore the dark image of the woman
at his side, inhaling her sweet scent, absorbing her
warmth, listening to the whispered sound of her steady
breathing, relishing everything from the soft hair
between her legs that caressed his thigh to the intimate
closeness of her face nestled in the crook of his neck,
feeling tenderness and anticipation fused with hot,
agonizing desire. . . .

Touch me . . .
Let me feel you . . .

Make love to me . . .
Please—

Ian sat up at once, blinking hard, confused and momentarily uncertain where he was. Then memory collided with what remained of the fantasy, jarring him back to reality. He shivered from the cold perspiration that bathed his body, then scrubbed a palm down his face and swung his legs over the side of the leather sofa, recalling suddenly why he'd come back to Stamford and now found himself in his drawing room. At his arrival at the house he'd eaten a full meal, discussed a couple of estate matters with his butler, then only thought to lay his head down for a few minutes before planning the night ahead and returning to Viola. Clearly he'd been more exhausted than he'd realized. With a quick glance to the mantel, he checked the time on the clock: half past three. He'd been sleeping for more than six hours—and she had gone without food and water for nearly a day.

Viola. She was, without question, the woman in his dream, nude and willingly lying beside him, either before or after eagerly making love to him. What he didn't know, however, was whether his fantasy had been created from forgotten experience, a situation that had actually happened in the dungeon, or illusion borne of lust, his mind playing tricks because of the painting she'd created, because he wanted her sexually and she remained so close in thought and presence. The uncertainty nagged at him, and because doubts and desire lingered, it was time to take control and put them to rest.

Standing, all traces of the fog in his head finally cleared, he quickly left his drawing room. After washing up, changing into casual clothes, gathering a few supplies, and requesting a basket of foodstuff from the kitchen, he headed toward the cabin, this time on horseback. Silence loomed when he approached the small enclosure, and even if she heard him she didn't make a sound as he slipped the key into the lock and turned it. Of course he hadn't intended to deprive her of sustenance for any length of time, and although he tried to tell himself she deserved it, when he'd gone without everything but tainted beef broth and bread for five long weeks, he still felt a bit contrite over leaving her alone for so long.

Ian opened the door, allowed his eyes to adjust for several seconds, then spotted her sitting on the cot, her hands in her lap, her attention focused on him, though he couldn't read anything in her placid expression. He decided to attempt civility.

"Good evening, Viola."

"Is it evening already? I wouldn't know."

So she had a sour mood. He certainly wouldn't let that bother him. Placing the food basket and bag of supplies on the wooden floor, he left the door open so he could better see the room as he stepped inside.

"Would you like tea?" he asked, walking to the stove and lifting the tin of matches from the shelf beside it.

"Did you bring the china, your grace? Or am I to sip it from my hands?"

Clearly her mood went beyond sour to livid and sarcastic. It almost made him smile. For some odd reason he enjoyed bantering with her when she was angry with him.

"I brought two mugs. They're old, not worthy of the dining room or parlor, but they should do."

She huffed without reply. He closed the stove's iron door, allowing the coals to heat, then picked up the old teakettle from the shelf and a bucket beneath it, and strode back to the door. "I'm going to the well behind the cabin. Don't bother trying to leave—"

"Why on *earth* would I want to leave before *tea*?"

Suppressing a laugh, he nodded once and stepped outside. At least she was wise enough to know she had nowhere to go and if she tried to run he'd find her anyway. And hauling her back would make matters worse, he supposed.

Moments later he returned, and after closing the door and bolting it, he placed the kettle atop the stove and the full bucket beside it as the room began to warm.

"Did you also bring a tub so I could bathe?"

He turned to face her. "Viola, darling, did you bathe me while I lay chained in the dungeon?"

She eyed him candidly, her features as taut as her form was rigid. "Of course I did, and you very well know it."

Ian tried not to gape at her as that confession hit its mark. He'd never expected such an honest, forthright answer when he'd only been trying to exasperate her. And although he didn't exactly remember being bathed, he knew he hadn't been completely filthy and foul-smelling when he'd been rescued. There was something about being unclothed and cared for intimately by her that left him not only bemused but also deeply mollified.

"Is that how you got me aroused enough to get you pregnant?" he asked matter-of-factly as he picked up the basket of food and began to walk toward her.

Unmoving, she held his gaze as he approached.

"Did you bring a lamp, or do you expect me to answer all of your ridiculous questions in darkness after the sun sets?"

Her fearlessness in attempting to engage him in a fight when she remained at a clear disadvantage, even desperate for his care, continued to amuse, even charm, him in a manner—especially since she didn't seem at all frightened of him physically at this point. He wasn't sure if he should feel thankful or annoyed.

"My, you're certainly spirited today," he said, lowering himself to sit beside her on the cot.

She backed away slightly from his closeness, ignoring his comment as she tipped her head toward the basket. "I'm assuming you brought food?"

"I did," he admitted easily. "Are you going to answer *my* questions?"

"You'll find that a hostage responds better on a full belly, I'm sure."

"Something you learned from experience, no doubt."

"No doubt."

He smirked, opening the basket for her view. "I have cold chicken, apples, cheese, and a loaf of bread. Nothing warm but tea, I'm afraid."

"It's summer, your grace," she retorted, reaching for a slice of cheese with dainty fingers. "I'm starving, but hardly freezing."

"Ah, forgive me. I suppose I was thinking of the time you held me captive in winter and I *was* freezing."

She sighed, slumping into her stays, which she likely found incredibly uncomfortable after having them affixed to her ribs for nearly twenty-four hours.

"I never held you captive," she said, her tone slightly softer. She took a bite and chewed, then, after swallowing, added, "I tried my best to help you *endure* it. Why can't you understand that?"

He didn't reply for a moment as he spread a small tablecloth across the quilt between them and began removing the items from the basket, including two small plates, linen napkins, and the mugs, tea, and strainer. She watched him as he dished out servings for both of them, her outrage radiating from her like a tangible thing, though she began to eat with gusto the moment he handed her a plateful of generous portions.

They supped in silence for several minutes until finally, between bites, she asked, "How long do you intend to keep me here?"

The kettle began to steam. "Until you tell me everything," he answered without pretense as he lifted the mugs and tea and returned to the stove.

"So we are at an impasse."

He didn't comment on that obvious fact. "Sorry, but there's no milk or sugar."

Voice lowered, she maintained, "You can't keep me here forever, Ian."

Instead of arguing a point that clearly would get them nowhere, he poured the water, moved the strainer back and forth while the tea steeped, then turned at last and walked back to the cot.

"I've had dreams about you, Viola," he said very softly as he handed her a steaming mug.

She stopped chewing in midbite, then swallowed. "Dreams?"

He nodded as he sat next to her again, watching her closely. "Several dreams through the years, actually, though for a long time I had no idea I was dreaming of you."

That acknowledgment clearly troubled her. Frowning deeply, she placed her mug on the floor beside her, then turned her attention to her food once more, pulling a piece of bread apart with more force than needed.

"In fact," he added, "some of them were quite erotic."

A small mewl escaped the back of her throat, but otherwise she didn't comment or look at him.

"Can I ask you a question?" he prodded after a moment.

She swallowed. "I don't suppose I can stop you."

"No, I suppose not."

She shot him a quick, sideways glance. "What is it?"

He took a sip of tea. "If you didn't feel safe to have me rescued, but were instead, as you say, trying to help me endure my captivity, why didn't you bring me more food?"

A question so simple yet profound, and so unexpected that she stilled her movements as its significance dawned. Seconds later she licked her thumb, and after tapping her napkin across her lips, she lowered her plate of chicken and bread remnants into the basket. He waited, scrutinizing her as she reached for her tea, knowing he had cornered her but deciding to give her the chance to respond as she could, at her discretion.

Finally, staring down at her mug, she replied, "I did bring you food, Ian. I brought what I could, when I could, but since you were drugged most of the time, I found it hard to feed you when you had very little appetite, and I could only carry so much at each visit."

"How many visits?"

She blew across the rim, then took a small, cautious drink of the steaming brew. "Several."

"Several?" His brows shot up. "What does that mean? Once a week? Three times a week? Daily?"

She looked him up and down, her mug at her lips. "I didn't count."

"I'd bet my fortune that you did."

She almost smiled. He could see it in her eyes, at the curve of her lips. But then she hesitated, shying away from his steady gaze, taking another slow sip before continuing.

"The truth is, I tried to check on you every two or three days," she conceded, her tone contemplative. "I didn't want you to die. But you also must remember that I was just nineteen years old at the time, very sheltered, and under the control of a domineering mother and two older sisters, one hard and cruel, the other insane. Or so I thought. My greatest fear was getting caught and being tossed out onto the street with nothing. For a time I considered telling someone, having you rescued, but I didn't know who, and feared I would be arrested along with the conspirators. I was a country girl with no social standing, and truly felt my options were limited. Even if I were found legally innocent, my mother would surely disown me for bringing shame on my family by accusing them of despicable crimes, and again I would have nothing." She exhaled a heavy breath, then looked at him frankly. "I never did anything wrong, Ian, hadn't taken part in the abduction or in the planning of the event, but at that time in my life, I truly thought I had no options. I didn't see any way out. But I—I *could* help you. And that's what I did."

He felt a certain warmth spread within him, not necessarily from the events she described, which to him remained suspect, but from her gentle, innocent conviction. "Did your family know?"

"Eventually," she admitted without hesitation, "when I stole the key to your shackles from my sister and left it next to you the night you were found. Hermione and Mother were beside themselves, though I was somewhat forgiven in my mother's eyes when I agreed to marry Lord Cheshire and could support her until her death. They know I helped you escape, but none of them knew I visited you frequently, or nursed you. At least I don't think so. I never told anyone."

He nodded slowly, then asked, "And your sister who went to prison, do you hear from her at all? Has she forgiven you?"

Her brow creased suspiciously. "Why do you care?"

He shrugged. "Merely curious."

She almost snorted. "Well the answer is no," she said matter-of-factly, adjusting her sitting form on the cot and focusing once more on her tea. "Hermione was furious when she learned I staged your release, which, in her mind, prevented me from being prosecuted for the crime as she was. She despises me for many things, Ian, the greatest of which is my marriage into the peerage while she was transported to Queensland for a term of hard labor. I still put funds away occasionally for some future time when she might be given a reprieve, allowed to return and could need my financial help. But the last I heard she had attached herself to a gentleman as his courtesan, married him, and has since settled farmland. I doubt I'll ever see or hear from her again."

She raised her lashes to meet his gaze, hers narrowed, unyielding. "I made my choices, your grace, and must live with the consequences every single day. I truly believe I did what I could for you considering the circumstance, and I've paid for my family's crimes in many ways, even if not to your satisfaction. But I'd like to think you're alive today because I cared for you and refused to let you die." She let out a soft, bitter chuckle. "Ironically, aside from raising a charming son, it may be the only thing I've ever done, perhaps will *ever* do, that is in any way consequential or of redeeming value."

Ironically. Meaning that even as she'd lost her family, she'd given him back his life—only to have him hunt her down years later in a calculated attempt to destroy what she had made of hers.

Ian stared at her for several long, intense moments, as surprised by her candor as he was astonished at his own sudden feelings of remorse and compassion for her plight. He'd known that her sister had been sentenced to the western penal colony, and that her mother had died soon after the trial, yet he'd never before thought about these family hardships from anyone's perspective but his own. And maybe that had been wrong of him. Viola had no family alive to confide in, and as her husband had died, she truly had nobody who cared for her, who needed her, except her child, whom she obviously protected at all costs. Most remarkably, at this moment, and for the first time since he'd forced himself back into her life, he didn't suspect her of lying.

"What happened between us, Viola?" he asked quietly, subdued. "I need to know."

One side of her mouth tipped up fractionally. "Are you going to ravish me?"

He blinked, uncertain if he should find irritation or humor in that unanticipated question. With a sly smile, he replied, "Ravish is a harsh word, is it not?"

"That's not an answer."

He leaned forward on one hand, watching her eyes widen in surprise as he closed in on her. Huskily, he said, "Until you tell me the truth about us, I will do to you exactly what I believe you did to me. And until I hear otherwise, what I know is that you and your sisters violated me, Viola. You stripped me naked, touched me intimately—"

"We did no such thing," she cut in, light amusement turning to frustration as she placed her half-filled mug on the floor again and fairly jumped to her feet. She moved quickly across the room, then turned to face him, crossing her arms over her breasts protectively. "Nobody abused you like that, Ian, least of all me."

"No?" He stood to meet her gaze, his anger simmering once more. "So if I remember being touched and aroused, but you insist nobody molested me, are you then suggesting that you and I made slow, passionate love by mutual consent? As I lay chained and drugged in a dungeon? Tell me, Viola, which is easier to believe?"

"What do *you* remember?" she shot back defensively. "You said you've had dreams of me; did they include water and soap? Passionate *bathing* perhaps? Because that's what I did, I took care of you."

Irritated, he rubbed the back of his neck. "You're missing the point. Despite the bathing, I was either raped for a sinister purpose or seduced for some reason that isn't clear to me. Which was it?"

"You were nursed."

"Simple nursing is not typically how one gets pregnant with child, Viola."

"He is not your child," she insisted, her tone lowered, threatening.

Slowly, his patience nearly gone, Ian crossed the room to stand in front of her, taking note of her disheveled appearance, her pinkened cheeks and shining eyes, her wrinkled evening gown splattered with dried drops of sherry, her once perfectly coiffed hair, though still pinned, now an unruly mess. She regarded him as courageously as possible despite her predicament, and the sudden urge to kiss her, to try a different tactic and coax the truth from her lips with his, became nearly overwhelming. And yet the utter futility he felt at her continued denial and avoidance made him furious. She provoked the oddest combination of emotions in him, not all of them negative, though every one acute.

"Perhaps I need to make this clearer, Viola," he murmured in a husky timbre. "My dreams of my time in the dungeon may be dark, erotic, and confusing, but make no mistake: you are there as part of them. I remember your shadowed face next to mine, your soft voice in my ear, your warm body—"

"Your dreams are muddled, Ian," she cut in, shifting from one foot to the other as her anxiousness grew. "Desi and I looked very much alike then, and I'm sure you had difficulty telling us apart in the darkness, in your distress. You don't know *what* you remember."

With those words she'd been caught in her own contradiction, and he relished it.

"Are you now suggesting the woman in the painting you auctioned last night was your sister?"

That notion clearly flustered her. Her eyes widened, and she licked her lips with an embarrassment she couldn't hide if she tried. "That—that portrait—"

"Was of you, and you know it," he finished for her, suddenly feeling smug, and far more convinced that it was she alone who'd embedded herself so deeply in his memory. "You've already denied the fact that your sisters violated me. If that's true, it means it was *you* who touched me intimately. It means my dreams are memories of *your* breasts on my chest and *your* warm, caressing hands on my body—"

"No—"

"It was *you* who aroused me, stroked me, lay with me—"

"Stop it," she cut in, cringing. "This is disgusting."

"It's only disgusting if I was forced."

She shoved a palm against his chest, attempting to push him away. He quickly grabbed her wrist with one hand, wrapped his free arm around her waist, and yanked her against him.

"Every time I'm with you, I remember more," he continued, his voice rough with emotion as he gazed down to her flushed and startled face only inches from his.

"And in spite of the softness and warmth, in spite of my desire for you now and the confusion that continues to plague my dreams without clarity or peace, it's the thought that I might have been purposely aroused and stroked to climax that sickens me—"

"Stop it, Ian!" she whispered through clenched teeth, squeezing her eyes shut.

He shook her once in his arms, feeling a relentless need to push her to confession. "It's the thought that I might have been held captive and fondled until you could mount me, that you rode me until I left my seed inside you for your own selfish reasons, that *torments* me."

Tears beaded on her lashes as she shook her head vehemently.

"I was at your mercy, Viola," he whispered in a harsh breath of urgency, "and you became pregnant with my child. I saw his portrait, I know how a babe is conceived, and now I need you to tell me *why* you did it. I need you to *tell me how it happened*."

"No . . . ," she whispered in anguish. "Let it go, Ian. Please. Let it go. Let me go and leave me alone. I'll never bother you again. I swear it on my son's life."

Her unrelenting passion to hide the truth both riled and haunted him. She defied him more than he could ever understand, more than any woman ever had. He held her tightly, felt the heat of her body, her breasts crushed against his chest, ashamed and angry at himself for wanting her even now. He should despise her for every reason imaginable, and yet the most intense emotion, the most powerful urge he experienced at that moment in time, was to show her the agony and let her feel it for herself.

"Look at me," he said, his voice tight, daring.

For seconds she didn't respond. Then she raised her lashes, revealing tear-stained eyes filled with not only worry and grief but also fierce defiance. And that was all it took to convince him she would never give in to mere pleading alone. He would be forced to use extraordinary measures to get to the truth.

"Please . . . ," she whispered. "Ian . . ."

Very slowly, with meticulous intent, he whispered, "I will never let it go. . . ."

Then contrary to what she wanted, expected, contrary to what his body craved so desperately, instead of capturing her mouth for a searing kiss, lifting her and carrying her to the cot, he abruptly released her and stepped back.

She stumbled on wobbly legs, nearly crumpling to the floor before catching herself on the shelf beside the stove and pulling herself upright with both hands.

"What—" She swallowed, glancing around her, confused. "Why did you do that?"

Ian drew in a very deep breath, taking a moment for his pounding heart to still, his fired nerves to settle. Finally, in a voice thick with irony, he replied, "You were expecting to be ravished?"

Immediately, she blinked, stood upright, and wiped her palms down the waistline of her wrinkled gown. "I wasn't expecting to be *dropped,* your grace."

The side of his mouth tipped up a fraction. "And I wasn't expecting to be given more evasiveness and prevarication after opening myself to you as I did."

A cloud of guilt crossed her features, then quickly disappeared, replaced by obstinance and a measure of anger. "That's only your opinion. I thought I was rather forthcoming."

He couldn't believe she said that, or for that matter believed it. In a dark tone of warning, he murmured, "If that's your idea of forthcoming, then it's clear you need more time to consider your own memories, Viola."

That remark positively confounded her. Her forehead creased deeply; perspiration beaded on her upper lip as she looked him up and down. "What are you saying?"

He ran the fingers of both hands roughly through his hair, then offered her a vague smile. "You need more time alone, Viola. To consider why I brought you here—"

"We know *exactly* why you brought me here, your grace, and yet at the very moment you seemed to want to take me into a"—she waved a palm at him—"a passionate . . . embrace, you instead—you—you—"

She didn't want to say that he'd surprised her by his non-seduction when she'd expected it, nearly begged for it. For his part, he had no intention of explaining himself. Instead, Ian crossed his arms over his chest and continued to gaze into her eyes until she became so unbearably uncomfortable that she flushed bright red, shifted her weight from one foot to the other, and eventually glanced away.

Sighing, he moved away from her and strode to the bag of supplies he'd carried with him from the house. "I brought a few small items with me that I thought you might need for the night."

"The night?"

"Would you like me to help you undress? I'm very good with a corset."

She said nothing, either too furious or too shocked to do so.

"Very well, then." He dropped the bag on the cot, then turned and walked to the door. "I'll return at a later time, Viola. Sweet dreams."

Her eyes suddenly grew wide with panic. "No. Wait—"

Ian stepped outside, closing and bolting the door behind him, though he wouldn't have been able to hide the grin from his face if he'd tried.

Two hours. He'd give her two hours to wash up, change into one of Ivy's old nightgowns, slip beneath the covers, relax, and consider the night ahead. . . .

It would be the longest two hours of his life.

Chapter Sixteen

He touched me in places I have never been touched before, places on my body that I have never touched myself. I had always thought it shameful to do so, and yet he shared the pleasures of what married life is surely supposed to be. I know I am damned eternally in hell for committing so grave a sin in his arms, but I will surely go there happily, willingly, knowing that I have shared these sins with a man I've grown to love. . . .

*V*iola stared at the ceiling, somewhat restless and not at all sleepy after napping nearly half the day. After he'd left, she'd found a lamp on a corner shelf, though she'd decided not to light it since she hadn't a book to read or needlepoint to craft, and absolutely nothing with which to sketch or draw. He really was trying to re-create his time in the dungeon for her, leaving her with nothing but her thoughts, though to his credit, at least the mattress was clean and soft, and the cabin comfortably warm.

Still, the silence droned. After living for several years in the city, she'd grown accustomed to hearing street noise and traffic nearly all hours of the day, and without it the peacefulness of the country seemed almost deafening. Actually, in some strange manner, Ian might have been blessed by being drugged much of the time while in captivity. At least he hadn't had to contend with boredom; the passage of time had likely meant little to him when he couldn't possibly have comprehended it.

She'd paced for several minutes after his unexpected and rather speedy departure earlier this evening. Then, having decided it would do no good to chew her nails to the quick from continuous worry and frustration with her inability to convince him to just let the past be what it was and move on, she'd cleaned up the remnants of their meal, added water from the bucket to reheat a full kettle, portioning some for a second cup of tea while saving the rest to wash her face, neck, and intimate areas when it had cooled a little, and finally rummaged through the pouch of supplies he'd left for her on the cot. There hadn't been much, at least not what she'd expect or need as a lady, but at least he'd thought of the basic necessities.

She'd found a small bar of plain soap, a small towel and washing cloth, a toothbrush—no powder, though better than nothing, she'd supposed—a hairbrush, and a low-necked, short-sleeved, linen nightdress in pale pink that had to have belonged to his sister. It was a summer nightgown, elegant, pretty, simple of design, and looked not only soft and feminine but also *comfortable*. At this point, her ribs felt as if they'd been braced by a tight wrapping of wooden planks for a month.

She'd changed quickly, thankful she'd worn an evening gown that had allowed her to reach most of the buttons and wiggle out of easily enough, and a corset with front clasps. Then, after removing her petticoats, stockings, and shoes, she'd cleaned herself as best as she'd been able with her minimal toiletries, brushed her hair and teeth, pulled the nightgown over her head, and slipped beneath the covers on the cot.

Now, after lying alone with nothing but her thoughts for more than an hour, his parting words still gnawed at her. She had no need at all to consider her *own* memories. Her memories were far better than his, for heaven's sake, a fact that couldn't possibly have escaped him.

God, she'd nearly fainted for the first time in her life when he'd announced that he'd seen John Henry's portrait and recognized him. She'd realized they looked like father and son almost at his birth and had accepted at once that they could never, ever be allowed to meet face-to-face. She'd deal with the House of Lords later, since a possible confrontation between them as adults remained a problem years into the future. But an unexpected encounter in his childhood was something she'd considered on occasion, for which she'd taken a necessary precaution or two, and one reason she had immediately sent her son to the country when she'd learned that Ian had returned to the city and had come in search of her. But she hadn't prepared herself for recognition to happen now, and never because of a painting. And there could only be so much denying it on her part. The man certainly wasn't stupid; he could see his reflection in a portrait and recognize it. But he *was* being stubborn, selfish, and unthinking if he thought she'd simply admit to giving birth to his bastard child.

She wished she could tell him everything, wished she could explain her actions of so long ago, but even with her silence, even with the obvious fact that her son looked just like him, he should know why she didn't, why she couldn't. He should *know,* after all: the Duke of Chatwin was a bastard—his father was not the Earl of Stamford. His mother had lain with a man not her husband, resulting in the conception of Ian and his twin sister Ivy. Only a handful of people were aware of the indiscretion, including her, the former Viola Bennington-Jones—because she had heard every jumbled detail come from his tortured lips as he'd lain semiconscious in her arms all those years ago and she had put the details together, including the revelation that learning the truth in his twenties, at his mother's deathbed, had nearly destroyed him as a man bound by honor.

While it might have been possible that he didn't remember telling her anything of importance during his time in the dungeon, or have any notion that she would be aware of his greatest secret as a titled gentleman, the fact that *he* knew he was a bastard should have been enough to convince him that she would never want a soul to know *her* son could be one as well. He should *know* this. If she told Ian everything and offered him details—as much as she wanted to, simply to relieve her own guilt and give him a measure of comfort in learning he hadn't been violated as he feared—there remained the tiniest possibility that he would still use the information against her, perhaps even try to take her son away from her or have her arrested for some sort of attempted fraud or extortion. He'd threatened as much before. Honestly, she had no idea if he had legal grounds to do any such thing without the ability to prove parentage, but she couldn't possibly go to Mr. Duncan, broach the issue, and ask for his advice. The subject went beyond delicate to deceit and perhaps even criminal action. In the end, all would simply be best for everyone, especially her and John Henry, if Ian would just leave the past alone. Even if he cared nothing for her child, which she didn't expect and would never demand, at the very least he should have some sympathy for the difficulties of a bastard should anyone among the peerage learn the truth. Society could be very cruel, and she could only hope to God that if she continued to deny his being John Henry's father, he would eventually let it go. He would simply have to accept it.

Viola snuggled down deeper into the blankets as dusk finally gave way to nightfall and darkness filled the cabin. Strangely, she didn't feel a trace of fear. Maybe it was the bolt on the door and the sturdiness of the shelter itself, or the fact that she simply felt secure on Ian's land, but even without him in the room, it comforted her to know he remained close by and at least wasn't going to let her starve. And if he wasn't going to let her starve, and had been attentive enough to bring her a nightgown and hairbrush, he probably thought she was safe.

She closed her eyes, nearly smiling as she remembered the look on his face right before he'd released her from his embrace. He had wanted desperately to kiss her, and it had been difficult for him to let her go without doing so. Oh, yes. And shamefully, she had been just as eager. It had been so many, many years since she had been kissed by a man, touched by a man, and the memory of it, being so close to that same feeling this afternoon, the same sensations she'd discovered as a virgin of nineteen in his arms, made her shiver beneath the covers. Her husband had been a caring lover, had made certain she'd found her pleasure in his bed, but there had been nobody but Ian in her dreams, in her fantasies, and with her in memory all those lonely nights when she'd lain by herself and dared to touch those secret, sinful spots that he had found and kindled for her all those years ago. He'd made her cry, and then cry out, and only Ian had given her such inexplicable, intimate joy and the desire to share that joy through her art when she'd no longer been able to share it with him.

She sighed, feeling suddenly sensual, wanting more and wishing he hadn't left her so quickly. It truly hadn't taken much to convince her that being with him again wouldn't be so awful, certainly wouldn't be a distasteful ravishing, and would satisfy so many hidden longings! She always felt guilty when she touched herself, as ladies were never supposed to do such sinful things. But the scent of him inside the cabin still lingered, the feel of his hard body holding her still scorched her, and the pull of her own sexuality seemed too great to ignore this time.

Viola ran the fingers of both hands over her nipples, enjoying the tingling sensation, suddenly craving his lips on her breasts, his palms skimming every inch of her body. She felt the rush of heat between her legs, the growing need to be gently stroked by the fantasy, and finally, after lifting her nightgown to her waist, she pressed two delicate fingers between her intimate folds and began to caress the wet, warm softness as her desire for him began to intensify.

Ian . . .

The bolt on the door clicked.

Viola's eyes shot open; her heart stopped. Then suddenly light filled the cabin as he entered, carrying a lamp, looking straight at her from the doorway.

"I hope you're not asleep," he drawled.

Her entire body flushed with fire, but she didn't dare move, since he might see her lift her hands and know exactly what she'd been doing. For the first time in her life, she wanted to cower in pure mortification.

"Viola?"

"What?" she whispered, though it sounded like a croak.

He chuckled, closing and bolting the door behind him. "Sorry. Did I interrupt your prayers?"

Her mind clearing, she ordered, "Turn around."

"Turn around?" he repeated, slowly walking toward her.

"A lady needs a moment, your grace," she said through gritted teeth.

"Ah." Instead of doing her bidding, he strode to the stove and placed the lamp on the shelf, at an angle and height that brightened most of the room.

Quicky, she lowered her bunched nightgown to her ankles and sat up a little, pulling the blankets decently to her neck. "What are you doing here, Ian?"

He turned to her once more and, smiling slyly, walked confidently to the cot. "I wanted to show you something, and I assumed since you'd napped most of the day you probably weren't tired."

Skeptically, she asked, "What on earth would you need to show me now?"

He lifted a small satchel he'd brought with him. "Something that might help with your memories."

She didn't trust that rather vague explanation at all. "You shouldn't be here. It's not appropriate. I'm in my nightdress. In . . . bed. If one could call this a bed."

The smile slowly faded from his handsome face as he gazed down at her, studying every feature on her face. Then he lowered his body and sat beside her. "Let me see your hand."

She could feel her heartbeat begin to quicken, both from his closeness and his scrutiny. "My hand? Why?"

"Just let me see it, Viola. Don't argue."

With slight hesitation, she did as he ordered, pulling her left hand from beneath the blankets and offering it to him, palm up. "Are you going to tell me what this is about?"

His eyes narrowed a fraction as he wrapped his fingers around her wrist. "You can't guess?"

She swallowed, noting the firmness of his grasp, his confidence, and suddenly she felt a tinge of uneasiness course through her. "No. Am I supposed to?"

For several long seconds he continued to watch her, his thumb caressing her palm. Then he leaned over to the floor, reached into his satchel, and pulled out a thin, red satin ribbon about five feet long.

"What are you doing?" she asked, her growing discomfiture now spilling into her voice.

He didn't reply. Instead, he quickly wrapped the middle of the ribbon around her wrist three times, then lifted it with her arm and quickly began tying it to the metal post at the top of the cot.

"What—" she gasped in stunned disbelief. "Ian, stop this! You can't possibly think to tie me up like an animal!"

"As you did me?" he replied matter-of-factly, securing the ends in a tight knot.

"I did no such thing! And you're a gentleman. This is—" She pulled at the ribbon to no avail; awkwardly, she attempted to raise herself to a full sitting position. "This is *absurd*."

Complete in his effort, Ian sat back and studied his work. Viola just stared at it. Her arm was loose enough to move down to a right angle, and her wrist was snugly wrapped, though not enough to lose feeling in it. He'd tied the ends of the ribbon in a triple knot, attaching her to the post until he saw fit to release her. Or until she could manage to pick the entanglement apart with the fingers of her right hand.

He'd apparently thought of that, however, as he reached into his bag one more time and produced another ribbon, exactly the same length as the first.

"Now the other one."

Her eyes widened in startled fury. "Absolutely not," she seethed. "Ian, this is ridiculous. Your point is taken. You were badly treated. I have fully admitted that. But I refuse to give in to you and simply allow—"

He cut her off by standing suddenly, whipping the blankets off her body, and grabbing her right hand so quickly that she wasn't even aware of all that was happening until he'd wrapped the satin rope around her wrist and begun tying the end to the opposite iron post at the right of her head.

"I should think you'd be happy these aren't chains," he maintained with a casual air as he checked the knot and reinforced the tightness in both of them before standing back to observe her.

Viola cringed inside. Never had she felt so humiliated and exposed, so utterly helpless as she did now. Aside from the thin summer nightgown that she'd thankfully been able to lower to her ankles, she lay on the mattress completely at his mercy, tied up by both wrists as he gazed down to her with dark, daring eyes that seemed to linger on every curve as his gaze raked her form from her toes to her mussed hair that spilled across the pillow.

"Now we're going to talk, Viola," he murmured, his tone almost velvety as he reveled in his power. "And I think your being the captive this time will help *both* of our memories."

She shivered, mouth dry, unable to think clearly. "You're insane."

He chuckled. "Now *that's* funny."

"Funny? Are you going to keep me tied up for weeks? Feed me bread and broth? Leave me here to die?"

All humor left his face as he once again sat beside her, arms crossed over his chest. "While I think it's true that only an insane person could kidnap a nobleman and keep him chained to a wall for weeks, feed him nothing but tainted broth and bread crumbs, I would never hurt you like that, Viola. And believe it or not, it pains me to hear you suggest that I might do such a thing to you after all we've shared, good and bad." He paused, then leaned forward to whisper, "Especially knowing you're the mother of my son."

A strange feeling of warmth enveloped her, coupled with a good dose of guilt, which he no doubt intended to shove down her throat. But truthfully, she didn't feel threatened bodily by him at this point, only apprehensive of his immediate intent.

"Now," he began, "I am going to ask questions, and you are going to answer them, truthfully and completely."

Hoping he wouldn't notice, she lightly pulled at one of the ribbons to check its strength. It didn't budge.

"I want to know," he continued, staring directly into her eyes, "if you took advantage of me intimately, in a . . . sexual manner, while I was unconscious in the dungeon."

Her pulse began to race. "Of course not. I told you this before. I—I cleaned you when I could, nursed you. That's all."

His dark gaze narrowed shrewdly as he drew in a long breath, but he never looked away. "What about while I was semiconscious or aware of you?"

She swallowed. "No."

The side of his mouth ticked up a fraction. "And yet, as we discussed earlier today, I remember being stroked by a woman's hand until I climaxed, Viola. Why would you lie to me now rather than just admit it?"

Thoroughly embarrassed by his explicit language, she felt her face flush with color and she closed her eyes, shook her head in denial. "Aside from the fact that your memory is foggy, Ian, I refuse to discuss something so utterly private and inappropriate."

For seconds nothing happened. And then she felt the slightest touch of his fingertips as they slowly skimmed her linen-covered left breast.

She gasped in complete shock; her eyes flew open. He stared at her, his gaze no longer just focused but remarkably intense.

"My memory may be foggy," he replied huskily, "but I definitely recall a woman's hand on my body. I'd very much like to think it was yours. Now, tell me again what *you* remember."

She squirmed a little, unable to move her body even minutely from his touch. "Ian, please, let's not—"

He cut her off by turning his hand over and brushing his knuckles across the same breast with slightly more pressure, making her nipple harden beneath the fabric and her breath catch in her chest.

"Viola?"

She understood his intention now, knew he would continue to deliciously assault her until she gave him every piece of information he wanted. She could lie, of course, or tell him what he longed to hear, or she could let him make love to her like this, surrendering herself to him as she lay tied helplessly to a bedpost in a cabin with nobody around for miles. Five years ago she'd possessed in her hands the power to love him or release him, and now he carried it in his. And he knew it. This total control over her, to use her and ruin her should he so desire, had been his plan from the beginning.

Giving in at last, watching him closely, she murmured, "You begged me to touch you, Ian."

For a moment or two he seemed unable to grasp the meaning in her words. Then he sat up a little, pulled his hand from her breast as his brows creased in a frown.

"Begged."

He said it as a statement, not a question, and she could tell by the look on his face and the tone of his voice that her unexpected answer had not just utterly surprised him; it had also perplexed him.

She sighed. "Perhaps it's more accurate to say you pleaded with me to stay with you, to . . . comfort you."

"I see." He ran his fingers through his hair, noticeably uncomfortable. "And you just accommodated my physical needs at my request?"

Why did he make it sound so base and disgusting? Irritated, she returned, "It wasn't like that. It wasn't vulgar, or . . . immoral to care for you, and there was nothing carnal about it at first. You were alone, and afraid. You . . . you were . . ." She paused, bit her bottom lip. "You really can't remember any of this?"

He shook his head minutely. "Not all the details. Probably only enough to know if you're lying."

Although she had no choice but to believe him, her nose itched, and suddenly she cursed him within for being an overbearing ass and putting her in such an unladylike predicament.

"There really are no more details to tell, Ian," she continued, exasperated. "You were in a desperate way. You'd been there for a few days' time, sometimes conscious, sometimes not. I had bathed you, lain beside you, warmed you on occasion when you were especially cold, hugged you when you needed someone close and asked me to. Eventually one thing led to another, and at some point, while I was next to you, you—you became . . ."

"Aroused?"

Heat suffused her, but she resisted the urge to tear her gaze from the starkness of his. "You asked me to help relieve your . . . discomfort, then when I hesitated, you took my hand and . . . it—it just happened . . ."

His brows rose and he almost smiled. Almost. "That's very sweet, Viola."

She squirmed again. "Yes, well, now you know the *details,* so let me go. Please. Keeping me tied up like this is absolutely ridiculous. Truly appalling behavior for a gentleman."

He ignored her demand. "Did you enjoy the intimacy as well?"

She'd feared he'd ask something like that. With a brave lift of her chin, she replied matter-of-factly, "I was nursing you, your grace. I didn't want you to be miserable, and I didn't want you to die. I considered it more of a duty."

He burst out laughing.

She wanted to cower beneath the blankets. "Would you please untie me and *leave.* Better yet, just take me home."

"Oh, not on your life, sweetheart," he said through a chuckle. "We're just getting started."

"God, there isn't anything more to *say,*" she insisted through clenched teeth.

His laughter faded as he continued to study her. Finally, he said somberly, "You are a gem, aren't you?"

She shoved her head back onto the pillow, a wave of melancholy washing over her. "A gem unpolished is just another rock."

For several long seconds he said nothing, then, "Where did you hear that?"

"From my mother," she replied without pause. "Reminding us always that my sisters and I were not born ladies and so instead had to infiltrate society by learning their secrets and pretending to be one." She smirked, glancing to one of the ribbons, then the cabin wall. Voice overflowing with frustration, she added sarcastically, "And for all my effort to please her, just look where I am now. She would truly be appalled."

Exhaling a fast breath, he leaned forward to capture her gaze with his. "Actually, if there's one thing I very much admire about you, Viola, it's that you are quite polished. Beautifully so. Every time I lay eyes on you I don't see a rock but a ruby, or a diamond or emerald. Shining, lovely, sophisticated. You've managed to make yourself into a lady from a country miss, a feat not easily accomplished." Carefully, he placed a palm on her stomach, caressed her ribs with his thumb. "You are one of the most breathtaking women I've ever known, and I daresay it wasn't something you learned and are pretending to be. It's who you are."

The tenor of his voice enraptured her, melting her inside, making her feel, at least for the moment, like a beautiful, desirable woman. And no matter how much he might despise her as a person, regarding this, he meant every word. She knew that instinctively.

"Now," he fairly whispered, "I want you to tell me if you enjoyed the intimate caressing as I did."

She hesitated. "Ian, I don't want to talk about—"

He cut her off by raising his hand from her stomach to her breast, closing his palm over it gently, unmoving.

Her breath caught; her eyes widened.

"You were saying?"

"I—didn't know."

"Didn't know?"

"At the time." She licked her lips. "I didn't know what was happening or what to do."

"Because you were a virgin."

She nodded minutely.

He paused, then very gently drew his thumb over her nipple, back and forth, and a sudden heavy heat converged between her legs. Embarrassment flooded her, but she couldn't bring herself to look away.

"Did I teach you anything?" he asked huskily, seconds later.

"You . . . showed me," she replied. "I—I just held you and you did most of the . . . moving."

"I see."

His eyes had darkened and his breathing had quickened as he'd listened to her, as he'd continued to lightly caress her. He was slowly becoming as aroused as she, and although it felt delicious, it scared her as well.

"How many times did this happen?" he continued.

"I don't—"

He lowered the top of her nightgown, exposed her full breast, and covered it with his warm hand.

Eyes wide with growing alarm, she mumbled, "I think three times. Ian, please."

"Please, what?"

She swallowed. "Please don't hurt me. . . ."

His expression turning grave, he asked in a husky timbre, "Does this hurt?"

She blinked, confused. "No . . ."

He smiled vaguely. "Then you can be sure I'm not going to hurt you, Viola."

She said nothing to that, just tried in vain to squirm away from him. He continued to watch her intently as his fingers began a slow caress of her breast, skimming the nipple in faint, small circles. In a matter of seconds she could hardly breathe.

"Did I beg you all three times?"

She was beginning to find it very difficult to understand him. "Wh-what?"

"Did I beg you to stroke me all three times, or did you take the initiative on occasion?"

She couldn't remember. Really. "I don't know, Ian. I don't. Honestly."

He abruptly pulled back, and a small moan escaped her throat.

"Now, let's talk about that painting."

Flustered, she glanced down to notice that he'd left her exposed. "Would you please offer me a bit of decency and lift the nightgown?"

He lowered his gaze. "I don't think so." Then with very swift fingers, he pulled the top of her nightdress down to expose the other. "You have beautiful breasts, Viola." Seconds later, he leaned over and kissed the space between them, nuzzling her cleavage.

She moaned. "God, Ian, please stop this. Please."

He raised his head a fraction and glanced up. "Then tell me about that painting."

"What—" she gasped. "What do you want to know?"

Without pause, he asked, "Was it of you and me, to-gether?"

"No," she stated emphatically.

His tongue found her nipple, nearly jolting her off the mattress. Obviously, he didn't believe her.

"It was a fantasy," she whispered.

Seconds later, he raised his head once more and looked at her. "We never made love like that?"

"No, I swear it."

He watched her closely, trying to decide if she offered him the truth. Then he asked softly, "Was it something you envisioned us doing?"

She hesitated, and just as she felt his palm begin to lift her nightgown at her ankles, she admitted, "It was my dream, Ian, yes. I wanted to be with you like that. But it was a long time ago, when I was young and naive."

He smirked. "The painting certainly doesn't depict that of a naive artist."

She looked at the ceiling.

"So," he continued, "if we didn't make love in that particular . . . pose, how then did we do it?"

She didn't respond.

He sighed. "Viola, we both know your child is also mine. How was he conceived?"

She closed her eyes. "He is not your child."

For a long time, it seemed, he remained still and silent beside her. She could feel his gaze on her, as if he was trying to penetrate her mind, perhaps trying to decide if he should continue this ridiculous game or release her knowing he'd never get her to divulge her secrets. And then, just as she was about to suggest a truce, she felt his fingers pulling at the hem of her nightgown as he very slowly began to lift it.

She raised her lashes; her mouth went dry as she gazed into his eyes once more, a witness to a defiance she'd never seen in him before.

"Since you refuse to tell me the truth, much less the details," he murmured, "it appears I'll have to try to remember it myself."

"There is nothing to remember," she said, attempting to be rational.

He ignored her, continuing to raise the soft linen past her calves, her knees.

"Please don't do this, Ian," she whispered, though she knew the words sounded more like forced, ladylike appropriateness than pleading despair.

He never dropped his gaze from hers, though he paused in his movements when his fingers reached her thighs. "Then tell me honestly: did I teach you passion, Viola? Did I touch you the way you touched me?"

She really didn't think it mattered now if she lied or not. "Yes."

The slightest flicker of surprise crossed his features. "Did you beg me?"

Heat flowed through her veins as she shook her head. "No. I—I didn't know."

"Didn't know?"

For seconds she said nothing, then again felt his fingertips begin to trace a line of tender circles up her thigh. "I didn't know what to expect. I didn't know anything."

He drew in a long breath. "I see. You didn't know what an orgasm was?"

Squeezing her eyes shut, she whispered, "I can't talk about this."

He continued to caress her. Then in a soothing, velvety voice, he asked, "Did I give you your first orgasm, Viola? Make you come for me?"

She shook her head.

"I wasn't able to pleasure you?"

He sounded almost incredulous. With a growing sense of guilt, embarrassment, and desperation, she said, "I don't remember, Ian, it was so long ago—"

His chuckle cut her off. "You're lying again, my dear Lady Cheshire. I may not be the world's greatest lover, but I am not inept, even when physically hindered, as I was then. And if I made you climax, you *would* remember."

She whimpered just as she suddenly felt him push his fingers up and under her nightdress so that they brushed against her intimate curls. Now exposed nearly to her hips, she instinctively crossed her legs.

"That won't work," he said. Using both hands, he pressed them between her knees, pulled them apart with little effort, leaned over one leg and braced his body between them—propped up by his elbow—to keep her wide open for his view. "God, this is a lovely sight. I could stay here and stare at this all day."

She wanted to cry, to scream, bewildered as to why a man would want to look at a lady's private parts for *any* length of time, and completely unable to tell if he was teasing or serious or just trying to torture her with continued mortification. But most of all, she desperately wished he would lean forward five inches and kiss her there.

"Is your goal to utterly humiliate me?" she managed to whisper as each passing moment under his scrutiny grew ever more intolerable. "Because you're doing a stupendous job, your grace."

When the silence continued to linger, she bravely raised her lashes to find him watching her, his eyes narrowed and focused intently on her face.

"I can smell your scent, Viola."

She stilled inside. It wasn't as if his words shocked her more than any others, but rather his tone had changed so abruptly, altered so dramatically in its intensity, that she realized he'd suddenly remembered something intimate about her and their time in the dungeon. Nerves afire, she licked her lips and said nothing.

And then she felt his finger, one finger on her, tenderly brushing the curls, as if he was trying to discover a treasure beneath the folds. She inhaled sharply as her breath caught, but she couldn't drop her gaze from his.

"Answer my question," he said, his voice low and rough.

She couldn't remember the question at all. "I can't . . . think, Ian."

His jaw twitched. "Did I pleasure you?" he asked again, his finger still teasing her intimately.

"God, why are you doing this?" she asked through a whimper.

His touch grew bolder as he moved in closer. "You're getting so wet now," he said. "Tell me what I want to know and I'll stop."

She didn't want him to stop! But she couldn't move at all, couldn't resist, couldn't defy him. Closing her eyes once more, she turned her head to the side. "Yes . . ."

Pausing, he pulled back a little. "Yes? I made you come?"

"Yes."

A soft groan escaped him, and she couldn't decide if he was disturbed by the revelation for some reason or feeling rather triumphant as a man. But she didn't dare look at him.

"Please leave, Ian."

"No."

He said the word so softly that she almost didn't hear it. And then she felt his finger slide up and down her intimately again, then two, then three fingers.

He began to stroke her slowly. She whimpered, shook her head, eyes squeezed shut. "Ian . . . no . . ."

"I have another question," he whispered, leaning over to brush his lips against her thigh.

She shivered.

"When you touch yourself now, like this, do you think of me?"

She pulled against the ribbons, moaned lightly, tried to lift her hips to shove him away even as she knew he'd pinned her so well beneath him that the act was fruitless.

"Viola?"

The tension began to coil within. Her breath quickened, her pulse raced. Finally, she raised her lashes again just enough to find him staring at her face, his gaze focused, grave.

"Do you ever think of me making love to you?" he asked in a deep whisper. "Do you stare at your paintings and touch yourself and think of me?"

She couldn't believe he was asking her this, stroking her intimately, watching her as he took her to the heights of bliss with a purpose so fervent she could see it in his expression, feel it radiate from him. Suddenly it became clear how desperately he wanted her to want him. Then, and now.

"Always," she breathed, "and only with you . . ."

He hadn't expected that. For a slice of a second he hesitated, his features going slack as genuine surprise crossed his face. Then he swallowed hard and glanced down to where his fingers caressed her.

And without warning or expectation she felt his lips on her, then his tongue, and she softly cried out in exquisite delight. He ignored her shock, her breathless wonder as he spread her knees wider apart to give him better access.

Finding his rhythm, he began to stroke her, to make love to her with his mouth, and she gave in to the pleasure, raising her hips to meet his every move. It took only seconds for the tension to once again build to delicious heights. She gripped the ribbons with her hands, whimpered as he brought her closer to the edge, and just as she felt his finger glide into her, the pressure exploded within.

She arched back, moaning, feeling each powerful pulse course through her. He continued his glorious assault for several long seconds until he felt her begin to relax, heard her breathing slow. Finally he pulled away and sat up a little. He wiped the sheet across his mouth and stared down at her flushed face.

"You're very beautiful, Viola," he said contemplatively.

Senses returning, she suddenly felt exposed, overwhelmed, embarrassed. She closed her eyes and turned her head away again, having no idea what to say.

"Tell me what happened. Tell me he's my child."

His voice remained quiet, but beneath the masculine bravado, she could sense his frustration, his longing, and a bit of resentment. It took all that was in her not to blurt out the truth.

"I suppose you want to take me now, tied up and at your whim?" she asked without looking at him.

After several seconds of strained silence, she heard him reach into his satchel. She opened her eyes to see him remove a six-inch knife. Quickly, he leaned over her and cut both ribbons at mid-stream.

"Sleep well, madam," he said flatly.

With that, he gathered his things and left the cottage without another glance in her direction, locking her inside once more, alone with only her thoughts.

Chapter Seventeen

Today was the end of my innocence, in every way. It was an end he sought, but to which I yielded, with compassion and desire and love in my heart, and now that it's over, I have no regrets, only memories to last a lifetime. . . .

Ian paced the floor of his study, too anxious to sleep, unable to focus on anything but her and the miserable position he'd put himself in when he'd decided to tease her, taste her, then leave her instead of having his way with her delectable body and relieving the sexual tension that had been building inside him since Fairbourne had introduced her to him weeks ago as the beautifully sensual, grown-up Lady Cheshire. Now, after hours of trying to rationalize it all, he felt all the more confounded by his behavior toward her, and angry for denying his own needs for the sake of . . . what? His honor? *Her* honor? What a damnable laugh.

He couldn't get her out of his mind. Her scent lingered on his skin, the sound of her breathless climax both soothed and irritated his senses, making his head hurt more than the half bottle of whiskey he'd downed since he'd left her. And all of it stirred his forgotten memory, turning his usually practical, intelligent brain into a muddy puddle of acute distraction and mild bewilderment.

Making love to her had not been his prime objective when he'd gone to the cottage to confront her, his ribbons in tow. He'd merely wanted to put a bit of fear in her, to demonstrate his power over her, to let *her* experience how it felt to be restrained and at someone else's mercy. And he'd no doubt accomplished his goal. His plan had worked perfectly, at least at first. Using sexually suggestive touch had been well and good, an added bonus of manipulation, his intention to take her so far she'd beg for release, at which point he'd leave her to her own frustration and musings. Arousing her to climax had never been his intent—until he'd sat there and made her body come alive at his touch, felt her wetness, smelled her, tasted her, and experienced the heart-pounding measure of his own desire. Couple that with the knowledge that they had once been together intimately, and suddenly he'd wanted nothing more than to give her the ultimate physical pleasure and watch her enjoy it.

He would have made love to her all night, too, taking his slow time inside her, had she not sounded so practical and unaffected by him in the wake of his attention, waiting to be used as if he'd picked her up for a price at the docks. Then again, perhaps she had a point, as they both knew he'd initially brought her to Stamford to get answers and make her his without her consent.

He simply didn't know what to do with the lovely, obstinate, desirable Lady Cheshire anymore, which was undoubtedly why he now found himself alone and drinking unsatisfying whiskey in his study in the middle of the night instead of sexually sated and sleeping peacefully in her arms.

Still, it was his reaction to her that gnawed at him the most. True, he needed a woman, but he wasn't so desperate that he should have to lose himself to this one particular female as if he'd been caged for five years without any diversion at all from the gentle sex. And for the life of him, he couldn't understand why she, of all the ladies in the land, had to be the one to capture his thoughts and engage his lust so totally as if none other would do, or even existed. He knew he didn't despise her as he'd once thought he had. He couldn't possibly despise a woman and at the same time admire her charms and want so badly to be with her physically. Frankly, he had no idea at all what he felt for her aside from absolute confusion.

He couldn't even say he wanted to ruin her anymore, which, in itself, disconcerted him. Ruining her had lost all meaning, he supposed, the moment he'd discovered the face on the portrait of her child to be his mirror image. Destroying her would destroy her son, and truthfully, he didn't have it in him to do either. For a fleeting moment marriage to her crossed his mind, but it quickly vanished. She would probably never agree anyway, especially after his telling her that he'd rather see her die in prison than take his name; she didn't need his money or title, and she resented him totally. Besides, he'd lived his life these last years knowing he had to marry well, needed to marry a noblewoman of pure line descent. He was a bastard, and learning that truth as a grown man had only solidified what he expected for his future. Marrying a common woman, regardless of the title she herself had once married into, would remind him every day of the lie he lived, and he wanted more for his legitimate children. But what about the boy? What should or could he do—what did he *want* to do—about his bastard son? Especially when she *still* wouldn't admit he was his?

Jesus, what a damn mess.

Ian stopped pacing in front of his desk, took a long, full swig from his bottle, then, squinting, glanced at the clock over the mantel. He thought it said nearly three, but it was hard to tell. Too much whiskey and not enough light. He swore loudly and scrubbed a palm down his face.

At this point the only thing he did know with any certainty was that he was fast growing tired of the games. Tired of trying to coerce the truth from her. Tired of not understanding why his own feelings suddenly didn't seem at all rational. He wanted answers, and more than anything, right this moment, he wanted her.

Always, and only with you . . .

Ian groaned and placed what remained of his whiskey on his desk. Then he combed his fingers through his hair and left his study—confident, edgy with renewed desire, and ready for a fight.

"Wake up, Viola."

She stirred, uncertain if she was only dreaming she heard his voice, felt his presence, until she blinked and caught sight of his shadowed face. He stood above her, holding a dimly lit lamp as he towered over her form on the cot.

"Why are you here?" she mumbled, sitting up a little, brushing loose strands of hair from her forehead and cheeks. "What time is it?"

"About half past three," he said rather casually. Stepping away, he walked to the stove, placed the lamp on the cold surface, then turned back and faced her squarely. "I couldn't sleep after our last . . . encounter, though I see you didn't have trouble."

That flustered her a little. She couldn't read his mood, mostly because he'd awakened her from a dead slumber and she had yet to fully gather her wits.

"If you'll recall, your grace," she said through a yawn, "you told me to sleep well when you departed. I was only too pleased to do as you ordered, so are you trying to haunt even my dreams?"

In a tone low and rough, he maintained, "I hope so, Viola, since you've managed to haunt my dreams for five long years."

She'd been half-joking, but he remained somber, apparently ready to continue a discussion of their past. That meant he'd probably come back for an argument. But why now? She eyed him candidly for a moment or two, noting his tense form, his mussed hair. He still wore the same dark trousers and casual linen shirt, but they were both wrinkled now, his sleeves loose and pushed up to the elbows, the neckline unbuttoned to show a scattering of chest hair. He looked quite troubled about something, and although his gaze never strayed from hers, in a sudden explanation of everything, he swayed on his feet when he reached up to rub the back of his neck.

"Are you drunk, Ian?"

He gave her a half grin. "Not really. Only numb enough to make me reflect on how lonely life can be alone."

She snorted, rolled her eyes. "If that actually makes sense to you, then you're quite drunk."

"I should think," he remarked softly, "that you of all people would understand just how much loneliness can be felt without imbibing at all."

Her shoulders slumped as that statement hit its target. Depending on how much liquor he'd consumed, this conversation could sting bitterly. But if he wanted a fight, she supposed she couldn't stop him, and it would probably be better to stand up to him instead of cowering. Seconds later she pushed the covers to her ankles and stood to face him unafraid, hands on hips.

"So get to the point. Why are you here?" she asked again, her tone firm from her own growing irritation.

Immediately, his eyes flashed with a noticeable sexual hunger. His gaze slowly traveled down and then up the length of her body, making her suddenly wish she'd never left the cot.

"It really should be illegal," he drawled, "for a lady who looks like you, dressed in barely nothing, to stand in front of a man who hasn't been bedded by one in ages."

She faltered, feeling her pulse begin to race. Crossing her arms over her breasts, she shifted from one foot to the other as the real reason for his unexpected return began to dawn on her and she realized at once just how exposed she truly was.

"So, that's it," she stated flatly, lifting her chin in feigned confidence. "You've come to bed me now, to take me at a time of *your* choosing, catching me off guard because I was sleeping, proving some sort of complete control by waking me for it."

He smirked. "Why would you assume the only thing I want from you right now is to bed you?"

Treating her like an idiot irritated her even more. "Because there's nothing else to do here?" she replied sarcastically. "Because of the way you're looking at me?" She paused, then added, "It is what you want, isn't it? Or did you come back for more tea?"

"I came back to be with you."

That huskily whispered statement thoroughly rattled her. It was unlike him to be so evasive and say something in the intimate manner a lover might use. She could only blame it on the drink. "To be with me?"

He shook his head. "Viola, you're making this very difficult—"

"I'm making *what* difficult?" she cut in, incredulous that he would accuse her of anything right now, especially when he was the one not making any sense at all. "You can't possibly expect me to believe you came back to chat about the warm summer weather, or go fishing with you at sunup." She shook her head slowly, finally understanding his late-night ploy. "No, your grace. You came back to annoy me, to gloat in your power over even my ability to rest by awakening me, to take pride in the fact that I am locked up at your command, and then to use my body to satisfy your carnal desire, the first of many times you might feel the need to seduce me at your whim until you tire of me and decide to send me home. Am I right?"

She apparently hit a nerve as she deliberately touched on every one of his motives. His eyes grew stormy and his jaw hardened as he pressed his lips together.

"Why do you make it sound so offensive?" he asked, his voice taut. "As if all I want from you is to lie there like a rag doll while I use you for some sort of passionless physical release?"

Back rigid, shoulders squared, she decided at that moment to lay her feelings bare; she had nothing left to lose.

"Because, Ian," she disclosed in a near-whisper, her tone spilling over with raw emotion, "at the very heart of everything between us there is only pain and sorrow, regret and, for you, revenge. We're not lovers, and I think you know I'm not the kind of woman who needs or wants to become any man's mistress. You may desire me, but that's just male lust. We both know the last thing you want to do is make slow, passionate, *meaningful* love to me. You didn't bring me here for that purpose, and I'm not naive enough to ever expect it from you."

For seconds he seemed stunned, perhaps even appalled by her candor as he once again looked her up and down. Then suddenly his features hardened as the air around them charged with a static she could positively feel.

"My, that's . . . quite a deduction," he enunciated in a thick, cold whisper. "Remarkable insight considering your apparent lack of understanding."

Lack of understanding? She frowned slightly, her uncertainty growing with his sharp change in focus and shift in mood. Still, she refused to cower to him. "I'm not an idiot, Ian."

He smirked. "But you are naive if you think the only reason you're here is for passionless coupling."

"Oh, I know it's more than that," she shot back in quick defense. "It's also about control, humiliation."

"You're dead wrong if you think your captivity is about my satisfaction and need for revenge." He shook his head slowly, his mouth turning down in bitter contempt. "This isn't about me, it's about you."

"You're talking in riddles," she said, eyeing him carefully as her pulse began to race. "Go back to the house, to your drink, and leave me alone."

With renewed purpose he began to walk toward her, all apparent drunkenness gone, replaced with determination.

"You really don't know why I brought you here, do you?" he asked, his tone now icy, controlled.

A wave of uneasiness washed over her, and very subtly she began to retreat from his slowly approaching form. He was attempting to confuse her, catch her off her guard, but his ultimate intent remained unclear.

"Answer me, Viola," he whispered.

Exasperated, bewildered, angry, she threw her arms wide. "I don't know what you're *asking,* what you expect me to *say.*"

He didn't respond immediately. Instead, he continued closing the space between them until he stood directly in front of her, towering over her, his eyes narrowed to slits, jaw tense, shoulders bunched involuntarily, which tightened his linen shirt around the muscles of his chest and arms. She swallowed, held his gaze, hardly able to breathe as she realized he'd backed her up against the wall, cornering her next to the foot of the cot.

"You think you know what I experienced five years ago," he murmured, his voice low and brimming with grief. "You think that because you still feel some sort of empathy, a bit of guilt for what your family caused, that you *understand*. But guilt isn't anything like helplessness, Viola, like hopelessness. Guilt isn't anything like *terror*."

She cringed inside as it began to dawn on her that he had every intention of making her feel his pain, a heartache she would do anything to avoid. He didn't know the depth of her feelings for him, how the memory of that time long ago had affected her entire life, how terror was experienced by everyone who loved the one tormented.

"You've never experienced the nightmares that still haunt me," he continued, "the anxiety that cloaks me still when darkness falls and I'm alone in silence with memories that seem like yesterday. You don't awaken in the middle of the night, awash with panic, filled with rage you can't ignore or explain because every single day you're reminded of the time you were *violated* by an unseen demon—"

"Stop it, Ian," she pleaded in a whisper, pressing her palms against his chest as she attempted to push him away.

Instead, he moved closer, brushing his entire frame against hers. Totally at his mercy, she could smell the faint trace of whiskey and heady male musk, could feel the heat of his body emanate from every tight muscle as he overpowered her with his strength, as his chest grazed her breasts and the warmth of his breath caressed her cheek and jaw when she turned her head in some attempt to avoid him.

"I want you to feel my fear, Viola," he maintained relentlessly. "I want you to feel my helplessness, to experience the raw terror of having everything you are as a person of dignity taken away from you."

"I'm sorry—"

"I don't want you to feel *sorry* for me," he seethed through clenched teeth. "I want you to know what I experienced, to *know* the depth of my anger." In a sudden burst of anguish, he slammed his fist into the wall beside her. "*I want you to feel what I felt!*"

Tears filled her eyes. She started trembling, struggling against him in a vain attempt to break away from his clutches. He wouldn't let her budge. Instead, he grabbed her jaw with his palm, forcing her to face him, to look at him.

"I'm a *man,* and until five years ago, I lived the life of one entitled, a respected lord and heir to a wealthy earldom. And then two common country girls managed to outwit me, drug me, chain me, and by doing so, steal my manhood—"

"That's not true," she whispered.

"Your sisters *emasculated* me, Viola. Whether physical or only deep in my mind, they *violated* me. And during that time of horror, you came along and took my seed without my consent or complete awareness—"

"Please, Ian, stop," she begged, tears rolling down

her cheeks as she squeezed her eyes shut. "It didn't happen that way—"

"It happened that way *to me!*"

She shook her head fiercely, though he continued to hold her firmly in his control. And then, to her great astonishment, he pushed his hips into hers, forcing her to notice his rigid erection as he pressed it into her belly. She whimpered as a sudden heat suffused her, as her breathing quickened and her legs weakened beneath her.

"I sought you out to ruin you, to make you suffer as I did," he said, his voice choked with emotion. "But meeting you again has disoriented me, stirred my passions, made me crazy with need that I don't understand." Leaning in, he whispered in her ear, "Can you feel what you do to *me,* sweetheart? Can you now understand *my* confusion, *my* humiliation and outrage when you, one of the women who stole my manhood, continues to arouse it like this?"

Abruptly, before she could utter a response, he released her jaw and threaded the fingers of both hands tightly through her hair, pinning her head to the wall.

"It's always part of me now," he said as he rubbed the tip of his nose along her ear and temple, his voice a husky mixture of anger, frustration, and hot desire. "And what infuriates me most of all is that in five long years you're the only woman who haunts me, awake and asleep. You're the only woman I want to satisfy my lust. Can you imagine anything more absurd?" He chuckled with disgust. "You're the demon of my nightmares, Viola, and yet my greatest personal fault is that I can't bring myself to hate you. And when I touch you like this, have you close to me like this, nearly naked and all to myself . . ." He placed his face in the crook of her neck and inhaled deeply, then ran his tongue up the side of her throat. "When I can taste you and smell you and feel you like this, I fear I'll never be able to rid myself of you, that you'll go on haunting me night after night forever."

Moaning softly, she pushed her hips into his. "Please—"

"Please, what?" he murmured in her ear. "Let you go? Or take you here, fast and hot like this, and satisfy us both?"

"Ian—" She gasped when he reached down with one hand and pinched her nipple, then ran his thumb across it.

"It's only simple lust between us, anyway," he remarked bitterly, his lips grazing her jawline. "You said you don't want or expect passionate, *meaningful* lovemaking from me, but I can take you just like you did me five years ago, satisfy your desire, make sure you enjoy it." He pressed his erection into her again, gently bit her earlobe. "Is that what you want, Viola? Do you want me to make you come?"

She couldn't breathe, couldn't think, could hardly move in his tight grasp, his body flattened into hers, one hand threaded through her hair, the other caressing her breast. He made her insane with need, desperate for him to just kiss her, to touch her everywhere and tease her to oblivion. But above all, she absolutely felt every measure of his frustration and hopelessness within her, his anger at being used and unable to forgive his captors of so long ago, and suddenly she realized that the only way she knew of to help him save his soul was to now, and like this, accept his feelings as he wanted her to experience them.

Squirming a little in his arms, she lifted one hand and cupped his chin with force. He pulled back just enough to look into her eyes.

In a voice of sheer terror mixed with a sultry desire she hoped to God he recognized, she murmured harshly, "I want to *feel* what you *felt*."

For a slice of a second surprise flickered in his stark gaze. And then he groaned low in his chest and released her, flipping her around so fast and unexpectedly that she gasped. Before she could even begin to predict his intention, he flattened her arms on the wall, her palms to the sides of her shoulders, then lifted her nightgown with ease and bunched it at her ribs, exposing her below her waist. Quickly, he wrapped his arms around her and pulled her body toward him an inch or two to give him access, shoving one of his hands up to clutch a breast while lifting her right leg at the knee and resting her foot on the edge of the cot for support with the other. When he had her in place, he pressed his lips to her neck and boldly reached down until the fingers of his free hand began to explore her from behind.

He inhaled sharply when he finally touched her intimately; she shivered from the contact, so heated and fast, so shocking and totally out of her control. He seemed lost with purpose, driven by the moment, relentless in his pursuit, caressing her breast with one hand while using whisper-soft movements to tease her apart and explore her more fully with the fingertips of the other.

He began to kiss her neck and shoulder in gentle pecks, suck her earlobe as he caressed her with ever-increasing intensity. He held her captive to his whim, unable to move, to face him, to look into his eyes and witness his feelings as he purposely pushed her closer to the edge of sanity. It took only seconds for her breathing to become fast and erratic, her body to succumb to his rhythm, to focus on each touch, each play of his fingers on each delicate, sensitive spot on her body, as he brought her nearer and nearer her crest—

Suddenly he released her. She moaned in blissful agony, though just as quickly, he brought his hand from her breast and wrapped it in her hair, coiling his fingers through her long tresses.

"You're so wet, so aroused," he whispered, his tone low and thick. "Do you feel what I felt, sweetheart? Stroked by someone unseen until you're brought to the brink of pleasure?"

She wanted to hit him, run from him, plead with him to make love to her all night. Instead, he had her trapped, needing him, desperate for release, to feel him inside of her. And he knew it.

Drawing a shaky breath, she murmured over her shoulder, "Truthfully, I've never wanted a man more, Ian. But unlike you in that dungeon, I will never, *ever* beg for it."

It took seconds, it seemed, for him to grasp what she said. And then very slowly, she felt his fingers tighten in her hair to the point of gentle pain. She squeezed her eyes shut, half expecting to be thrown across the room in a venting of his rage. Instead, he groaned deeply in his throat, wrapped his free arm around her hips, and yanked her into his nude body.

She nearly squealed at the contact, so warm and erotic and unexpected. She had no idea when he'd removed his clothes, though when he then nestled his hard and hot erection into her bottom such an irrelevant, banal consideration evaporated.

Suddenly his fingers were in her intimate curls, playing, stroking, moving lower to tease her apart and find the nub of her pleasure. He tugged her head back a little so that he could access her face, pressing his lips to her jaw, sucking her earlobe, her throat and shoulder. His hot breath grew erratic, mixing with hers as he very quickly brought her once more to the edge.

She began to move her hips in rhythm, whimpering softly, leaning back on his shoulder to give him access to her neck and jaw. His lips teased her soft flesh, sucking, kissing, licking, until at last, as she began moaning, her body growing tense, her mind reeling as she neared the heights of ecstasy, he pulled on her hair again, just enough to turn her face so he could capture her mouth with his in a searing kiss.

He groaned again, inflaming her pleasure. And then suddenly she felt him move the tip of him between her legs.

Viola relaxed into him even more, adjusted her foot on the cot to give him better access, uncertain what to do in this position, but at the edge of orgasm and desperate for him to be inside of her. She'd never made love standing, been taken from behind, and all of it, with Ian, made for the most carnal, explosive experience of her life. She moaned softly as he kissed her, sucked her tongue, caressed her with an arm wrapped around her, his fingers between her legs, stroking, preparing—

And then he thrust once, twice, and continued pushing upward until he filled her. She gasped, pulled away from his mouth, the pain not as intense as her first time with him, but sharp enough from years of celibacy to cause her body to tense.

He remained still once deeply embedded, untangling his fingers from her hair and wrapping his arm around her, clutching her breast as he began to tease her nipple. Within seconds the pain subsided and he once more began stroking her between her legs, quickly taking her again to the edge.

Viola closed her eyes, losing herself to the feel of him behind her, touching her, inside of her as he held himself steady to bring her to climax first. And just as he began to run his tongue up her throat, moan in her ear with a warm breath of his own increasing desire for her, she reached her peak and the pleasure burst within.

She cried out; her arms flew back to clutch his head, her fingers squeezing together tightly in his hair. He stroked her, held her as she trembled against him, clung tightly to her breast and leg as he began thrusting steadily inside her.

"Jesus, Viola . . ." He sucked in a breath, teeth clenched. "Just feeling you—makes me—"

He let out a growl, coming fast and hard within her, sucking her neck, clinging to her with a wild possession that made it nearly impossible for her to breathe. She gulped for air as he shuddered against her, thrusting upward into her a final time, panting, his face buried in her hair.

She remained still, fighting a sudden urge to cry, though she had no idea why she should want to. They hadn't made love; there was nothing romantic or emotionally close in what they'd done, and yet as they stood together, still joined physically against the wall of a fishing cottage, she felt more bound to him than to any other man ever in her life. Something more than poor luck or chance or a strength of two wills kept bringing them together, and the saddest part of all was that nothing meaningful, or even good, could possibly come of it. There was no affection between them, no hope of a future of happiness. He despised her and desired her at the same time, a combination that brought nothing but heartache and regret. She had always loved him, but she found it far easier to stay away from him than he did her. If only God would listen to her prayers and quell his insatiable need to haunt her to the grave. . . .

"Viola?"

She shivered against him, tried to push him away with her shoulder. He didn't seem to notice as he continued to hold her tightly, running his nose along her hairline at the base of her neck, inhaling deeply.

"I don't think I'll ever be able to forget your scent," he said, his tone low and contemplative.

She had no idea how to reply, whether he thought her particular smell good or bad, though as she finally felt him slip out of her a measure of relief that they were no longer joined intimately settled in.

"Are you going to say something?" he drawled, slowly releasing her and backing away to reach for his clothes.

With a level of modesty, and without offering him

even a glance, she lowered her leg from the cot as she shuffled her nightgown until it dropped to the floor.

"I'm not sure what to say," she answered truthfully, noting how the moment had suddenly become so awkward that she felt like crawling out of her skin.

He didn't reply to that as he began to dress. She ran her fingers through her hair, then sat on the edge of the cot and folded her hands in her lap, staring at the floor but positively feeling his gaze focused on her, watching, waiting.

"What are you thinking?" he asked solemnly, seconds later.

Irritated, she ran a palm across her forehead. "That my mind is a jumble right now, Ian. That my nerves are raw, and that when I think of you, I just don't know what to feel anymore."

She'd said the words with absolute honesty, without much clear thought, but the moment they were out of her mouth, she regretted them.

He cleared his throat. "I suppose I wasn't expecting you to say what a marvelous lover I am."

Her head shot up. Their gazes locked and she glared at him.

He chuckled, running his fingers through his tousled hair. "Sorry."

It hadn't occurred to her that he might find the entire episode awkward as well, and his apparent sheepishness surprised her, even warmed her heart a bit.

"I want to go home," she said very softly.

To her relief, neither his anger nor bitterness resurfaced, though his easygoing expression slowly faded as he began to walk toward her. She held her ground, sitting up a little straighter, completely uncertain of his mood. When he stopped directly in front of her, he reached out for a lock of her hair, lacing it through his fingers as his brows gradually creased in contemplation.

"Maybe I'm not ready to let you go," he finally replied in a near-whisper.

She had no idea what to make of that statement, though under the circumstances, she could only assume he meant to keep her even longer in this hovel as his plaything. She would never last five weeks, as he had in the dungeon. For the first time in two days, she felt the weight of helplessness start to settle in the pit of her stomach.

"Ian, please, enough," she said, hoping to sound stern and not desperate. "I need a bath, clean clothes, to see my son. I cannot stay here another—"

"Viola, lie down," he cut in gently.

She frowned. "What—Why?"

He sighed and untangled his fingers from her hair. "We're both tired and I don't want to talk about this now."

She hesitated only until he grabbed her elbow, lifted her arm, and began to pull her toward the top of the cot. Then, to her surprise, instead of leaving, he walked to the lamp and extinguished the light before lowering himself beside her.

"We need to discuss—"

"Mmmm . . . go to sleep. . . ."

She turned to face the wall and he scooted in to conform to her backside, laying the quilt over them both, then draping his arm over her waist and planting his face in her neck and hair. The last thing she recalled was the comforting sound of his slow, steady breathing before sleep quickly overtook her once more.

A sharp knocking at the door jolted her awake. Startled, she abruptly sat up, uncertain where she was for a moment until she brushed stray hair from her face and her eyes adjusted to rays of bright sunshine beaming through the bars in the window.

The lock clicked just as she remembered that Ian had been with her when she'd fallen asleep at dawn. He must have stepped out while she'd slept, though why he'd knock upon his return—

"Pardon me, Lady Cheshire," came a meek female voice from the doorway as it slowly creaked open.

Viola clutched the quilt to her neck. "Who are you?"

A girl of about sixteen entered, smiling prettily, her blonde hair tightly knotted at her nape, her clothes clean and perfectly pressed. In one hand she carried a small picnic basket, in the other a large leather valise over which was draped what appeared to be a gown covered in a linen travel bag. She quickly placed the items on the floor, wiped her hands once on her skirts, then curtseyed.

"Name's Missy Stone, my lady. So sorry to disturb you, but his grace sent me from the house to see to your needs this morning."

Viola blinked, confused. "To see to my needs?"

"Yes, ma'am." Missy closed the door behind her and locked it, then walked swiftly to the stove to light it. "He was called away from the estate urgently at dawn and asked me to let you sleep till at least ten. 'Tis half past ten now. I've brought blueberry scones, cooked bacon, and tea for brewing. If you'll give me a moment, I'll get the water heating."

A bit dumbfounded, Viola watched the girl putter around the small cabin, realizing she should be relieved that he'd gone, but instead feeling more than a little saddened and irritated that he'd left her without even a brief explanation or apology.

"I've also brought one of Lord Chatwin's sister's good day gowns for you to wear, and I'll have your evening gown cleaned and returned to you, as he ordered," the girl continued cheerfully as she began removing items from the valise. "After you've eaten, I'll help with your toilette, and then at your leisure, Larson will drive you to the city and take you any place you wish to go."

So that was it, she realized with a sinking heart. Their tryst had ended with not even a good-bye. Just cold breakfast, a borrowed dress, and a ride home.

"You needn't worry, my lady," Missy added seconds later, scrutinizing the expression on her face. "Lord Chatwin hires only those servants who are extremely discreet."

"Of course," Viola said at once, ignoring the heated flush in her cheeks and trying to sound indifferent as she finally rose from the cot. She needed to use the chamber pot and she wanted to wash herself, but she preferred to wait for the water to warm. And she was ravenous of a sudden. "You said you brought scones?"

"Yes, ma'am." Missy turned her attention to the picnic basket and rummaged inside. "They're quite delicious, if I do say so myself. My mother bakes them for his grace every—"

"So where *did* his grace run off to so quickly this morning?"

Missy's gaze shot up from the basket, a grin of understanding breaking out across her wide mouth. "I'm sure I wouldn't know, my lady."

Viola almost kicked herself for her absolute stupidity. She wasn't testing the girl; she truly wanted the answer, *needed* the answer for all the complex reasons that escaped her at the moment, regardless of whether it was any of her business.

But in the end, his doings remained his matter or he would have told her himself. She wasn't a relation, his wife, his mistress, or even his obligation. He'd finished with her, obviously washed his hands of her, and now he just needed to see her packed up and taken home as soon as possible.

So, on that confusingly dismal thought, she grew silent, allowed herself to eat his—yes—delicious scones, to be dressed and primped by the Duke of Chatwin's maid in his fishing cottage, of all places, knowing his entire household would soon be privy to the account but would keep his mysterious, two-day liaison with the Lady Cheshire of London below stairs on his country estate. Probably.

In any case, the affair was over, and he had, at last, gotten what he had wanted all along. He would likely soon forget her as a sexual triumph and trophy won. A revenge complete.

She needed now to just get back to the routine of her own busy life—and do her best to try to forget that she'd ever met the bastard Ian Wentworth.

Chapter Eighteen

Hermione accused me of trying to help him escape today. I denied it, of course, but she has become suspicious of my visits now and threatens to tell Desi. He is ailing, and I must do all that I can to get him out of there. The masquerade is next week, and with a full house, I'm hoping to think of a plan to have him rescued so that nobody gets hurt.

Hold on, Ian. Help is coming. Please, my brave man, hold on. . . .

From the upstairs balcony, Ian stared down at the growing crowd, trying to remain inconspicuous before being formally announced at Lady Isabella Summerland's August soiree. Viola had already arrived, he knew, and although he had yet to see her, he watched with diligence, knowing he'd spot her instantly among the guests the second she took to the dance floor below.

It had been nearly three weeks since their intimate encounter, and in that time he'd thought of little else—

their passionate, if enlightening, conversations, the scent of her skin, her breathless sighs and moans of ecstasy, and the innocent beauty of her face when she'd slept. He'd watched her for a long while that morning before he'd left the cottage. His intent had been to stray from her side only long enough to arrange a warm breakfast for both of them before engaging her in another round of lovemaking, knowing he'd imprisoned her far too long and needed to take her home. But when he'd arrived at the house he'd received the note that had called him away so quickly and unexpectedly. He'd wanted to explain, but there hadn't been time. And now, as he'd finally arrived in London to discuss things with her and apologize for his hasty exit that morning, he had no idea how to approach her, or even what to say. Which was why he now found himself acting like an inexperienced schoolboy with jittery nerves, hiding behind the pillars above the dance floor just to have a look at her first.

Still, wondering if she thought about their last time together as much as he did kept him in the most suspense. He'd never in his life made love to a woman standing, having all the control, and with so much obsession and power and animalistic hunger. And every time he thought about how she had abandoned herself to his will and taken him, had accepted all of his hurt and anger, had permitted him to express his deepest emotions and compelling, confusing need for her in such a raw manner, his heart was truly soothed. At that moment Viola had totally understood him, had allowed him to show her a part of himself he'd hidden from everyone for five long years. And the most shocking thing of all was how now, after almost a month since he'd left her, instead of feeling sexually sated and proud of accomplishing his goal of humiliation and revenge, ready to rid himself of his past and move on with his life, all he could think of was how much he wanted to be with her again. Not like before, not brutally fast and with erotic domination, but slowly, in a soft, luxurious bed, making slow, passionate, meaningful love to her—something that probably meant different things to the two of them but *mattered* nonetheless. It was now very clear to him that his future remained just as tightly tied to the lovely Lady Cheshire as it was to the shy Miss Viola Bennington-Jones all those years ago. But, God help him, he had no idea what to do about it.

"Thought I'd find you up here all by yourself."

Ian half-smiled, thankful for the interruption of thoughts too complicated, though he didn't turn to look at his friend who slowly walked to his side.

"Evening, Fairbourne," he replied. "I despise these things."

Lucas sighed. "As do I."

"So why are you here?" Ian asked, moving a little to his right to give the man room to stand beside him.

Lucas leaned his elbows on the balcony and clasped his hands in front of him, peering over the edge to the scene below. "The same reason you are, I expect."

Ian almost snorted. "To fill your belly with Lady Tenby's food?"

Lucas chuckled. "You don't lie well, Chatwin."

"Well, I know you're not here for the dancing," Ian maintained, turning slightly to eye his friend askance.

"No, I'm here for the food," Fairbourne said, grinning. "Fired my French chef last week."

"Right," Ian retorted, glancing back to the dance floor. "You don't lie well, either."

"True enough," Lucas admitted. "I wanted to remind you I'm still waiting on payment for that painting I purchased for you at Brimleys."

God, the painting. He'd forgotten about that.

"How much?"

Fairbourne grinned wryly. "Plenty. But it is a beauty. You'd think I'd purchased an original Rubens the way society has been aflutter with gossip these last weeks, everyone wondering what it's worth, what I'd paid, if I'd sell, and of course, if you were the . . . uh . . . subject." He chuckled again, raking his fingers through his hair. "Had to hide it in my attic just to keep the staff from gaping then disappearing to fulfill their own fantasies."

Ian groaned and looked away, stretching his neck in a circle as he suddenly felt uncomfortable in his clothes. "I'll send someone for it next week, along with a bank draft."

Lucas cleared his throat. "Think you'll hang it?"

He snorted. "Maybe around Lady Cheshire's smooth and lovely neck."

"Funny," Fairbourne said through a chuckle, "I rather thought the good widow has been dragging you along for quite some time now with her lascivious paintings tied around your—"

"Don't say it, Fairbourne," Ian cut in, "or next month you'll find a nude portrait of you at auction." He tossed a grin to his friend. "The lovely widow can be easily persuaded to paint quickly and sell."

Lucas nodded once and gave in. "Always good to know, my friend."

A few moments of silence fell between them, then Lucas nodded toward the far doorway and murmured nonchalantly, "There she is, just entering."

Ian immediately focused on the north entrance, at first seeing nothing but a swirl of colorful skirts and blur of dandies attempting to make the perfect conversation to impress. And then, as if drawn by some inexplicable power, he spotted her, and his breath caught in his chest.

She looked radiant, dressed entirely in sea blue, her gown hugging a tightly drawn corset and tied at her left hip with a large cream-colored satin bow that matched the flounces of her skirt, her long silk gloves, and the wide brim of her hat. He couldn't see her hair or eyes, but he had no trouble identifying the line of her jaw and the lusciousness of her pink lips now tipped up in a rather seductive, playful smile.

Ian's pulse began to race as he felt his body break out in sweat. True, he was nervous, for reasons he more or less understood, but suddenly he was also quite furious when he realized she walked arm in arm with Miles Whitman, using that seductive smile on him like warm honey—warm, sweet honey flowing over crusty old bread.

All at once, inexplicably, nothing in his life made sense, nothing in his *head* made sense.

"You've been gone a long time," Lucas murmured, his tone thoughtful.

"Three weeks is not a long time," he charged in fast return, unable to take his eyes off Viola until she walked beneath the balcony and disappeared from view.

Lucas shrugged and stood upright again. "Maybe that's true. It's probably more accurate to say that a lot can change in a very short time."

Ian turned his complete attention to his friend, careful not to give anything away in his expression. "What are you trying to tell me, Fairbourne?" he asked cautiously.

Lucas held his steady gaze, pausing only long enough to gather his thoughts. "It seems Mr. Whitman has taken a fancy to Lady Cheshire."

"The gentleman has admired her for a time, as many do," Ian replied somewhat defensively. "So?"

Lucas reached up and scratched the back of his neck. "I've heard, however, that he has escorted her to every social event in the last three weeks, and that she's made it quite obvious to all that should he ask, she would accept his offer to become his wife."

Become his wife . . .

"That's absurd," Ian said in a gruff, near-whisper.

Lucas shook his head. "I don't think so."

Ian felt the world stop, as if he'd been living in some freak, horrific play that had just ended with tragedy, no satisfying resolution, no applause to come. And with its tragic ending came nothing but agony and strangeness and confusion for all who watched, all who participated. His mouth went dry; he couldn't move, couldn't breathe. Time simply stopped as the gods looked on and laughed at him in mocking silence.

And then everything reeled—the tumultuous clashing noise of the ballroom below, the loud pounding of his heart in his chest, the blood rushing through his veins. He heard laughter below and knew at once it wasn't the gods but his peers, snickering at him—his life and the joke it had become.

"Who told you this?" he asked at last, his voice quiet and remarkably steady.

Fairbourne studied him closely. "Lady Isabella mentioned it when I arrived about an hour ago."

Ian's eyes narrowed as his mind began to churn with questions. "Lady Isabella?"

"In fact," Fairbourne continued, his lips curling up slyly, "I believe she was waiting for me at the door. I can only surmise that she expected me to relay the news to you as soon as possible."

"To me," Ian repeated. He stiffened and inhaled deeply, shoving his fists in his pockets. Flatly, he asked, "And why do you suppose she'd expect that?"

Lucas nonchalantly pulled down on his cuffs. "Maybe Lady Cheshire's friends don't think a marriage to Mr. Whitman would be in her best interest. And if they're under the assumption he's going to propose soon, perhaps they're a bit . . . concerned."

"And do you suppose," Ian continued, his tone sardonic, "that they would think I'd be inclined to save her by proposing to her first?"

Fairbourne's eyes widened in a depth of surprise he couldn't hide. Then he laughed softly and shook his head. "I truly doubt it, Chatwin. I can't imagine there's a soul on earth who would think you'd have the least bit of interest in *marrying* Lady Cheshire, especially Lady Cheshire. Bedding her, certainly; taking her for a mistress, maybe. But never marriage. You've exposed her as a fraud and clearly despise her. At least . . . that's what you've led her and her friends to believe."

Which was probably the truth, as Ian considered it more fully. If she'd been any other scheming society miss, he could have believed they were all trying to coerce him into proposing to a woman he desperately wanted, just to keep her from marrying another. But not Viola. He'd never given her any indication he might consider pursuing her as a wife. In fact, everything he'd done since he'd come back into her life had supported just the opposite. He'd even said as much. She would never, in countless years, expect him to ask for her hand.

But Jesus . . . marriage to Miles Whitman? Just remembering how she had smiled seductively at the man moments ago, and the thought of Viola in bed with him, moaning as he touched her intimately, stroked her, aroused her, entered her . . .

Sweat broke out on his upper lip and he shakily wiped it away with the back of his hand. He felt nauseated of a sudden, desperate and thoroughly bewildered.

"So what in Christ's name do they think I'm supposed to do about it?" he grumbled, staring down at the dance floor again, seeing nothing.

"I've really no idea. You know how ladies plan things that make absolutely no sense."

"But—why now?" Ian asked, more to himself as he stared off into the distance. "And Miles Whitman? He's not titled, not wealthy, and she told me she's not interested in marrying again anytime soon."

Lucas stepped closer to him and lowered his voice to say carefully, "Maybe she needs to."

Ian felt his body grow cold; his eyes shot back to lock with Fairbourne's. "What are you implying?"

Lucas inhaled deeply and slipped his hands into the pockets of his jacket. "If you can't figure it out, or simply don't want to be bothered, you can always go back to the country and relish in the fact that if she's anxious for a husband, she must be desperate. Desperate women will marry even penniless men, those socially beneath them, or those for whom they hold absolutely no affection, which I suspect is the case with Whitman. If that is indeed what's happening, then you, my friend, should be very pleased. You can savor the fact that in the end you got the *ultimate* revenge."

With that, Fairbourne brushed by him and sauntered away.

It took Ian only ten minutes or so to find her in the crowd, sipping champagne as she stood next to a sideboard, huddled with several ladies, including the apparently conniving Lady Isabella. He needed to get Viola alone but decided it might help to break the ice between them if she was forced to be polite.

And so, with a deep breath in an attempt to calm his nerves, he straightened, pulled down on the edges of his waistcoat, and casually walked toward the gossiping group.

Lady Isabella noticed him first and stopped speaking in midsentence, her eyes opening wide in surprise.

He stopped directly behind Viola and clasped his hands behind his back. "Good evening, ladies," he drawled.

Viola whirled around at the sound of his voice, gaping at him, unable to hide her surprise in her pinkened cheeks. The others remembered their good breeding and curtseyed appropriately.

"Why—what are you doing here?" Viola stammered.

He almost smiled as he glanced around the ballroom. "It's a party, and I believe I was invited."

She tossed a glare at Isabella, who demurely shrugged and faintly shook her head.

He cleared his throat. "Lady Cheshire, may I have a word in private?"

He watched her bite her bottom lip and frown very slightly in hesitation, and for a second or two, he thought she might actually decline his invitation. But when her friends said nothing to dissuade her and refused to come to her defense, she realized she had no choice.

Planting a false smile on her lovely face, she nodded once. "As you wish, your grace."

"Please excuse us, ladies," he said, feeling a genuine sense of relief as he raised his elbow.

Avoiding his gaze, she gingerly placed her gloved palm on his forearm, and with that, he led her away from the safety of her companions and toward the south-facing, opened French doors.

"Where are you taking me?" she asked stiffly as they walked out onto the balcony.

"I thought a little fresh air and privacy would be nice," he replied after a moment.

"Nice for what?"

He sighed. "Must you always feel compelled to argue with me, Viola?"

To his great surprise, she didn't answer, though she

remained aloof and stiff in posture, keeping a fair distance from him as they walked side by side.

The cool breeze welcomed him, helped him breathe easier, relax a bit, concentrate on what he wanted to say, even though he really had no idea how to begin. She saved him the trouble by suddenly breaking free of his arm and moving quickly away to stand by the balcony wall.

"What do you want, Ian?" she asked cautiously, turning to look directly at him.

He paused in front of her and stuffed his hands in his coat pockets. After a slight pause for confidence, he murmured, "You look beautiful tonight."

She smiled wryly. "Thank you. But surely you didn't bring me outside to tell me that."

"No." He glanced out over the lawn below, noting footmen lighting torches as darkness began to fall. Then peering back into her eyes, his tone grew serious. "How are you?"

Her brows rose. "I'm very well, thank you."

Her politeness was beginning to irritate. "Stop being coy, Viola."

"What do you *want,* Ian?" she repeated, her own annoyance coating her words.

He took a step closer, staring down at her face. Finally, he said huskily, "I suppose I want to apologize."

That confession seemed to make her uncomfortable. She glanced away from him, shuffling from one foot to the other as she crossed her arms over her stomach.

"For which part?" she asked softly.

He thought about that for a moment, then decided to just be honest. "I'm probably most sorry that I left you in bed that final morning when all I wanted was to make love to you again."

If he'd expected her to sweetly succumb to his charm and truthful disclosure, he'd sorely miscalculated. Instead, she snickered caustically, raising the back of her gloved hand to cover her mouth as she did so.

He stiffened. "You find my honesty amusing, madam?"

She cleared her throat. "I'm sorry, your grace," she said, straightening and glancing around them to be certain they weren't overheard. Dropping her voice to a near-whisper, she added, "But really, of all the . . . questionable things you did to me in the course of two days, held hostage in your fishing shack—"

"Cottage."

She nodded once. "Cottage. Of all those things, you're apologizing for leaving me in bed that morning and not *making love* to me again?"

The manner in which she overpronounced the words, and the tremble in her lips, which she squeezed together to keep from laughing again, thoroughly deflated and embarrassed him. And experiencing such unexpected feelings where Viola was concerned, when he only wanted to explain himself, left him somewhat bewildered—and irritated beyond measure.

"Ian, please," she said through a sigh, cutting into his thoughts. "If you've nothing more to say—"

"Oh, I have plenty to say, Lady Cheshire," he drawled, attempting to recover his dignity before she left him to expose him to her friends as a foolish nitwit, or worse, a lovesick puppy—which he would be unable to deny without sounding ridiculous. He stepped even closer to her, fairly trapping her against the wall, drawing satisfaction in watching her merriment fade. "Do you know, this is the same balcony we stood in front of months ago, when we met again at a party just like this one and I asked you to paint my portrait?"

She said nothing, just eyed him nervously after casting a fast look over the wall and down to the lawn below.

"Even that night," he continued matter-of-factly, raising a hand to rub his chin with his fingers, "I felt the strangest attraction to you, Viola. I didn't at all understand how I could so thoroughly despise you, want to see you ruined both socially and financially, and yet on that evening suddenly feel the need to take you in my arms and kiss you passionately. It made no sense, and truly angered me, but I did want to kiss you then, and I was very much aware at the time that you were anxious for me to do it, too."

She faltered with that admission, blinking quickly as she began to wring her hands together in front of her stomach.

"And that's what I found even more uncanny," he continued in a husky whisper, watching her closely. "Beneath your nervousness and confusion at seeing me again, you radiated a very strong attraction to me."

She swallowed, seemingly mesmerized by his gaze. Then, recovering herself, she lowered her lashes and shook her head matter-of-factly.

"No, Ian, that's wrong. What you felt from me then was fear and desperation in knowing I'd been discovered. I also felt confused, true, because I didn't understand why you didn't recognize me, but that's all. Anything else is part of your imagination."

"You're lying, Viola," he said, ignoring the tinge of hurt at her passionate denial as he tossed a quick glance toward the ballroom. Then, looking back into her beautiful eyes, he squeezed his palms together in his pockets to keep from reaching out to her. "You cannot convince me that even now we don't desire each other. I feel it, and so do you."

She smiled snidely. "You're so arrogant, your grace. I don't *desire* you at all. Isn't that perfectly clear? Can't you just leave me alone, as I am attempting to do with you?"

"No."

That simple answer, spoken so quietly and quickly, caught her totally off guard. Even in the dusky glow of a late summer evening, he could see her body start to tremble.

"Have you thought about me these last few weeks?" he asked gently.

She looked away from him, rubbing her upper arms with her palms. "To be honest, I've been very busy. John Henry is back in town and—"

"Are you carrying my child, Viola?" he whispered.

She seemed to still before him, then very, very slowly turned to gaze at him once more, her eyes now wide and frightened, her skin suddenly pale.

"Is that why you're so anxious to marry Miles Whitman?" he added before she could offer an excuse of a reply. "Because you think you have to?"

He waited for what seemed like decades for her to answer, his heart pounding harder with each passing second. Finally, she straightened and dropped her arms to her sides, smoothing her skirts as if ready to walk away from him.

"That is not something I would even know yet, your grace," she said flatly. "Now if you'll excuse me—"

He reached out and grabbed her by the elbow, pulling her closer to him. "Then why suddenly plan to marry a man who does nothing to advance you socially or financially?" Lowering his voice to a whisper, he added, "I know you're not in love with him."

She gazed up into his eyes, her expression now taut with tightly controlled fury. "Why did you leave me in the cottage?"

The question took him aback. "That's not an answer. You're changing the subject."

"No, I'm not. It's *the* answer."

He didn't at all understand her female mind, and the more she evaded his very easily answerable questions, the more annoyed he became. Inhaling deeply to stay his temper, he replied, "I left for the reasons you were told, Viola."

Her brows rose as she looked him up and down. "You have exemplary servants, your grace. I wasn't told anything."

Very slowly, Ian released her elbow, as stunned by the admission as he was infuriated that his staff had neglected to inform her that he had not in fact left her to rot in bed and be shuffled home like a tramp after a drunken night's tryst. And to think that for nearly three weeks—

"Jesus, Viola, I'm sorry—"

"I'm not," she snapped, taking a step away from him. "Under the circumstances it's probably a very good thing they're so discreet. I'm home now, and it's forgotten. It's your business where you go—"

"You don't understand," he cut in, reaching up to rub the back of his neck with tense fingers. "My sister had gone into labor and there were complications. Her husband sent word to me, fearing she would die. Because I spent the night with you in the cottage, I didn't get the message from him till morning. By then I feared I was already too late and wanted to leave at once. I did, however, leave explicit instructions for you to be told the reason for my hasty departure." He shook his head, reaching out to touch her warm cheek with the back of a finger. "Please believe I would never just make love to you and leave you except in such a dire family emergency."

Although she didn't flinch from his touch, she did pull away from him slightly.

"What we did was not lovemaking, Ian."

"But it was intimate, and went beyond simple coupling," he replied softly. "You must admit that."

She didn't, just shifted her body nervously, glanced to the ballroom again.

"How is Lady Ivy?"

Through a sigh, he maintained, "Doing better. She and Rye have a son and now a healthy new daughter, so I don't know that they'll have more children. The birthing was very hard on her and she barely survived."

"I'm very glad to hear she did," Viola said wistfully. "I know what it's like to suffer like that. Thank God the baby is healthy."

He had forgotten her story of how she'd experienced such a difficult birth herself. Now that he knew she'd suffered delivering his son, thinking about it from such a perspective melted his heart a little. He actually had to stop himself from reaching out and drawing her against him.

In a deep, quiet voice, he returned to the most nagging point of all. "Why in God's name do you want to marry Miles Whitman? *Miles Whitman?*"

She looked back into his eyes, her gaze softened, though the crease in her brow revealed a tension within her he wished he understood.

In a voice filled with sadness, she replied, "Because you left me, Ian."

He rubbed his eyes briefly with his fingers and thumb, shaking his head. "I don't understand you."

Bitterly, she whispered, "Then you need to *think* about it, because you of all people *should* understand."

The fact that she talked in circles, on purpose, only managed to increase his irritation. For a moment it crossed his mind that she might be trying to make him jealous by allowing Whitman to court her openly, as any other lady in her position might, but that didn't make sense, either. She hadn't known he'd come back to the city, and there was no reason for her to think he'd have any interest in her romantically, especially the wild notion that he might ask for her hand when he learned of Whitman's—or any other gentleman's— interest. No, there was more involved here, something deeper and more complex, and she expected him to discover it without being told.

He stepped closer to her so that her gown swept around his lower legs. "You do realize, madam, that you'll be required to succumb to his needs."

Her eyes flashed in anger and she fisted her gloved hands at her sides. "And you must realize, your grace, that what I and my husband do privately is none of your business."

"True enough," he agreed soothingly, smiling slyly, "but I wonder if he'll know that when he takes you as his wife you'll be thinking of another man."

That infuriated her. He could see it in her eyes, in her tight expression and rigid form. For a moment, he suspected she might strike him.

Reaching up with his hand, he ran his forefinger across her bare shoulder. "Have you considered that, Viola? Did you think of me while I was away?"

She started shaking, though from rage or desire or fear, he couldn't guess.

Finally, in a raw voice charged with emotion, she disclosed, "I have thought of you every single minute of every day for the last five years, Ian. And just because I know it will cut you to the bone, I want to tell you this: Every single time Miles takes me as his wife, climbs into my bed and makes love to me, the memory of you will haunt me, even as I am willing and faithful to him as my husband whenever he needs me for intimacy. I can only hope that such a thought of me, lying naked and satiated in his arms, will haunt you, too—every day, every night, for the rest of your life."

Before he could begin to let those words sink in, she turned her back on him and walked away, her head held high, brushing him off with dignity and grace as a princess might dismiss a disgusting cad who tried to steal a kiss.

Her words haunted him now, only hours after she'd said them. In fact, just the slightest image of Viola in bed with Miles Whitman, or truthfully, any man, distressed him so thoroughly that he could only conclude the damn woman had put him under some kind of female, sexual spell. Or something of the kind. But he couldn't deny any longer that thinking about her in the arms of another man made him crazy, and she apparently knew it, which made him irritable. But in the end it didn't matter. He refused to see her wed to Miles Whitman—unless Miles Whitman would prove to be an excellent husband and father to her son. At least that's what he told himself. And so in the interest of learning the man's intentions, he forced himself to stay at the party much longer than he'd intended and discover what he could from the man himself.

The crowd in the ballroom had thinned as midnight had approached. Most of the ladies had retired, including Viola more than two hours ago, and most of the gentlemen were in the smoking room or near the sidebar and buffet, stoking their inebriation and filling their stomachs. He'd watched Miles fairly cling to Lord Tenby, their host, for the last forty-five minutes, and had considered interrupting to call the man out to the patio for discussion, but he didn't want to seem obvious for Viola's sake. Or, perhaps more honestly, for his own sake, should he fail in his endeavor to learn the level of intimacy between the two of them. But at last Tenby managed to make his own escape, and Whitman, hands stuffed into his coat pockets, strolled toward the balcony entrance, giving Ian his first opportunity to corner the man alone.

A misty rain had starting falling, both chilling and freshening the air, and Ian drew a deep breath to clear his head for the conversation to come. He followed Whitman toward the same railing where he and Viola had conversed just hours before, strolling up to stand beside the man as he peered down to the garden below.

"Good evening, Whitman," he said casually.

The older gentleman whirled around, a look of genuine surprise sweeping across his portly face. "Good evening, your grace," he said with a nod, patting down on his waistcoat. "Fancy meeting you on the balcony at midnight."

Ian couldn't read the man's disposition after he recovered his bearing, or whether he meant to be derisive by his statement. Frankly, he'd never thought Miles Whitman clever enough for sarcasm and underlying meaning, humorous or otherwise.

"Thought I might have a private word, and so I followed you out, actually," Ian replied, deciding to get directly to the point. Wasting time chatting about the rain or other nonsense with a museum curator seemed most unappealing at the moment.

Whitman smiled flatly—a smile Ian assumed he used officially when dealing with pesky business transactions and those who annoyed him. "Of course, Lord Chatwin, I am at your service," he said with another slight nod.

Ian rubbed his chin with his palm, thinking. Or at least wanting to give that impression. "Of course, as gentlemen I don't have to mention that anything said confidently between us will be kept as such."

Whitman frowned so deeply that his eyebrows became one thick line across his forehead. "Oh, absolutely, your grace. I'm sure you know my prominence in the art world wouldn't be what it is today without my solid reputation for discretion."

"Of course," Ian agreed, again wondering if Whitman meant to be intentionally snide or if he was just a man who had expertly learned how to pacify the aristocracy. In any case it didn't matter. He needed to get to the point, remembering that he had the advantage in knowing things about Viola this man did not and never would.

"Mr. Whitman," he began, looking at the man frankly, "I learned this evening that you might be considering asking Lady Cheshire for her hand in marriage. Is this true?"

Whitman's mouth dropped open slightly and then closed again as his eyes narrowed suspiciously. "I'm sorry, your grace, but that's . . . I really don't think that's any of your concern."

Ian hadn't expected such an arrogant response, but he didn't let it faze him. Leaning an elbow on the balcony rail, he gazed out across the lawn below. "And yet, the fact that I raise the issue should mean that it is a concern."

Whitman chuckled. "Why is that, your grace?"

Again, Ian found himself stumped by the man's shrewd attitude, especially considering their difference in station. Shrugging nonchalantly, he replied, "I guess the only reason I mention it is because Lady Cheshire's friends were discussing it earlier this evening and it surprised me. I thought perhaps I'd ask you myself."

"Her friends? Lady Tenby's daughter?" Whitman asked stiffly.

Ian brushed over clarification as he looked back at the man. "Is it true?"

Whitman drew in a long breath and attempted to puff out his chest. "I am considering it, your grace, if you must know. But only because Lady Cheshire seems . . . quite willing to accept an offer should I decide to propose."

"I see." Ian tapped his fingertips on the railing. "I never realized you had just an affection for Lady Cheshire. At least not deeply enough to propose marriage."

Whitman laughed. "I have a deep and abiding affection for Lady Cheshire and her . . . assets, shall we say."

Ian didn't know whether to be intrigued or appalled. "Assets? You mean financial?"

Whitman patted down the top of his oiled head, eyeing him speculatively as his laughter gradually faded. "Come now, your grace, you and I both know there is more to marriage than doting companionship as one ages. Where Lady Cheshire is concerned, I will no doubt enjoy her good devotion in the marriage bed, just as I will expect her undivided attention at the museum." He smiled. "And as an educated and . . . worldly gentleman, I'm certain you're aware of how her late husband's good name can help us acquire pieces we might not have been able to before. And then there is his private collection, which will no doubt be a fabulous asset to the museum, or the auction house should we decide to sell."

He frowned in the darkness. "Private collection?"

Whitman paused as if unsure how much to reveal,

then said, "Lady Cheshire's private artwork. I'm sure you're aware her late husband left her with a substantial income from the priceless pieces he collected through the years."

Ian nodded, attempting to appear unruffled while a cascade of alarming thoughts began to flood his mind. He had no idea if the late Baron Cheshire had collected any art beyond Viola's prized and secret erotic work, or if Whitman knew something about Viola's finances he didn't. But trying to imagine Viola giving Miles Whitman access to her fortune as she willingly gave him access to her beautiful body made Ian's skin crawl. He just wasn't sure now what to do about it when he really had no right to do anything. If Viola truly wanted the man for a husband, he couldn't very well stop her from accepting a proposal from him. And he could think of no reason on earth how he might talk Miles Whitman out of a marriage to Viola when Viola had nearly everything an untitled man could want in a wife. Nor was it Ian's place to do so, unless all Whitman really wanted was her fortune. In such a case, Ian could probably talk himself into believing he was honor bound to save her from just such a union because he'd learned of it. He wouldn't want to see an innocent widow robbed blind.

"So, I assume you've discussed this arrangement with Lady Cheshire," he stated rather than asked, keeping his gaze on the lawn below.

Whitman sighed. "A bit, I suppose, especially during the last fortnight or so since I've seen her fairly frequently. It's an excellent match between us, really, and she couldn't agree more."

The last fortnight. She'd been purposely allowing him to court her for a fortnight. Why? Why, why, *why*?

Because you left me, Ian. . . .

"Did you expect to hang the baron's private collection in the museum?" he asked, thinking furiously.

Whitman cleared his throat. "Some of it, especially the respectable artwork. But I'm sure there will be pieces, including any other Bartlett-James works, that will need to be sold."

That explained it all. Ian couldn't be certain whether Whitman knew Viola was the famed erotic artist—in fact, he probably did not, as there wasn't any way for him to discover her secret short of her telling him. But he either knew or suspected she had other items, sketches and paintings to sell at auction, which would be the key to his financial gain through marriage. Or so he thought.

"What makes you think she has others?" Ian asked cautiously.

The older man smirked. "Lady Cheshire has acknowledged that her late husband had long been a fan of Bartlett-James and his work, and being a collector of fine artwork in general, one can only assume she has several excellent pieces."

"But, Mr. Whitman," Ian said, his voice lowered with feigned concern, "if that be the case, aren't you a bit worried that the . . . unconventional artwork Lady Cheshire mentioned might be forged? You were there at the small gathering in my home where the sketch she sold me was . . . exposed."

Whitman stared at him starkly, his jaw set rigidly as he pulled a pipe from the breast pocket of his evening jacket and tapped it lightly on the railing.

"Your grace, I may not be of your class, but I am an educated man, especially where good art is concerned," he replied with thick enunciation. He chuckled again knowingly, then remarked, "We both know the sketch you presented at your party was, in fact, an original Victor Bartlett-James."

Ian tensed, feeling his stomach tighten into a knot of repulsion. Miles Whitman was indeed clever, and knew exactly how every word he spoke would be taken. He might not be an unsatisfactory husband for a lady, but he would never prove to be a trustworthy one. And he would never be deserving of Viola.

"Did you realize the sketch was original at the time?" Ian asked as an idea began to quickly formulate.

Whitman shrugged. "I suspected as much. I know there seemed to be a good deal of tension between you and Lady Cheshire. And the fact that you purchased it, then had it authenticated by an Englishman whom even I, in my profession of twenty years, had never heard of, in front of your peers, seemed a bit . . . odd, shall we say?"

Odd, indeed. And as Ian thought about it in retrospect, terribly unfair to her, when she had done nothing at the time to deserve such sudden, unflattering exposure. He understood now why he'd never truly enjoyed that evening, and how revenge ultimately disgraces the honorable.

After exhaling a full breath, he said, "You are correct, Whitman. You are an educated man and I congratulate you on discovering something I'd hoped would remain confidential. For Lady Cheshire's sake, of course. And since we both care about her continued excellent reputation, I expect you to keep this matter between us this evening."

That outright compliment followed by more mystery stumped the man. He blinked; his brows twitched.

Ian shoved his hands in his pockets again and looked at his feet, crushing beneath the sole of his shoe a nighttime insect that had once dared to crawl across a darkened patio.

"Yes, the sketch is original," he explained, his voice filled with deep concern, "and I purchased it, in good faith. And that's when I learned the truth about Lady Cheshire and her husband's assets. Before the party, I had my solicitor contact hers, a Mr. Leopold Duncan, to discover if Lady Cheshire actually owned the piece or if, as I wondered, it belonged to her husband's estate." He smiled bleakly. "A buyer of such an extravagant and expensive piece of art cannot be too careful."

Whitman shifted his large stature on the patio, clearly agitated and suddenly uncertain. He tapped his pipe on the railing again, though he never reached for tobacco to fill it, just let it hang at his side.

"We're both gentlemen," Ian continued, "so you'll understand why I, as a gentleman, chose to arrange for someone to declare the sketch a forgery, deciding it would be better to expose Lady Cheshire with a light rebuke than have someone learn she sold property she does not own. She could have been jailed for fraud."

Ian watched Whitman closely. Although the torches remained lit in the garden below, and the lights still blazed from the ballroom to their right, the darkness surrounding them still made it difficult for him to gauge the man's expression. But he did notice him squeezing the pipe in his hand repeatedly.

Whitman didn't understand. And he was too arrogant to admit it.

Seconds later Whitman forced another chuckle and shook his head, apparently recovering his pomposity.

"I'm sorry, your grace," he said as he reached up to rub his neck with his palm, "but I don't see what your dinner party and one lone Bartlett-James sketch has to do with my marriage to Viola."

The fact that he used the lady's given name while touting an upcoming marriage as if it was a given event implied an intimacy meant to challenge Ian's claim of knowing Viola and her intentions more. It was a calculated statement, evoking jealousy and possessiveness, and they both knew it.

Keeping his raw anger in check, Ian merely stared at the man as if he'd been an idiot.

"Mr. Whitman," he disclosed gravely, "Lady Cheshire has no artwork to sell. Her late husband left his entire estate and all of his wealth to his son. She receives a stipend each month, an excellent amount according to her solicitor who oversees it, to pay her dressmaker and purchase other small female sundries she might need." He paused, then ran his fingers through his hair. "Naturally I wouldn't know such . . . personal information had I not investigated the Bartlett-James sketch, and naturally up until this moment, I've told no one. It's not a gentleman's business to pry into the financial status of a widow who is not a relation. But in this unusual case her solicitor, who would normally be silent on such a matter, agreed that Lady Cheshire could be putting her good name and reputation in danger. I only exposed her the night of her party to protect her. She may have been embarrassed and looked foolish, but looking foolish is a far cry from being socially disgraced, or worse, arrested."

"This is preposterous," Whitman said, swallowing hard. "Why would Lady Cheshire take such a risk? I cannot believe it."

Ian shook his head, frowning. "Why do ladies do anything? They're all quite frivolous, I'm sure you know. And maybe up until that time she wasn't aware of her limitations. Perhaps after my party, when she learned she couldn't sell the sketch, she decided a marriage to you would help her in her ability to sell her still-life paintings and family portraits, or perhaps hang them in your modern history museum? In that regard, it makes perfect sense why she's suddenly thought of you as a good match and is considering marriage to you now. Aside from her monthly stipend, Lady Cheshire is practically penniless."

The air seemed to crackle between them, and for a second or two, Ian thought Whitman might strike him. Or attempt to. The man's entire body had gone as rigid as stone. Even his pipe looked as if it might be crushed inside his suddenly tight fist.

But Ian's calculation worked. Whitman looked furious, confused, and had no idea what to say, or do. He also knew he had no manner at his disposal to prove the truth behind Ian's claims. Her solicitor wouldn't speak, Viola would be livid, but even if she denied it, the man could never be sure of the situation until after they'd spoken their vows. Her title meant nothing to him aside from having a titled wife, and if she had no fortune, he could ultimately be saddled with not only her brat to raise but also her debt—and a London town house full of glorious artwork he would be forced to admire every day but from which he could never profit.

Suddenly, marriage to Lady Cheshire seemed unpalatable to Miles Whitman. Ian could read it in his hardened expression, see it in his piercing gaze. And because he felt no real love for Viola, realized he might only have her own trivial artwork to sell, this new revelation that she might be using *him* for gain settled the deal for him. Her paintings of still life and sketches of puppies wouldn't pay for his shoes.

"Well," Whitman said, his tone raspy, "I appreciate such candid information, your grace, and naturally it will remain between us. Now if you'll excuse me, I remember telling Lord Tenby I'd meet him for cards at half past twelve, and I wouldn't want to keep him."

Then, without waiting for a reply, Whitman nodded stiffly, brushed by Ian, and walked once more toward the ballroom.

Chapter Nineteen

The party is tomorrow night. Somehow I will see him rescued, even if I have to defy my family and destroy my future. I cannot let him die. He means too much to me now. . . .

$\mathcal{V}$iola waited as patiently as she thought humanly possible for the Duke of Chatwin to greet her in his stunning green salon. She was trying not to fidget or cry, tears not of sadness but of anger and frustration, and even a bit of fear for what she was about to do. She'd come to his home unexpectedly today, hoping to catch him by surprise, but instead he'd kept her waiting for nearly twenty minutes, no doubt purposely, as it was his nature to torture her with agitation at every step.

She stared out the long windows to the green garden beyond. Although it was still early afternoon, pouring rain obscured the view, as it had all day, the miserable weather matching her mood and what she feared might now be a dismal future.

"Viola."

She turned abruptly at the sound of his voice, as surprised that she hadn't heard his footsteps from the hallway as she was at the intimate manner in which he softly said her name. He stood leaning against the doorway, watching her candidly, arms crossed casually over his chest, the expression on his handsome face one of soft speculation. She couldn't begin to guess how long he'd been standing there before he'd revealed himself, and the thought made her stomach flutter, her skin tingle.

"Your grace," she replied, offering him a curtsey as she forcefully tempered her nerves. "I didn't hear you come in. I hope I'm not troubling you."

The side of his mouth ticked up in mild amusement as he stood upright and sauntered into the room. "Not at all." His gaze traveled up and down the length of her. "You look well."

Heat suffused her cheeks, but she ignored it. "Thank you. As do you," she returned properly, noting how he didn't look just healthy; he looked marvelously handsome in casual navy trousers and a light gray shirt unbuttoned at the neck, the sleeves rolled up to his forearms. And although God might strike her down for vanity, she suddenly felt rather thankful she'd chosen to wear her low-cut plum gown and a tightly waisted corset for this meeting. At least she felt better prepared for battle dressed in something she thought would please him visually.

"So what can I do for you today?" he asked as he strode toward her side.

She straightened, bravely holding his gaze. "This is not a pleasant social call."

He exhaled a long breath. "Well, after our encounter at Lord Tenby's ball last week, receiving a pleasant social call from you had not occurred to me."

He stood so close to her now that even the faint traces of his cologne disconcerted her. Shaking herself, she stepped away from him as nonchalantly as possible and walked to the other side of the room to stand behind one of the brown leather wing chairs. Turning to face him, she placed her palms on the back of it for comfort.

With fearless determination, pulse racing, she said, "Ian, I want you to tell me exactly what you said to Mr. Whitman that made him decide I would make an unworthy wife."

For seconds he didn't say anything. Then he tipped his head to the side a fraction and asked cautiously, "What makes you think I said anything?"

A flash of anger sliced through her. "Destroying my life is a game to you, isn't it?"

He seemed to think about that for a moment, then, dropping his arms to his sides, he replied, "Viola, no matter what I say to you in answer, you wouldn't believe it."

She swallowed. "That's probably the most honest thing you've *ever* said to me."

He almost smiled. Soberly, he admitted, "If it's truth you want, then it's true I came to the city, back into your life, to destroy it."

Her heart lurched and her throat tightened with the sudden raw emotion of hearing it.

"But that's not what I want for you now," he continued in a husky near-whisper. "Believe it or not, you've taught me a lot about myself in these last few weeks, and whether I recognize why I do certain things, I do know I care about your future. I just . . . didn't want to see you married to Miles Whitman."

"It's none of your business who I marry," she said, squeezing the back of the chair, "much less whether I choose to do so or not."

"That's true," he admitted.

"So why did you involve yourself in something that's not your concern?" she asked after seconds of incredulity.

He ran a palm down his face. "I can't answer that right now."

She shook her head and shrugged a shoulder. "Or perhaps you're lying about everything. How would I know at this point?"

His eyes narrowed as he regarded her closely. "I'm trying to be honest with you, Viola. But there are some things between us that need discussing, that we need to resolve. It won't help if you can't believe me when I tell you that being with you again has helped me clearly see that destroying your future won't change my past. Or make me happy."

Her lips thinned in disgust. "None of this is about you except where you enjoy the power you've had in changing my future to destroy any security or happiness I may have found with Mr. Whitman."

He smirked. "I think we both know you wouldn't have found any happiness married to the man."

She narrowed her eyes to glare at him. "So is that why you disclosed to Mr. Whitman that I am Victor

Bartlett-James? Because you care so much about my *happiness*?"

His entire face went slack. "I told him no such thing."

She would not be undaunted. "He said he knows the sketch I sold you was an original, and that he can't possibly court a lady who cannot be trusted to know her place where the sale of good art is concerned."

Ian chuckled, and she nearly picked up the lamp at her side to throw at his handsome face.

"You find that funny? He could tell anyone—"

"He knows nothing," he soothed as he came even closer.

"What did you say to him, Ian?" she asked again.

"Sit down and I'll tell you," he ordered.

She didn't move, just clasped her hands in front of her, keeping her gaze locked with his.

"Please," he said, pointing to the sofa as he softened his request.

Reluctantly, she stepped in front of it and lowered her body onto the cushion with grace, fluffing out her skirts around her legs and feet more out of habit than need. As she feared, he sat beside her, though thankfully keeping himself at a respectable distance. She waited, her body stiff, hands in her lap, watching him, smelling his cologne again, wanting very badly of a sudden to reach forward and touch his face.

"I spoke with Whitman," he admitted quietly, eyeing her closely, "not only because your friends were concerned about him, but because a marriage to him seemed oddly timed—"

"That's none of your business," she cut in, irritated.

He raised an arm and laid it flat across the back of the sofa. "None of my business, true, and yet I care."

She shook her head fractionally, confused. "Care so much that you destroy my reputation?"

"I did no such thing." He sighed, then said, "Miles Whitman admitted without any reservation that he intended to marry you for your art collection, mostly to sell. He wanted you only for financial gain, Viola. I merely told him all the artwork he thought you owned actually belongs to your son. He knew the sketch was original because he knows good art, that's all. He doesn't know you're the artist Bartlett-James, at least not from anything I told him."

Viola continued to gaze into his lovely eyes, seeing no deception, yet perfectly aware he could be keeping details from her for his own benefit.

"You had absolutely no right to step in like that, Ian."

He blinked. "The man wanted to marry you for your fortune. He was quite honest about his purpose."

"Perhaps such a fact is irrelevant to me," she shot back, eyes flashing. "It's not your place to interfere with my future. I didn't interfere when you said you were anxious to court Lady Anna, a lady who, by the way, is absolutely wrong for you in every regard."

"Is she," he stated rather than asked.

Feeling a sudden rush of heat to her cheeks, she quickly countered, "But, again, it's not my place to determine your needs in a wife. Who you choose is your business."

"Ah." He cleared his throat. "Well, just so we're clear on the matter, I never had any intention of courting, or marrying, Lady Anna," he revealed, tone lowered. "I admit that implying an interest was a means to get to you. But even if I'd found her remotely engaging, she cannot compare to your elegance, your wit, and level of passion. She is, as you say, absolutely wrong for me in every regard."

Viola squirmed a little in her stays, finding his honestly compelling yet totally unable to grasp his ultimate purpose. Her female instincts urged her to ask what he thought of her wit, elegance, and level of passion, as if they mattered horribly, but her sensible nature won the battle.

"I don't understand you," she said, returning to the point. "You have no intention of marrying me, have even explicitly stated that you'd rather see me dead than take your name, and yet you purposely interfere in my life to deny me a marriage to a man of my choosing." She threw her arms out in wonder. "Do you still think to keep me as your mistress? Is bedding me at your whim the underlying impetus behind your desire for control? Do you think I have no say in such a matter?"

His brows furrowed slightly and he hesitated. For a moment it seemed to her that he actually looked torn by indecision. Then he sighed softly and reached out for her hand, taking it into his own and caressing her fingers as he looked down at them.

"That was a truly horrible thing to say to you, Viola," he whispered huskily. "Please know that I spoke so rudely from anger and a misunderstanding of your intent at the time. I didn't actually believe what I said." He drew a sharp breath and looked back into her eyes. "I have no desire to control you, either, but for reasons that baffle me, I do want to be with you. I just don't know what that means yet."

She felt a stirring within of her own sorrow and regrets, wanting to believe him wholeheartedly because his voice and words expressed nothing but honest confusion and remorse. Still, even with such a heartfelt apology, he had yet to explain his manipulation of her future with any understanding she could grasp.

"Now it's time for total honesty from you," he said, cutting into her thoughts.

In nervous response, she tried to discreetly pull her hand from his, to no avail as he moved his palm to her wrist and gripped it.

"I would like to know," he continued slowly, holding her gaze, "why you once said, not too long ago, that you have little desire to marry again, and yet only weeks after that statement, you pursued with vigor the opportunity to marry Miles Whitman?"

A trace of terror sliced through her. She remembered their conversation in her studio, how she'd tried to be so vague about her past *and* her future, not realizing how intently he'd listened to her babbling and would one day request her to answer for it. But she had no intention of revealing too much now. It could only make matters worse.

With dignity, she stood. "It doesn't matter, though if you must know, I simply changed my mind. Ladies do it all the time."

His cheek twitched in a half smile. "True," he agreed, raising his body to stand beside her, though keeping her at arm's length by refusing to release her wrist. "But I want you to tell me, without prevarication, what *happened* to change your mind."

She swallowed back tears of frustration, refusing to look away from his challenging gaze. "So you can mock me?"

"So I will know what's in your heart."

Melting within, she relented. "*You* happened, Ian."

His eyes widened minutely, as if he didn't quite believe she offered him that truth so simply. And then his expression clouded, and, quite unexpectedly, he reached up and ran his thumb very gently over her lips. She shivered and lowered her head.

"We're an odd pair, aren't we?" he said seconds later, his voice silky, reflective. "I want to rid you from my mind and I can't stop thinking of you. You are happily widowed, but I come back into your life and you suddenly want to marry a man you don't love or desire or need for any reason, a man who wants only your fortune, just to rid yourself of me."

"Ian, stop. It's more complicated than that."

"I agree, but I can't stop," he whispered. Slowly he began to rub his thumb across her wrist in feathery strokes. "I know there is something missing between us, but I'm unsure of what it is. Sometimes I think we both long for each other but we're afraid of it and what acting on it might do to us. Our history together stems from a thing so wretched. Sometimes I think bedding you again is the answer, but I know it will only leave me wanting more, and in the end the void will still be black, and the nights lonely."

She tried to pull away again, but instead of releasing her, he wrapped his free arm around her waist and drew her against his hard body.

"But the one thing I want most, Viola," he whispered, leaning in to nuzzle her ear, "is to see you happy, to hear you laugh, not from sarcasm or anxiousness, but from joy. I have dreams of it, maybe memories of it. I don't know. But since I've come back into your life, I have never once heard you laugh from sheer happiness, and nothing, right now, haunts me more."

He began dropping tiny kisses onto her neck, running his lips along the delicate skin, and her legs went weak. He must have expected her to crumble against him, because he seemed to be bearing her weight suddenly as his lips found hers.

She couldn't resist should she try. Being with Ian felt like joy in the morning, and never had it been so sweet and precious as it felt right now. He kissed her with a mixture of passion and tenderness, urgent desire and gentle need, his tongue teasing softly, his fingers brushing her cheek as if he found her priceless to his touch. And when at last she moaned softly and whispered his name against his lips, he pulled away, resting his forehead against hers for several long moments before leaving soft kisses on her brow, her lashes and nose and cheeks.

"You're so beautiful, and soft. . . ."

She whimpered, uncertainty filling her as she gently pushed against his chest. "I have to leave, Ian," she said shakily.

Through a low sigh he relented, gradually releasing her.

A feeling of deep loneliness enveloped her when he

finally let her go. Unable to look at him, she tipped her head toward the wall next to the doorway. "I brought your portrait, completed and, I think, an excellent likeness." Drawing a long breath for confidence, she added, "And I wanted you to know that John Henry and I are going to be leaving the city soon."

When he didn't say anything to that, she finally raised her lashes and dared to look into his eyes. He studied her intently, his face still flushed from their kiss, his eyes still smoldering beautifully, and it took all that was in her not to throw herself into his arms again.

Slowly he straightened and formally clasped his hands behind his back, his features growing hard. "Where are you going?"

She swallowed every torrential emotion that threatened to surface. "First to Cheshire for the winter. After that, I don't know, though perhaps somewhere on the Continent."

"I see." Seconds later he asked, "May I ask why?"

Trying to sound brave and matter-of-fact, she said, "With this portrait finished, I have no other financial obligations here, and John Henry needs to be in the country where he can ride and play and thrive in greater space. And to be perfectly honest, your altering of my future by ruining the chance of a perfectly good marriage for me is the last battle I want between us. I've come to tell you I surrender, Ian. You have won the war."

"I haven't won anything," he maintained in sudden, quiet fury, "if you take my son away before I even meet him."

That statement, uttered in such heartfelt anguish,

melted her to the bone. And perhaps because of all they'd shared so recently, perhaps because she'd always cared so deeply for him for reasons she'd never fully understood, this time she truly sensed his hurt and couldn't bring herself to deny it.

Lowering her lashes to avoid his penetrating gaze, she turned her back on him and walked out of his gorgeous green salon for a final time, his sweet kiss still lingering on her lips, the memory of which she hoped would last a lifetime.

Chapter Twenty

I am very frightened, for both of us. I am three weeks
late for my monthlies, and now fear I carry his child.
Everything right now seems so bleak, though I am
praying for his rescue as I leave for the masquerade
ball. Please, God, be with us both this night.
    It is time....

After days of overcast skies and generally dreary
weather that matched her mood, the sun shone brightly
upon waking this morning, and Viola decided she
would take John Henry to the park with the nanny. It
would do them both good to get some sunshine and
fresh air, and getting the opportunity to sketch for the
first time in ages might take her mind off her troubles.

She didn't want to leave the city, or England. Frankly,
she didn't want to leave Ian, but she couldn't deny the
anxiety he roused just knowing the power he had over
her when it came to her son. But it would all soon be
in the past. This morning, she vowed, with the chill of
autumn in the air, and the warmth of the sun on her

face, her life stood on the verge of beginning anew and she would enjoy it.

Viola sat on a wooden bench, watching John Henry play with several other children near the sandbox. Thankfully plenty of other mothers and nannies had taken advantage of the beautiful day and ventured out as well, allowing her the opportunity to just sit and watch and enjoy the quiet moment by herself.

She couldn't help but smile when she watched her son play. In many ways he took after her, especially with his creative mind, the manner in which he thought about the world, and his very talkative nature. But in other ways, primarily physical mannerisms, there could be no doubt he was Ian's child. Every time her son became angry about something his brows would pinch together and he would scowl at her with his head tilted in exactly the same angle his father did, his hands in tight fists at his sides. When he grinned, she could see the same dimple in his left cheek, and when he contemplated something she said that he didn't understand, his forehead would crinkle and he would stare at her as if she had no brain. And they both had the same small, key-shaped birthmark high on their left thigh.

There were times like this when she would grow melancholy and dream of a different life, where Ian raised his son and loved her and married her and they lived a life full of differences of opinion, joy, and surprises.

And then reality would interfere with her daydreams, as it did now, when John Henry began crying and stomping his feet, tugging on a shovel as he fought with two small girls for possession.

"Would you like me to rescue them?"

The sound of Ian's voice from behind her so shocked her that she gasped aloud and jumped from the bench, turning quickly to face him, gaping, heart pounding.

He stood leaning against a tree, dressed casually in a cream-colored linen shirt and brown trousers, his arms crossed over his chest, hair tousled from the light breeze.

He smiled at her mischievously, almost . . . intimately, scrutinizing every feature, every curve, as if seeing her for the first time.

Suddenly she felt hot color flood her cheeks, and she crossed her arms over her breasts in mild self-protection.

"How long have you been standing there?" she asked defensively, her voice raspy.

He shrugged. "For a time."

"A *time*?" She glanced worriedly at John Henry, who had managed to strip the girls of the shovel but now didn't care about it as he stared curiously at Ian.

"Are you following me?" she asked, looking back into Ian's eyes.

"A man can't stroll through the park on a beautiful day?" he countered, pulling himself upright and moving closer to her.

She stood her ground. "Forgive me, your grace, but you weren't strolling."

"Ah, quite right, Lady Cheshire," he agreed as he stopped in front of her. "But I was enjoying the view."

Her brows rose. "Of the back of my head?"

His smile faded as he lowered his voice. "Of that, and watching my son play in the dirt and flirt with girls for the very first time."

A certain fear gripped her, causing her to sway on her feet, look nervously over her shoulder toward John Henry again, rub her arms with her palms.

"It's all right, Viola," he said soothingly. "I'm not here to interfere."

"Why are you here?" she asked as her nervousness rose. John Henry began to skip in their direction.

"Last time we spoke you said you were moving to the Continent," he replied, watching the boy approach. "Is this still a consideration?"

Viola could feel her heart pounding hard in her chest. Her mouth had gone dry as her nerves had caught fire, and every instinct she possessed as a mother told her to grab her son and run. Instead, curiosity won for the moment and she remained composed, licking her lips before replying, "Yes, why?"

Ian nodded, unable to take his eyes off the child as he hopped to her side and wrapped his arms around her thickly skirted legs.

"Well, before you leave," he said in a rather faraway voice, "you'll need to address the problem with my formal portrait, Lady Cheshire."

She stared at him, uncertain, confused, and now, without warning, experiencing the greatest fear in her life she'd sworn to avoid—the moment Ian would meet his son. And she could think of absolutely nothing to say.

Ian raised his gaze, and then his brows, in stark question. "Are you going to introduce us?"

She didn't know if she should feel manipulated and furious, or thrilled and relieved. But with a mock smile, she replied, "John Henry? May I introduce Lord Chatwin. Use your manners, please."

The boy peeked out from her skirts. "See porting?"

She playfully rubbed his head, the smile on her face turning to a genuine grin. "He thinks he is."

Ian looked from one to the other. "Porting?"

"He asked if you're important."

"Ah." Ian held out his hand. "And who are you?"

Shyly, the boy glanced up to her for direction, and with a nod she gently urged him on. "John Henry, Lord Chatwin is a very important gentleman. What are you supposed to do?"

Seconds later the boy put his little hand in Ian's, shook once, and bowed stiffly. "I'm John Henry Cresswald, Baron Cheshire, and someday I will be porting, too."

"I see," Ian muttered, amused. "Well, then, Lord Cheshire, I am very pleased to meet someone of your prestige."

He looked up at her. "Whas a pesteege?"

Smiling, she clarified, "*Pres*-tige. To be very prestigious is to be very important."

John Henry giggled, then released Ian's hand and flipped his body over, planting his head on the grass to view the world upside down.

Ian looked at her curiously. She shrugged. "He does that, I'm afraid. He's only just five, you know."

"Yes, I know."

For several long seconds he gazed starkly into her eyes, until she shook herself and returned to the moment. "So, forgive me, your grace, but what is this about a problem with the portrait?"

Brows furrowed, he drew in a long breath and crossed his arms over his chest. "Well, although it's an excellent likeness, as you said, it seems the colors are completely wrong and . . . not what I had hoped. The hues don't match the decor of the room in which I'd like to hang it."

She gaped at him. "I beg your pardon?"

He dropped his gaze to John Henry, watching the boy as he suddenly jumped twice, then ran back to the sandbox.

"I'm sure you realize, Lady Cheshire," he explained, shifting his attention to her once more, "that I paid a great deal of money for the portrait and expect it to meet with my approval."

"You—you want me to paint another portrait because you're dissatisfied with the color hues, shades of which, I might add, you initially approved?"

He shrugged with total innocence. "If that's what it takes. We could start tomorrow if you like, at say . . . ten o'clock?"

Never in her life had Viola been so utterly outraged by what she considered a direct attempt to bait her. The color was entirely satisfactory, and the portrait as a whole lovely. She'd even considered keeping it for herself and painting him another so that she could have something to glance at when she worked in her studio each day. The only reason she'd decided against such a notion had had as much to do with her own heartache as it had with the knowledge that as John Henry aged, he, and anyone else who happened to catch a glimpse, might wonder at the resemblance. It would simply be too much.

But this ridiculous concern of his seemed nothing more than another tactic to unsettle and wound her. And she'd had about all of the inner turmoil she could take from the Duke of Chatwin.

"Why are you doing this, Ian?" she murmured in a voice low enough that only he could hear.

Smiling faintly, he replied, "I just don't want you to leave until I'm satisfied that everything between us is settled."

She hadn't expected such a quick and honest response. But the unsaid, underlying meaning threading his words vibrated through her, causing her to shiver and stumble over a reply. She wrapped her arms around herself for comfort, tossing a fast glance to her son, who had once again started quarreling loudly with the girls in the sandbox. A well-born lady and her nanny, who was pushing a buggy, stepped past Ian, and he moved to his left, off the path and so close to Viola that she could suddenly feel the heat of his body.

"I think now," he murmured good-naturedly, "before I risk a scandal by taking you in my arms and kissing you in public, I am going to go to the sandbox and teach my son that I've learned it's much easier to win a lady's admiration by building her a castle than by fighting and making her cry."

That said, he winked at her, turned, and walked away.

Made speechless, and flustered to the bone, Viola sat again on the bench and watched in wonder as the Duke of Chatwin took charge of the box and in minutes had the boys and girls together making castles in the sand.

Chapter Twenty-one

They rescued him last night, and although I helped to free him, doing so made it necessary to expose my sisters and the evils they've committed. I have disgraced my family and fear I may remain disowned and alone. With his baby inside of me, I can only hope to find a husband quickly. All of our futures now rest in God's hands. . . .

*H*e had no idea how to seduce her. Or where, or at what time. He'd been meeting her once a day for the past week for sittings, but she'd been cordial and polite, not particularly eager to take up conversation about informal topics, and certainly unwilling to discuss anything personal between them. So unwilling, in fact, that for nearly the entire time, one or more servants had meandered through her studio—an interruption which, he suspected, had been thoroughly staged.

But each day he sat before her, listening to her talk of trivialities, watching her try to stay focused on her work when he so obviously unnerved her by his presence, he grew more desperate to hold her, make love to her, and show her how without trying at all she had managed to transform his feelings for her. Into what, he wasn't altogether sure, but he desperately wanted to discover it. He wanted to tell her how just the sound of her voice carried with it an instant blanket of comfort, and the thought of her leaving his life forever sent a wave of dread through him so powerful that it hurt. He had no explanation for this new ray of emotions he'd never experienced before, and he frankly couldn't put them into words if he tried, but they certainly went beyond lust, and he wasn't stupid enough to dismiss them. He wasn't about to throw away something within his grasp simply because he'd for so long been mistaken and thought differently about the woman at the center of it. It was clear that his assumptions about her role in his captivity had been, if not completely wrong, then altered by vague memories and his own misguided craving for revenge.

Yet much could change, *had* changed, in five years. She had cared for him long ago, but he needed to learn the certainty and depth of her feelings for him now, and the way to that discovery had, until today, eluded him. It had taken him a week of consideration and indecision before deciding on a plan of action. Abducting her again would only prove what *hadn't* changed between them, and asking her to simply tell him how she felt would only lead to more evasion, argument, and mistrust. But he'd bet his fortune she wouldn't be able to hide her feelings if he made love to her.

So tonight, with such a plan in mind, he awaited her arrival at his town house, pacing the floor of his drawing room, his heart thumping hard from anxiousness as he looked again to the clock on the mantel. He'd sent a note requesting a meeting after eight, and it was now nearly half past the hour. He'd chosen the time specifically, wanting to make it late enough to dismiss all but essential servants for the evening. Braetham would greet her, tell her driver to make himself comfortable, then order the rest of the staff to remain below stairs until morning. It was an excellent plan—if she bothered to call on him at all.

Ian strode to the window and gazed out to the driveway beyond. Much of it remained obscured by oak trees and the darkness of night, but after a moment or two of attempting to breathe deeply and contemplate different options for seduction should this one fail, he saw her coach round the corner and pull to a stop next to the stone steps.

Stepping quickly away from the window, he walked to the center of the room and composed himself, waiting with his hands clasped behind his back, feeling surprisingly nervous and worried about his ability to seduce the one woman on earth whose refusal would trouble him indefinitely. He had to make it matter.

Suddenly her footsteps echoed on the marble flooring of his entryway. His mouth went dry and his heartbeat raced, and he faced the opened door as he feigned a calmness he didn't feel at all.

"Your grace," Braetham said after a courtesy knock, "Lady Cheshire to see you."

"Show her in," Ian replied, his voice remarkably steady.

His butler moved to his right, and seconds later she glided into his drawing room.

Ian's breath caught when he saw her, looking beautifully polished and seemingly unworried, but he managed to hide his admiration of her figure with a droll smile and a nod. "Lady Cheshire. I'm so glad you could visit on such short notice."

She raised her brows and managed to appear somewhat amused, if not overly curious. "You said it was important."

Ian glanced at Braetham, who stood in the doorway looking appropriately staid. "That will be all for now," Ian informed him.

The man bowed. "Of course, your grace." Then he turned and shut the door behind him, leaving them alone and enclosed in the silent drawing room.

She glanced around her for the first time, fingering the strings of her tiny reticule in her only display of discomfiture. He eyed her speculatively, noting how lovely she looked in a low-cut, tightly drawn evening gown of bronze satin and pale yellow flounces, her hair upswept in curls. He wished he had a brilliant golden topaz necklace and earrings to give her to complete the picture, then with her on his arm, take her to meet the queen. And by the looks of it, he decided with some humor, such an introduction at court might be faster to accomplish than getting her out of the contraption she was wearing. He couldn't wait to see her corset—

"Your grace?"

He blinked. "I'm sorry?"

Her lips thinned in annoyance. "I asked if there is something I can do for you this evening?"

Oh, sweetheart . . .

Smiling, he began to walk slowly toward her. "You look lovely tonight," he remarked offhandedly. "I hope I didn't pull you away from an important social function."

"Just dinner," she said, watching him through slightly narrowed eyes.

"I see." He waited, and when she didn't offer anything else, he couldn't help himself from prying. "With another prospective husband?"

Her suddenly suspicious gaze grazed the length of him. "With Lady Tenby and several of her guests, if you must know."

He wasn't about to go so far as to ask about Lady Tenby's guests, no matter how curious he was to know if she'd been escorted by another gentleman. Hopefully, and with any luck, it wouldn't matter by morning.

Standing before her now, he looked down into her wary eyes and smiled. "Well, then, I apologize for the interruption, but I am very glad to know you weren't swallowed up in a long night of meaningless gossip."

She sighed into her stays. "Ian, why am I here? What is so important it must be discussed tonight?"

He felt a swift, instantaneous panic slice through him. Never in his thirty-one years had he truly felt as if his future rested on the fate of one event, as he did now. It was time to stop his own meaningless chatter and get to the meaningful lovemaking.

"I need to show you something," he revealed softly.

Her brows furrowed as she scanned each feature of his face. "*Show* me something? Here?"

"Yes." He raised his elbow. "Follow me?"

She hesitated for a second or two, then placed her gloved palm gently on his forearm and allowed him to lead her from the drawing room and into the foyer.

"Where are we going?" she asked as they neared the large marble staircase.

He grinned down at her. "Up."

"Up?"

"To the top floor—"

"Ian, I don't think—"

"Trust me, Viola," he urged in a whisper.

She nervously glanced around the silent house, then, without further pause, lifted her skirts with her free hand and began to climb the steps alongside him.

Silently, he led her up to the third landing, then down the long hallway to the closed door at the very last room.

He could sense her growing concern. Part of that, no doubt, stemmed from the lack of obvious help. If she screamed, no one would come to her rescue. He could only hope that soon he would have her screaming from pleasure, in which case she would be absolutely thankful he'd fairly vacated the house.

"Why do you keep smiling?" she asked suspiciously.

He paused in front of the door. "Smiling?"

"You're not going to murder me up here, are you?" she shot back flatly.

"Not tonight," he replied as he reached for the latch and pushed it downward.

Eyeing him askance, unable to hide a wry grin of her own, she walked inside—then stopped short so quickly that her skirts bounced back into his shins.

She stared at the mantel ten feet in front of her, where the first sketch he'd purchased from her hung in all its glorious beauty, lit on both sides by lamplight as the focal point of the entire room.

"This is your bedchamber, isn't it?"

"Yes." Very quietly, he closed the door behind him, locked it, and stood in front of it to block her exit should she try to run before he had his say.

She glanced to her left, noting his large four-poster bed for several long seconds before twirling around to glare at him.

"It's a lovely room," she said in a daring breath of anger. "Why am I here?"

This is the moment. . . .

"I wanted to show you where I've chosen to hang your sketch."

She shook her head minutely, confused. "Why? If I say it's unattractively displayed above your fireplace, will you give it back to me?"

He chuckled. "Absolutely not. I want it to be the last thing I see before I sleep every night." Growing serious once more, he added, "It reminds me of you."

That bold statement made her uncomfortable. She took a step away from him, glancing to the bed, then back again, her features dark and haunted by lamplight.

"Did you bring me here to seduce me, Ian?" she asked softly.

Moment of truth . . .

"I brought you here for much more than that."

She fidgeted with her reticule strings again, and he reached out to take the small pouch from her, dropping it on the nightstand behind him.

"I won't be your mistress," she said shakily, defensively.

He sighed. "I would never bring a mistress to my private bed, Viola."

"Then why am I here?"

Very slowly, he began to pull at the fingers of her glove. "I wanted to begin by apologizing for taking you to my cabin against your will."

"You didn't have to apologize for that in your home, much less your bedroom."

He read skepticism in her voice, but she didn't pull her hand away when he managed to slip the glove off and reach for the other.

"True," he said, concentrating on removing lace from her fingers. "But this is a very intimate setting, and what I have to say, and do, requires intimacy."

She said nothing to that, but he could feel her gaze on his face, studying his expression. When he finally had her gloves removed, he tossed them onto the nightstand with her reticule, then lifted both hands so he could place his lips on first one wrist, then the other.

She shivered. "What are you doing, Ian?"

He looked into her eyes and whispered against her soft skin, "I'm kissing you."

Her brows creased in a frown. "I know that, but I mean—what intimate thing could you possibly want to say?"

Although she tried to sound matter-of-fact, he noticed her breath quickening as her guard lowered. Gently, he pulled her toward him, close enough that her skirts blanketed his thighs. "I want to thank you," he said huskily, his mouth still brushing her wrist, "for helping me all those years ago."

She swallowed hard, mesmerized of a sudden. "You needed help."

He pulled back a little and smiled into her eyes, then wrapped an arm around her waist to draw her even closer. "I want to *show* you what it meant to me."

With a shaky exhale, she murmured, "You want to make love to me. . . ."

"I do."

For a timeless moment she gazed into his eyes, her own troubled, searching. He felt his heart beating hard in his chest, knowing that as he'd laid bare his desire for her, she could very well step back and walk out on him. If she did, he realized, it would be one of the greatest disappointments of his life.

And then, as if accepting the destiny that brought them together, she lowered her lashes, leaned forward, and placed her lips on his.

It took him several long seconds to realize she was giving herself to him without reservation or argument, if only this one time, and with a sudden urgency that staggered him, his body came alive.

He wrapped his arms around her and pulled her forcefully against him, relishing in the softness of her lips, the sweet, flowery scent of her skin. She lifted her hands to lightly grasp his cheeks as his mouth lingered on hers, tasting, caressing, taking the time to savor. His tongue flicked across her top lip and she opened for him, giving him access as she pressed her body into his with her own growing need. He restrained his eagerness, afraid to move too quickly—until she moaned softly and pushed her hips forward in her demand for more.

Quickly, he broke their kiss and lifted his head, gazing down at her flushed face.

"Turn around," he whispered, his voice gruff. "I'm going to undress you."

Her lashes fluttered open and she looked at him, her eyes conveying a hint of hesitation. He lowered his hand to the ruffled neckline of her gown, then closed his palm over her satin-covered breast.

She gasped lightly when he started caressing her. He watched her closely as her desire intensified, and then in one swift move, he grasped her upper arm with his free hand and turned her himself, his palm never leaving her breast as he pulled her back against his chest.

He leaned over to leave gentle kisses on the nape of her neck, her bare shoulder, while he began to expertly pry each button apart with nimble fingers.

Eagerly, she began to help him, slipping her gown over her arms as it loosened. He nipped her earlobe, flicked it with his tongue, then drew his lips down her neck to the top of her shoulder. Within seconds, her evening dress pooled at her feet, and to his great surprise, she unfastened her white lace corset in the front and dropped it to her side.

Ian pulled back a little and once again turned her to face him. She stood unashamed, her breasts exposed but the remainder of her body covered from the waist down in lacy fabric. With nimble fingers he unbuttoned his own shirt and slipped it off, all the while staring into her eyes, a witness to her uncertainty even as she boldly held his gaze.

He glanced down to her lovely, exposed breasts, each nipple hard from the chill in the room, and carefully closed his hands over both to warm, caress, tease each peak with the pads of his thumbs.

She moaned softly and closed her eyes, leaning her head back as she gave in to the moment.

"Tell me what you like," he said in a husky timbre.

Without lifting her lashes, she whispered, "With you I like everything. Kiss me, Ian. . . ."

He needed no other urging. Lowering his head, he captured her mouth again, playing with her lips, her tongue, relishing in her softness, her quick breaths, her warm palms gently framing his cheeks as their mutual passion grew in intensity. Then in a sweeping fashion, he reached down and lifted her into his arms, carrying her to his bed and easing her onto the coverlet before releasing her luscious lips in an effort to draw a string of feather-soft kisses down her jaw and throat, her chest and the valley between her breasts.

She arched her back in response, raking her fingers through his hair as he took one nipple into his mouth and began to lightly suck, to tease it to a taut peak with his tongue and then trace it with his lips.

She began to whimper, to push her hips toward him in abandonment. In one quick action, he raised himself just enough to pull at the top of her petticoats, loosen them and draw them and her stockings down her hips and legs to expose the length of her beautiful body to his view.

She was stunning by lamplight, and he caressed each curve and shadow with his gaze, then lowered his head and dropped a kiss on the mound of dark curls between her legs.

She inhaled a sharp breath and shivered.

"Are you cold?"

"A little," she replied in a silky whisper.

He reached up and yanked down the coverlet. "Get under the blankets."

Without looking at him, she did as ordered, and just as quickly he unfastened the buttons of his trousers, slipped off the remainder of his clothing, and snuggled in beside her, covering them both to their necks.

They lay side by side on his pillows, facing each other, though she kept her eyes closed. He stared at her for several seconds, still not quite touching, his mind a sudden jumble of mixed emotions, all of them both troubling and wonderful. Then, as if sensing his gaze on her face, she lifted her lashes and looked into his eyes.

He smiled, and she did the same, making his heart lurch in his chest.

"Warmer?" he whispered.

"Much."

His smile fading, he asked, "What are you thinking?"

For seconds she said nothing, just studied the features of his face. And then she reached up and very gingerly placed her splayed palm on his bare chest so close to her own.

"I'm thinking," she whispered, "that although it's dangerous for me to be here, I trust it because I've never felt safer in my life than in your arms."

His throat constricted as a rush of tenderness swept

over him. He wasn't expecting anything so intimate, so thoroughly honest, and he had no idea what to say.

Offering him a hesitant smile, she added shyly, "And I don't want to disappoint you."

Something deep inside of him melted at that moment. He couldn't begin to understand it, or put words to it, but it took his breath away.

"Viola . . ."

She leaned forward and placed her lips on his. He responded with a lingering kiss, heightening the passion slowly, reveling in her desire to give herself to him fully despite the risks. She caressed his chest with her fingertips as he moved his own hands, one to her breast, the other to the back of her head, his fingers threading through her silky hair.

He teased her nipple once more to a peak and squeezed it gently, listening to the sound of her quickening breaths and soft moans of pleasure as his own heart began beating fast and hard again.

He stretched his leg out a little to cover hers, pulling them toward him to bring her closer. She flicked her tongue across her top lip, and in answer he plunged deep to grasp hers and suck it. She whimpered and raised her hand from his chest to his cheek, then moved it behind his head to hold him tightly.

He caressed, tasted, teased as she did, and finally, when he could take the wait no longer, he reached down, grabbed the back of her knee, and lifted it while pulling her against him so her thigh covered his hip and his thick erection nestled into her soft, feminine curls. With a gasp, she drew her lips from his, raised her lashes, and looked into his eyes.

At that second, a spark of a memory flickered, captured him. And in it, a whisper from a fragment in time long ago—

I love you, Ian. . . .

He sucked in a sharp breath as disbelief and wonder, confusion and a sense of belonging pierced his mind, his heart.

So beautiful . . .

She watched him intently, face flushed, eyes dark with desire, her brows creased minutely as she sensed the strange and glorious turn in him. Then she brought her hand forward and touched his lips with her fingers.

He kissed them, brushed his lips along the pads, held her vivid gaze as he drew her ring finger just slightly into his mouth to gently suck. She inhaled shakily when he began tracing small circles over her nipple with the pad of his thumb, then grazed it with his knuckles before cupping the soft flesh with his palm.

She moaned again, absorbing every sensation to its fullest. Blood rushed through his veins, his heart raced at the sound of her voice, the sight of her pleasure, and suddenly, urgently, he needed to be inside her.

Reaching down, he took hold of the base of his erection, adjusted his hips so that her knee lifted a little, and pushed himself between her legs.

She cradled him instinctively within the warm, wet walls of her cleft. For several long seconds he held himself steady, afraid to move, to breathe, lest he lose himself too quickly. He'd never made love side by side before, yet everything about their closeness—her face inches from his, eyes able to behold, hands and fingers able to freely touch and give and accept—managed to intensify his need.

As if sensing his thoughts, she licked her lips, and either from instinct or pure arousal, began to stroke him by gingerly rocking her hips into his, smothering him with slick, wet heat. He clenched his jaw and groaned low in his chest as she purposely baited him, silently begged for him to enter her. And then, with the delicate lift of her thigh to give him access, he did as she wanted, as he desperately craved, and pressed upward, finding the center of her, and very slowly glided inside her sweet, warm walls.

She whimpered, briefly tensed. He reached for her knee and raised it toward his chest, allowing him to fill her deeply. For seconds neither of them moved, though she kept her gaze locked with his, as if she needed to see his every reaction to such exquisite torture. With one hand still caressing her breast, he moved the other from her leg to her cheek, cupping her face, brushing his thumb along her lips.

"I could stay like this forever," she murmured softly against his sensitive skin.

He swallowed hard, unable to put his feelings into words. Never in his life had he experienced a moment of closeness more perfect than this one.

"Viola . . . ," he said in a far-off whisper, "so beautiful . . ."

A trace of confusion flickered in her eyes. And then they filled with tears.

Cradling her head, he captured her mouth once more, tasted the sweetness of her lips, felt her quick, warm breaths on his face, sensed the presence of longing within her. She pressed her hips into his, then began to move them as desire returned anew.

He lowered his hand from her head to her bottom, pulling her as close to him as possible, allowing her to set the pace. He caressed her breast, thumbed her nipple, traced his tongue across her lips, then plunged deeply as she whimpered again in abandonment. He felt his own passion growing with each slight thrust of her hips, each soft moan to his ears, and knew that within moments she'd bring him to the edge.

Suddenly she tore her mouth from his and gasped. She looked into his eyes, held his gaze, rocked her hips faster.

"Ian . . ."

He bit down hard to hold himself back, watching her climb to the brink of her release.

She moaned, opened her eyes wider, squeezed the muscles of his chest.

"Yes," he breathed.

"Ian—"

And with that she cried out in pleasure, clinging to him, staring into his eyes.

He witnessed the emotion, felt each pulse of her orgasm within, gripping him, pulling him along with her.

"Oh, yes, sweetheart . . ." He tensed. "Oh, yes—"

He exploded inside, squeezing his eyes shut, groaning through each wave of ecstasy, holding her tightly as he thrust into her again and again with total abandonment. His breath mingled with hers, the moans from his throat matched her own, and they clung to each other through each rock of her hips, with each movement of legs and hands, each brushing of lips and fingertips, until at last their bodies, together, grew still.

Ian allowed his heartbeat to slow, then wrapped his arms around her and pulled her head into the crook of his neck, turning just enough to make them comfortable but not enough to slip out of her. Then resting his head on hers, he cupped her face with his palm and stroked her cheek, listening to the soft sound of her breathing until sleep overcame him.

The softness of her lips on his stirred his senses.

"Wake up, Ian," she whispered from above.

He opened his eyes, blinked quickly, and then remembered everything as he looked into Viola's beautiful face illuminated by lamplight.

"What time is it?" he asked groggily, noting of a sudden that not only was she standing beside his bed but she'd also managed to do an adequate job of dressing herself without his help.

"It's nearly dawn, I think," she said, straightening.

He sat up and wiped a palm down his face. "You don't have to leave."

Casting him a wry smile, she reached for her gloves and reticule on the nightstand. "Of course I have to leave. I should have left hours ago."

"No," he countered, "you should be in this bed and ready for another round of lovemaking."

Her smile faded as she gazed at him squarely. "It was wonderful, but one night in your bed doesn't change anything. You should know that. And I have to get home before the staff wakes. My hair is a mess and—"

"Your hair is a beautiful mess. Come back to bed."

She bit her bottom lip in hesitation, then murmured, "I can't."

Her desire to leave so quickly after the intimacy they'd shared bothered him more than he wanted to admit. He didn't give a damn about her hair, her staff or his. He wanted her back in bed with him now, naked and willing.

Tossing the blankets aside, he swung his legs over the edge and stood to face her.

"Yes, it was wonderful," he agreed huskily, "and it's sure to be wonderful the next time. I need you, Viola."

Frowning negligibly, she reached up and delicately touched his face. "*I have* to *leave.*"

He placed his hands on his hips, exhaled a fast breath. "Why are you so nonchalant about what happened last night?"

Her eyes widened and she pulled her hand away, thoroughly surprised. "Nonchalant? I'm not being nonchalant, I'm being practical. It's nearly morning and I have a child, a studio, a social schedule and household to run."

Groaning, he rubbed his eyes with his fingertips. "Then I'll bring you back tonight."

She gave a soft laugh as she donned her gloves. "Now *that's* impractical. I'm not your mistress to order around, Ian, and I can't wander in here at your whim night after night. Even if I had no other engagements, think of the trouble, the inconvenience for both of us, not to mention the scandal it might create for me should we be discovered, or worse."

Or worse. He knew what she meant. Getting her with child again, even as she still refused to acknowledge her son as his.

They'd come to a stalemate, obviously, and the fact that she seemed so reluctant to throw caution to the wind and become his ready lover irrationally irked him. She wanted—*needed*—him as much as he did her. He was sure of it. Yet he couldn't possibly seduce her again and again; she would have to come to him willingly.

"What of desire?" he murmured.

Her light humor faded. "Desire is a fleeting thing. Commitments and practicalities are not. You know that as well as I."

That statement's harsh truth gnawed at his gut. "You could marry me."

The air between them electrified at once. She blinked, then shook her head minutely, as if she couldn't comprehend what he'd said.

He swallowed; his heart began to pound. The words had slipped from him as smoothly as the flow of silk, and yet as he boldly stared into her large, stunned eyes, he couldn't regret them. Everything had changed between them since he'd begun his absurd quest for revenge, since he'd learned of and then met their son. And if she married him, she wouldn't be able to just leave the city, or country, at will. Yes, he decided, marriage between them made very practical sense.

"Viola?"

"I'm not— Is that a proposal?" she asked, bewildered.

Nervously, he massaged the back of his neck. "Yes. I suppose."

"You suppose?"

He felt suddenly ridiculous, standing nude before her, realizing it wasn't the most romantic way to ask for a lady's hand, nor the most suitable moment, and yet it seemed to him she should still be pleased. "It would be a good match," he answered decisively.

For several long, uncomfortable seconds she stared at him. And then very softly she nodded and replied, "Yes, it would be an excellent match, quite sensible, really, for a variety of reasons."

Relief coursed through him—until she lowered her lashes and turned toward the door.

"Where are you going?"

"I'm going home, Ian," she said. "Good-bye."

Without another glance at him, she straightened her shoulders, lifted her chin a fraction, and regally strode out of his bedroom.

Chapter Twenty-two

I close this diary by omitting the gravest secret he whispered in his delirium. I cannot mention what I know, for if anyone should learn the truth behind his family secret, it would surely ruin him. I love him too much to risk disclosing all. . . .

Ian walked into the parlor, decidedly irritable simply because his sister, Ivy, the Marchioness of Rye, tried so hard to make the room frilly and cheery, and he didn't feel at all like being cheery. Especially when he'd had to travel to the southern coast to see her and he hadn't been keen on leaving the city after his seduction of Viola three days ago had turned so horribly wrong. They still had much to discuss, whether she knew it or not, but Ivy's note had said she needed to speak to him quickly. As her twin, he'd always felt close to her, concerned when something needed to be addressed urgently, and she couldn't very well have left her home with a newborn in tow to visit him.

The room was decorated in peach, yellow, and some

odd shade of pink he'd never seen before. He succumbed to his exhaustion and walked directly to a white velveteen settee, fairly falling on it and spreading his arms out wide, closing his eyes as he leaned his head back on the cushion, hoping his sister wouldn't keep him waiting.

She didn't disappoint. Only moments later he heard her footsteps on the parquet floor as she stepped quickly into the parlor—and suddenly stopped short.

"Didn't Mason offer you tea?"

He smiled, though he refused to open his eyes when they felt like lead. "I don't want tea. I want a bath and a night's sleep."

"Oh, for heaven's sake—"

"Just sit down, Ivy."

She huffed and moved toward him. "Why are you so cross?"

He opened his eyes wide. "I'm *tired*."

"Ridiculous," she countered, leaning over to kiss his cheek. "I'm the one who gets almost no sleep at all. You may whine when you have a newborn babe in the nursery. And yes," she added as she backed away and lowered her body with cultured grace into the chair opposite his relaxed form, "you do need a bath."

He gave her a droll smile. "Thank you for such hearty agreement."

She cocked her head to the side a little, growing serious. "You do look tired. You're not sleeping well, are you?"

Irritated, he sat up and crossed one leg over the other, then ran his fingers harshly through his hair. "You need to worry about yourself. How are you, by the way?"

She waved a palm through the air. "I'm fine. Rye is a doting husband, actually, so I'm as good as new, and the baby is perfect."

With heartfelt relief, he offered her a genuine grin. "I'm pleased. You look happy."

She grinned in return. "I am immeasurably happy, thank you."

"But you didn't ask me to urgently come to Rye to tell me that," he drawled.

Sheepishly, she replied, "No. I wanted to talk about something else, actually."

She fidgeted, sitting perfectly straight in her chair, and for the first time he noticed she carried two items that looked like slender books with her, now clutched in her lap as if she feared he might grab them and run.

"What are those?" he asked with a nod.

"Umm . . . I'll tell you that in a moment."

He waited, watching her forehead crease. She studied the tea table in front of them, gently biting her bottom lip as she often did when she worried about informing him of momentous news, and his intrigue began to grow.

He sighed with impatience. "Ivy—"

"What do you remember about your time in the dungeon, Ian?"

The temperature in the parlor seemed suddenly hot and thick, stifling his ability to breathe, and he pulled at the collar of his shirt to loosen it.

"Why?" he asked seconds later.

She looked at him candidly. "There is something about your recovery that I never told you, but I'm going to now because . . . new information has come to light and I think it's important."

"New information about what?" he asked cautiously, tamping down a spark of dread.

She paused for a moment, then murmured, "During those first few hours after you were rescued, when I sat by your bedside and you were delirious and so close to death, I nursed you and held your hand, and tried to feed you broth. Do you remember?"

Agitated, he tapped his thumbs together in his lap. "Not really. Get to the point, Ivy."

"You wept, Ian," she said, lowering her voice with concern. "And you kept asking for Viola."

His entire body tensed reflexively. He had no idea what to say to such a revelation, or even what to feel. But he would never doubt his sister when it came to his horrible experience five years ago. She had saved him, and he lived today because of her.

"At the time," she continued, "I didn't know what to think of anything you said while you were incoherent; most of it was muffled and confused. I just wanted to keep you alive, to help you gain strength and nurse you back to health. I thought perhaps you called out for Viola Bennington-Jones, but that didn't make sense to me because she took part in your abduction—"

"*She* did not," he countered. "Her sisters did."

Ivy tilted her head to the side a fraction, looking at him inquisitively. "I see. Well, then perhaps all this makes sense."

"What makes sense?"

She twisted her wedding ring nervously, then sighed.

"I know you moved from Stamford to Tarrington Square for the season because Lady Cheshire had come out of mourning."

Ian felt as if she'd knocked the wind from him with that disclosure. His sister had never been one to interfere with his dalliances, few though they'd been since his abduction, and she'd always been rather silent on his decision thus far to remain unmarried. So this stunning acknowledgment on her part left him wondering if he should ask her to explain herself or mind her own damn business. Curiosity won.

"What makes you think I went to London because of her?"

"Did you?"

He studied her for a moment, his irritation bubbling to the surface. Lowering his voice, he said, "Why don't you tell me what concerns you."

"*You* concern me, Ian." She slumped a little into her corset. "Did you intend to court her or ruin her?"

"Why would you ask me that?" he shot back brusquely.

Without skipping a beat, she smiled faintly and replied, "Because love and hate are both passions that can be easily blurred, especially when the memory is affected."

Nerves fired, Ian bolted from the settee. He had no idea why Ivy was involved now, but the mention of his past, the dungeon, and learning his sister knew something about his intentions toward Viola and the intimacy between them made him feel like jumping out of his skin. And his lack of control in the matter infuriated him.

Walking stiffly to the window, he leaned his palms on the pane and stared out to the freshly cut lawn below. His nephew, James, now nearly four years old, stood with his father and two footmen as Rye lectured, with some displeasure on his face, about the sophistication of properly using a bridle. Or something. Suddenly the boy burst out crying, and seconds later, Rye scooped him up in his arm and lifted him onto his shoulders. It was enough training for the day, apparently, as the marquess dismissed the footmen with a wave of his hand. Then, as his son wiped his tears and hugged him with his cheek to the top of his father's head, the two of them headed toward the house, Rye talking and consoling, until they passed below the window and out of sight.

"What are you looking at?"

Dreams that come true for other people. . . .

"Nothing," he said, turning to face her. He leaned his hip on the windowsill and crossed his arms over his chest. "Why did you need to see me so urgently, Ivy?"

Sighing, she replied, "I'm not sure of your intentions toward Lady Cheshire, and it's certainly none of my business—"

"True."

She gazed at him as she often did, her expression firm, as if ready to scold. He almost smiled. Thank God for Ivy in his life.

"As I was saying, your paramours are not my concern."

"Lady Cheshire is not anyone's paramour."

Ivy's mouth tipped up minutely. "I'm sure she's not. However, three weeks ago, I received a package from your home in Chatwin. It contained a lovely evening gown, plum colored, with beautiful embroidery on the skirt, cleaned and pressed."

He frowned, thinking. "So?"

"It's not mine." She cleared her throat and sat up straight again. "You have exceptionally diligent servants, your grace, but they are apparently confused about the ladies in your life."

Viola's gown. He remembered her wearing it the night he took her from Tarrington Square to the fishing cottage at Chatwin. She'd borrowed one of Ivy's old nightgowns, then a day gown when she'd left, and now he remembered telling one of the young maids to have it cleaned for her, to try to remove the sherry stains from the skirt—a spill he'd caused. Clearly, during the process, one of his servants, unaware of Viola's stay, had assumed that Ivy had left an expensive evening gown on her last visit and would want it returned to her. And Viola had never mentioned this to him, possibly forgetting it, or, more likely, assuming he wouldn't care enough to have it sent to her. Or she'd simply wanted to forget the experience entirely. In any case, the error by his staff had exposed his deplorable actions to his sister.

"What makes you certain it's Lady Cheshire's gown?" he asked quietly.

She offered him a proud grin. "Because, darling brother, I contacted the good dressmakers in London and sent inquiries. It's a unique gown, very beautiful, and if it were mine, I'd want it returned to me."

So that was it. His clever sister had connected dots and in so doing had drawn a very good picture of his affair.

"I hope you didn't say anything . . . improper in your keen investigation," he drawled.

She scoffed. "Of course not. I merely said I'd seen the gown at a party, couldn't remember who'd worn it, and since I was considering having one made in a similar fashion and by such a good dressmaker, wanted to talk with the lady who owned it."

Ian exhaled a long breath and wiped a palm down his tired face, then stood erect and walked back to the settee to sit again. Slumping against the cushion, he stared at his smugly smiling sister. "Don't tell me you asked me here simply to give me the dress to return to her."

"No," she said softly, her expression growing serious again. "But in learning who owned it, I began to understand more of what happened to you all those years ago, and I started to worry about you, and your intentions toward Lady Cheshire. It was then that I remembered something found in the dungeon when Rye had it sealed."

He nodded toward the books in her lap. "Those?"

She glanced down at them. "These have been in a trunk in my attic for four years, Ian. When we discovered them long after your rescue, we could only guess at their meaning, and we decided it was best not to expose anyone, or return them to their owner. She had just lost her husband, and her son, now the Baron Cheshire, deserved a life unencumbered by his family's horrible past. We also weren't certain that if we did give them back to her, she wouldn't use them against you in some way unimaginable. But, as you'll see, we just couldn't bring ourselves to destroy them."

His curiosity piqued, he sat forward at once, hand outstretched. "Give them to me."

"Wait," she said, clutching them to her breast. "One more thing."

He didn't move. "What is it?"

"Before you look at these, please know that we never meant to keep anything from you. It wasn't a matter of protecting you, or even her, it was a matter of letting the past go. And nobody has seen these books but Rye and me—"

"Ivy, so help me God—"

She thrust them forward, into his waiting hand, then stood.

"I'll leave you alone to peruse them. When you're ready I'll have Mason draw you a bath and send you up a meal to your usual room." Giving him a final smile filled with love and concern, she added, "I suspect you'll want to leave for the city at dawn."

That said, she turned and walked from her parlor, closing the door behind her.

For several long moments Ian stared at the two books, realizing his hands trembled slightly when he pulled them apart to study them individually. One was a journal or diary of some kind, the other a sketchbook, which he chose to open first.

His breath caught in his chest when he turned to the first sketch, created by Viola's gifted hand, and recognized the manor house in Winter Garden that Rye now owned, beneath which he'd been held captive for five long weeks. It was an innocuous drawing of the outside of the building, and yet it sent an instant stab of trepidation though his body.

He closed his eyes briefly, drawing a deep, full breath, then turned to the second page.

And there he was, sketched in perfect form, chained and lying on the cot in the dungeon, apparently asleep.

He swallowed, feeling suddenly overwhelmed by emotions that ranged from fear to helplessness, rage to heartache.

He began to flip through the pages, each one more graphic than the last, until he came to the first one of them together—he and Viola, embracing on the cot.

Ian stared in absolute awe, astonished by the sensual beauty. He held her, both of them nude, his right arm shackled, but his left encircling her at the waist, her right breast hidden, her left breast resting on his chest as she lay sideways across the length of him. Tenderly, she cupped his head with her palms, resting her forehead on his temple, her lips gently pressed against his cheek, their eyes closed as they seemed to melt into each other. But the most revealing aspect of the sketch for him showed her left leg crossed over his waist, exposing a shadow of her cleft, his right leg raised so that he could keep his erection tightly encased within her.

It was the most erotic drawing he'd ever seen in his life, and it was of him, and Viola, making love. He knew it now because he had remembered it just days ago when she'd lain in his arms in his bed. He'd sensed the familiar, the two of them lingering, holding, embracing, touching, caressing, and remaining joined, side by side, as lovers who were not yet ready to pull apart. Not a quick and passionless coupling, but *meaningful*. And they had shared it years ago, as they had recently.

Shaken, he closed the book of sketches, feeling suddenly raw and exhausted and exposed, realizing now what Ivy had meant when she'd said only she and her husband had seen these and had kept them from exposure. She had saved him possible scandal, and yet he couldn't help but be embarrassed to know she'd seen a sketch of him nude and in a carnal position, regardless of its accuracy. Still, it hadn't been put up for auction at Brimleys, thank God.

Without pause, he moved on to the diary, opening it to the first written page. Immediately his trepidation turned to amazement, then to silent shock as he began to read:

> *It's so dark inside, so cold, and in his sleep he weeps. Although I wish I could, I cannot help him. . . . Watching him struggle makes my heart ache so. . . .*

Ian felt his mouth go dry, his heart began to pound. He turned the page and read more.

> *I spoke to him at last, whispered words of comfort as I tried to soothe his brow. He first called me Ivy, then opened his eyes when he realized a stranger sat beside him. . . . I put the candle behind me today, so he couldn't see my face inside my cloak. He asked me my name, but I didn't dare speak. He is frightened, and his heartache is so intense. . . .*
>
> *I stole the key to the dungeon today, and went to him just after she drugged him. I could finally*

*nurse him and care for his needs without him
knowing. . . . He begged me not to leave him. . . . I
risked everything and went to him, lying down on
the cot beside him to lend him my warmth. . . .*

"Jesus . . . ," he whispered. His entire body trembled
now, felt cold inside. He started flipping through the
pages faster, processing the truth as quickly as he could,
trying to place the information, to wrap it around his
own veiled memory.

*I tried to bathe him today, while he slept from the
drug. He is so masculine, so handsome, but he is
beginning to lose strength. I want to help him, but
they will keep me from him if I do anything else.
He needs me, but I am so afraid. . . .*

   *I couldn't stop looking at him today, and when
I finally touched him to care for him, his body
responded and he reached for my hand, pleading deliriously for me to caress him. I have never
experienced anything so shocking, so intimate, in
my life. . . .*

   *. . . I'm afraid for him when he's alone. Much of
the time I'm only there to listen to him speak. . . .*

   *I wonder what would happen to my life if I
helped him escape. My future seems as bleak as
his. . . .*

   I sat beside him for a long while today. . . .

   I think I could stay in his arms forever. . . .

   His body responded. . . .

   *. . . he needed me, begged me, and I couldn't
resist the desire to be with him. I've never felt*

anything so intense and wonderful, and doubt I ever will again. . . .

He touched me in places I have never been touched before, places on my body that I have never touched myself. . . . I have shared these sins with a man I've grown to love. . . .

Today was the end of my innocence, in every way. It was an end he sought, but to which I yielded, with compassion and desire and love in my heart, and now that it's over, I have no regrets, only memories to last a lifetime. . . .

He is ailing, and I must do all that I can to get him out of there. . . . Hold on, Ian. Help is coming. Please, my brave man, hold on. . . .

The party is tomorrow night. Somehow I will see him rescued, even if I have to defy my family and destroy my future. I cannot let him die. He means too much to me now. . . .

I am very frightened, for both of us. I am three weeks late for my monthlies, and now fear I carry his child. . . .

"Viola . . . ," he breathed, touching the words with his fingertips as if they'd been part of her.

They rescued him last night, and although I helped to free him, doing so made it necessary to expose my sisters and the evils they've committed. I have disgraced my family and fear I may remain disowned and alone. With his baby inside of me, I can only hope to find a husband quickly. All of our futures now rest in God's hands. . . .

And then, at long last, he came to the answer to everything:

I close this diary by omitting the gravest secret he whispered in his delirium. I cannot mention what I know, for if anyone should learn the truth behind his family secret, it would surely ruin him. For now, as a new journey for me begins, I will live in silence, with the knowledge that I, a common lady of modest means, saved the life of the noble Earl of Stamford. My new husband has agreed to keep my secret and raise my bastard child as his own, providing I paint and sketch lascivious art for him to sell. He is practically penniless, but is titled, and Mother insisted on the match for that reason. She—no one—will never know the truth, but it matters little to me as long as I have my baby. Pray God, thank you for giving me this precious life inside to cherish always, conceived from the heart of the man who will never know his child, but will forever be my greatest desire and deepest love. . . .

Shakily, his mind numb, Ian closed the journal and wrapped both arms around it as he held it tightly against his chest. For a long while he just stared vacantly, unblinking, at the tea table in front of him, seeing nothing through the blur of tears that filled his tired eyes.

Chapter Twenty-three

$\mathcal{T}$he invitation to the unveiling party said seven, but Ian had arrived early, wanting to get a few moments alone with his son before he talked to Viola. Ian wasn't exactly sure what he'd say to the boy, who was just barely five years old, but he assumed conversation with John Henry wouldn't be too difficult. Or perhaps the opposite would be true. He really had no idea, since he seldom found himself in the company of children.

He'd returned from Rye with Viola's books and gown, intending to use them as an excuse to see her should he need it, but on arriving back at Tarrington Square two nights ago, he'd received his invitation. She'd finished a second portrait, the one they were about to view in some dazzling display she'd planned, and now he had his own display and would use this night to reveal it. It was time for truth, for decisions to be made, and for him, the first would begin with his son.

Fortunately, he didn't have to ask to meet the boy inside the home, a situation that would no doubt field speculation and gossip among her staff. As soon as his coach pulled into the drive, he noticed John Henry in the small garden to the side of the house, hanging from a swing by his belly as two servant girls chatted nearby. A perfect opportunity.

Ian stepped out the moment his driver stopped, then walked the path back the way he'd come. He spotted the child just as the girls, probably no older than sixteen, noticed him entering through the wrought-iron gate. They stopped talking at once, both of their mouths hanging open in surprise.

"I'd like to speak with Lord Cheshire alone," he said, coming to a standstill beside the swing. "I'll bring him to the house with me in a few minutes."

The girls looked momentarily confused. Then, apparently gathering their wits, each one curtseyed, replied meekly, "Yes, your grace," and quickly exited the garden through the gate.

He glanced down to the boy, who had now twisted the swing's rope so tightly that it lifted him to his tiptoes. Suddenly, he jumped, pulled his feet off the ground, and twirled, giggling as the twisted rope swung him round a half dozen times before spinning back in the other direction.

"Is that fun?" Ian asked, amused.

John Henry looked up, grinning. "'Course!"

God, he looked like Ivy. Or, probably more accurately, he looked like him. Others would notice, some would talk, but in the end none of that mattered. He wanted his child in his life as much as he wanted the child's mother.

"Are you going to the party?" John Henry asked.

Smiling, Ian clasped his hands behind his formal dinner jacket. "How can you guess?"

John Henry giggled. "Mama says you're gonna be sapized."

Frowning, he clarified, "Surprised?"

John Henry started swinging again, concentrating on his feet. "Sa-pized when you—see the painting."

That thoroughly intrigued Ian. "Is that so? Have you seen it?"

The boy looked up at him, grinning. "Yes. It's funny."

"Funny, eh?" For a second it occurred to him that she'd actually done the unthinkable and painted a formal portrait of him in all his naked glory, intending to reveal it tonight. It would no doubt be the ultimate humiliation in front of friends and social acquaintances who didn't need to know the size of his privates according to her imagination. That would surely make everyone laugh. But such a notion quickly vanished, for two reasons. First, if she planned to humiliate him, she would never do so in front of her son, or with his knowledge. And secondly, they had moved beyond trying to hurt each other. Whatever the future held for the two of them, from now on it would only include contentment and delight that satisfied them both. He would make certain of it.

"I have something to ask you, Lord Cheshire," he said very formally. "And you must keep this a secret between gentlemen. Do you think you can do that?"

John Henry suddenly flipped over on his swing, then stood upright and hopped onto the wooden seat to watch him.

"I s'pose."

Ian cleared his throat and lowered his voice. "I was wondering if you'd like to come and live with me in the country for a little while. I have a big house and lots of horses to ride. I even have a nephew about your age who probably knows a lot about swings and toys and climbing trees outside. I'm sure he'd like to meet you."

John Henry leaned on the rope, eyeing him suspiciously, his little face pinched as he considered the offer. "Can Mama come, too?"

"I sincerely hope she does," Ian replied through a long exhale. "But you must keep it a secret until I ask her myself. Is that understood?"

John Henry grinned again and began swinging upright. "A secret 'tween gel-men?"

Ian nodded. "Exactly. It's a secret between gentlemen."

John Henry flipped over again, then jumped back and fell onto his bottom into the dirt. Ian reached out and offered him his hand.

"Did that hurt?" he asked, amused.

The boy pulled himself up. "No. I fall sometimes."

"Ah."

John Henry rubbed his backside, then leaned over onto his head again to stare at the world upside down.

Ian smiled. "Shall we go inside, John Henry? I'm starving."

The boy immediately stood upright. "I am, too. 'S-go."

Without prompting, John Henry reached out to take Ian's hand, then skipped along beside him as they wandered through the garden toward the house.

Viola made her way to her drawing room to take note of the evening's arrangements and make certain all was in order. Now nearly six, she had little more than an hour before guests would begin arriving for the event. The gathering would be small, with only twelve people or so, but she wanted it to be a night to remember, especially for Ian. That's what terrified her.

She hadn't seen or spoken to him in the week since she'd left his bedroom after his ridiculous marriage suggestion, and truthfully, she couldn't wait to see him again. She missed him, a revelation of her own that grew sharper every day. She only wished she knew the depth of his feelings for her, and where, dear heaven, they would go from here.

Part of her realized he had fallen in love with her, though whether that had happened years ago or recently, she couldn't guess. But she couldn't just tell him what, or how, he felt. He had to recognize it for himself. And maybe he never would. She had seen it when he'd made love to her, when he'd been inside of her and had experienced such a powerful connection of souls. Perhaps only a woman could understand, but in the last few days she'd thought of that night frequently, recalling each intense moment, each delicious sensation and the expression of feelings between them, and if there was one thing she knew as fact, it was that he didn't want to live without her.

For tonight, though, she would do her best to entice him as any smart woman would do when she wanted the attention of the man she loved. She'd decided on the very same scarlet gown she'd worn to Lady Tenby's party on the night she'd met him again, this time adding ruby earrings and a ruby teardrop necklace to draw his attention to her uplifted breasts, made as obvious as possible by her tightly drawn corset. With her hair swept up in curls, she decided to wear the tiniest trace of rouge on her cheeks and kohl on her eyelids to enhance her color under candlelight. In the end, she looked sophisticated, confident, and radiant. She only hoped he noticed.

Viola stepped into her drawing room, already smelling of cinnamon and cloves, and surveyed the surroundings. Two servants were busy setting the buffet with hors d'oeuvres and champagne in one corner, and in the other, next to the mantel, stood the easel on which rested her painting, covered in a drape of red velvet. After a quick consultation with the cook's daughter, Molly, her staff quit the drawing room, leaving her alone with her thoughts.

The day had been rather warm for late August, so she walked to the wide French doors to the west and opened them, stepping onto the patio for a bit of fresh air. Though it was not yet dark, the sun had set behind the trees, and the lights of the city had begun to glow. She stood at the railing and closed her eyes.

"You look stunning, madam."

Viola twirled around to the sound of his voice, her heartbeat quickening at the sight of his gorgeous form standing alone in the doorway, dressed entirely in black save for his gray-and-white-striped cravat. His hair had been combed back to expose all of his clean-shaven face, and when a trace of his spicy cologne reached her, she had to fight the sudden urge to walk into his arms.

"Viola?"

She blinked, feeling a rush of heat fill her cheeks as she realized she was staring. With a swift curtsey, she mumbled, "I beg your pardon, your grace, but—when did you arrive? Why were you not announced?"

"I wanted to speak with you before the party began," he replied with a gentle shrug, "and asked to see you alone. Needham escorted me to the drawing room and told me where you were."

The entire situation confused her. Her butler should have introduced him, but that was suddenly beside the point. Ian seemed different in manner, subdued, smiling faintly as he slowly looked her up and down, taking in every curve as if he'd never seen her before. It made her incredibly uncomfortable.

"I take it you didn't look at the painting?"

He stepped away from the French doors and out onto the patio. "Would I still be here if I had?"

She almost laughed, but her inability to grasp his mood kept her cautious. "I doubt it."

He strode easily to her side, covered the railing with his palms, and glanced out over the garden below. "What kind of portrait are you going to expose to the world, Viola? Should I fear you may have painted me . . . too small?"

She grinned, clasping her lace-covered hands together in front of her as she turned to face him. "It's not a nude, Lord Chatwin, rest assured. But I did alter the background, since you seem to have trouble with color contrasts and hues."

His mouth ticked up a fraction as he cast her a sideways glance. "I have no trouble with color contrasts and hues, sweetheart," he drawled. "In fact, let me just say that you look truly breathtaking in that shade of red."

Her heart skipped a beat, and for a moment she had no idea what to say.

He inhaled deeply and turned to her, keeping his distance, though lowering his voice. "Is Miles Whitman attending tonight?"

"No. Would it matter if he was?"

"Not anymore."

She pulled back a little. "What does that mean?"

With a vague smile, he replied, "I now realize how needless it was to worry that another gentleman might steal your heart."

She studied him again, his thoughtful expression, his intimate manner that implied nothing. Something very substantive had changed in him since their last encounter, since she'd walked out on him after he'd made love to her. And she had absolutely no idea what to think of it, or where his thoughts were leading.

"I don't understand," she murmured.

Stepping closer to her, he glanced down to the ruby hanging between her uplifted bosom, then reached for it, cradling it in his fingers as he stared at the intricate diamond-shaped cut of the stone.

Softly, thoughtfully, he said, "A gem unpolished is just another rock."

She stilled as a certain uneasiness budded within.

"I think," he added seconds later, raising his gaze to meet hers once more, "that no truer words were ever spoken."

"What's happened, Ian?" she asked, her voice low and grave.

Abruptly, he dropped the ruby. "I want to tell you something about me, Viola. Something I've never told anyone."

She said nothing, just watched him.

He stuffed his hands in the pockets of his evening coat and turned his attention to the garden again, staring out across the trees to the city park beyond, engrossed in his thoughts.

"I've always blamed your sisters, and even you, for my capture," he began. "But the truth is, I was partly to blame, because I was there at the time."

"Ian—"

"Just listen," he soothed, casting her a quick glance.

She nodded, relenting.

He sighed. "I had been on a destructive path for a long time, and finding the diamonds had become an obsession for me."

The Martello diamonds, she remembered. Stolen by Benedict Sharon, the man who'd owned the property in Winter Garden. Ian had returned there, following Sharon to confront him and retrieve the jewels, only to find him dead. That's when her sisters had surprised Ian, struck him down, and dragged him to the dungeon beneath the house. Viola had discovered him the next day.

"When I awoke and found myself lost," he continued, subdued, "chained to the wall by my wrist in absolute darkness, I realized my life was probably over. I could see no way out and expected to die, and all for a handful of polished rocks. During the first day, before they began to drug me, I had nothing but hours in cold, total blackness to dwell on my past, and a future that might have been. It was a horrific time, and the fear immeasurable."

Her throat constricted with emotion, and she clutched

her hands together in front of her to keep from reaching for him.

"During that time of fear and uncertainty," he disclosed, dropping his voice to just above a whisper, "I was able to reflect on every mistake, every decision that might have been, and I realized the only reason I had become so intent in the quest, had allowed myself to be captured, first by brilliant jewels and then by your sisters, was because I had lost faith in what mattered, lost faith in myself." He looked back into her eyes, his gaze intense. "And I lost faith in myself, Viola, became a wandering, reckless man, because of my mother's simple deathbed confession just a few short years earlier, when Ivy and I learned we were not the legitimate children of the Earl of Stamford. I was a bastard, a fraud who carried the title in name only, and for years a confused man who couldn't share the anguish and anger with another living soul." He reached out and touched her cheek with his fingertips. "Until you."

She started trembling. Tears filled her eyes and she lowered her gaze from his, hugging herself with her arms closed over her stomach.

He took a step closer, his legs pressing into the folds of her skirt, the pad of his thumb brushing back and forth across her lips.

"I told you in the dungeon, didn't I?" he whispered huskily. "And to this day you've never mentioned it to anyone."

Bravely, she straightened and shook her head. "It doesn't matter, Ian, and even if I told everyone I knew, nobody would believe me and it wouldn't change a thing."

"You're wrong," he stressed with utter conviction. "You would never have told anyone because you'd fallen in love with me and cared enough to keep my secret as your own. And your love, your devotion, is what matters. It mattered to me then, and it matters even more to me now."

The intensity behind his words took her breath away. Instinctively, she reached up and placed her gloved palm on his chest, over his beating heart, closing her eyes to the teardrops that threatened on her lashes.

With that, he reached out and wrapped his arms around her waist, drawing her into him.

"You were so young," he whispered fervently, "so brave, and you must have been so scared. And yet you gave yourself to me when I needed you, accepting the risks, offering me a last hope of passion and comfort." He inhaled a shaky breath, then cupped her chin and tilted her head up. He dropped gentle kisses on her wet lashes, her cheeks, and finally her lips before pulling back again and resting his forehead against hers.

"You loved me, Viola," he said in a breath of longing, "and I needed that love to save me. And when you realized you carried my bastard child, you did the only thing you could and married a man who offered to raise him in exchange for drawings and paintings he could sell. It's why you were so anxious to marry after I left you at the cottage, afraid I might have left you carrying again with no hope of a future with me."

"Ian . . ."

"And I know," he admitted at last, "that this is why you could never tell me your beautiful boy is mine. A mother's love is inherently protective, and the wounds caused by such a revelation are too great. You learned as much from me. But even if he will be known by all as the Baron Cheshire, you and I will always know and keep the secret that he was conceived in love and is my son."

She raised a palm to her lips, squeezing her eyes shut as tears began rolling down her cheeks.

He hugged her against his chest, his cheek resting on top of her head.

"I'm so sorry I ever hurt you, sweetheart," he said, his voice thick with emotion no longer controlled. "But I realize now an apology for all I've done to you will never be enough. I need to ask for forgiveness instead."

She melted into him, listening to the sound of his beating heart, absorbing his warmth.

"I love you, Ian," she whispered into the quiet, cool evening.

His breath caught sharply, and then he whispered in return, "I love you, too. . . ."

They all stood in front of the red-velvet-draped portrait resting up on the easel in her drawing room. Ian stood next to Viola, who managed to look dignified and lovely even as she must have still been reeling inside from his confession an hour ago. He very much wanted to touch her, to take her in his arms, but that would come later.

As everyone grew quiet for the viewing, Viola said a few words regarding her new endeavor at artistic flair, then nodded to a footman. After a second or two of anticipation, he grasped the drapery at the bottom, then raised it quickly to the gasps of everyone in attendance.

For seconds silence reigned. Then Fairbourne's low chuckle from the back of the room broke the ice and everyone began laughing at once.

Ian couldn't help himself. He started chuckling, then broke out into his own hearty laughter at the funniest damn painting he'd ever seen in his life.

It was a portrait of him, beautifully done. He sat on a stool, but rather than evening attire, he wore a baker's apron. In his two uplifted hands, he held two steaming pies, while on his face, he wore the silliest, most ridiculous grin that exposed both rows of large, gleaming teeth.

It was monstrously appalling, and hysterically funny. And he supposed he deserved it for having made her paint it. Yes, she had worked for pie.

Flushing with his own keen embarrassment, Ian turned his gaze on Viola, who huddled next to Lady Tenby and her daughter Isabella.

He cleared his throat as he bit down hard to hide his humor. "Just where, madam, do you suppose I hang it?"

Viola broke out in her own fit of giggles, and through them managed to snort, "In the kitchen?"

"Remind the cook every day of your importance," Lord Tenby offered.

That brought another roar of snickering from the group, and with it, Ian decided he loved the sound of her honest and cheerful laugh almost as much as he loved her.

In two strides he was upon her. Before she realized

his intention, he grasped her head and plunged his fingers through her hair, fairly yanking her into him and planting a hearty kiss upon her mouth.

Lady Tenby screeched. Isabella gasped and whispered, "Oh, my . . ."

He pulled back and stared down to her flushed face, grinning wickedly.

"It's quite all right, Lady Tenby," he said. "Lady Cheshire has consented to become my wife. I'm simply thanking her for such a thoughtful betrothal gift."

Viola's eyes flashed in amusement. "Perhaps, your grace, I'd rather just sell this masterpiece—"

He cut her off with another sweet touch of his lips to hers. Scandal be damned.

Ian stared at the portrait in front of him. The real portrait she'd completed and revealed to all her guests following the joke that had played so well hours ago. This one, by comparison, would hang with pride in his home, alongside one she would paint of herself as the Duchess of Chatwin, and their children. She'd taken the original he'd obstinately rejected and changed the background so that he now stood dignified at the window in his green salon, in front of his vivid garden forest. She'd outdone herself, and the final result proved magnificent.

Alone at last, he turned to study her by candlelight.

"You're beautiful," he whispered.

She glanced at him askance. "You're not angry?"

"At my complete humiliation in front of my peers? Of course not. It happens frequently where you are concerned, and I'm growing rather amused by it. Besides," he added sheepishly, "I deserved it after offering you such a ridiculous marriage proposal the first time."

She grinned and reached for his hand. "I couldn't marry you for pity, or lust, Ian. But I will marry you for love. I just wish we could start from the beginning, do everything over. I wish we hadn't lost five years."

He drew her against him, wrapping an arm around her waist and cupping her chin to hold her gaze.

"The hurt has made us stronger, taught us so much," he replied. "And if we can love each other through everything we've shared, we can love each other through anything. I've never been more hopeful of the future."

She smiled softly and touched his face. "Neither have I. . . ."

Coming August 2010

Last Night's Scandal

**By *New York Times* bestselling author
Loretta Chase**

*Peregrine Dalmay, Earl of Lisle, spent years living
dangerously in Egypt, yet nothing could've prepared
him for London's greatest peril: Olivia Wingate-
Carsington. The devious redhead was trouble as
a child, but now a voluptuous woman, she's more
dangerous than ever. The* ton's *darling, Olivia has a
string of broken engagements in her wake, and she
is determined to have at least one adventure before
settling down. When Lisle's family sends him north
to rid their Scottish estate of ghosts—Olivia sees her
chance. It's just too bad the stone-hearted wretch is
the one man in the world she can't wrap around her
finger . . . or so easily dismiss.*

The crowd was so thick that at first all he could see was the fashionably absurd coiffure rising above the men's heads. Two birds of paradise seemed to have their beaks stuck into a great loop of . . . red hair. Very red hair.

Only one girl in all the world had that hair.

Well, then, no surprise to find Olivia at the center of a crowd of men. She had rank and a thumping great dowry. That would more than make up for . . .

The crowd parted then, giving him a full view. She turned his way and he stopped short.

He'd forgotten.

Those great blue eyes.

For a moment he stood, lost in a blue as deep as an Egyptian evening sky.

Then he blinked, and took in the rest, from the ridiculous birds hanging over the stiff loops of red hair to the pointed slippers peeping out from under the ruffles and furbelows at the hem of her pale green gown.

Then his gaze went up again, and his brain slowed to a crawl.

Between coiffure and shoes appeared a graceful arc of neck and smooth shoulders and a creamy bosom more than amply on display . . . and lower down, an armful of waist curving out gracefully into womanly hips. . . .

No, that had to be wrong. Olivia was many things. *Beautiful* wasn't one of them. Striking, yes: the fatally blue eyes and the vivid hair. Those were hers and no one else's. And yes, that was her face under the absurd coiffure . . . but no, it wasn't.

He stared, his gaze going up then down, again and again. The room's heat was suddenly beyond oppressive and his heart was beating strangely and his mind was a thick haze of memories where he was searching to make sense of what his eyes told him.

He was dimly aware that he was supposed to say something, but he had no idea what. His manners had never been quite so instinctive as they ought to be. He was used to another world, another clime, other kinds of men and women. Though he'd learned to fit in this one, fitting in didn't come naturally to him. He'd never learned to say what he didn't mean, and now he didn't know what he meant to say.

At the moment, everything anybody had ever done to civilize him was lost. He beheld a vision that stripped away all the rules and meaningless phrases and proper ways to look and move and shredded them to bits and blew them away.

"Lord Lisle," she said, with a graceful dip of her head that made the birds' plumes flutter. "There's a wager on, as to whether you'd turn up for Great-Grandmama's party."

At the sound of her voice, so familiar, Reason began to slog its way through the muck of confusion.

This was Olivia, Reason said. Here were the facts: her voice, her eyes, her hair, her face. Yes, her face was different because it had softened into womanliness. Her cheeks were softer, rounder. Her mouth was fuller. . . .

He was aware of people talking, of this one asking that one who he was, and another answering. But all of that seemed to be in another world, irrelevant. He couldn't see or hear or think anything but Olivia.

Then he discerned the glint of laughter in her eyes and the slight upturn of her mouth.

He came back to earth with a *thunk* that should have been audible on the other side of the great ballroom.

"I wouldn't miss it for the world," he said.

"I'm glad to see you," she said, "and not merely because I've won the wager." She gave him one slow, assessing look that slid over his skin like fingertips and sent heat arrowing straight to his groin.

Ye gods, she was more dangerous than ever.

He wondered whose benefit that look was for. Was she simply exercising her power or was she trying to provoke all her admirers simultaneously by pretending he was the only man in the room?

Excellent work, either way.

All the same, enough was enough.

She wasn't a little girl anymore—if she'd ever been a little girl—and he wasn't a little boy. He knew how to play this game. He let his gaze drift down again to her breasts. "You've grown," he said.

"I knew you'd mock my hair," she said.

She knew he wasn't referring to her hair. She knew *exactly* what he'd meant. One thing Olivia had never been was naïve.

But he took the hint and dutifully regarded the coiffure. Though it towered over many other men, he was tall enough to look the birds in the eye. Other women wore equally fantastical hair arrangements, he was aware. While men's fashions had grown increasingly sober in recent decades, women's had grown increasingly deranged.

"Some birds have landed on your head," he said. "And died there."

"They must think they've gone to heaven," said a male voice nearby.

"Looks like rigor mortis," Lisle said.

Olivia sent him a fleeting smile. Something curious happened inside his chest. Something else happened lower down, not at all curious and all too familiar.

He willed the feelings into oblivion.

She couldn't help it, he told himself. She was born that way, a Dreadful DeLucey through and through. He mustn't take it personally. She was his friend and ally, practically his sister. He made himself picture her as she'd been on the day when he first met her: a skinny twelve-year-old who'd tried to brain him with his sketchbook. A provoking, dangerously fascinating girl.

"I dressed for *you*," she said. "In honor of your Noble Quest in Egypt. I ordered the silk for my gown to match the green of the Nile in your watercolors. We had to use birds of paradise because we couldn't find ibises."

Voice dropping to a conspiratorial tone, she leaned toward him, offering a nearer and fuller view of alabaster flesh, curved precisely to fit a man's hands. At these close quarters he was acutely aware of the faint sheen of moisture the ballroom's heat had brought to her skin. He was aware, too, of the scent of a woman arising therefrom: a dangerous blend of humid flesh and a faint, flowery fragrance.

She should have warned him, drat her.

Think about the skinny twelve-year-old, he counseled himself.

"I wanted to dress like one of the ladies in the copies of the tomb paintings you sent," she went on, "but that was *forbidden*."

The scent and the stress on *forbidden* were softening his brain.

Facts, he told himself. *Stick to facts, like . . .*

Where were her freckles?

Perhaps the room's gentle candlelight made them less obvious. Or maybe she'd powdered her breasts. Or had she bleached them with lemon juice?

Stop thinking about her breasts. That way madness lies. What's she saying? Something about tomb paintings. He filled his mind with images of flat figures on stone walls.

"The ladies in the tomb paintings are not, technically speaking, dressed," he said. "When alive, they seem to be tightly wrapped in an extremely thin piece of linen."

The costume left nothing to the imagination, which was probably why even he—who preferred to stick to facts and leave the realm of imagination to his parents—

had no trouble at all picturing Olivia's curvaceous new body wrapped in a thin piece of linen.

"Then, when they're dead," he went on, "they're overdressed, tightly wrapped in layers of linen from head to foot. Neither form of attire seems practical for an English ball."

"You never change," she said, drawing back. "Always so *literal*."

"Leave it to Lisle to throw away a golden opportunity," said another male voice. "Instead of complimenting the lady—as any man with eyes must do—and trying to win her favor, he must wander into a boring lecture about pagan customs."

Yes, because it's safe there.

"My attention has not wandered, I assure you, Miss Carsington," Lisle said. "At present it could not be more firmly fixed."

He'd like to fix his hands on the throat of the fiend who'd given her this face and body—as though she needed any more weapons. It must have been the Devil. A trade of some kind, sometime in the five years since Lisle had last seen her. Naturally Satan, like anyone else, would have had the worst of any bargain with her.

In a corner of his mind, the voice that warned him of snakes, scorpions, and cutthroats lurking in the darkness said, *Watch out.*

But he already knew that, because he knew Olivia.

She was dangerous. Beautiful or striking, with or without breasts, she exerted a fatal fascination. She drew to her otherwise intelligent men, most of whom had already seen her destroy the peace of other equally intelligent men.

He knew that. Her letters had been filled with her numerous "romantic disappointments," among other things. He'd heard other stories since entering this ballroom. He knew what she was like.

He was merely temporarily unhinged because he was a man. It was a purely physical reaction, completely natural when one encountered a beautiful woman. He had such reactions all the time. This was disturbing only because he was reacting to *Olivia*.

Who was his friend and ally, practically his sister.

He'd always thought of her that way.

And that was how he'd continue to think of her, he told himself.

He'd had a bit of a shock, that was all. He was a man who encountered shocks nearly every day of his life, and thrived on them.

"Having fixed my attention for the moment," he said, "perhaps the lady would be so kind as to grant the next dance."

"That's mine," said one of the men hovering at her shoulder. "Miss Carsington promised."

Olivia snapped her fan shut. "You may have another, Lord Belder," she said. "I haven't seen Lord Lisle this age, and he'll soon be gone again. He's the most elusive man in the world. If I don't take this dance, who knows when I should have another? He could be drowned in a shipwreck. He could be eaten by crocodiles or bitten by a viper or a scorpion. He could succumb to plague. He's never happy, you know, except when risking his life to advance our knowledge of an ancient civilization. I can dance with *you* any time."

Belder looked murder at Lisle, but he smiled at Olivia and yielded his claim.

As Lisle led her away, he finally understood why so many men kept shooting each other on her account.

They all wanted her and they couldn't help it; she knew it and she didn't care.

Unforgettable, enthralling love stories, sparkling with passion and adventure from Romance's bestselling authors

At Avon Books, we know your passion for romance — once you finish one of our novels, you find yourself wanting more.

May we tempt you with . . .

- **Excerpts** from our upcoming releases.

- Entertaining **extras**, including authors' personal photo albums and book lists.

- Behind-the-scenes **scoop** on your favorite characters and series.

- **Sweepstakes** for the chance to win free books, romantic getaways, and other fun prizes.

- Writing **tips** from our authors and editors.

- **Blog** with our authors and find out why they love to write romance.

- **Exclusive content** that's not contained within the pages of our novels.

Join us at
www.avonbooks.com

AVON
An Imprint of HarperCollins*Publishers*
www.avonromance.com

Available wherever books are sold or please call 1-800-331-3761 to order.

FTH 0708